Vow To Redemption

LACI MAE WYLD

I want to dedicate this to all the incredible authors in the Books and Bitches Down Under community. You're all incredibly supportive, generously offering advice to help those with less publishing experience. I doubt I would have managed to persevere through some tough times without your amazing support lifting me up. Thank you so much.

Contents

Afganistan 2007

Riley's voice crackles in my earpiece. "We doing this or just standing here with our thumbs up our asses?" Across the sand and dust-strewn street, his face is tight with anticipation, that familiar half-smile that always appears before we breach. I press my com.

"Hold position. Too many civilians. Something's wrong." The hair on my neck stands up, that sixth sense they can't teach you in training. I scan the windows again, counting shadows, movements. I catch Fynn's eye, motion toward base. He understands, checks in with command. Seconds drag like hours while my pulse hammers in my throat. I taste copper, feel sweat trickling down my spine despite the cool morning air. Fynn's thumb jerks up. Green light from command.

"Lock and load," I growl, chambering a round with a satisfying click. "Move in. Now."

The building's first floor, empty. Too empty. The silence has a weight, pressing against my eardrums. Our boots barely whisper on the stairs when they appear. Six tangos materialize on the landing above, weapons already raised. I register their faces in that frozen moment, young, determined, and worst of all, expecting us.

"COVER!" I scream, diving sideways. The air explodes with gunfire, a deafening symphony of death. Concrete splinters inches from my face, dust filing my nostrils. I return fire, but it's too late. Riley takes three to the chest, his body jerking with each impact. He drops like a stone, eyes still open, still seeing. Fynn's head snaps back in a red mist that spatters across the wall behind him. Johnson's screaming, clutching at his throat where an artery pumps his life onto the floor.

Blood sprays the wall behind me, my blood, hot and sticky. Pain tears through my chest and my arm, like being branded with white-hot iron. I'm still firing, the rifle bucking against my shoulder, when the civilian appears in the doorway below, a small boy trailing behind him. The man's eyes widen in horror. I try to shout a warning, but my mouth fills with blood.

I collapse against the wall as consciousness slips away.

ONE
The Debt Collector

Mason

The clock on my office wall reads 11:42 PM. I've been staring at the same security protocol for twenty minutes, the words blurring together like watercolors left in the rain. My eyes burn. My neck complains with every slight turn of my head. But these physical discomforts are nothing compared to what waits for me at home, the empty rooms, the silence, the memories that always find me in the dark.

"Phillips Security Solutions," I mutter, reading my company letterhead for the thousandth time. Sometimes I still can't believe I built this from nothing after leaving the service. After everything.

The screen in front of me glows with the security assessment for a tech billionaire's summer home in Lake Geneva. Three access points need upgrading. Two blind spots in the camera coverage. Personnel recommendations: minimum four-man team during peak occupancy. I make these observations with the detachment of a surgeon, clinical and precise. Security is math, and math doesn't care about your feelings.

I tab through the next client file. A diplomat with enemies in three countries. I start typing notes, my fingers move like they're still required to file reports at 0400 hours, with a commanding officer waiting to tear apart any sloppiness.

My desk is a landscape of organized chaos—stacks of folders arranged by priority, clients' names tabbed and color-coded. A half-empty coffee cup sits on a coaster, never directly on the wood; that's how rings form, and rings mean decay, and decay means loss of control. My laptop displays multiple windows: security schematics, personnel rotation schedules, threat assessments.

The only personal item is a silver frame, face down. I don't need to see the photo to know every detail of it. Kerry's smile. My arm around her shoulders. The beach behind us. The ring catching sunlight on her left hand. I keep it down because looking at it hurts, but putting it away hurts more.

I rub my eyes, feeling the grit of exhaustion. My neck makes a sound like gravel when I rotate my head. The building is quiet around me. The cleaning crew came through at nine, nodding respectfully when they saw me still working. They know not to touch anything on my desk. They know I notice things move even a centimeter.

"Finish the job, Phillips." I tell myself the same words I've used since my first mission with the SEALs. I force my attention back to the screen, clicking through the last of the protocols. I triple-check the alarm codes, the emergency response times, and the contingency plans. In my line of work, missed details mean dead clients.

When I finally power down my computer, the ritual begins. I align the folders in perfect right angles. I empty the coffee cup in the small sink in the corner, rinse it twice, set it upside down on the rack. I check that my desk drawer is locked - inside are three handguns, two knives, and credentials that still get me into places most civilians can't go.

The Navy taught me efficiency; survival taught me precision. I straighten the pens in their holder, adjust my chair to be perfectly centered at the desk, and turn off the desk lamp. The office falls into shadow, illuminated only by the city lights bleeding through the blinds.

The walls around me are sparse - a framed Navy SEAL emblem, my security consultant licenses, and a single commendation letter from a government agency whose name has been carefully redacted. Nothing about Afghanistan. Nothing about the ambush. Nothing about a little boy named Juan or his father, who saved my life when my entire team died around me.

As I shrug on my jacket, I catch my reflection in the darkened window - broad shoulders, short-cropped hair, a face that's settled into permanent vigilance. At forty-three, I look older around the eyes. Those are the parts that have seen too much.

The security guard at the front desk nods as I pass. "Another late one, Mr. Phillips?"

"The usual, Ray." My voice comes out gravelly from disuse.

"You ever sleep, sir?"

I offer him the smile I use for civilians - professional, distant, revealing nothing. "Sleep's overrated."

What I don't say: sleep means nightmares. Sleep means Kerry's voice calling my name as machines flatline. Sleep means the faces of my team in Kandahar, their eyes accusing me of surviving when they didn't.

Outside, Chicago's night air hits me with its particular blend of exhaust, restaurant grease, and lake moisture. I stand straighter, scanning the street with automatic caution, I check parked cars, rooflines, shadows. Old habits. Necessary habits, to me at least.

My firm has twenty-eight employees now. Ex-military, mostly, with a few former intelligence analysts. They respect me because I've seen what they've seen, done what they've done. I never ask them to take risks I wouldn't. I never sugar-coat the realities of the job. Protection isn't about being a hero; it's about anticipating the worst and preventing it through sheer force of will and planning.

I check my watch - nearly 1 AM. Another day of keeping other people safe while my own life remains on permanent lockdown. I don't date. I don't make friends. Relationships mean vulnerability, and vulnerability gets people killed. Kerry taught me that lesson with her last breath.

As I lock the building door, my fingers brush against the security panel I designed myself. Triple redundant, connected to response teams that can be on-site in under four minutes. I protect what matters. I control what I can. And I try like hell to forget what I can't change.

Tomorrow will be the same - client meetings, security assessments, training sessions with new hires. Routine is sanctuary. Routine is control. And control is the only thing standing between me and the chaos that claimed everyone I ever loved.

I take one last look at the darkened office - at the life I've built from the ashes of what came before - and turn away. The night spreads before me, empty and predictable. Just the way I need it to be.

The apartment door recognizes my fingerprint with a soft click. Forty-two floors up, the city spreads below me like a circuit board, all light and electricity and movement, none of it touching me. I step inside the motion sensors trigger soft recessed lighting, illuminating my fortress of solitude. Floor-to-ceiling windows showcase Chicago's glittering skyline, but I barely glance at the view I pay seven thousand a month for.

I make a beeline for the bar cart in the corner, tonight's first priority established.

The keys land on the granite countertop with a metallic clatter that echoes through the open floor plan. My footsteps are muffled by the plush rug as I cross to where the crystal decanters wait like old friends. I choose the bourbon without hesitation, Blanton's, Kerry's favorite. My hands don't shake anymore when I pour, not like the first year after she died. Progress, my therapist would say, if I still went to therapy. It's only taken nearly ten years.

The first pour goes down like liquid fire, a familiar burn that does nothing to warm the cold spot behind my sternum. I don't even wince anymore. I pour a second, more generous this time, and carry it to the leather chair angled toward the windows.

The apartment is magazine-perfect, sleek furniture, minimalist art, everything in its place. And utterly devoid of life. No dirty dishes in the sink, no shoes kicked off by the door, no half-read books splayed open on the coffee table. Just the pristine emptiness of a showroom, not a home. Kerry would have hated it. She was all color and clutter and spontaneity, cups of tea forgotten on windowsills, earrings dropped on every surface, notes scribbled on the backs of receipts.

I sip the second drink slower, feeling the alcohol begin to dull the sharp edges of the day. My reflection in the window stares back at me, a man holding it together through sheer force of will. Behind me, Kerry's collection of military insignia patches sits in a display case I maintain with obsessive care, dusting it weekly, making sure the lighting hits it just right. Sometimes I think it's the only thing keeping me tethered to the world.

When the glass is empty, I push myself out of the chair with a soft grunt. My body feels heavier at night, weighted down by memories and regrets. The bedroom beckons, king-sized bed made with military corners, pillows arranged with perfection, sheets changed weekly regardless of use. Sleep hygiene, another therapist called it. As if clean sheets could scrub away the nightmares.

I go through the motions: shoes placed neatly in the closet, suit on a hanger, shower hot enough to turn my skin red. When I finally slide between the sheets, the silence of the apartment presses against my eardrums like deep water.

Sleep comes reluctantly, then betrays me instantly.

The hospital room materializes around me with perfect clarity, the antiseptic smell burning my nostrils, the fluorescent lights casting their sickly glow over Kerry's pale skin. The steady beep of the heart monitor provides the rhythm to which I count her breaths, each one shallower than the last. Her hand in mine feels small, the bones delicate as a bird's wing. The engagement ring I gave her six months earlier catches the light, mocking me with its promise of a future we'll never have, one I insisted the nurses allow her to keep on.

"Mason," she whispers, her voice a paper-thin version of the one that used to call orders across naval vessels. "Not your fault."

But it was my fault. My hands on the wheel. My eyes that missed the SUV running the red light. My body, which somehow survived when the passenger side took the full impact. My parents in the back seat, gone before the ambulance arrived.

The crash replays in high definition, the screech of tires as I slammed on the brakes, the sickening crunch of metal giving way, the world spinning in slow motion as the SUV T-boned us. The shattered glass catching the streetlights like diamond dust in the air. Kerry's scream cut short by the impact. Then silence, so profound it seemed to swallow the world, before the chorus of car alarms and distant sirens filled the void.

In the nightmare, I'm always frozen, unable to reach for Kerry, unable to check on my parents in the back seat. Just trapped in my own body, watching helplessly as blood spreads across Kerry's white blouse like spilled wine.

Back in the hospital room, the monitors suddenly scream in electronic panic. Her hand goes limp in mine as medical staff flood the room, pushing me aside, their voices urgent but distant, as if I'm hearing them from underwater. "Clear!" someone shouts, and Kerry's body arches with the defibrillator's current once, twice, three times.

Her chest doesn't rise again. The flat line on the monitor extends into infinity, a horizon I can never cross to reach her.

I jolt awake with a gasp, sheets twisted around my legs like restraints. Sweat plasters my t-shirt to my chest, and my heart hammers against my ribs like it's trying to break free. The digital clock reads 2:37 AM, less than an hour of sleep. My fists are clenched so tight my nails have left half-moon impressions in my palms.

My breathing comes in ragged bursts as I fight to separate memory from reality. The shadows in the room seem to pulse with each heartbeat, stretching toward me with accusatory fingers. I swing my legs over the side of the bed and press my bare feet against the cool hardwood floor, trying to ground myself in the present.

"Name five things you can see," I mutter, using the technique my last therapist taught me before I stopped going. "Nightstand. Lamp. Window. Closet door. Hands." My hands, still strong despite everything they've failed to hold onto.

The panic recedes gradually, leaving me hollow and scraped raw. I know sleep won't return tonight, it never does after the nightmare. I push myself up and pad back to the living room, where the city lights offer the illusion of company.

Standing at the window, I press my forehead against the cool glass. Forty-two floors below, tiny cars move along prescribed paths, people living their orderly lives, leaving nightclubs, unaware of the man watching from above. I wonder how many of them are awake at this hour, haunted by their own ghosts.

The bourbon bottle beckons, promising temporary oblivion, but I resist. Physical control is all I have left some nights. Instead, I stand sentinel at the window, keeping watch over a city that doesn't know it's being protected, much like the clients who hire me without ever truly understanding what they're buying, not just security protocols and personnel, but the hypervigilance of a man who knows exactly how quickly everything can be taken away.

The private phone vibrates against the glass coffee table, its screen illuminating the darkness like a miniature lighthouse. 3:18 AM. Nobody calls this number. I stare at it for three full seconds before picking it up, my mind cycling through worst-case scenarios. Unknown sender. No caller ID. Just a notification for a video file attachment, 237 seconds long. In my line of work, unexpected messages at ungodly hours never bring good news.

My thumb hovers over the screen. This phone isn't connected to any cloud services, has no social media apps, and only has five contacts, all emergency backups. It's a digital ghost, untraceable by design. Whoever sent this message went to considerable trouble to find it.

Security protocols say to ignore it. Delete without viewing. But something, instinct, curiosity, or the restless energy of another sleepless night makes me tap the attachment.

The video buffers for a moment, then fills my screen with a face I haven't seen in years, though it's haunted plenty of my nightmares. Emelio Zentarra. The man who saved my life and lost his son in the process.

"Mason." His voice comes through tiny and strained, lacking the commanding presence I remember. His face is haggard, the once immaculate hair now disheveled, silver strands catching light from what appears to be a car's interior dome light. His eyes dart sideways repeatedly, checking something outside the frame. "I don't have much time."

I sink onto the couch, a cold weight settling in my gut. Emelio Zentarra doesn't scare easily. As one of the largest arms dealers in North America, he's faced down cartel leaders and warlords without blinking. Seeing fear in his eyes is like watching a mountain tremble.

"Sierra is dead." He says it flatly, but I catch the slight break in his voice. Sierra, his wife. The woman who nursed me back to health in their compound after Emelio pulled me, half-dead, from that bloodbath in Kandahar. "Not an accident. They made it look like one, but..." He shakes his head. "They're coming for me next. Probably already on their way."

My mind immediately shifted to tactical assessment. They. Unknown hostiles. Multiple, based on his level of concern. High-level threat if they could get to someone as protected as Sierra Zentarra.

"I've moved Yelana to the estate outside Los Angeles. Security is tight, but..." He looks away from the camera, his profile sharp against the darkness outside the car window. "I don't trust anyone right now. Not my security team, not my business partners. There's a traitor in my organization, and until I find out who..."

He turns back to the camera, his eyes suddenly burning with the intensity I remember.

"Remember Afghanistan, 2007? When my son Juan died saving you after your SEAL team was ambushed?"

My chest tightens at the mention. How could I forget? The ambush that killed my entire team. We walked into the trap because our intel was compromised. The moment I prepared to die, surrounded by bodies of my brothers, only to have Emelio Zentarra appear like some avenging angel, guns blazing. Then, after, his boy, Jesus, just a kid, running toward his father, caught in the crossfire.

"I need you to honor that blood debt now," Emelio continues, his voice dropping to an urgent whisper. "You're the only one I trust to keep my daughter alive."

The video shakes as he adjusts something, and for a brief second, I glimpse what looks like a weapon on the seat beside him.

"If you're seeing this, I'm probably already dead." His mouth twists into a grimace that might have been attempting to be a smile. "Ironic, isn't it? I've spent my life selling the means to kill, and now..." He shakes his head. "Doesn't matter. What matters is Yelana. She doesn't know about any of this, the danger, the business, all of it. Sierra and I sheltered her. My mistake."

He leans closer to the camera, his face filling the screen. "They'll come for her, Mason. Not just for revenge, but because she's the heir. They think she knows things, account numbers, client lists, supplier contacts. She doesn't, not yet, but they won't believe that. They'll take her, and they'll make her suffer trying to get information she doesn't have."

I find myself sitting straighter, my body responding to the command in his voice even after all these years. The bourbon's effects have evaporated, leaving my mind cold and clear.

"I've arranged for you to have full access to the estate security. The staff knows to expect you." He pauses, conflict visible in his expression. "Yelana..she may not welcome you. She knows about Afghanistan, about Juan, but not everything. Not the part where I chose to save you. She just knows her brother died there."

The knowledge sits like a stone in my stomach. Of course, she wouldn't welcome me. In her eyes, I'd be the American soldier her brother died trying to save, a death that shaped her entire childhood.

"She's all I have left, Mason." Emelio's voice breaks for real this time, the facade of the hardened arms dealer cracking to reveal the father beneath. "She's headstrong, reckless. Doesn't understand the danger. You have to protect her, even from herself if necessary."

He looks over his shoulder again, tension visible in every line of his body. "My enemies will come for her. The Costa organization, others. They think she's soft, an easy target. Prove them wrong." His eyes harden again. "Whatever it takes. Whatever it costs. I'm calling in the blood debt."

The video ends abruptly, freezing on Emelio's face, those eyes that have seen too much now fixed on me across digital space and time.

I set the phone down carefully, as if it might detonate. My hands are steady, but my mind races, professional assessment battling with personal history. Emelio Zentarra, arms dealer, war profiteer, supplier to groups that have killed thousands. A man whose merchandise has destabilized governments and fueled conflicts across three continents.

Also, the man who carried me, bleeding and broken, to safety when he could have left me to die. The man who lost his son because of it. The man whose wife tended my wounds for weeks while I recovered in their home.

I stand and move to the window again, staring out at the city below. The moral calculus is impossible. Helping Emelio means protecting the daughter of a man whose life's work has been selling death. It means potentially getting involved in a war between criminal enterprises. It means putting myself in the crosshairs again after years of carefully controlled distance.

Not helping means breaking a blood debt, the most sacred promise there is in the world of men like Emelio. It means leaving an innocent young woman to face killers alone.

My reflection stares back at me from the window, superimposed over Chicago's glittering skyline. In the glass, I see not just my face now, but the shot of who I was then, a broken SEAL lieutenant watching a seven-year-old boy die because his father chose to save a stranger.

"Fuck," I whisper to the empty room, the decision already made despite my internal protests. Some debts can never be repaid, but you should be willing to die trying.

The city is starting to wake up outside my window, delivery trucks making their rounds, early commuters catching trains, the eastern sky lightening to a dull gray. I pace the length of my living room, seven steps each way, like a caged predator. Emelio's face stays with me, his words echoing: "blood debt," "only one I trust," "keep my daughter alive." Every instinct I've cultivated since leaving the service screams this is someone else's war, someone else's problem. But debts like mine to Emelio transcend good sense and self-preservation. They're written in blood, a boy's blood, spilled in Afghan dust.

My mind drifts back to the Zentarra compound outside Kandahar, where I spent weeks recovering after the ambush. I remember little Yelana at maybe three years old, all enormous dark eyes and serious expression. She'd sneak into my room when her mother wasn't looking, carrying a plastic first aid kit filled with bright pink Band-Aids. "You're broken," she'd announce with the solemn certainty of a child, carefully placing Band-Aids over my visible wounds, and sometimes over perfectly intact skin, just to be thorough.

"Papa says the bad men hurt you," she told me once, her tiny fingers surprisingly gentle as she stuck a bandaid across the bridge of my nose. "I'm making you better."

I never had the heart to tell her that her father was the one who supplied the weapons to those same "bad men." Even then, I understood the complicated morality of Emelio Zentarra, a man who armed conflicts for profit while maintaining his own rigid code of honor.

The memory shifts, fast-forwarding four years to my last visit to the Zentarras. Seven-year-old Yelana was a different creature entirely, all wild energy and stubborn pride. I'd come to discuss security concerns with Emelio, and she'd burst into his study unannounced, demanding attention. When Emelio firmly sent her away, the tantrum that followed was spectacular, all stamping feet and flashing eyes and declaration that she hated everyone, especially the "Stupid American soldier."

I stop pacing and calculate: she'd be about twenty-one now. A young woman, not a child. Heir to an arms empire she apparently knows nothing about. Target for enemies I can only begin to guess at. If Emelio was right—he rarely wasn't when it came to threats—she's in immediate danger from people who make their living in violence.

Christ. What am I even considering here? Dropping everything to fly across the country to protect the spoiled daughter of an international arms dealer? Getting myself entangled in whatever war Emelio was fighting when he recorded that desperate message?

But the debt remains. My life for Juan's. An exchange I never asked for but can't deny. And beneath that obligation runs a deeper current, the memory of failing to protect Kerry. Of watching helplessly as she slipped away in that hospital bed. The thought of another death on my conscience makes my chest constrict painfully.

"Not this time," I mutter to myself, "Not losing another one."

The decision crystallizes, bringing with it a clarity I haven't felt in months. I move with renewed purpose toward the bedroom, pulling my duffel bag from the closet. My hands remember this dance from countless deployments, efficient, economical movements as I pack only what's essential. Three sets of clothes. Extra socks.

Toiletry kit. Spare boots. Tactical gear disguised as civilian sportswear.

From the safe behind my closet's false wall, I retrieve my personal arsenal. The SIG P365 goes in my shoulder holster - compact but reliable. The Glock 19 gets checked, cleaned, and secured in a hidden compartment in the duffel. Backup piece at my ankle. Two knives with ceramic blades that won't trigger metal detectors. Garrote wire disguised as a leather bracelet. Tactical flashlight that doubles as a striking weapon.

Each item gets inspected with mechanical precision, muscle memory taking over from conscious thought. I'm no longer the security consultant watching the sunrise from a luxury apartment. I'm Lieutenant Phillips again, preparing for hostile territory, calculating threats and responses, mapping contingencies.

On my laptop, I pull up everything I can find about the Zentarra estate outside Los Angeles, satellite images, property records, and nearby access roads. If I'm walking into a potential war zone, I need to know the terrain. I study the layout, identifying defensive positions, potential vulnerabilities, escape routes. The muscle in my jaw tightens as I spot at least three security weaknesses from these preliminary images alone.

My phone requires only a few taps to book a direct flight to LAX, leaving in three hours. First class, not for comfort, but for the priority boarding and extra privacy. I arranged for a rental car under one of my alternate identities, selecting an unremarkable sedan with decent acceleration and a reinforced frame.

The sky outside has lightened to pale blue by the time I finish my preparations. I stand in the center of my apartment, mentally checking my readiness. The duffel by the door contains everything I need for the mission ahead. My civilian passport and three alternate IDs are secure in my inner jacket pocket. Cash in various denominations is distributed throughout my luggage and clothing.

I move to the display case holding Kerry's insignia collection, resting my fingers lightly on the glass. "Wish you were here to tell me I'm being an idiot," I whisper. The silence that answers feels less empty than usual.

Before leaving, I send two encrypted messages, one to my second-in-command at Phillips Security Solutions, delegating my client load for the foreseeable future; another to an old Navy contact who might have additional intelligence on the Costa organization Emelio mentioned.

At the door, I hesitate for one final moment, looking back at the life I've built since Afghanistan, since Kerry's death. The ordered, controlled existence that keeps the chaos at bay. I'm about to trade it for unknown dangers, for the messy complexity of the Zentarra world, for the protection of a young woman who probably resents everything I represent.

But as I shoulder my duffel bag, my steps are lighter than they've been in years. Having a mission, a purpose beyond maintaining my own carefully constructed walls, feels like coming up for air after being underwater too long. The grief and guilt that normally weigh me down seem temporarily suspended, replaced by the cold focus of operational planning.

"Not losing another one," I repeat to myself as I lock my door, the words becoming both promise and prayer. I may not be able to save Emelio or bring back Kerry or undo what happened to Juan, but Yelana Zentarra will not die on my watch. Whatever it takes.

I straighten my shoulders and head for the elevator, feeling the familiar pre-mission calm settle over me. Time to pay a blood debt.

TWO
The Heiress

YELANA

The security footage plays for the ninth time on my tablet. My mother's final moments, caught in the cold precision of a camera she never knew existed. I watch her walk to her car, elegant as always in her tailored suit. The shadow that moves behind her. The sudden tension in her shoulders when she senses something wrong. Too late. Always too late. I don't flinch anymore when the silenced bullet catches her at the base of her skull, when she crumples like a marionette with cut strings. I've gone numb, sitting here in my father's —my—leather chair, breathing in the lingering scent of his Cuban cigars.

My fingers tremble as I rewind the footage again. Not from grief —I've cried myself hollow over the past two days—but from rage. Cold, precise rage that demands focus. Someone betrayed my family. Someone close enough to know my mother's schedule, to disable the security perimeter, to approach without raising her suspicions until the final second.

The study remains exactly as my father left it. Leather-bound ledgers stacked with mathematical precision on the credenza. The crystal tumbler still bears the ghost of his fingerprints. His reading glasses folded neatly beside a half-finished report. Behind the mahogany paneling to my left, security monitors blink with reassuring regularity, showing every angle of the estate's grounds through the hidden door my father showed me only six months ago.

"Just in case," he'd said, his face uncharacteristically grave. "Knowledge is security, Yelana."

I didn't understand then. I do now.

The call came at 4:37 this morning. My father's body was found in his car with three bullets to the chest. "Professional hit," the police detective said, his voice carefully neutral when he learned my surname. Even law enforcement treats the Zentarra name with cautious respect, though I've never understood why.

My eyes sting but remain dry. There are no tears left in me. Just this hollow space where my heart should be, and the growing certainty that I'm next.

I pause the footage on my mother's face, that final moment of dawning comprehension before death claims her. She was always so vibrant, so full of fierce intelligence and cutting humor. Now she's a frozen image on a screen, already beginning to feel less real with each passing hour. And my father, the mountain of a man who filled every room with his presence, reduced to a police report and the echo of his voice in my head.

The scent of his cigars clings to the leather chair, to the heavy drapes, to the books lining the walls. I breathe it in deeply, desperately, knowing it will fade too soon.

The soft knock at the door pulls me from my thoughts. Three precise taps, Kendrick's signature. In the chaos of the past forty-eight hours, the butler's unwavering routine feels like the only solid ground beneath my feet.

"Enter," I call, quickly locking the tablet screen. Some things aren't meant for loyal staff to see.

Kendrick steps in with that perfect posture that makes me wonder if he sleeps standing up. Not a silver hair out of place despite the hour, his black suit impeccably pressed. His face betrays nothing, though I know he loved my parents in his reserved way.

"Miss Zentarra," he says, using my surname with the formal address that still sounds wrong. That's my mother's title. Was my mother's title. "Mr. Mason Phillips has arrived as expected."

The name hits me like cold water. Mason Phillips. My father spoke that name often over the years, always with a strange mixture of respect and something darker. "The only man I truly trust," he'd say, usually after too much bourbon on the anniversary of Juan's death.

My brother Juan. Dead in Afghanistan before I could form proper memories of him. And somehow, this Mason Phillips was there. Connected to that loss in ways my parents never fully explained.

"He claims your father sent for him," Kendrick continues, his tone carefully neutral. "He's carrying significant...hardware." The slight emphasis tells me all I need to know about what kind of 'hardware' our visitor brings.

Vague memories surface, a tall man with hard eyes who visited our home when I was small. Me placing pink bandages on his wounds, thinking I could fix what was broken. My father speaking with him in hushed tones behind closed doors. My mother's tight smile whenever his name was mentioned.

"How convenient that he arrives the day of my father's murder," I say more to myself than to Kendrick.

"Indeed, Miss." Kendrick's expression remains unreadable. "Shall I send him away?"

I straighten my shoulders, feeling the weight of the Zentarra name settling onto them like a heavy cloak. My silk blouse feels too light, my skin too thin for what lies ahead. But I am my father's daughter, even if I don't understand half of what that means.

"No," I decide, pushing back from the desk. "Show him in."

Kendrick hesitates, just a fraction of a second, but enough for me to notice. "Are you certain that's wise, Miss? Perhaps Mr. Jackson should—"

"I said show him in, Kendrick." My voice drops lower, finding that tone my father used when he would not be questioned. "Ken doesn't need to be present for every conversation."

"Of course, Miss." He bows slightly and withdraws, closing the door with a soft click.

Alone again, I rise and move to the window, looking out at the manicured gardens below. Armed guards patrol the perimeter, doubled since my mother's murder. Ken Jackson's doing. My father's right-hand man has barely left my side since the news broke, managing security, fielding calls, keeping the vultures at bay. His concern seems genuine, his grief for my father palpable.

And yet.

My father's voice echoes in my memory: "Trust no one completely, mijita. Not even those who seem most loyal."

I return to the desk, sinking into the leather chair that still feels too large for me. My hand slides beneath the polished wood, fingers finding the cold metal shape secured there with magnets. The gun my father insisted I learn to use on my sixteenth birthday. "Just in case," he'd said then too.

I've never fired it outside the shooting range. Never needed to. But my fingers check the safety automatically, a movement drilled into muscle memory by hours of practice I'd complained about at the time.

The clock on the wall ticks loudly in the silence. Seconds stretching into eternity as I wait for a stranger my father trusted.

A man connected to my family's first great loss, now arriving in the wake of our latest.

I steel myself, forcing my features into the mask of control my mother perfected. Back straight, chin lifted, emotions locked safely away where they can't betray me. Whoever Mason Phillips is, whatever he wants, he will not find Yelana Zentarra weeping or afraid.

He will find a Zentarra ready for war.

He fills the doorway like a storm front, broad shoulders, watchful eyes, danger wrapped in a deceptively simple black suit. Mason Phillips. The name my father whispered with respect. The man somehow connected to my brother's death. I remain seated as Kendrick announces him with typical formality, my fingers still resting near the hidden gun. Phillips doesn't wait for an invitation to enter. He steps into the study, his gaze sweeping the room in a practiced pattern: windows, corners, exits, me. Assessing threats. Identifying tactical positions. Only after this swift inventory does his attention settle fully on my face.

"Miss Zentarra." His voice is gravelly sandpaper, deeper than I expected. The kind of voice that's seen too much, said too little.

I study him coldly. Mid to late forties, maybe, with close-cropped dark hair graying at the temples. A thin scar bisects his left eyebrow, another traces his jawline. His hands hang loosely at his sides, deliberately non-threatening, yet ready to move in an instant. The slight bulge beneath his left arm confirms what Kendrick mentioned: he's armed. And he's also kind of hot. I wonder if he knows about my own weapon inches from my fingertips.

"My father was killed last night," I say without preamble, watching his reaction. Testing him.

Something genuine flashes across his face, shock, then a swift cascade of emotions too complex to name. His jaw tightens, cords standing out in his neck. His hands clench briefly before deliberately relaxing. Not the reaction of someone who already knew. Not the controlled mask of someone who arranged it.

"Jesus Christ," he breathes, shaking his head slightly. "When? How?"

"Three bullets to the chest. Professional hit, according to the police." I keep my voice clinical, detached. The way my mother taught me to discuss difficult matters. "Found in his car near the marina. Security footage conveniently missing."

Phillips takes another step forward, then stops, seeming to recalibrate his approach. "I received a message from your father two days ago," he says, each word measured. "He sent a video saying your mother had been killed. That he was next. That he needed me to protect you."

I arch an eyebrow, irritation flaring through the numbness. "Protect me?"

"He believed someone inside his organization had betrayed him," Phillips continues. "He didn't trust anyone here to keep you safe."

"So he sent for you." I can't keep the edge from my voice. "A man I've never met?" I lie testing the water. "A stranger connected to my brother's death."

His expression doesn't change, but something shutters behind his eyes. "We've met, actually. When you were younger."

"Pink Band-Aids," I say before I can stop myself. The childhood memory surfaces unexpectedly, me standing on tiptoes to place colorful bandages on this man's wounded face. "You were hurt."

A small smile begins to form, but doesn't reach his eyes, then he nods once, a barely perceptible movement. "Afghanistan, 2007. Your father saved my life when my team was ambushed."

"The same ambush where my brother died." The words hang between us, heavy with unspoken history.

"Yes."

One syllable, carrying the weight of so much pain. I search his face for deception but find only a weathered kind of honesty. Not comfort, not pity, just acknowledgement of a shared wound.

"And now my father summoned you to, what? Babysit me?" I stand up, needing the leverage of height, even though he still towers over me. "I have security. I have Ken Jackson, my father's most trusted advisor. I don't need some—"

"With respect, Miss Zentarra," Phillips cuts in, his voice low but firm, "your father believed someone close to him ordered the hit on your mother. Someone with inside knowledge of security protocols, access codes, and schedules. He didn't know who to trust anymore."

"Except you." I can't keep the bitterness from my voice. "A man he hadn't seen in what, fifteen years?"

"Fourteen," Phillips corrects quietly. "We stayed in contact though, more than you know, and more than we should have."

This catches me off guard. What else about my father's life remains hidden from me? How many more secrets will death reveal?

"He left a message for you," Phillips says after a moment. "For your eyes only. Said it would explain everything, but you would need me to access it."

Despite myself, interest prickles beneath my skin. "What message?"

"On a secure drive. I'll need to authenticate it before turning it over." His hand makes a small motion toward his jacket pocket. "Your father was very specific about security protocols."

I let out a sharp laugh that sounds nothing like humor. "Of course he was. My father and his secrets." I turn away, moving to the window where I can see the gardens, the guards, the high walls that have never felt like enough protection. "Did he tell you what I know about his business, Mr. Phillips? About why someone might want him dead?"

In the reflection of the glass, I watch Phillips consider his words carefully. "He said you were unaware of certain aspects of his operation."

"Aspects," I repeat, turning back to face him. "What a delicate way to phrase it. Let me be clearer: I know my father sold weapons, Mr. Phillips. I'm not a child. I've known since I was sixteen and found documents he thought were well hidden. I just never confronted him about it. It was easier to pretend."

Surprise registers briefly in his eyes before he masks it. "Then you understand the kind of enemies he made."

"I'm beginning to." I move back to the desk, running my fingers along the polished edge. "What I don't understand is why you're here. What debt could possibly make you drop everything to fly across the country for a dead man's daughter?"

Phillips takes a breath, something raw and painful crossing his face. "Your brother died because your father chose to save me."

The admission hits me like a physical blow. My parents never shared these details, just that Juan died in an accident while we were in Afghanistan for my father's import business." The room suddenly feels too small, too stuffy with the ghosts of family secrets.

"Blood debt," Phillips says quietly. "In your father's world, in my world, that means something."

Before I can respond, the study door flies open. Ken Jackson bursts in without knocking, his face flushed with anger, his tall frame vibrating with barely contained fury. Behind him, Kendrick hovers apologetically.

"I tried to inform Mr. Jackson that you were in a meeting, Miss—"

"What the hell is this outsider doing in Emelio's study?" Ken demands, his eyes locked on Phillips with naked hostility. His hand drifts toward the weapon I know he carries beneath his tailored jacket.

Phillips doesn't move, doesn't even blink, but something in his stance shifts subtly. The air between the two men crackles with potential violence.

And just like that, I'm caught between my father's oldest ally and his final choice, neither of whom I truly know, both claiming to protect me from shadows I'm only beginning to understand.

Ken's body blocks my view of Phillips, his broad back forming a human shield between us. The gesture might seem protective if not for the white-knuckle tension radiating from him; clearly, it has bruised his ego. His hand hovers near the slight bulge under his jacket, the Glock 19 he's carried for as long as I can remember. Across the room, Phillips hasn't moved an inch, but something has changed in his posture. The casual readiness has crystallized into something more focused, more dangerous. Two predators sizing each other up in my father's study, while I'm caught in the crossfire of their silent assessment.

"What the hell is this outsider doing here?" Ken demands again, his voice dropping to that dangerous register I've heard him use with people who disappoint my father. "This is Zentarra business."

Phillips' eyes flick from Ken to me and back again, cataloging everything, missing nothing. His hand doesn't drift toward his weapon, but I sense his awareness of exactly how many steps it would take to reach Ken, exactly how many movements to neutralize the threat.

"Mr. Phillips was invited," I say, but Ken doesn't turn to look at me, his attention fixed wholly on the stranger.

"By who? Not by you." Ken's voice carries an accusation. "Not with Emelio's body barely cold. You think I don't recognize a vulture when I see one? These types always appear when they smell vulnerability."

Phillips remains perfectly still, but his eyes harden. "I'm here at Emelio's request," he says, his voice so level it seems artificially controlled. "Made two days ago. After Sierra's murder."

"Convenient timing," Ken spits. "You expect us to believe Emelio just happened to call in some long-lost friend right before his death? That doesn't strike you as suspicious, Yelana?"

My father's chair suddenly feels too large, the leather too slick beneath my palms. I push myself up, spine straightening inch by inch until I'm standing at my full height. Let's be honest, I am not tall, or physically imposing like these men, but a Zentarra nonetheless.

"He's here because my father sent for him," I state, my voice dropping to a commanding pitch I didn't know I possessed until this moment. Both men turn to look at me, identical expressions of surprise quickly masked. "And I don't recall asking for your opinion, Ken."

Ken's face flushes deeper, a vein pulsing at his temple. "Yelana, be reasonable. Your father would want me to protect you. Bringing in strangers during this vulnerable transition puts the entire organization at risk. We don't know who we can—"

"Trust?" I cut him off, stepping around the desk. "Isn't that interesting? Mr. Phillips was contacted by my father specifically because he didn't know who to trust anymore; he suspected someone inside our organization had betrayed him."

Ken's eyes widen fractionally before narrowing. "That's absurd. Your father trusted me with everything. I've been by his side for twenty years."

"And yet he sent for Phillips," I observe, letting the implication hang in the air between us.

Ken's jaw works as he struggles to contain whatever he wants to say next. I've known him my entire life—the uncle who taught me to ride a bike, who brought me ice cream after piano recitals, who looked at me with sad eyes on the anniversary of Juan's death. But the man standing before me now seems almost a stranger, vibrating with an anger I don't fully understand.

"Yelana," he tries again, his tone gentler but still rigid with tension. "Your father was under enormous stress after Sierra's death. He wasn't thinking clearly. We need to circle the wagons right now, not invite unknown elements into our home."

I move until I'm standing directly between them, a position that feels both vulnerable and powerful. "My father trusted this man," I say, nodding toward Phillips without looking at him. "That's enough for now."

"You don't even know him!" Ken protests, gesturing sharply. "You have no idea what his real agenda might be."

"I know my father saved his life," I reply evenly. "I know there was a blood debt between them. I know enough to understand why he's here."

The study falls silent except for the soft ticking of my father's antique clock. Three strangers bound by the ghost of Emelio Zentarra, each with our own version of who he was.

I take a breath, feeling the weight of the Zentarra name settle more firmly on my shoulders. "Mr. Phillips will be staying to help identify the traitor who killed my parents. That decision is final."

Ken's posture shifts, his expression cycling through disbelief, hurt, and finally, a grudging submission. "As you wish," he says stiffly. "But I strongly advise against it. And I'll be watching him." He directs this last part at Phillips, who meets his gaze without flinching.

"I expect nothing less," Phillips replies, his voice neutral.

"If you'll excuse us," I say to Ken, making it clear the conversation is over. "Mr. Phillips and I have matters to discuss."

For a moment, I think Ken might refuse to leave. His body remains rigid, his presence a wall of disapproval. Then he gives a curt nod, his eyes never leaving Phillips.

"I'll be right outside," he says, the words carrying an unmistakable warning. "Call if you need anything."

"Thank you, Ken." I soften my tone slightly, aware that I need allies, not enemies. "We'll speak more later."

With obvious reluctance, he backs toward the door, turns with military precision, and exits. Kendrick, who has been standing forgotten in the doorway throughout this exchange, gives me a questioning look.

"That will be all, Kendrick," I say quietly. "No more interruptions, please."

"Very good, Miss." He closes the door with a soft click, leaving me alone with Mason Phillips.

We regard each other across the study—me, a twenty-one-year-old thrust into leadership I never wanted; him, a scarred stranger carrying my father's final trust. Neither of us speaks for a long moment. His eyes are the color of burnished steel, giving away nothing, yet somehow seeing everything.

"You don't trust me," he says finally. Not a question.

"I don't trust anyone," I correct him, returning to my father's chair. "But my father did, for whatever reason. And right now, that's the only currency that matters."

Phillips nods once, accepting this fragile truce for what it is—not trust, not partnership, just mutual necessity bound by a dead man's wishes. He moves to the window, positioning himself with his back to the wall, where he can see both the door and the gardens outside.

"So," I say, folding my hands on the desk, my right still within reach of the hidden gun. "Tell me about this message my father left me."

THREE
The Final Message

Mason

I run my thumb along the edge of the secure drive in my pocket. "The message isn't something I can just hand over. Your father was specific about where and how it should be accessed." I meet Yelana's eyes across the desk, seeing Sierra in the sharp angle of her cheekbones, Emelio in the unflinching stare. "We need to go to his secure room."

Her jaw tightens at my presumption that I know about a place in her home she might not. "Fine," she says after a moment, rising from her father's chair with fluid grace that can't quite hide the exhaustion beneath. "Follow me."

I step aside to let her pass, keeping a careful distance. Her perfume catches me off guard – something light and expensive that reminds me of her mother. Sierra wore the same scent, I realize. A daughter trying to hold onto what's lost.

Yelana leads me through corridors lined with artwork worth more than my annual income. I catalog every turn, every security camera, every potential choke point. Old habits. Three armed guards patrol this wing alone – one near the main staircase, two by the east corridor. Their eyes track me with professional suspicion. Good training, but not good enough. I spot at least two blind spots in the coverage, places where someone with the right knowledge could slip through undetected.

"Your security has gaps," I say, keeping my voice low as we pass a guard who stands a little straighter at our approach. "East corridor, second floor landing, junction near the kitchen."

Yelana doesn't turn around. "Is that your professional assessment, Mr. Phillips?" Her voice drips with disdain.

"Yes."

"Then I'll add it to my list of concerns, somewhere below my parents' murders."

Fair enough. I fall silent, focusing instead on the back of her head, the rigid line of her shoulders. She moves with purpose despite the weight I know must be crushing her. Twenty-one years old and suddenly responsible for an empire she doesn't fully understand. I've seen hardened soldiers break under less.

We descend a narrow staircase hidden behind what looks like a supply closet. The air grows cooler, the lighting more utilitarian. My palm slides against the wall, feeling the transition from plaster to concrete. We're entering the fortress beneath the mansion – Emelio's true domain.

My mouth goes dry as we approach a steel door at the end of the corridor. Sweat beads along my hairline despite the chill. I've been in war zones that triggered less physical reaction than this threshold to Emelio's inner sanctum. My eyes dart to a framed photo on the wall – Emelio standing beside a helicopter in some desert landscape, his face younger but his eyes the same. Watching me even in death.

"This is it," Yelana says, stopping before the door. She turns to me with narrowed eyes, her stance defensive. "Now what?"

I step forward, acutely aware of her gaze tracking my every movement. My heart pounds against my ribs as I approach the security panel beside the door – a state-of-the-art biometric system paired with keypad entry. The old war room, as Emelio called it. The place where he planned operations I pretended not to know about, made deals I convinced myself weren't my concern.

"Your father gave me access," I explain, my finger hovering over the keypad. "For emergencies."

Her eyebrow arches skeptically. "And what was the emergency fourteen years ago that required you to have access to my father's most secure room?"

I don't answer immediately, instead punching in the code – a date seared into both our memories, though she doesn't realize its significance to me. June 17, 2007. The day Juan died. The day Emelio saved my life. The blood debt beginning.

The panel beeps once, then prompts for a verbal authentication.

"Kashmir," I say clearly. The code word Emelio and I established years ago – the name of the village near where it all happened. A place neither of us would ever forget.

Yelana watches with tightly controlled surprise as the security system accepts my credentials. The heavy door slides open with a pneumatic hiss, releasing a rush of climate-controlled air that carries the ghost of Emelio's cigars – Cuban, expensive, unmistakable.

"How—" she starts, then stops herself, squaring her shoulders. "Never mind. Let's just get this over with."

I follow her into the room, fighting the urge to check over my shoulder. Being in this space feels wrong without Emelio's permission, like trespassing in a tomb. The room is exactly as I remember it – military precision in every detail. One wall is lined with display cases containing weapons behind bulletproof glass – everything from ancient ceremonial daggers to cutting-edge prototypes that shouldn't exist outside of classified military programs. Another wall holds tactical maps on digital screens, currently dormant but ready to display global operations at the touch of a button.

A large desk dominates the center of the room, its surface clear except for a single computer terminal and a humidor made of polished mahogany. Behind it, a custom gun safe large enough to walk into stands partially open, revealing glimpses of an arsenal that would make some small nations envious.

What catches me off guard are the personal touches – things I hadn't noticed during my previous brief visits. A child's drawing framed beside operational maps of the Middle East. A worn baseball displayed in a glass case. A row of photographs – Yelana at various ages, Sierra in evening wear, Juan in his baseball uniform with a gap-toothed smile. These glimpses of Emelio the father, not Emelio the arms dealer, hit harder than I expected.

"Where's this message?" Yelana demands, her voice sharper than necessary, betraying her own discomfort in this space.

I pull the secure drive from my pocket, approaching the computer terminal. "Here. Your father said it would only work on this system, with both our biometric confirmations."

As I set up the drive, I notice a small wooden box beside the monitor, hand-carved with intricate patterns. Without thinking, my fingers brush against it – a mistake. The touch brings a rush of memory: Emelio showing me this box during my last visit, explaining it contained sand from the place where Juan died. "To remind me of the price of my choices," he'd said.

I withdraw my hand as if burned, focusing instead on the task at hand. The system boots up, demanding fingerprint authentication. I place my thumb on the reader, watching as the screen fills with lines of code, verifying my identity against parameters Emelio established.

"Your turn," I say to Yelana, stepping back from the terminal.

She approaches cautiously, looking at the machine like it might bite. When she places her finger on the reader, the screen flashes green, and a video file appears – Emelio's final message to his daughter, delivered through the man he trusted with her life.

The room seems to shrink around us as we stare at the frozen image of Emelio Zentarra's face on the screen, both of us momentarily united in the knowledge that whatever comes next will change everything.

Yelana circles the desk and lowers herself into her father's chair, her movements deliberate, as though sitting there requires permission even now. I position myself by the computer, far enough away to give her space but close enough to reach the controls. Our eyes meet briefly across the expanse of polished wood. I see the unspoken question in hers: How bad is what I'm about to hear? I have no comfort to offer, so I simply nod once and press play. Emelio's face fills the screen.

He looks exhausted, the lines in his face deeper than when I last saw him. His eyes are shadowed, but the intensity that always made men twice his size step back remains undimmed. He's recording from this same room—I recognize the gun display behind him—but the timestamp shows this was made just three days ago.

"Yelana, mija," he begins, his accent thickening with emotion. "If you're watching this, I'm gone, and things have happened exactly as I feared." He leans closer to the camera, his face filling the frame. "I've arranged for Mason Phillips to protect you. You must listen to him. Trust him as I have."

Beside me, Yelana stiffens in her chair, her knuckles whitening as she grips the armrests. But she remains silent, eyes locked on her father's image.

"Phillips and I have history," Emelio continues. "A debt that goes back to before you can remember. I've never told you the full truth about Juan's death, about Afghanistan." He pauses, rubbing a hand across his face. "It's time you knew."

My throat constricts. This is it—the moment of truth that can't be taken back. I force myself to breathe evenly, to maintain the rigid control that's kept me alive through worse situations than this. But somehow, facing Yelana's reaction feels more dangerous than any combat zone I've survived.

Emelio's voice drops lower. "In 2007, I received intelligence about a SEAL team ambushed near the Afghanistan-Pakistan border. One survivor—Lieutenant Mason Phillips." He glances off-camera briefly. "I had business interests in the region. Went to investigate personally, brought Juan along to learn the operation. We found Phillips barely alive, surrounded by his dead team."

Emelio's eyes find the camera again, finding his daughter across time and death. "The men who ambushed the Americans came looking later, mijita. We engaged them. During the firefight, Juan —" His voice breaks for just a moment before he regains control. "Juan ran to help me when I was pinned down. He was killed trying to reach me."

The room goes utterly still. Yelana doesn't move, doesn't blink, her breathing so shallow she might be carved from stone. On screen, Emelio continues, explaining more details about the aftermath, about bringing me to their compound to recover, about the promise I made to him—but I'm barely listening now. My focus has narrowed to Yelana, tracking the minute changes in her expression as shock transforms into comprehension.

"The blood debt between Phillips and our family cannot be measured," Emelio says, his voice pulling my attention back to the screen. "He knows this. He has carried this weight for years. Now I call upon that debt one final time. He must become your shadow, Yelana. He must protect you from what's coming."

Yelana's breathing changes—quickens, shallows. The first visible crack in her composure.

"Someone close to me betrayed us," Emelio continues. "Sierra's death was not an accident. By now, they've likely come for me too. They will come for you next. Phillips is the only one outside our organization I trust completely. Let him help you. Let him repay the debt he owes our family."

The message continues, but Yelana isn't listening anymore. She rises from the chair slowly, like someone in a trance. Her eyes find mine across the room, wide and glittering with something more dangerous than tears.

"You're the reason Juan is dead?" Her voice is barely audible, a whisper that somehow fills the entire room. "And my father kept this from me for eighteen fucking years?"

I don't move. Don't defend myself. Don't offer excuses. There are none. "Yes."

The single syllable detonates her composure. She crosses the space between us in three quick strides and slams her palms against my chest. I absorb the impact without stepping back.

"You!" The word explodes from her like a bullet. "My brother is DEAD because of YOU!"

She shoves me again, harder this time. I let her, keeping my hands at my sides, accepting each blow as earned penance.

"All those years, those stories about an 'accident,' about Juan being in the wrong place—" Her voice rises, fractures. "It was YOU! He died saving YOU!"

She paces away, then whirls back, hair flying wild around her face. The controlled, composed woman from her father's study is gone, replaced by raw fury in motion. Her hands cut through the air as she speaks, her entire body vibrating with rage.

"And you just, what, showed up at our house? Let my mother nurse you back to health? Accepted our family's hospitality while my brother was being buried?" Her laugh holds no humor, just broken glass. "Did you sit at our dinner table, eating our food, sleeping in our beds, while Juan was rotting in the ground because of you?"

I stand perfectly still, back straight, shoulders squared. Each word lands like artillery fire, accurate and devastating. My jaw clenches tight enough to crack molars, but I keep my face neutral through years of practiced control. She deserves this outlet. Deserves to hurt me with these truths.

"Answer me!" she demands, moving back into my space, close enough that I can see every detail of her face—the flush of anger across her cheekbones, the slight tremble in her lower lip, the unshed tears making her eyes shine like wet obsidian.

"Yes," I say, the word costing me more than she'll ever know. "I recovered at your family's compound for six weeks. Your mother changed my bandages. Your father kept watch while I slept. You brought me pink Band-Aids from your toy medical kit. Every day, I wished it had been me instead of Juan."

My honesty seems to fuel her anger rather than diminish it. She circles me like a predator, her movements sharp and unpredictable while I remain motionless at the center of her orbit.

"And now my father thinks I need YOU? The man who got my brother killed? The man whose life my father valued more than his own son's?" She snatches a crystal paperweight from the desk and hurls it against the wall where it shatters impressively. "Fuck you, Phillips. And fuck my father for bringing you here."

She paces the length of the room, hands alternating between wild gestures and raking through her hair. I track her with my eyes only, keeping my body still. Each outburst strips away another layer of the sophisticated facade, revealing the wounded child beneath—the little girl who grew up with a brother-shaped hole in her life, never knowing the full truth.

"Get out," she finally spits, pointing at the door. "Get the fuck out of my house."

Behind her, Emelio's frozen face watches from the screen, his final message paused mid-sentence. Warning undelivered. Threat unexplained. I remain where I stand, weathering her rage like a stone enduring a hurricane, knowing the storm must exhaust itself before we can move forward.

Because despite her fury, despite her hatred, I know what she doesn't yet understand: leaving isn't an option. Not with Emelio's killers still out there. Not with the threat he tried to warn her about still hanging over her head.

The blood debt demands payment, and I intend to pay in full—even if it costs me everything.

I don't move toward the door. Instead, I reach for the computer and unpause the video. "Before you throw me out, hear the rest of what your father has to say." My voice is steady despite the storm of emotions churning beneath my rigid exterior. Yelana opens her mouth to object, but Emelio's voice fills the room again, and her attention snaps back to the screen almost against her will.

"—not just any betrayal, mijita," Emelio continues mid-sentence, his face grave. "Someone in my inner circle. Someone with access to security protocols, to our schedules, to the estate's weaknesses." He leans forward, his eyes intense. "Sierra discovered something. Financial discrepancies. Weapon shipments that didn't match our records. Communications with the Costa organization."

Yelana's breathing is still ragged from her outburst, but her focus has shifted. She takes an unconscious step closer to the screen, her rage temporarily eclipsed by her father's warning.

"Three days before she died, your mother told me she had identified the traitor." Emelio's jaw tightens visibly. "Before she could tell me who, she was killed. Made to look like an accident, but we both know better, don't we, mija?" A bitter smile crosses his face. "Your mother was too careful for accidents."

I ease away from the computer, positioning myself near the door. Not to leave, but to give Yelana space while maintaining tactical awareness of our surroundings. My mind races, analyzing the security implications of what Emelio is revealing. An inside man changes everything. The estate isn't just vulnerable—it's compromised. Every security protocol, every safe room, every escape route potentially known to the enemy.

"I've been investigating quietly," Emelio continues. "Keeping my suspicions hidden, feeding different information to different people. But they're closing in. I can feel it." He runs a hand through his hair, a gesture of frustration I'd never seen from him in life. "Sierra's files were encrypted. I haven't been able to access them yet. The answers are there—who's behind this, who in our organization is working with them."

Yelana sinks back into the desk chair, her earlier fury now tempered by dawning comprehension. The floor has shifted beneath her twice in minutes—first learning the truth about her brother, now understanding that someone she likely trusts is responsible for her parents' deaths.

"Trust no one inside the organization right now," Emelio warns. "Not until you find Sierra's evidence. Not Ken, not security, not household staff. No one." His eyes seem to find mine through the screen. "Except Phillips. His debt to our family is absolute. And he has no connections to our business that could compromise him."

I watch Yelana carefully, gauging her reaction. Her knuckles are white where they grip the chair arms, but the wild rage has crystallized into something colder, more focused. She's beginning to think like her father's daughter—calculating threat levels, prioritizing immediate dangers over personal feelings.

"The safe deposit box at Cayman United," Emelio continues. "Sierra kept a backup there. Account number and access codes are in the humidor, under the false bottom. Third cigar from the left releases the mechanism." He pauses, something like regret flickering across his features. "I'm sorry, Yelana. I should have prepared you better. Should have told you everything years ago. But I wanted to protect you from this life."

The video continues with Emelio providing more operational details—names of allies she can potentially trust outside the organization, locations of emergency resources, contingency plans—but my attention is on Yelana herself. The transformation happening before my eyes is remarkable. Beneath the grief and rage, I can see her mind working, processing, adapting. In this moment, she reminds me less of the little girl with pink bandaids and more of the tactician her father was.

When the video finally ends, the room falls into weighted silence. Yelana stares at the blank screen for several long moments before turning her attention back to me. Her eyes are still hard, but the focus has changed.

"Why would he trust you with this?" she demands, her voice hoarse from shouting. "Why would he trust my safety to the man responsible for Juan's death?"

I meet her gaze directly, not hiding from the accusation in her eyes. "Because I owe your family a debt I can never repay." The words come out rough, scraped against the gravel of old regrets. "And because I won't fail again."

Something in my tone makes her look at me more closely. "Again?"

I don't elaborate. Some wounds aren't meant to be displayed. Kerry's ghost stays mine alone. Instead, I hold Yelana's stare, letting her see the resolution behind my words. I failed Juan. I failed Kerry. I failed my team in Afghanistan. But I will not fail this mission, even if it costs me everything.

Our eyes lock in silent confrontation across the room—her fury against my determination. I can almost see the calculation running behind her eyes, weighing her hatred for me against the reality of her situation. Her father's murdered. Her mother's murdered. A traitor lurks in her inner circle. And the only person she can trust, according to her father, is the man she has every reason to hate.

Finally, something shifts in her posture—not softening, but recalibrating. "Stay if you have to," she says, her voice like steel wrapped in silk. "Help me find who killed my parents. Help me find my mother's evidence." Her eyes narrow, boring into mine with unflinching intensity. "But understand this—I'll never forgive you for Juan."

I nod once, accepting these terms without argument. Her forgiveness isn't something I've ever expected or felt I deserved. "I understand."

She moves toward the door, posture rigid with barely contained emotion. "Then we have work to do."

I follow her out of the secure room, maintaining a respectful distance. The pneumatic door hisses closed behind us, sealing away Emelio's inner sanctum once more. As we climb the stairs back to the main house, I'm acutely aware of the fragile alliance we've just formed—not built on trust or friendship, but on the pragmatic recognition of mutual necessity.

She hates me for her brother's death. I'm bound to her by a blood debt I can never fully repay. But for now, we're moving in the same direction—toward whoever murdered her parents, toward the traitor in her midst, toward the danger that still threatens to claim another Zentarra life.

And as we emerge into the main hallway, where Ken Jackson waits with poorly disguised impatience, I feel my operational mindset snap fully into place. My personal feelings—the guilt, the grief, the regret—all neatly compartmentalized and set aside. From this moment forward, Yelana Zentarra's survival is my only mission.

A mission I cannot, will not fail. No matter the cost.

FOUR
An Uneasy Alliance

YELANA

I spread funeral brochures across my father's desk, no, my desk now, arranging them in neat rows like I'm organizing battle plans instead of burial details. The mahogany surface gleams beneath the soft study lights, still bearing the water ring from my father's last bourbon glass. His cigars still perfume the air, as if he might walk in any moment and scold me for disturbing his papers. I've been at this for hours, methodically selecting programs, floral arrangements, burial plots, transforming unbearable grief into manageable logistics to prevent myself from completely shattering.

My finger traces the embossed lettering on a sample program. "Emelio & Sierra Zentarra, Beloved Parents." Not "arms dealer" or "criminal mastermind" or whatever titles the whispers behind cupped hands might assign. Just parents. My parents. Gone in the span of three days.

The door swings open without a knock. Mason Phillips strides in with the confidence of someone who believes every room belongs to him. I straighten my spine, irritation flaring hot beneath my skin.

"We need to discuss funeral security," he announces, already spreading diagrams across my carefully arranged brochures. "The cemetery presents multiple vulnerabilities we need to address."

"Please, come right in," I mutter, not bothering to hide my sarcasm. "I wasn't in the middle of anything important."

He either misses or ignores my tone. His finger taps a spot on what I now recognize as a topographical map of Evergreen Cemetery. "The chapel has limited egress points. Two main doors, windows too small for practical evacuation. The tree line here—" his finger traces a perimeter around the building, "—offers multiple concealed positions for long-range weapons."

My irritation falters as his words sink in. Long-range weapons. Concealed positions. I look up from the diagrams to his face, finding nothing but cold professionalism in his expression. No grief, no sympathy, just tactical assessment.

"The funeral is in three days," I say, hating how young my voice sounds. "I'm still selecting the casket lining."

"The casket lining won't matter if you're joining them in it." His bluntness slices through the room like a knife. He pulls another diagram from his folder—this one showing the cemetery's main pathway. "The walk from the chapel to the gravesite exposes you for approximately ninety seconds. No cover, multiple angles of approach."

The words "joining them" echo in my head as Phillips continues his assessment, pointing out choke points, identifying optimal positions for his security personnel, mapping escape routes with the precision of someone who has planned too many last stands.

"We'll need at least six men positioned here, here, and here." He marks spots on the diagram with a red pen. "Two advance teams sweeping for devices or planted threats. Counter-sniper positions on these three elevations." More marks appear on the map, transforming the peaceful cemetery into a battlefield. "Your vehicle needs to be armored, parked here for immediate extraction if necessary."

My eyes follow his pen, watching as he systematically dismantles any illusion that this will be a normal funeral. That I can simply grieve like a normal daughter. That I am anything but a target.

"My parents deserve a proper service," I say, fingers curling around the edge of a brochure showing peaceful angels and tasteful floral arrangements. "Not some...militarized operation."

Phillips looks up, his steel-gray eyes meeting mine directly. "Your parents deserve to have their daughter survive their funeral."

The blunt truth of his statement hits harder than any sympathy could. I glance down at the security diagrams, really seeing them now. The Xs mark potential sniper nests. The dotted lines show paths of vulnerability. The harsh reality of my new existence mapped out in red ink.

My shoulders tense as a new thought forms. If Phillips believes these precautions are necessary, then he believes the threat is imminent. The same people who murdered my parents are still out there, watching, waiting for the perfect moment to complete their task. And what better opportunity than a public funeral where everyone knows I'll be present?

"You think they'll make a move at the funeral," I say. Not a question

"It's what I would do." His voice is matter-of-fact. "Large gathering. Predictable movements. Emotionally compromised target." He pauses, then adds, "You."

I swallow hard, feeling suddenly exposed despite the solid walls of my father's study surrounding us. My fingers begin arranging the funeral brochures into even straighter lines, a pointless bid for control.

"Can we secure it or not?" I ask, proud that my voice doesn't waver.

Phillips studies the diagrams again. "Yes. With the right preparations and your cooperation." His emphasis on the last two words makes his meaning clear—he expects me to follow his instructions without argument.

I look down at the sample program in my hands. My parents' names stare back at me, gold leaf catching the light. For a moment, I imagine another program, another funeral, mine. My name in gold lettering, the same cemetery map marked with an X where I fell.

"What do you need from me?" The question costs me, each word extracted like a splinter.

Something shifts in Phillips' expression, not softening, exactly, but a slight recalibration. Recognition of concession. "Final guest list by tonight. Approval for additional security personnel. Your agreement to wear body armor beneath your clothes. And no deviations from the planned schedule or routes."

Body armor. At my parents' funeral. The absurdity almost makes me laugh, but the sound dies in my throat before it can form. This is my reality now. Security assessments and escape routes, bulletproof clothing, and counter-sniper positions.

"Fine," I say, pushing aside a delicate floral arrangement catalog to make room for more of his tactical diagrams. "Show me the evacuation routes again."

Phillips nods, seemingly satisfied with my acquiescence. He pulls another diagram from his folder, this one showing the cemetery grounds with three different colored lines marking potential exit strategies.

As he explains each route in meticulous detail, I find myself studying his face instead of the maps. This man, this stranger who carries my brother's death on his conscience, now holds my life in his hands. The irony isn't lost on me. But beneath my lingering resentment, a reluctant understanding begins to form. He knows what he's doing. Each word, each movement speaks of experience paid for in blood.

My father trusted him enough to call in a blood debt. For now, that will have to be enough for me, too.

He looks up, and our eyes lock. Suddenly, the room around us is nothing but static. I can see his professionalism, but I also see pain and something else.

The moment is shattered when the door crashes open with enough force to rattle the hinges. Ken Jackson strides in like he owns the damn place, his tailored suit failing to disguise the tension rippling through his shoulders. His eyes lock onto Phillips, narrowing to slits as he takes in the security diagrams spread across my father's desk. The temperature in the room seems to drop ten degrees as the two men assess each other, neither bothering to hide their mutual distrust. Ken has been by my father's side for twenty years, but in this moment, he looks like a stranger, territorial and dangerous.

"What the hell is this?" Ken gestures toward the papers, his voice deceptively controlled. "Funeral plans are being made without consulting me?"

Phillips doesn't straighten from where he's leaning over the desk, doesn't offer any deference to Ken's seniority in my father's organization. "Security preparations," he says flatly. "Time-sensitive."

Ken's jaw tightens as he turns to me, "Yelana, we discussed this. My team has handled Zentarra security for two decades. We don't need outside interference." The emphasis on 'outside' carries a weight of accusation.

"Your team failed to prevent two assassinations in as many days," Phillips observes, his tone clinical rather than accusatory. The implied failure hangs in the air between them like a grenade with the pin pulled.

Ken's face flushes dark red. "You sanctimonious bastard. You think you can waltz in here after all these years and take over? Based on what? A debt Emelio mentioned when he'd had too much to drink?" He steps closer to Phillips, invading his space. "I know your type, military has-beens who think their tactical training translates to real-world protection."

"And I know yours," Phillips counters, not backing up an inch. "Security chiefs who get comfortable. Who mistake familiarity for effectiveness. Who develop blind spots precisely where they should be most vigilant."

The testosterone in the room thickens until I can practically taste it. Two apex predators circling each other, neither willing to show submission. I remain silent, studying both men with new eyes. There's history here I'm not privy to—resentments that predate the current crisis.

Ken snatches one of the diagrams, scanning it with a professional eye before tossing it back onto the desk. "Ridiculous. You've got visible security positioned all along the chapel approach. Might as well put up a neon sign announcing we're expecting trouble."

"Because we are expecting trouble," Phillips replies, tapping the map with one finger. "Visible deterrence is half the strategy."

"It's security theater," Ken scoffs. "Advertises weakness, makes guests feel uncomfortable, and doesn't prevent a determined attack. Our approach has always been subtle integration, security that blends with the environment."

"Your subtle approach got Emelio and Sierra killed," Phillips says, his voice dropping dangerously low.

Ken's hand twitches toward his hip, where I know he keeps his Glock, before he catches himself. "You know nothing about what happened.

"You weren't here. You haven't been here for years."

"Which makes me the only person in this room guaranteed not to be compromised," Phillips counters.

The implication lands like a physical blow. Ken's face hardens into something I barely recognize, this man who taught me to ride a bike, who brought ice cream after piano recitals, suddenly transformed by fury and suspicion.

"You're suggesting I had something to do with Emelio's death?" Ken's voice is barely above a whisper. "After twenty years of loyalty?"

Phillips doesn't answer directly, turning instead to lay out another diagram. "The gravesite needs coverage from these three positions. Long-range team here, mid-range here, close protection detail within five feet of Miss Zentarra at all times."

"Absolutely not," Ken interjects. "You'll turn a solemn ceremony into an armed camp. Emelio has business associates attending who won't appreciate being treated like potential threats."

"Everyone is a potential threat," Phillips states, as if reciting a fundamental law of physics. "Including business associates. Especially business associates."

I watch them volley arguments back and forth, each insisting his approach is superior. Ken advocates for hidden security, plain-clothed personnel, and minimal disruption to the ceremony's dignity. Phillips pushes for overlapping visible and hidden assets, restricted access points, and pre-vetted attendees only. Neither man seems to remember I'm in the room. Neither bothers to ask what I want.

The argument escalates, their voices rising with each exchange.

"Your approach leaves at least four blind spots in the coverage," Phillips says, marking areas on the map with sharp jabs of his pen.

"Your approach creates panic and makes my security team look incompetent," Ken fires back.

"Maybe they are incompetent, given recent events."

"You arrogant son of a—"

My palm slams against the mahogany desk with enough force to make both men jump, the sharp crack splitting their argument in half.

"Enough." My voice emerges colder than I expected, harder, carrying an echo of my father that surprises even me. Both men turn toward me, momentarily startled out of their territorial display.

I stand slowly, drawing myself up to my full height, filling the space between these two much larger men. "Let me make something abundantly clear. My parents are dead. I am alive. And I am in charge now."

Ken's expression shifts, softens into something apologetic. "Yelana, I'm just trying to—"

"I'm not finished." The steel in my voice stops him mid-sentence. "You will both remember that this is my family's organization, my family's funeral, and my life at stake. You don't get to posture and argue over my head like I'm some prized territory to be claimed."

Phillips' face remains impassive, but something in his eyes changes, a reassessment, perhaps even a flicker of respect.

"Ken, you've been loyal to my father for twenty years, and I value that. But Phillips is right, someone got past our security twice. Something needs to change." I turn to Phillips before Ken can respond. "And you. You may have my father's trust, but you haven't earned mine. Your security measures need to respect the dignity of this occasion while keeping everyone safe."

I sweep my gaze between them, letting my words sink in. "You will work together. You will compromise. You will remember who you're serving. Am I understood?"

Ken's jaw works silently for a moment before he nods. "Yes, Yelana."

Phillips gives a single, clipped nod. "Understood."

The atmosphere in the room shifts perceptibly. Nothing is resolved between these two men; the distrust remains palpable, but the dynamic has changed. I am no longer the object they're fighting over. I am the authority they answer to.

I sit back down, gesturing to the diagrams. "Now. Show me what you both propose, and we'll find a middle ground that keeps me alive without turning my parents' funeral into a military operation."

As they reluctantly begin to outline their respective approaches, I feel something solidify inside me, the weight of the Zentarra name taking root, transforming from burden to armor. My father cast a long shadow. Perhaps it's time I stopped standing in it and started casting my own.

The soft clink of china against silver cuts through the tension. All three of us startle and turn toward the door where Kendrick stands, impossibly silent despite the loaded tea tray in his hands. I swear that man floats rather than walks, a skill he's used since my childhood to catch me sneaking cookies or eavesdropping on my parents' conversations.

His expression betrays nothing as he sets the tray on the side table, but I don't miss how his eyes sweep across the security diagrams spread over my father's desk, lingering just a beat too long on the evacuation routes Phillips has outlined.

"Refreshments, Miss Zentarra," Kendrick announces with that proper British inflection that hasn't softened in the twenty years he's been in California. "I thought you might require something to sustain you through your...discussions."

His emphasis on the last word is subtle, yet unmistakable, a gentle rebuke for the raised voices that surely carried beyond these walls. The butler's immaculate appearance, from his pressed shirt to his polished shoes, seems almost obscene against the chaos of our situation. As if proper service can somehow normalize the fact that we're planning how to avoid assassination at a funeral.

"Thank you, Kendrick," I say, watching as he arranges the cups with a precision that he has mastered.

Phillips hasn't moved, but his attention has shifted entirely to Kendrick. I catch the almost imperceptible tightening around his eyes, the slight adjustment in his stance, subtle changes that transform him from security consultant to predator assessing a potential threat. He's watching Kendrick the same way I am, noting how the butler's gaze keeps returning to our security diagrams despite his affected disinterest.

My father's words echo in my head: "Trust no one inside the organization right now."

Kendrick has been with us for as long as I can remember. He's seen me at my best and worst, holding back my hair when I had stomach flu at seven, discreetly removing wine stains from my dress at sixteen, standing silent sentinel at my graduation while my parents beamed with pride. The idea that he could betray us seems absurd.

And yet.

"Will there be anything else, Miss?" Kendrick asks, his hands clasped behind his back, his posture perfect.

"No, that's all." I force a small smile. "Thank you."

Kendrick nods, then glides from the room as silently as he entered, pulling the door closed with a soft click. Phillips and I exchange glances, a moment of unspoken acknowledgment that even the walls might have ears now.

Ken clears his throat, clearly uncomfortable with the new thread of suspicion woven into our already tense conversation. "As I was saying, we need a balance between security and propriety. The Zentarra name demands a certain dignity."

"The Zentarra name won't mean much if the last Zentarra is dead," Phillips counters, but his tone has lost some of its edge. He taps the chapel diagram. "We can compromise on the visible presence if you'll agree to these sniper countermeasures and the advanced security sweep."

Ken frowns, studying the adjusted plan. "The metal detectors?"

"Non-negotiable," Phillips says.

"Disguised as part of the entry archway," I interject, finding a middle ground. "Tasteful, but functional. No wands, no obvious scanning."

Both men consider this, then nod reluctantly. For twenty minutes, we continue negotiating each detail, placement of personnel, evacuation protocols, and communications systems. Ken agrees to integrate some of his team with Phillips' external resources. Phillips concedes on keeping certain measures more discreet. Neither man looks happy, but the plan taking shape is stronger than either of their original proposals.

"I still don't like having an outsider running point on this," Ken says finally, gathering his notes. "But, I'll coordinate with my team based on these revisions." He turns to me, his expression softening into the avuncular concern I remember from childhood. "You should rest, Yelana. You look exhausted."

"I'll rest when my parents' killers are found," I reply, the words coming out harsher than intended.

Ken's lips press into a thin line. "Of course." He shoots one last suspicious glance at Phillips, then strides from the room, his displeasure evident in every line of his body.

As the door closes behind him, the study falls into a weighted silence. Phillips moves to the window, positioning himself so he can see both the gardens outside and the door, his back never fully turned to any entry point. Always vigilant, always ready. I wonder if he sleeps that way too, or if he sleeps at all.

"We should review the guest list next," I say, pulling a folder from beneath the scattered funeral brochures. "My father had...complicated business relationships."

Phillips nods, returning to the desk. "I'll need details on anyone you're uncertain about."

"That would be most of them," I admit. "My father kept his business separate from family life. I recognized names, faces at events, but details were..." I trail off, realizing how naive this makes me sound.

"Intentionally limited," Phillips finishes, no judgment in his tone. "Emelio was protecting you."

"Well, fat lot of good it did me," I mutter, flipping open the guest list. "Now I'm planning his funeral without knowing which attendees might want to add me to the program."

For the next hour, we work methodically through the names. Phillips knows more about my father's associates than I do, which ones are genuine allies, which maintain connections to rival organizations, and which have violent tendencies that make them high-risk attendees. I find myself reluctantly impressed by his knowledge and his focus. No wasted time, no unnecessary words. Everything precise, everything purposeful.

The tension between us hasn't disappeared, but it's transformed into something more functional. We're not friends, I don't think that would ever be possible, but we're finding a rhythm as reluctant collaborators. I still hate what he represents, still blame him for Juan, but I can separate that from his undeniable competence.

"That should cover it," Phillips says finally, after we've flagged the highest risk attendees for special monitoring. "We'll have security profiles on everyone by tomorrow morning."

I nod, reaching for the funeral brochures I'd been organizing before the interruption. My hand betrays me, trembling visibly as I gather the glossy papers. I clench my fist, willing the weakness away, but not before Phillips notices. His eyes flick to my hand, then away again quickly, pretending not to have seen my momentary lapse.

The kindness in that pretense catches me off guard. It would be easier if he remained the callous intruder, the unwelcome reminder of my brother's death. Instead, he keeps revealing these small, human moments that complicate my determination to hate him.

"We should finalize the program," I say, my voice steady even as my insides quiver with exhaustion and grief and fear. I spread the sample layouts before us, focusing on font choices and paper weight like they're matters of national security. As if the right combination of elegant typography and tasteful borders can somehow make sense of this nightmare.

Phillips doesn't focus on this obvious displacement activity. He simply stands beside me, offering practical input when asked, otherwise letting me work through my process. His presence in simultaneously intrusive and grounding, a stranger who knows too much about my family, yet the only person who seems to truly understand the danger I'm in.

I hate that I need him. Hate that my father trusted this man with my life. Hate that he's probably right about the security risks. But beneath that resentment, a cold pragmatism is taking root. I can hate Mason Phillips and use his expertise at the same time. I can work with the man responsible for Juan's death while never forgiving him for it.

"I need to survive long enough to find who killed my parents," I say finally, looking up from the funeral arrangements to meet his steady gaze. "After that, all debts are paid."

His expression doesn't change, but something flickers in his eyes, "Understood."

It's not friendship. It's not even trust. It's a transaction, his protection for my cooperation. A blood debt balance against a temporary alliance. For now, it will have to be enough.

FIVE
The Warning

Mason

I slide into a corner table at a beachfront cafe in Los Angeles, angling my chair to keep my back to the wall and my eyes on every entrance. The morning crowd mills around us, tourists with sunscreen and flip-flops, locals with laptops and designer sunglasses, all oblivious to the currents of danger flowing beneath their ordinary day. Waves crash against the shore beyond the patio, providing cover for our conversation. Miguel Loretta sits across from me, his espresso cup already half-empty, the knuckles of his right hand bearing the scars of a man who's delivered as many messages with his fists as with his words.

"You look like shit, Phillips," Miguel observes, his voice carrying the rough edges of too many cigarettes and not enough sleep. "Though I guess planning a fortress around a funeral will do that to anyone."

I don't bother responding to the jab. Miguel and I have history, the kind forged in places where diplomatic solutions failed and men like us were sent to clean up the mess. Now he moves in circles adjacent to the Zentarra organization, collecting information like a spider at the center of a web.

"Talk to me about the landscape," I say, scanning the cafe while a waitress approaches. I order black coffee, waiting until she's out of earshot before continuing. "Who's making moves?"

Miguel leans forward, forearms on the table. His eyes never stop moving, a habit we share. "Emelio's death has blown the whole thing wide open. Power vacuum like you wouldn't believe. Everyone from the Costa family to the Hernandez cartel is testing boundaries, looking for weaknesses."

"And inside the organization?"

Miguel's mouth twists. "That's where it gets interesting. Several lieutenants who've been chafing under Emelio's control for years. They smell blood in the water." He takes a sip of his espresso, watching me over the rim of the tiny cup. "Word is, nobody expected the daughter to actually take control. They all figured it was a formality, that someone else would run things behind the scenes."

The waitress returns with my coffee. I wait until she's serving another table before asking, "Ken Jackson?"

The subtle tightening of Miguel's jaw tells me everything I need to know before he even speaks. "Jackson's been with Emelio for decades. Right-hand man, trusted advisor. Word is he expected to inherit operational control when Emelio stepped down or died." Miguel's voice drops lower. "Some say he's been making arrangements toward that end for years."

I sip my coffee, letting the bitter heat clear my head. "Arrangements?"

"Building his own network within the organization. Siphoning off resources. Making quiet deals with people Emelio wouldn't approve of." Miguel shrugs. "Nothing concrete enough to move against him, Emelio trusted him too much for that, but enough smoke to suggest fire."

The pieces start shifting in my mind, forming new patterns. Ken's hostility toward me goes deeper than territorial posturing. If he expected to take control after Emelio's death, my arrival represents a direct threat to plans years in the making.

"Tell me about Yelana," I say, keeping my voice neutral.

Miguel raises an eyebrow at the shift but follows my lead. "Ivy League educated. Double major in international business and political science. Speaks four languages fluently. Sharp as a fucking tack." He gestures with his cup. "Emelio may have shielded her from the dirty side of the business, but he's been grooming her to take over the legitimate operations since Juan died. She's run their front companies for the past year, turned profits that impressed even the old-timers."

I absorb this information, mentally adding it to my assessment of Yelana Zentarra. The grieving daughter may not be just the spoilt brat I thought her to be; perhaps she's also a competent businesswoman, all existing in the same volatile package. Both sides are genuine; both sides are relevant to her survival.

"She's got her father's head for strategy," Miguel continues, "and her mother's ability to read people. Problem is, she's twenty-one and female in an organization built on old-world machismo. Some of these guys would rather burn everything to the ground than take orders from Emelio's little girl."

The waitress passes close to our table. We both fall silent, adopting the casual postures of friends having morning coffee. When she's gone, Miguel leans in closer.

"Look, the funeral's going to be a shitshow no matter how you play it. Every player in the game will be there, watching for weakness, making calculations." He drains his espresso. "But the real danger is closer to home. Someone gave up Emelio's schedule, his security protocols. Someone on the inside."

I nod, having already reached the same conclusion. "Ken isn't the only possibility."

"Not by a long shot." Miguel's eyes meet mine directly. "The household staff has access to everything, schedules, security codes, daily routines. That butler, Kendrick? Been with the family for decades. Seems loyal, but who knows what resentments build up over twenty years of service? And there's Martina Hascada, who runs the household staff. She knows every movement within those walls."

I catalog each name, adding them to the growing list of potential threats. My coffee grows cold as Miguel outlines the various factions within the Zentarra organization, the external rivals circling like vultures, the complex web of alliances and grievances that Emelio navigated with expert precision.

"The Costa family is making the boldest moves," Miguel says, keeping his voice low. "They've wanted Zentarra territory for years. Rumor is they've already flipped someone high up in the organization, but no idea if it's true or a rumor they created to destabilize the Zentarra's."

I check my watch, aware that I've been away from the estate and Yelana for nearly an hour. Too long. "Anything else I should know?"

Miguel studies me for a moment, something like curiosity flickering across his weathered face. "Why are you doing this, Phillips? This isn't your world. You've built something legitimate, something clean. Why risk it all for the daughter of an arms dealer?"

The question hits closer to home than I care to admit. I keep my expression neutral, but my mind flashes to the desert sand of Afghanistan, to Juan's blood on my hands, to Emelio's face as he carried me to safety.

"Blood debt," I say simply, knowing Miguel will understand the weight of those two words.

He nods slowly, respect and something like pity crossing his features. "Well, I hope it's worth it." He slides a folded paper across the table. "Names and locations of Costa's top people. If they make a move, it'll come from one of these quarters."

I take the paper, tucking it inside my jacket pocket without looking at it. "Appreciate it."

"Don't die for these people, Phillips," Miguel says as I stand to leave. "The debt isn't worth your life."

I leave cash on the table to cover both our drinks and a generous tip. "Some debts you can't calculate," I say, then turn and walk away, already scanning the parking lot for threats, my mind racing with new information and heightened suspicion.

A blood debt demands payment in full. No matter the cost.

I drive through the gated entrance of the Zentarra estate, nodding to the guards who recognize my vehicle. Their postures are too relaxed, their attention divided between me and their smartphones. Strike one. I make a mental note to address security protocols after the funeral arrangements are finalized. The scent of Mediterranean pines wafts as I wind up the driveway, the morning sun casting long shadows across manicured lawns. Everything looks peaceful, orderly, secure. Everything is a lie.

The main house stands like a fortress at the end of the curving drive, its Mediterranean architecture belying the security measures hidden within its elegant exterior. I park in the circular driveway, performing a quick scan of the surroundings before exiting the vehicle. The morning dew still clings to the grass as I cut across the lawn.

Yelana isn't in the study where we'd arranged to meet to finalize funeral details. Kendrick informs me that "Miss Zentarra requested some private time," but offers no location. I don't press him; the fewer people who know Yelana's exact whereabouts, the better. Instead, I follow instinct; there were snippets of conversations that we had yesterday that I think might be where I find her.

The eastern section of the grounds, past the rose garden and behind a row of cypress trees, holds a private area Yelana had insisted remain unpatrolled during the funeral. "Family only," she'd said with quiet firmness that brooked no argument.

Morning fog from the sprinklers hovers just above the grass as I walk the perimeter, staying alert for any movement that doesn't belong. The estate is quiet except for distant gardeners and the occasional security guard making predictable rounds. Too predictable. Another vulnerability to address.

I find her exactly where something inside me knew she would be —at Juan's memorial—his body rests in a family plot elsewhere, but a tribute created in the place where he reportedly spent hours practicing his baseball swing. A simple stone plaque set into the ground, weathered by sun and rain, with a scuffed baseball cap resting on top. The tribute of a sister to a brother she barely had time to know.

Yelana stands with her back to me, shoulders stiff with the effort of containing her grief. Even from this distance, I can see the slight shake in her hands, the mascara straining her cheeks. She doesn't turn at my approach, though I know she hears me. My training doesn't allow for silent movement unless necessary, and something in me doesn't want to startle her in this moment of vulnerability.

"I used to hide here when I was little," she says as I draw closer, her voice steadier than I expected. "After Juan died. My parents would find me asleep next to his plaque." She doesn't wipe away the tear tracks on her face, doesn't try to hide the evidence of her grief. "I thought if I stayed here long enough, he'd come back and teach me to throw a baseball like he promised."

I stop at the edge of the plaque, close enough to read the simple inscription: "Juan Carlos Zentarra. Beloved Son and Brother. Forever a child."

"He had a good arm," I say, the words slipping out before I can consider their impact. "Strong and accurate for his age."

Yelana's head turns slightly, just enough to see my face in profile. "You saw him play?"

"Once." My throat tightens around the memory. "At the compound in Kandahar. There was a makeshift diamond the local kids had set up. Juan jumped right in, organizing a game between your father's security team and the village boys."

She's fully facing me now, her eyes rimmed with red, but her gaze direct; the sight crushes something inside me. "My parents never told me details like that. Just that he was brave, that died in an accident." Her voice hardens on the last word.

"Not an accident," I confirm, meeting her gaze despite the urge to look away, to escape the weight of this moment. "Your father and I were pinned down by enemy fire. Juan was supposed to stay back with the vehicle, but when he saw your father under fire..." I swallow hard, forcing myself to continue. "He ran to help. Straight into the crossfire. Trying to reach your father."

The words hang between us, trembling on the morning air. I can see her processing this information, adding it to what she learned from her father's video message, assembling the full picture of that day in Afghanistan.

"He died saving you," she says finally, her voice flat.

"He died saving his father," I correct gently. "I was just...there. Wounded. The original target." I look down at the weathered plaque, at the baseball cap that's faded from red to a dusty pink in some places. "Your father chose to save me. I've carried that choice and its cost every day since."

Yelana's expression remains like marble for several heartbeats, then shifts into something harder, more defined by pain than stone. "Did you know my parents never spoke of you after you left that time...I think I was seven or eight. Not once. But every year on the anniversary of Juan's death, my father would lock himself in his study and drink bourbon until he couldn't stand." She turns back toward the plaque. "Now I understand why."

The silence stretches between us, filled with the weight of shared knowledge and separate grief. The morning sun climbs higher, burning away the sprinkler mist that had lingered on the grass.

"I'll comply with my father's wishes," Yelana finally says, her voice gaining the steel edge I recognize from our previous interactions. "I'll accept your protection because he believed it necessary." She turns, looking me in the eye, her spine straight, her chin lifted in defiance of her own vulnerability. "But I will never forgive you for being the reason my brother died."

I don't argue or defend myself. There is no defense. Instead, I give her the only thing I can—honesty. "I don't expect forgiveness. I don't deserve it. Especially when I won't forgive myself. But I promise you this: nothing will happen to you while I'm alive to prevent it." The vow forms itself, heavy with the weight of blood debt and personal redemption. "I failed Juan. I won't fail you."

She holds my gaze for a long moment, something unreadable passing behind her eyes. Then she turns away, moving past me toward the house, her body a study in controlled tension. I watch her go, noting the rigid set of her shoulders, the precise placement of each step, the way her hands still tremble slightly despite being balled into fists at her sides.

The scuffed baseball cap stares up at me from Juan's memorial, a silent witness to promises made and broken. I reach down, straightening it slightly before turning to follow Yelana at a respectful distance. Close enough to protect, far enough to respect the boundaries her grief and anger have established between us.

The blood debt remains. And debts must be paid in full.

SIX
Security Measures

Mason

The morning air holds a chill that won't last once the California sun climbs higher. I've been in the courtyard since 5:30, clearing space, laying out training mats, planning the session in my head. Teaching a civilian, especially one as stubborn as Yelana, requires different tactics than military training. I can't rely on ingrained respect for rank or fear of pushback. She'll question everything, challenge every instruction. Good. Questions mean engagement. Challenges mean she's paying attention. Both increase her chances of survival, which is the only metric that matters.

At 6:02, Yelana emerges from the house. I'm surprised she's only two minutes late; I had expected a small act of defiance or at least a half-hour late arrival. She's dressed in black leggings and a fitted gray tank top, hair pulled back in a ponytail that exposes the clean lines of her neck and jawline. She looks nothing like the Yelana I have encountered so far. I force my eyes away from the curve of her hips, focusing instead on her footwear, running shoes, not the best choice, but better than I had hoped for.

"You're late," I say, keeping my voice neutral.

"By your watch, maybe." She drops her water bottle at the edge of the mat. "Most normal humans consider 6 AM to be the middle of the night."

I don't respond to the bait, just move to the center of the mat and gesture for her to join me. "We'll start with the basic stance and strikes. The goal isn't to win a fight, it's to create enough space to escape."

Yelana rolls her eyes but steps onto the mat. "I took a women's self-defense workshop in college."

"Forget everything they taught you," I tell her, positioning myself in front of her. "Those courses are designed to make women feel empowered, not to actually protect them."

Her jaw tightens, but she doesn't argue. I demonstrate the basic stance, Yelana attempts to mirror me, but her posture is stiff, her balance off-center.

"Wider stance," I instruct. "Lower your center of gravity."

She adjusts, still incorrect. Without thinking, I move behind her, my hands finding her hips to reposition them. The contact is professional, impersonal, the same corrections I've made with hundreds of trainees. But something electric passes between us at the touch, a sudden awareness that has nothing to do with combat training. I feel her stiffen, then forcibly relax under my hands.

"Like this," I say, my voice rougher than intended as I adjust her posture, fingers pressing lightly against her hip bones. "Power comes from the ground up."

I step back quickly, putting professional distance between us again. "Now, basic strikes. Palm heel to the nose or throat." I demonstrate in slow motion. "Elbow to the solar plexus. Knee to the groin."

Yelana mimics the movements, her execution stiff and ineffective. Frustration tightens her features as she repeats the sequence.

"You fight like someone who's never had to," I observe after her third attempt.

Her eyes flash. "And you teach like someone who enjoys watching people fail."

I ignore the barb. "Again. This time, imagine I'm the one who killed your parents."

The words are calculated cruelty, but they have the intended effect. Something shifts in her eyes, grief crystallizing into focused rage. Her next strike sequence carries real intent, her body moving with newfound purpose.

"Better," I acknowledge. "Now with a partner."

I position myself in front of her, arms raised to simulate an attacker. "I'll come at you slowly. Use the palm strike, then create distance."

As I reach for her, Yelana executes a clumsy but effective strike toward my face, pulling back at the last moment.

"Don't pull your strikes," I say sharply. "In a real fight, hesitation gets you killed."

"I'm not actually trying to break your nose, Phillips," she retorts.

"My nose has been broken four times. It can handle your best shot." The corner of my mouth twitches in what might almost be a smile. "If you can land it."

Her eyes narrow at the challenge, a small smirk playing at her lips. "Is that permission to hit you? Because I've wanted to do that since you arrived."

"Give it your best shot, princess," I say, trying to get a rise out of her.

We continue through basic defense sequences, each repetition bringing marginal improvements. Despite her initial clumsiness, Yelana is a quick study, adaptable, determined, with better natural coordination than most civilians I've trained.

"When someone grabs you from behind," I explain, moving to demonstrate, "the instinct is to pull away. That's wrong. You move toward the threat first, then create separation."

I position myself behind her, arms wrapped around her upper body in a bear hug. "I've got your arms pinned. What's your move?"

Her body is tense against mine, her shoulder blades pressed against my chest. I'm acutely aware of our height difference, the scent of her shampoo, the controlled rhythm of her breathing.

"Break your grip, then run," she answers, her voice steady despite our proximity.

"Show me."

Yelana attempts the escape technique I taught earlier, dropping her weight, driving an elbow back. The execution is flawed but shows promise.

"Better, but you're still thinking too much," I tell her, releasing my hold. "Again. This time, don't think. React."

Our training continues, the physical contact becoming more fluid as she grows accustomed to the techniques. I notice Ken Jackson's arrival about thirty minutes in. He stands at the edge of the courtyard, arms crossed, watching with poorly disguised disapproval.

"Your stance is too wide," he calls out as Yelana practices a defensive posture. "Phillips has you looking like a street brawler, not someone with your background."

I continue as if I hadn't heard him. "Ignore distractions," I tell Yelana quietly. "In a fight, focus only on the immediate threat."

She nods, but Ken's presence has added tension to her movements, making her more self-conscious. He continues offering commentary from the sidelines, subtle undermining disguised as helpful suggestions.

"That technique might work for a man with his size," Ken remarks after I demonstrate a particular strike. "But you'd be better served with something that uses your natural advantages, Yelana."

I meet her eyes. "Your advantage isn't your size or gender. It's that they'll underestimate you. Use that."

Something like appreciation flickers across her face. We move to ground defense, techniques for when an attacker has pinned her. This requires even more physical contact, my body hovering over hers as I demonstrate how to create leverage from a disadvantaged position. I keep my instructions clinical and professional, but can't help noticing the flush spreading across her cheeks, the way her eyes occasionally meet mine with something more complex than simple concentration.

"Bridge your hips, create space, then escape," I instruct, aware of Ken's scrutiny from the sidelines.

Yelana executes the move with surprising effectiveness, nearly knocking me off balance. I catch the flash of triumph in her eyes, the slight curl at the corner of her mouth that might almost be a smile.

"Not bad," I acknowledge, offering a hand to help her up. Our palms press together for a moment longer than necessary.

Kendrick appears with fresh water bottles, his silent approach once again setting off warning bells in my tactical assessment. The butler's eyes track our movements with more intensity than casual interest would warrant, lingering on the self-defense techniques I'm teaching Yelana.

"Your refreshments, Miss Zentarra," he says, placing the tray at the edge of the mat.

"Thank you, Kendrick," Yelana replies, breathing heavily from exertion.

I watch as the butler's eyes catalog every detail of our training setup, every technique we've practiced. Not the casual observation of a household staff member, but the calculated assessment of someone gathering intelligence.

"We'll take five," I tell Yelana, moving to the water bottles. I position myself between her and Kendrick without making it obvious, a protective instinct I don't bother analyzing.

When we resume training, Yelana shows marked improvement; her movements are more confident, her strikes carry genuine force. During one sequence, she executes a complex escape from a rear chokehold, creating distance exactly as I taught her. The move brings her face inches from mine, and we are both breathing hard, a moment of connection that transcends our antagonistic dynamic. My mind loses focus for a split second. She sees it. She takes me down, straddles me, and puts her forearm to my throat.

"Not bad for a spoiled princess," I say, lowering her arm from my throat and standing to reset the training scenario.

A small, genuine smile breaks through her usual defensive facade. "Not bad for a drill sergeant with a god complex."

The exchange carries none of our usual bite; instead, something that might almost be mutual respect colors the words. I file away the moment, refusing to examine it too closely. My job is to keep her alive, not to catalog the precise shade of brown in her eyes or the way her rare smiles transform her face.

"Again," I say, refocusing on the task at hand. "This time, faster."

Two A.M. and sleep is a memory from someone else's life. I prowl the perimeter of the estate like a ghost with a purpose, checking door locks, window latches, and security camera angles. The guards I've positioned at strategic points nod as I pass, straightening their postures when they spot me. Good. No comfortable slouching on my watch. My boots make no sound on the stone pathways as I complete my third circuit of the night, the weight of the SIG at my shoulder a constant, comforting presence. Then I hear it; the rhythmic thud of fists against canvas, coming from the east wing. The gym. Someone's awake besides me, and I don't like surprises.

I move toward the sound, keeping to the shadows out of habit. The estate is a maze of corridors and hidden passages, a security nightmare I've been mentally redesigning since arrival. I pass through the darkened kitchen, noting the half-empty wine glass by the sink, condensation still fresh on its surface. Someone's been up recently. My hand hovers near my weapon as I approach the gym, though my instincts aren't screaming danger.

The door stands ajar, warm light spilling into the hallway. I position myself to see inside without being seen. My breath catches slightly at what I find.

Yelana moves with focused intensity against the heavy bag, her form imperfect but determined. She's traded her usual designer clothes for black leggings and a gray tank like she wore that morning; the top is now darkened with sweat between her shoulder blades. Her hair is pulled back in a messy ponytail that swings with each strike. Left jab, right cross, left hook, the combination I taught her this morning. She's been practicing.

I stay motionless, assessing her technique with professional detachment. Or trying to. Her form has improved since our session, but she still telegraphs the hook, still drops her guard after the second strike. Makes her vulnerable to a counter. My eyes track the lean muscles in her arms, the determined set of her jaw, the intensity in her eyes that reminds me so much of Emelio it's almost unsettling.

Something tightens in my chest that has nothing to do with security protocols or blood debts. I push it away, locking it down with everything else that doesn't serve the mission. She's a client. She's twenty-one. She's Emelio's daughter. Three strikes that should be enough to kill whatever inappropriate awareness is trying to surface.

She spins suddenly, executing a decent roundhouse kick, and freezes mid-motion when she spots me. Her chest heaves with exertion, a slight flush coloring her cheeks.

"Checking if I'm sneaking out?" she asks, reaching for a towel draped over the weight bench. The question lacks its usual sharp edges.

I step fully into the doorway, crossing my arms. "If you were sneaking out, you wouldn't be making enough noise to wake the dead."

She wipes her face, something like embarrassment crossing her features before she masks it. "Couldn't sleep."

I nod, understanding more than she realizes. Sleep and I have been strangers since Afghanistan. Since Kerry. "Your form's improved. But you're still dropping your guard after the second strike."

She turns back to the bag, throwing the combination again. "Like this?"

I shake my head and approach her, professional assessment overriding personal boundaries. "You're leaving yourself open here." I gesture to the space between us. "May I?"

She hesitates, then nods once. I position myself behind her, close enough to correct her stance but maintaining what space I can. Even so, I catch the scent of her, expensive shampoo mingled with honest sweat. It hits something primitive in me that I immediately suppress.

"When you throw the cross," I say, my voice deliberately neutral, "your shoulder drops here." I touch her elbow lightly, adjusting her position. "It telegraphs the next move and leaves your ribs exposed."

She stiffens slightly at the contact but doesn't pull away. She adjusts her stance according to my guidance. "Show me again."

I move to face her, demonstrating the proper technique in slow motion. "Tight. Controlled. Every movement has purpose." I throw the combination at half-speed, watching her eyes track each motion with sharp intelligence. "Now you try."

She mirrors my movements, her focus absolute. We fall into a rhythm—I demonstrate, she follows. I correct, she adjusts. The antagonism that's defined our interactions since my arrival fades into the background, replaced by the shared language of combat training. For these moments, we're just teacher and student, not grieving daughter and the man who owes her family a blood debt.

"Better," I say when she executes the combination cleanly. "Now add the defensive counter I showed you this morning."

She nods, concentration etched into every line of her face. When she executes the sequence—strike, block, counter—I catch myself almost smiling at her progress. She's a quick study, this Zentarra princess with her expensive education and sheltered upbringing. There's a fighter in there that Emelio saw but never fully unleashed.

"Like that?" she asks, a hint of something almost like eagerness in her voice.

"You tell me," I counter, stepping toward her with deliberate intent. "Defend yourself."

I telegraph my movements clearly, coming at her with a slow-motion attack that matches what we've practiced. Her eyes widen momentarily before narrowing in concentration. She executes the defensive sequence with surprising precision—block, step, counter. Her fist stops just short of my solar plexus.

“Pretty good for a spoiled princess," I say, echoing my comments from earlier, and something unexpected happens. The corner of my mouth twitches upward.

She catches it, and for a flickering moment, something passes between us—not quite humor, but its distant cousin. The ghost of a smile touches her lips.

"Not bad for a drill sergeant with a god complex," she retorts with a smirk, but the words carry none of the venom from our earlier encounters.

We step back from each other, the moment fragile as spun glass. She pushes a stray strand of hair from her face, and I notice the delicate curve of her neck, the way her eyes shine with exertion and something like satisfaction. Beautiful. The thought ambushes me from nowhere, unwelcome and dangerous. I mentally shove it away, locking it behind the walls I've built to keep such complications at bay.

"You should ice your knuckles," I say, retreating to safer territory. "And get some sleep. We have the final security walkthrough at the funeral home tomorrow."

She nods, fatigue suddenly visible in the slump of her shoulders. "This helps," she says quietly. "Hitting things. Makes me feel less..."

"Helpless," I finish for her. Our eyes meet in shared understanding.

"Yeah." She begins unwrapping the tape from her hands. "Thanks. For the pointers."

I head for the door, needing distance from whatever just shifted between us. "Same time tomorrow?" I ask, keeping my tone professional. "You need more work on your defensive positioning."

"Same time," she confirms.

I leave her there, the sound of her steady breathing following me into the hall. Something's changed tonight—a microscopic crack in the wall between us. Not friendship, not forgiveness, but something that might eventually become respect. For the mission, it's progress. For everything else, it's complicated.

I resume my patrol, forcing my thoughts back to security protocols and threat assessments. Safer ground than noticing the curve of Yelana Zentarra's smile or the fire in her eyes when she lands a perfect strike. The blood debt demands focus, not distraction.

Even if the distraction has surprising hooks.

SEVEN
Funeral Preparations

Yelana

The funeral home smells like lilies and lies. Artificial scents pumped through hidden vents, trying to mask the formaldehyde and grief that seep from the walls. I sit with my spine straight in a chair designed for slouching mourners, surrounded by glossy brochures of caskets with names like "Eternal Rest" and "Peaceful Passage." My fingernails dig crescents into my palms beneath the table while I discuss the most efficient way to put my parents into the ground with a stranger whose sympathy I thought would be as practiced as a handshake. But his sympathy and grief are more real than I care to admit.

"The Monterey model offers a premium velvet interior," the funeral director says, his voice a carefully modulated dirge. His name tag reads "Thomas," but I've already forgotten it three times. "Many families find the burgundy lining particularly... dignified."

I stare at the casket. "My mother hated burgundy."

Mason sits beside me, a solid presence in a charcoal suit that fits him too well, I hate that I notice that. He hasn't spoken except to ask pointed questions about the service's security arrangements. His knee occasionally brushes mine under the small consultation table—accidental contact that shouldn't register through two layers of clothing but somehow burns like a brand every time.

"Perhaps the Celestial model then," Thomas offers, flipping to another page of gleaming hardwood and polished brass. "It comes in navy."

I try to picture my father, powerful, dangerous Emelio Zentarra, confined in this glorified wooden box. My mother, elegant, razor-sharp Sierra, reduced to ashes in one of the urns displayed on shelves like macabre trophies. The absurdity of it all threatens to crack my carefully maintained composure.

"Two Celestials," I say, my voice betraying nothing. "Navy for both."

"An excellent choice," the funeral director nods, making a note. "Now about the programs..."

My focus drifts as he prattles on about paper weights and font choices. Instead, I find myself acutely aware of Mason's breathing beside me, steady and controlled, a metronome keeping time in a world spinning out of control. I catch him watching me from the corner of his eye, his gaze less clinical than yesterday. There's something else there now, something that makes my skin tighten with awareness that has no place in a funeral home, and I hate how much he is keeping me grounded right now.

I flip through sample programs, but the words blur together. My fingers tremble slightly, a weakness I despise but can't seem to control. I press my palm flat against the glossy paper, willing the shaking to stop.

"I'll just retrieve the necessary paperwork," the funeral director says, rising with solemnity. "Take your time with the selections. This is a difficult process."

The moment the door clicks shut behind him, the mask I've been wearing threatens to slip. My exhale comes out shakier than intended, the sound loud in the quiet room.

Mason's hand slides over mine without warning. His palm is warm, slightly rough with calluses. He doesn't speak, doesn't offer empty platitudes or ask if I'm okay when I'm obviously not. He just covers my trembling fingers with his steady ones, anchoring me to something solid.

I know I should pull back. This man is the cause of Juan's death. He embodies everything that's gone wrong in my life. Yet my body betrays me, soaking in his warmth like a desert thirsting for rain. His thumb briefly brushes my knuckles—so fleeting I might have imagined it—and heat rushes up my arm, spreading through my chest.

My mind flashes to yesterday's training session. His hands positioning my hips, adjusting my stance. "Power comes from the ground up," he'd said, his voice rougher than usual. Later, in the gym at two AM, the careful way he'd touched my elbow to correct my form. Not treating me like I might break, but like someone worth teaching properly.

The memory of his body behind mine, solid and warm as he guided my movements, sends an inappropriate flush across my skin. There had been a moment, just a fraction of a second, when his fingers had lingered at my waist, when his breath had caught slightly before he stepped away.

What the hell is wrong with me? My parents are dead. I'm planning their funeral. And I'm thinking about the way my skin heated when a man I should hate touched me?

I stiffen but don't pull my hand away. The contact feels like the only thing keeping me from floating off into the void that's opened inside me since finding out my parents were murdered. I hate that it's him providing this anchor, hate that my body responds to his proximity when my mind is still filled with Juan's memorial plaque and pink Band-Aids that couldn't fix what was broken.

The door opens, and Thomas returns with a stack of forms. Mason withdraws his hand smoothly, no acknowledgement of the moment passing between us, nothing to suggest it meant anything beyond professional support. The loss of contact leaves my skin cooler, but the memory of warmth remains.

"Just some signatures required," Thomas says, placing papers before me. "Take your time to review everything."

I sign where indicated, my fountain pen scratching across paper that will authorize the disposal of my parents' remains. The mundane legality of death feels obscene. I initial here, sign there, check this box, the bureaucracy of grief proceeding in orderly fashion while nothing inside me feels ordered at all.

As we prepare to leave, Mason moves to the window, seemingly casual but with that predatory awareness I've come to recognize. His shoulders tense slightly, a subtle shift in posture that signals something's wrong. His gaze fixes on something in the parking lot, and his hand drifts toward where I know he keeps his weapon.

"Time to go," he says, his voice carrying a new edge that sends warning prickles across my skin.

I rise, funeral arrangements complete, death neatly packaged and scheduled. But the look on Mason's face tells me that death might not be finished with the Zentarra family yet.

Mason's hand at my elbow guides me through the funeral home's glass doors, his touch light but insistent. The parking lot stretches before us, ordinary and innocent in the midday sun, but his body language screams danger. He opens the SUV door for me, scanning our surroundings with eyes that miss nothing. I slide into the plush leather seat, the luxury suddenly absurd as he closes me in like precious cargo being secured for transport. When he takes the driver's seat, he's transformed; the man who touched my hand with unexpected gentleness has vanished, replaced by something harder, more predatory.

"Put your seatbelt on," he says, voice clipped as he starts the engine. My father's Range Rover purrs to life, its bulletproof glass and reinforced frame suddenly less of a rich man's paranoia and more of a necessity.

I buckle in, watching Mason's hands on the wheel, the same hands that steadied mine on the funeral brochures, that adjusted my stance during training yesterday, that made my skin hum with unwanted awareness. Now they grip the leather with controlled tension, ready to react to threats I haven't even identified.

The rearview mirror captures his attention every few seconds. Three cars back, a black sedan with windows dark as oil slicks maintains perfect distance. Not close enough to be obvious, not far enough to lose us. I wouldn't have noticed it without watching Mason watch it.

"We have a tail," I say, more statement than question.

His eyes flick to mine, a millisecond of surprise before refocusing on the road. "Yes."

The simple confirmation sends ice through my veins. Not because of the danger—though that's real enough—but because of how calmly he says it, like being followed by potential killers is Tuesday's weather report. This is his world, I realize. Has been for decades. The man who trains me to fight, who corrects my stance with careful hands, lives permanently in the space where violence is always one wrong move away.

We turn onto Wilshire Boulevard, merging into midday traffic. Mason's movements are precise, his attention divided between the road ahead and the mirror reflecting our shadow. His jaw flexes, a decision crystallizing behind his eyes.

Without warning, he cranks the wheel hard left, throwing me against the door as we careen across three lanes and down a narrow one-way street—in the wrong direction. Horns blare, tires squeal, and pedestrians scatter as we barrel toward oncoming traffic.

"What the fuck are you doing?" I grab the door handle, knuckles white with sudden terror. A delivery truck looms ahead, its horn a constant scream as we hurtle toward it.

"Confirming our tail," Mason replies with infuriating calm, swerving at the last second into an alley barely wider than our vehicle. The side mirror scrapes against brick, sending sparks into my peripheral vision. "Black sedan took the turn. Definitely following us."

My heart pounds against my ribs like it's trying to escape. "So your solution is to kill us first?"

His mouth twitches—almost a smile if it weren't so grim. "If I wanted you dead, I'd let them do it." Another sharp turn throws me against his shoulder despite the seatbelt. The brief contact burns through my blouse. "I'm making them show their hand."

We emerge onto another street, this one residential. Mason accelerates, weaving between parked cars with impossible precision. In the mirror, the black sedan remains, closer now, its pursuit obvious with pretense abandoned.

"Who are they?" I demand, bracing myself as we take another corner too fast.

"Could be Costa's men. Could be someone else your father pissed off." His eyes never stop moving, calculating angles, escape routes, threats. "Doesn't matter who. Only matters what they want."

"Which is me."

"Yes."

One syllable, loaded with implication. They want me dead—or worse, alive for questioning. The reality I've been avoiding since my parents' murders crystallizes in the space between heartbeats. This isn't a bad dream. This is my life now.

Mason's hand shoots out, pressing me lower in my seat just as we pass under a bridge. "Stay down."

I comply, fear overriding indignation. Through the windshield, I watch his face—completely transformed from the man in the funeral home. His features sharpen, eyes cold with lethal focus. This is Lieutenant Phillips now, the soldier who survived Afghanistan, not the security consultant who held my trembling hand.

We approach an intersection, yellow light flashing to red. Instead of slowing, Mason accelerates. I bite back a scream as we blast through, narrowly missing a crossing SUV. But before we can clear the intersection, a second vehicle—matte black with tinted windows—screeches into our path from the right.

Mason swears, a single harsh syllable, as he slams the Range Rover into reverse. The transmission screams in protest, but the vehicle responds, lurching backward before being thrown forward again like a battering ram. Metal crunches as we slam into the blocking vehicle.

Two men in tactical vests exit their car, weapons drawn. Not random thugs—trained professionals with dead eyes and purposeful movements. One circles wide to flank us while the other approaches head-on.

"Stay in the car. Lock the doors when I'm out." Mason's voice cuts through my frozen panic. Before I can respond, he's out of the driver's seat, moving with a fluid speed that doesn't register as human.

The first attacker raises his weapon, but Mason is already inside his guard. Their bodies connect, a violent dance of precise movements. The gun clatters to the pavement. Mason's elbow drives into the man's throat, followed by a sweeping motion that sends him crashing down. The sound of bone meeting concrete reaches me through the closed windows.

The second attacker circles, knife now visible in his hand—a wicked curved blade that catches sunlight as he slashes. Mason weaves backward, his movements economical, nothing wasted. When the knife comes again, he deflects rather than blocks, using the attacker's momentum to throw him off-balance. Their bodies connect, separate, connect again in a brutal choreography.

Blood sprays across the pavement as Mason's fist connects with the attacker's face. I hear the crunch of cartilage even through the glass. The knife changes hands—now Mason has it, the blade disappearing into his grip as he drives his opponent backward. They grapple, fall, roll. More blood. A scream cut short.

I can't look away. This man who adjusted my stance with gentle precision yesterday is now unleashing violence with the same technical perfection. His face shows nothing—no rage, no fear, just absolute focus on the mechanical process of neutralizing threats. One attacker lies motionless by the rear tire. The second struggles briefly before going still beneath Mason's weight.

My stomach lurches, not with disgust but with a complicated mix of fear and something else—something I refuse to name. I've never seen actual violence before, only sanitized movie versions with dramatic music and artful camera angles. This is raw, efficient, terrifying. And he's doing it to protect me.

When Mason returns to the driver's seat, blood spatters his white shirt and a cut above his eyebrow drips crimson down his temple. His breathing is controlled, deliberate, as if he's manually regulating each inhale and exhale. He throws a man in the boot.

"Are you hurt?" he asks, eyes already checking me for injuries.

I shake my head, finding my voice. "Are they...?"

"One's no longer a threat. The other's coming with us." He throws the SUV into drive and maneuvers around the crashed vehicle. "We need answers."

As we pull away, I watch his bloodied knuckles on the steering wheel and realize with startling clarity that I've never been safer than I am with this dangerous man.

The abandoned garage smells like motor oil and neglect, paint peeling from concrete walls in leprous patches. Mason parks the Range Rover in the darkest corner, positioning it so the exit remains clear. His movements are precise, efficient, as if following a checklist for situations exactly like this one. I sit frozen in the passenger seat, watching him transform our kidnapped attacker from a threat to a source of information. The blood on his shirt has dried to rust-brown, the cut above his eye still seeping slightly. Yet his hands are perfectly steady as he pops the trunk with the key fob. "Stay in the car," he tells me, but I'm already opening my door. If this is my new reality, I refuse to experience it through glass and safety locks.

"Yelana." My name in his mouth is a warning, hard consonants wrapped in concern.

"I need to see." I meet his eyes, challenging him to force me back into protected ignorance. After a moment's assessment, he nods once, a decision made.

"Stay back." Not a request.

Mason approaches the trunk like a man who's done this before, too many times to count. The calculated way he positions his body, angled to minimize risk, weapon ready but not drawn, speaks of experience I can't begin to fathom. When he raises the trunk lid, I catch my first clear look at our attacker, younger than expected, early thirties maybe, with a face that would be forgettable if not for the blood crusting his split lip and the purple swelling already claiming his left eye.

His hands are secured with black zip-ties, too tight, judging from the discoloration of his fingertips. He squints against the sudden light, fear flashing across his face before being masked by defiance.

"Out," Mason commands, grabbing the man by his collar and extracting him from the trunk with clinical efficiency. Our attacker stumbles, off-balance with his hands bound, but Mason doesn't let him fall, just steers him to a rusty metal chair that I hadn't noticed before. He must have positioned it while I was still processing our surroundings.

I hang back near the SUV, close enough to hear but far enough to give the illusion of distance. The concrete floor is stained with substances I don't want to identify, decades of mechanical fluids and maybe worse things soaked into the porous surface. My designer boots seem absurdly inappropriate here, like I've wandered onto a movie set where I don't belong.

"Who sent you?" Mason's voice drops lower, shedding any pretense of civilization. This is the voice of a man who has extracted information in places where the Geneva Conventions don't apply.

The man spits blood onto the concrete between them. "Fuck you."

Without warning, Mason's hand shoots out, fingers pressing into a spot where the man's neck meets his shoulder. The effect is immediate, our attacker's face contorts in pain, a strangled sound escaping his throat though Mason's grip doesn't look particularly forceful. Pressure points. The realization hits me with a chill. Mason knows exactly how to cause maximum pain with minimal effort.

"Let's try again," Mason says, releasing the pressure slightly. "Who hired you?"

"Don't know," the man gasps, sweat beading on his forehead even with the garage's chill. "Hired through a cutout. Never saw the client."

Mason increases the pressure, his face impassive. "Details."

"Phone call...burner phone...instructions to grab the girl." Each word emerges through gritted teeth. "Paid half up front, cash. Rest on delivery."

"Delivery where?"

The man hesitates. Mason shifts his grip slightly, and a choked scream echoes against the concrete walls. I flinch but don't look away.

"Warehouse...San Pedro...I just had the address. Was supposed to call when we had her."

Mason searches the man with methodical thoroughness, retrieving a cheap flip phone and a wad of cash from his pockets. No ID, no wallet, no personal items. A professional, or at least someone trying to be.

"Costa organization?" Mason presses.

"Don't know. Swear to God." Fear has overtaken defiance in the man's eyes. "Just a job. Didn't ask questions."

I watch Mason's face as he processes this information, searching for tells that would indicate lies. Finding none, or perhaps deciding he's extracted all useful intelligence, he steps back slightly.

"The guy you were with. Partner? Or just for this job?"

"Just this job. Met him this morning." Blood dribbles from the man's lip as he speaks. "Look man, I'm just muscle. I don't know shit about who wants her or why."

I wrap my arms around myself, the reality of my situation settling over me like a shroud. Someone paid these men to abduct me. Would have paid them again when I was delivered like a package. If not for Mason, I'd be zip-tied in a trunk right now, headed toward God knows what fate.

My voice emerges before I can reconsider. "Are you going to kill him?"

Both men's heads snap toward me, as if they'd forgotten I was there. The attacker's eyes widen, real terror replacing the bravado. Mason's expression remains unreadable, but something shifts in his posture.

He studies the bound man for several long seconds. I find myself holding my breath, suddenly uncertain what answer I'm hoping for. Twenty-four hours ago, the idea of executing a bound prisoner would have been unthinkable. Now, watching the man who tried to abduct me and do god knows what, trembling under Mason's gaze, my moral compass wobbles on its axis.

"Not today," Mason finally answers, his voice neutral as if discussing dinner options.

Relief and something similar to disappointment war in my chest. I'm grateful he's not a cold-blooded killer, yet part of me wonders if mercy is a luxury we can afford. My father wouldn't have hesitated, I realize with sudden clarity. This was his world, with difficult decisions with life-or-death consequences. No wonder he tried to shield me from it.

Mason secures the attacker more thoroughly, using additional zip ties to bind him to the chair. He gags him with what looks like a clean handkerchief, then steps back to assess his work.

"Anonymous tip to police will have him found in a few hours," he explains, returning to where I stand. "Not immediately, but soon enough that he won't die of exposure or dehydration."

"But far enough removed that it can't be traced back to us," I conclude, understanding the calculation behind his decision.

Mason nods, something like approval flickering across his face. "Let's go."

As we return to the SUV, I find myself stealing glances at his profile. This man, who dispassionately interrogated our attacker, is the same one who held my hand in the funeral home. Who corrected my fighting stance with careful hands yesterday. Who killed one man and spared another today, all too protect me.

"Thank you," I say quietly as he opens my door. "For keeping me alive."

His eyes meet mine, steel gray and unfathomable. "It's my job."

But we both know it's more than that. It's a blood debt. A promise to my father. And something else that neither of us is ready to acknowledge.

My father's crystal tumbler trembles in my hand, amber liquid sloshing over the rim as I pour my third bourbon. The expensive alcohol burns a path down my throat, but doesn't touch the cold that's settled in my bones since the garage. I sink into my father's leather chair, my chair now, and watch my hands shake with a detached fascination. Adrenaline crash, Mason called it when he noticed in the car. "Perfectly normal response to combat situations." As if being hunted through Los Angeles streets, watching men try to kill us, and interrogating a bound prisoner in an abandoned garage could ever be considered normal. But for him, maybe it is.

Mason stands by the window, phone pressed to his ear, positioning himself to monitor both the grounds outside and the door to the study. The blood on his shirt has dried to a rust-brown stain, his knuckles raw and swollen where they split against our attacker's jaw. I should find his violence repulsive. Instead, I find myself studying the controlled economy of his movements, the way he maintains optimal positioning even while making a phone call. There's a comfort in his constant vigilance.

"Anonymous tip called in," he says after ending the call. "Our friend will be found within the hour." His gaze meets mine briefly, assessing. He doesn't ask if I'm okay, doesn't offer platitudes or comfort. Just honest evaluation. I appreciate that more than he knows.

"The warehouse he mentioned?" I ask, proud that my voice emerges steady, given the tremors in my hands.

"Being watched. If someone shows up expecting delivery, we'll know." He crosses to the desk, spreading out security diagrams with efficient precision. "We need to modify our approach. They're getting bolder."

I watch his hands move across the paper, the same hands that touch still linger on my skin from the funeral home. Hands that have killed and protected. Hands that make something flutter beneath my ribcage when they accidentally brush against mine.

The study door bangs open, Ken Jackson's imposing frame filling the doorway. His face is flushed with barely contained fury, eyes locking onto Mason with naked hostility.

"What the hell happened?" he demands, striding in without waiting for an invitation. His expensive suit is immaculate as always, making Mason's bloodstained shirt seem even more out of place in my father's tasteful study. "I get reports of a firefight downtown, our vehicle with front-end damage, and you two disappearing for hours!"

Mason doesn't straighten from the desk, doesn't give Ken the satisfaction of appearing defensive. "We were followed from the funeral home. Ambush set up on Wilshire. Two operatives, semi-professional. Neutralized the threat and extracted information."

"Extracted?" Ken's eyebrow raises, his gaze flicking to me as if concerned about what I might have witnessed. "And where is this valuable asset now?"

"Being picked up by LAPD," Mason replies, marking something on the security diagram.

Ken's face darkens further. "You should have brought him here for questioning. We have facilities for that."

I catch the implication immediately. My father had "facilities" for interrogation somewhere on the estate. Of course he did. Another piece of my childhood illusion crumbles away.

"Wasn't worth the risk of being followed," Mason counters, his tone maddeningly calm in the face of Ken's growing anger. "Decision made in the field."

"A poor decision," Ken snaps, moving closer to the desk, to Mason. "You let one get away. Should've broken more bones, gotten names, connections. That's how Emelio would have handled it."

I watch their standoff with new eyes, seeing beyond the surface antagonism to the deeper currents beneath. This isn't just about today's attack or interrogation methods. This is about territory, about control, about who truly speaks for my father's legacy. And I'm the prize they're fighting over.

"My father isn't here," I interject, but neither man acknowledges me.

Mason straightens slowly, facing Ken directly. "The survivor gave us what he had, hired through cutouts, paid cash, no direct connection to whoever ordered the hit. Breaking more bones wouldn't have changed that."

"You don't know that," Ken insists, his voice dropping dangerously. "In my experience, everyone breaks eventually if you apply the right pressure."

The door opens again, this time with Kendrick's signature silence. He glides in bearing a tray with fresh drinks, his expression betraying nothing as he surveys the tension-filled room. I watch him carefully, noting how his eyes drift to the security diagrams spread across the desk, lingering just a beat too long on the locations Mason has marked as vulnerable.

"Your refreshments, Miss Zentarra," he announces, placing the tray on the side table carefully.

"This wouldn't have happened on my watch," Ken continues as if Kendrick were invisible. "My men would have spotted the tail before you left the funeral home. Would have neutralized the threat without turning downtown into a demolition derby."

"Your men were supposed to be watching the funeral home," Mason points out, his voice cool. "They missed the surveillance team that was already in place when we arrived."

Ken's face flushes deeper. "My men—"

"Enough!" The crystal tumbler slams against the desk with more force than I intended, bourbon splashing across the polished wood. Both men turn toward me, momentarily startled out of their territorial display. Even Kendrick pauses in his silent ministrations.

I rise from the chair, summoning every ounce of my mother's imperious presence. "I'm still breathing, which means he did his job. Whatever you think of his methods, Ken, they kept me alive today."

Ken's expression shifts, softens into the avuncular concern I recognize from childhood. "Yelana, I'm only thinking of your safety. Phillips' approach is too volatile, too public. He's drawing attention we don't need right now."

"The attention was already there," I counter, surprised by the steadiness in my voice and the strength of my defiance against the man I have known so long. "They knew where we'd be. They were waiting."

A heavy silence falls as the implication sinks in. Someone knew our schedule. Someone from inside our organization.

"I've been saying we need to tighten the circle," Ken finally says. "Fewer people with access to your movements, stricter protocols." His eyes flick meaningfully toward Kendrick, who continues arranging drinks.

I catch Mason watching the butler's hands, the way they hover near the security diagrams as he reaches for my empty glass. When Kendrick straightens, his eyes meet mine for a fraction of a second, unreadable as always, yet somehow different than before.

"Will there be anything else, Miss Zentarra?" he asks, voice perfectly modulated.

"No, thank you, Kendrick."

He bows slightly and withdraws, closing the door with practiced silence. Even his footsteps fade away without sound, a ghost haunting my family's halls for two decades.

Ken gathers himself, straightening his already immaculate tie. "We'll continue this discussion later, when emotions aren't running so high." He shoots a final warning look at Mason before turning to me. “Call if you need anything. Anything at all.”

After he leaves, the study feels both emptier and less suffocating. I sink back into my father’s chair, the adrenaline crash hitting me again in a fresh wave of exhaustion.

“He’s right about one thing,” Mason says, gather the security diagrams into a neat stack. “We need to restrict information about your movements. Too many people knew our schedule today.”

I nod, watching his methodical organization with tired eyes. “Did you notice how Kendrick kept looking at your diagrams?”

A faint smile touches Mason’s mouth. “I noticed you noticing.”

Our eyes meet across the desk, something unspoken passing between us. I’m still furious about Juan, still conflicted about what Mason represents. But today, he kept me alive. Today, I saw him in his element—lethal, controlled, effective. And God help me, I didn’t look away.

“We’ll find who’s behind this,” he says, the promise carrying weight beyond the simple words.

I believe him. And that terrifies me almost as much as the men who tried to take me today.

EIGHT
The Inner Circle

Mason

I position myself three feet behind Yelana's chair, back to the wall, sight lines clear to both exits. The conference room's mahogany table stretches like a battlefield before us, each chair a potential position for friend or enemy, more likely the latter. I've cleared the room twice already, checking for surveillance devices, cataloging every object that could become a weapon. Old habits. The cut above my eye from yesterday's fight still throbs, a useful reminder to stay sharp. These people aren't soldiers, but they are dangerous in different ways. Politics and power plays can kill as effectively as bullets, and Yelana is about to walk into her first firefight as commander.

The door opens, and Ken Jackson enters first, punctual to a fault. His eyes sweep the room, lingering on me with poorly disguised contempt before he takes his seat at Yelana's right. He's dressed impeccably as always, his suit a silent statement of position and power.

"Phillips," he acknowledges with a curt nod. "Still wearing yester-day's blood, I see."

I don't respond. My shirt is fresh, but he knows that. It's a cheap shot meant to establish dominance. I catalog his posture instead, the way his right hand stays close to his concealed weapon, how his eyes flick repeatedly to the door. He's nervous but hiding it well.

The others filter in gradually. Sophia Reyes arrives next, her sleek bob and minimalist pantsuit projecting calculated efficiency. Head of distribution logistics, according to the files Emelio kept. Potential threat level: moderate. She's too smart for brute force, preferring subtle manipulations. She settles three chairs down from Ken, maintaining professional distance.

Marcus Webb follows, his massive frame filling the doorway momentarily before he squeezes into a chair that seems too small for his bulk. Financial operations. Former enforcer promoted to suit-and-tie work. His knuckles bear the permanent calluses of someone who's broken more than spreadsheets in his career. Threat level: high, but straightforward. If he betrays, it won't be with subtlety.

Victor Krane is last, deliberately so. Theatrical lateness as power play. European operations manager with connections to old-world arms dealers. His silver-threaded hair and casual confidence speak of someone who believes in his own importance. He doesn't acknowledge me at all, a deliberate slight. His gaze fixes on the empty chair at the head of the table with poorly concealed ambition. Threat level: immediate.

I track each of their movements, noting who places phones on the table, who keeps hands visible, and who sits with direct lines of sight to exits. Old SEAL team assessments, automatic as breathing.

The atmosphere shifts when Yelana enters. She's transformed from the woman I trained with yesterday, her usual designer jeans replaced with a tailored black suit that echoes her mother's style. Her hair is pulled back severely, emphasizing cheekbones sharp enough to cut glass. She meets no one's eyes as she takes her seat, letting the silence stretch until it becomes uncomfortable.

I catch the subtle straightening of her spine as she settles into her father's role, not mimicking Emelio, but channeling something of his presence. Pride mixes unexpectedly with my tactical assessment. She's a quick study in more than just combat training.

"Thank you all for coming," she begins, her voice cooler than I've heard before. No hint of the vulnerability I witnessed by Juan's memorial. "I appreciate your loyalty to my father. I expect the same loyalty will transfer to me."

Victor's scoff is barely audible, but in the silence of the room, it lands like a grenade. "With all due respect, Miss Zentarra," he begins, infusing her name with subtle condescension, "loyalty is earned in this business. Your father built this organization over decades. "You've been involved for...what? A year handling legitimate fronts?"

I tense, eyes tracking Victor's hands, body weight shifting slightly forward. But Yelana doesn't flinch. Her face remains perfectly composed, a skill she's obviously learned from Sierra. She catches my movement in her peripheral vision, the briefest glance in my direction carrying a clear message: Stand down. I force myself to settle.

"You raise a valid point, Victor." Her tone is diplomatic, almost warm. It immediately triggers my warning instincts. I've heard that tone before—in a commander's voice right before they order an execution. "Trust should be earned. As should the right to access company funds."

She slides a folder across the polished mahogany with deliberate slowness. Victor doesn't reach for it immediately, suspicion narrowing his eyes.

"Open it," she suggests mildly.

The room holds its collective breath as Victor finally flips the folder open. His face drains of color so rapidly, I wonder if he might pass out. Inside are bank statements, transfer records, and photographs that I can't see clearly from my position. Whatever they show, it's enough to transform Victor's arrogance into naked fear.

"These are copies, of course," Yelana continues in that same pleasant tone. "The originals are in several secure locations. Return the money by tomorrow, or I'll show you exactly how much of my father's daughter I am."

The threat lands with precision that was intended. Victor's Adam's apple bobs as he swallows hard. "There's been a misunderstanding," he manages, voice strained. "I can explain—"

"Tomorrow," Yelana cuts him off. "That's all the time you have for explanations."

My eyes drift to Ken, catching the quick smile he fails to fully suppress. It's gone in an instant, replaced with appropriate seriousness. but I file it away as suspicious. Is he pleased at Victor's downfall, or at Yelana proving herself? Or something else entirely? His hand has moved away from his weapon—another data point worth noting.

The balance of power has shifted palpably. Sophia sits straighter, reassessing Yelana with new calculation in her eyes. Marcus looks vaguely impressed, thick fingers drumming against the table. Victor stares at the folder as if it might explode.

Yelana transitions smoothly, outlining operational priorities with surprising command of details. She speaks of supply chain adjustments, territorial negotiations, and financial restructuring. Every sentence broadcasts the same message: I've been paying attention all these years. I know more than you thought.

Throughout her presentation, I notice her occasional glances in my direction, subtle checks for reaction or reassurance. She doesn't need either. She's handling these wolves better than veteran commanders I've served under. Each time our eyes meet, the connection lasts a fraction longer. Something is shifting between us, professional respect evolving into something I'm not ready to analyze too closely.

I find myself moving slightly closer to her chair as the meeting progresses, an unconscious decrease in our physical distance that mirrors our shrinking emotional one. By the time she concludes, I'm standing nearly at her shoulder, close enough to catch the faint scent of her perfume.

"That's all for today," she announces, closing her portfolio with finality. "Questions can be directed to me individually. Victor, I'll expect to hear from you by noon tomorrow."

They file out in silence, transformed from skeptical subordinates to, if not loyal supporters, at least wary respecters of the new order. Victor practically flees, folder clutched in his trembling hand. Ken lingers, offering a supportive nod to Yelana before shooting me a look I can't quite interpret.

When the door closes behind them, Yelana's shoulders drop a fraction of an inch—a tell only someone watching as closely as I am would notice. The commander recedes slightly, revealing the twenty-one-year-old woman beneath the armor. But she doesn't crumble. Instead, she turns to me with questioning eyes.

"Assessment?"

One word, loaded with meaning. She's not asking if they bought her performance; she knows they did. She's asking if I noticed anything suspicious, anything that might identify our traitor.

"We need to talk," I answer simply. "But not here."

I check the study for surveillance devices before letting Yelana enter, a routine we've established without discussion. The room feels different tonight, the ghost of Emelio Zentarra less present, the space gradually becoming hers. She claims her father's chair with growing confidence, her fingers drumming a nervous rhythm against the polished wood, the only outward sign that the commanding presence she projected in the meeting room took its toll. I pace the perimeter, muscles tight from standing motionless during the confrontation with Victor. The adrenaline hasn't fully dissipated; my body stays combat-ready even as my mind shifts to strategic assessment.

"Victor was too obvious," I say, stopping at the window to scan the grounds before turning back to her. "The real threat wouldn't show their hand like that."

Yelana nods, fatigue briefly visible in the slump of her shoulders before she straightens again. "He's always been ambitious, but not particularly bright. My father kept files on everyone, insurance, he called it." A small, sad smile touches her lips. "Apparently, I inherited his paranoia along with his business."

"Paranoia keeps you alive in this world." I move closer to the desk, resting my palms on its edge.

"Ken seemed pleased when you confronted Victor. Too pleased."

"Ken and Victor have been rivals for years," she says, looking up at me with new clarity in her eyes. The woman who emerged in that conference room hasn't fully retreated. "But you're right. We can't assume Victor is the traitor just because he's skimming funds."

I begin a systematic breakdown, my mind organizing threats the way I once planned missions. "Each of them has potential motive. Sophia controls distribution routes, perfect position to compromise shipments or leak schedules to competitors. Marcus handles finances, could be secretly funding another organization or preparing to break away with his own faction."

"And Ken knows everything," Yelana adds quietly. "Security protocols, safe houses, contacts. My father trusted him completely."

"Which makes him the most dangerous if he's turned." I straighten and begin pacing again, the movement helping me think. "We need to flush out the traitor without tipping our hand."

Yelana watches me move, her eyes tracking my path across the study. There's something different in her gaze now, not the hostility from our first meeting nor the grudging cooperation of recent days. Something closer to genuine interest, perhaps even respect. It's distracting in ways I can't afford.

"What do you suggest?" she asks, leaning forward slightly.

I approach the desk again, closer this time, and spread out a blank sheet of paper. "We feed different information to each of them. Tell Sophia about a weapons shipment arriving through an unusual route. Tell Marcus about specific financial transfers to offshore accounts. Tell Ken about changes to security protocols at certain safe houses."

"See which bait gets taken," Yelana finishes, understanding immediately. She reaches for a pen, her hand brushing mine in the process. The brief contact sends an unexpected current up my arm. I pull back slightly, maintaining professional distance.

"Exactly." My voice remains steady despite the lingering sensation of her skin against mine. "We craft each piece of information so that if it leaks, we'll know exactly which source it came from."

She begins writing, her elegant script filling the page with potential false intelligence. I find myself moving around the desk to stand beside her chair, pointing out details, suggesting modifications. Each time I lean in, I catch the scent of her perfume, something expensive with notes of vanilla and amber. The same scent that filled the SUV yesterday after the attack, when adrenaline and proximity heightened every sense.

"The shipment details should include a specific time," I suggest, reaching past her to indicate a spot on the paper. My arm accidentally brushes her shoulder, and I feel her slight intake of breath. "Something easy to verify if they're setting up an intercept."

"Like this?" She adjusts the text, shifting in her chair so that we're closer, our faces now only inches apart as we both focus on the document. I can see the faint freckle near her left temple, previously hidden by her hair. Can track the slight pulse at her throat. Details I shouldn't be cataloging but can't seem to ignore.

"That works," I manage, straightening to put necessary space between us. This growing awareness is dangerous—a distraction that could compromise my effectiveness as her protector. I need to maintain focus on the mission, not on the curve of her neck or the way her eyes change color slightly in different lighting.

We continue strategizing, our bodies gradually migrating closer as we work. The antagonism that defined our early interactions has evolved into something more complex—a partnership built on mutual necessity but increasingly tinged with genuine respect. Possibly something more, something I'm not ready to acknowledge.

"We'll need to deliver each piece of information privately," Yelana says, rising from the chair to stretch. "Make each of them feel specially trusted."

"And watch their reactions carefully," I add, forcing my eyes away from the graceful arch of her back. "First responses are hardest to fake."

She turns to face me, closer than necessary in the spacious study. "You're good at this," she observes. "The strategy, the manipulation. Not just the physical security."

"Different battlefield, same principles," I respond, holding her gaze. "Identify vulnerabilities. Exploit them. Maintain tactical advantage."

Something shifts in her expression—a new awareness, perhaps, that I'm more than just muscle. "Is that how you see everything? Everyone? Vulnerabilities to be identified?"

The question hits closer to home than she knows. "It's kept me alive," I answer simply.

The moment stretches between us, laden with unspoken complications. Her eyes drop briefly to the scar on my jaw, then back to meet mine. I find myself cataloging her vulnerabilities—not as tactical weaknesses, but as the human elements that make her more than Emelio's daughter, more than a protection assignment. The slight tremble in her hands after confrontation. The way she touches her father's desk for reassurance. The determined set of her jaw when she's afraid but won't show it.

The door opens with telling silence. Only Kendrick moves that quietly, appearing as if conjured by our focused conversation. He carries a dinner tray with practiced precision, his expression revealing nothing as he surveys us standing close together over the desk covered in strategic notes.

"Your dinner, Miss Zentarra," he announces, his British accent impeccable as always. "I thought you might require sustenance after your meeting."

I step back from Yelana, watching Kendrick's eyes carefully. They linger on our planning notes for precisely two seconds longer than necessary for a casual glance. His movements as he arranges the meal are too measured, too perfect—like someone performing surveillance while pretending to serve.

"Thank you, Kendrick," Yelana says, her voice neutral. "You can leave it there."

Only when the door closes behind him do we exchange a look. The same thought reflected in both our faces.

"He always seems to appear exactly when we're talking about something important," she observes quietly.

I nod, adding Kendrick to our mental list of potential threats. "Perfect timing is rarely coincidental in my experience."

Yelana moves to the tray, lifting the silver cover to reveal perfectly prepared food beneath. "Do you think it's safe to eat?"

The question carries weight beyond simple caution—it's an acknowledgment that her world has permanently changed. That safety is now relative, trust a luxury she can no longer afford.

"I'll taste it first," I say, the offer automatic. The need to protect her has evolved from professional obligation to something more personal, more essential.

She smiles slightly—the first genuine smile she's directed at me since my arrival. "Always the sentinel," she says, no mockery in her tone.

"Always," I confirm, the word carrying more meaning than I intended. A promise beyond the blood debt, beyond Emelio's final request. Something forming between us despite every reason it shouldn't.

We turn back to our planning, the proximity between us now feeling less like tactical positioning and more like chosen closeness. The traitor is still out there, the danger still immediate. But in this moment, the battlefield feels marginally less hostile with her beside me instead of across from me.

NINE
The Safe House

Mason

I keep one hand on the wheel and the other near my weapon as the Rover hugs each curve of the coastal highway. The storm-heavy clouds match my mood—dark, unpredictable, threatening to break at any moment. Beside me, Yelana stares out the window, her profile illuminated by flashes of lightning over the Pacific. The uncertainty about Ken has forced this move—this retreat to one of Emelio's off-book properties that even his own security team doesn't know about. Another layer of her father's world peeling back to reveal the paranoia beneath the empire. The same paranoia that's keeping her alive now.

"How much further?" she asks, breaking a silence that's lasted twenty miles.

"Five minutes." I check the rearview mirror for the third time in thirty seconds. Old habits. "It's not what you're expecting."

She shifts in her seat, the leather creaking beneath her. "What exactly should I be expecting from my father's secret beach house?"

"Not a beach house," I correct, slowing as we approach a nearly invisible turnoff. "More like a bunker with a view."

The narrow dirt road forces me to slow to a crawl, ruts and potholes threatening the Rover's suspension. Overgrown vegetation scrapes against the windows like desperate fingers. Nothing about this approach says 'Zentarra luxury'—which is precisely the point. The property disappeared under three layers of shell companies and false identities when Emelio purchased it a decade ago.

Lightning fractures the sky ahead, illuminating a rusted gate half-hidden by wild coastal scrub. Perfect camouflage—it looks abandoned, not worth investigating. I stop the vehicle, scan our surroundings, then step out into the first fat drops of rain to unlock the gate. The old padlock responds to a key Emelio gave me years ago, one I've carried but never used until today.

Back in the car, I catch Yelana studying me, questions forming behind those dark eyes. "My father gave you keys to a place I didn't know existed?"

"Insurance policy." I navigate the final stretch of rutted path. "For when everything else fails."

The house materializes through sheets of rain—weathered gray boards, salt-stained windows, sagging porch steps. Nothing like the Zentarra estate with its manicured gardens and Mediterranean elegance. This place was built to be forgotten.

I park as close to the entrance as possible, positioning the Rover for quick departure if needed. "Wait here until I clear it."

She raises an eyebrow. "You think someone's been here? Even you said nobody knows about it."

"I don't think anyone's been here," I explain, checking my weapon. "But I don't know for a fact."

The porch steps creak under my weight as rain soaks through my shirt. Three locks on the door—standard key, electronic keypad with a code that changes monthly, and a biometric scanner disguised as a rusted light fixture. Emelio's paranoia manifests in metal and circuits. I move through the security sequence, though I've only done it in theory before today.

The door resists when I try to push it open—warped wood swollen from ocean moisture. I put my shoulder into it, feeling the satisfying give as it surrenders with a groan.

"Emelio's best-kept trash bin," I mutter, gesturing Yelana forward from the car.

She darts through the rain, ducking under the shelter of the porch and then past me into the house. I follow, securing each lock behind us, then hit the light switch. Nothing happens. I try again before my eyes adjust enough to locate the backup generator controls on the wall. A few switches later, dim lights flicker to life, revealing what Emelio Zentarra considered an appropriate safe house.

"Jesus Christ," Yelana whispers, taking in the interior.

The front room serves as a combination living space and armory —rifles stacked neatly in racks along one wall, ammunition crates doubling as coffee tables, medical supplies organized in glass-fronted cabinets. A worn sofa faces the largest window, positioned to give clear sightlines to the approach. The kitchen area consists of a hot plate, mini-fridge, and stacks of MREs. Minimalist doesn't begin to cover it.

"Charming vacation home," Yelana says, running one finger along a dusty shelf and examining the gray residue with distaste. "Did he bring us here for Christmas, and I just blocked it out?"

I move through the space, checking windows, testing sight lines, locating all potential exits. "It wasn't built for comfort."

"Clearly." She picks up a tactical flashlight from a side table, turning it over in her hands. "Was anything in my father's life ever just... normal?"

The question hangs between us as I complete my security check. Her father lived in a world where safe houses equipped like military outposts were necessary. Where exit strategies and weapons caches were as essential as swimming pools and tennis courts are to other wealthy families. And now she's inherited that reality.

"Normal is a luxury in his line of work," I say, moving to the back door to verify its security. "In your line of work now."

The first real crack of thunder rattles the windows, followed immediately by a torrent of rain hammering against the roof. The storm has arrived in force, isolating us further from the world outside. I watch Yelana's reflection in the window as she continues exploring, her movements betraying both curiosity and revulsion. The elegant lines of her body seem out of place against the utilitarian backdrop—designer jeans and a cashmere sweater amid dust and weapons.

"We need to search everything," I tell her, turning back to the main room. "Your father wouldn't bring us here without a reason."

She nods, tucking a strand of hair behind her ear. "What are we looking for?"

"Information. Evidence against Ken, maybe. Or contingency plans." I begin methodically checking cabinets, looking for false bottoms, hidden compartments. "Emelio was old-school—he kept hard copies of important intel, didn't trust electronics."

We fall into a surprisingly efficient partnership, working opposite ends of the main room. I find myself watching her more than the search warrants—the focused concentration in her eyes, the way she bites her lower lip when examining something closely. Details irrelevant to security assessment but increasingly difficult to ignore.

Another lightning flash illuminates her face in stark relief, shadows accentuating cheekbones that remind me of Sierra. But the determination in her eyes is pure Emelio. In this dusty armory by the sea, with rain pelting the roof and danger at our backs, Yelana Zentarra is becoming something new—neither helpless princess nor her father's puppet. Something more dangerous, more compelling.

A flash of heat that has nothing to do with tactical assessment courses through me as she catches me watching her.

"Found anything yet?" she asks, either not noticing or choosing to ignore my gaze.

"Not yet." I return to searching, forcing my mind back to the mission. "But we will."

The floorboards near the eastern wall catch my attention—slightly uneven wear patterns, the rug positioned too precisely in a room where nothing else shows such careful arrangement. I cross to it, feeling the wood beneath the thin carpet with experienced fingers. Hollow. Different. A thousand hiding places in a thousand safe houses and bolt-holes have taught me to recognize the telltale signs of secrets beneath the surface. Emelio was better than most at concealment, but some patterns are universal among men who live with danger as a constant companion.

"Found something?" Yelana asks, frustration evident in her voice after an hour of fruitless searching.

I nod, pulling back the worn rug to reveal planks that match the others perfectly—almost perfectly. The seams are microscopically tighter, the wood aged with subtle artifice. "Your father had a talent for hiding things in plain sight."

"Like secret beach bunkers? Like traitors in his organization?" Her voice carries an edge that wasn't there before. "Like the truth about my brother's death?"

I don't answer, focusing instead on locating the mechanism that will open this particular secret. My fingers trace the edges of boards until I find it—a nearly invisible depression that yields slightly under pressure. Not enough. There's a secondary trigger.

"Hand me that tac knife from the table."

She does, our fingers brushing during the exchange. The brief contact shouldn't register through years of tactical discipline, yet somehow does. I insert the blade into the depression, applying pressure at precise angles until something clicks beneath the floorboards. A panel, approximately two feet square, rises slightly.

"There you are," I murmur, setting the knife aside and working my fingers into the gap. The panel lifts smoothly, revealing a compartment beneath. Inside, three waterproof cases sit nestled against each other, each secured with combination locks.

Yelana kneels beside me, close enough that I catch the lingering scent of her shampoo beneath the musty odor of the safe house. "More of my father's secrets." Her voice holds resignation rather than surprise.

"The combinations?" I ask, examining the first case.

She shakes her head. "I don't—" Then stops, eyes widening slightly. "Wait." Her fingers move to the locks, turning the dials with surprising confidence. "Juan's birthday. My birthday. My mother's birthday. He used them for everything important."

The first lock opens with a satisfying click. The second follows, then the third. I lift the cases from their hiding place and set them on the floor between us.

"How did you know they'd be here?" she asks as I open the first case.

"I didn't," I admit. "But I know Emelio. He'd want physical backups of anything critical, stored somewhere completely disconnected from his regular operations." My hands move methodically through the contents—waterproof folders, USB drives sealed in vacuum bags, handwritten notes protected by plastic sheeting. "This is his insurance policy."

Outside, the storm intensifies, wind driving rain against the windows in horizontal sheets. Thunder follows each lightning flash more quickly now, the storm directly overhead. I spread the documents across the floor, creating ordered piles as Yelana opens the second case.

"Offshore accounts," she reports, scanning a page of numbers and passwords. "Properties under shell companies. Contact information for people I've never heard of." She looks up at me. "Escape routes if everything failed."

"He was thorough," I acknowledge, reviewing what appears to be a complete organizational chart of Emelio's empire—names, positions, backgrounds, leverage points. Information that would be worth killing for in the wrong hands. Or the right ones.

We work in focused silence for several minutes, the only sounds the shuffling of papers and the storm's assault on the small house. I find myself watching Yelana's hands as she sorts through documents—elegant fingers with short, practical nails, moving with increasing confidence through her father's secret archives. Her eyes narrow with concentration, absorbing information at a pace that impresses even me. She's more like Emelio than she knows.

"Mason." Her voice sounds strange, tight with emotion. "Look at this."

She pushes a folder toward me, open to a page of handwritten notes. Ken Jackson's name appears repeatedly, circled in red pen, surrounded by question marks and cryptic notations. "Trust – maybe. Check again" is scrawled in the margins in Emelio's distinctive handwriting. Beneath that, a list of dates and locations corresponding to security breaches in the organization over the past year.

"He suspected Ken," I say, scanning the notes quickly. "Was building a case against him."

"Ken has been in our house since I was three years old," Yelana whispers, her voice hollow with betrayal. "He taught me to ride a bike. He brought me ice cream when I broke my arm falling out of a tree." Her fingers trace the red circles around Ken's name. "How could he—"

A blinding flash of lightning interrupts her, followed immediately by a thunderclap so violent it makes the windows rattle in their frames. The dim lights flicker once, twice, then die completely, plunging us into sudden darkness.

I move instantly, shifting positions to place myself between Yelana and the windows—the most vulnerable points in case the power failure isn't storm-related. My hand finds my weapon as my eyes adjust to the darkness.

"Don't move," I tell her, my voice dropping to near-whisper. "Stay low."

I listen beyond the storm, beyond the sound of her breathing, searching for anything that doesn't belong. Nothing. Just rain and wind and thunder. After thirty seconds of assessment, I relax marginally.

"Probably just the storm," I say, reaching for the tactical flashlight we'd found earlier. Its beam cuts through the darkness, illuminating Yelana's face—tension written in every line, but no panic. She's learning.

"There are candles in the kitchen drawer," I tell her. "And matches. The generator might have flooded—this place hasn't been maintained recently."

I navigate the darkened space with practiced ease, locating candles and matches where I'd noted them during our initial search. Muscle memory from countless operations in hostile territory makes darkness a minor inconvenience rather than a handicap. Within minutes, I've placed and lit candles around the room, creating islands of warm light that push back the shadows.

When I return to the documents, Yelana hasn't moved, still kneeling beside the evidence of Ken's potential betrayal. The candlelight plays across her features, softening the determination I've grown accustomed to seeing there. For a moment, she looks younger, more vulnerable—a woman discovering that her world is built on shifting sands, not the solid foundation she believed in.

I kneel beside her, closer than strictly necessary, and continue sorting through the files. The flickering light forces us to bend closer to read the documents, our heads sometimes nearly touching as we examine particularly dense pages. I find myself acutely aware of her proximity—the subtle warmth radiating from her body, the way her breath catches slightly when she discovers something significant, the faint scent of vanilla beneath the musty odor of old paper.

"We'll need to go through all of it," I say, my voice rougher than intended in the intimate quiet created by the storm and candlelight. "Every page. Every note."

She looks up, our faces suddenly inches apart over the scattered documents. Her eyes reflect the candle flames, dark pupils ringed with amber fire. "My father knew," she says softly. "He knew and he didn't tell me. Just like everything else."

The accusation hangs between us—not directed at me, but at the man whose secrets we're uncovering one page at a time. The man who connected us through blood debt and death. In the flickering light, surrounded by the physical evidence of Emelio's paranoia, we're closer than we've ever been, yet separated by the very reason I'm here.

"He was protecting you," I say, though the words sound hollow even to me.

"By leaving me blind? By trusting you to save me instead of trusting me to save myself?" Her eyes hold mine, challenging, fierce despite the betrayal evident in her expression. "That's not protection, Mason. That's control."

I have no answer for her—not one that wouldn't sound like defending a dead man's choices. Instead, I return to the documents, to the evidence, to the tangible problems we can solve. The storm rages on, trapping us in this moment of forced intimacy, surrounded by secrets finally coming to light.

The candlelight casts everything in shades of amber and shadow as we continue sorting through Emelio's files. Rain hammers against the roof with increasing fury, the sound occasionally punctuated by thunder that seems to shake the very foundation of this weathered safe house. I'm hyperaware of Yelana's movements beside me—the deliberate way she arranges documents into categories, the slight furrow between her brows when she concentrates, the brush of her fingers against mine when we reach for the same page. Each point of contact sends a current through me that I have no business feeling. Yet it persists, undeniable as the storm outside.

"Financial records," she murmurs, sliding a folder toward me. Our hands touch briefly, a whisper of contact that shouldn't register but does. "Offshore accounts in the Caymans, Singapore, Switzerland."

I nod, cataloging the information while trying to ignore the warmth lingering on my skin where her fingers brushed mine. "Your father was thorough. Multiple escape routes, resources scattered globally."

"Always planning for disaster," she says, her voice carrying an edge of bitterness. "Always preparing for the worst while pretending everything was normal."

Another folder yields security protocols for Zentarra properties I didn't even know existed—safe houses across three continents, each with detailed access instructions and emergency supplies. I add them to our growing map of Emelio's hidden empire, pieces fitting together like a puzzle we're assembling by flickering light.

"Wait." Yelana's voice changes, softens. She pulls something from between two financial statements—not a document but thicker paper, colorful even in the dim light. She stares at it, momentarily frozen.

"What is it?" I shift closer, the floorboards creaking beneath us.

She turns the paper toward me—a child's drawing, crude figures rendered in crayon. A house with a disproportionate chimney, three stick figures holding hands in front, labeled in careful but clumsy letters: "Daddy," "Mommy," "Lana."

"I drew this," she whispers, her voice suddenly young. "I was maybe five? Six? After Juan died."

I watch her face as she studies the drawing, her expression stripped of the hardened veneer she's cultivated since I arrived. The candlelight softens the angles of her face, illuminating something vulnerable I rarely see. She looks through more papers, finding two additional drawings tucked between financial records and weapons inventories.

"He kept them." Her voice holds wonder and confusion. "In his most secure files, with his contingency plans and blackmail material."

I remain silent, watching her fingers trace the childish lines of her own creation. This moment feels sacred somehow, a glimpse beneath the armor we both wear for different reasons.

"I used to draw him pictures all the time," she continues, speaking more to herself than to me. "I thought if I made enough beautiful things, he'd stay home more. Be a normal dad who came to school functions instead of disappearing for weeks on mysterious 'business trips'." She looks up, meeting my eyes. "I was always protected, always watched, but never really seen. Do you know what that's like? To be the most guarded person in the room and the loneliest at the same time?"

The question hangs between us, unexpectedly personal. I consider deflecting, returning to the documents, maintaining professional distance. But something in her expression stops me—a genuine need to be understood that cuts through my practiced detachment.

"Yes," I admit, surprising myself. "After Afghanistan, after losing my team... being the only one who survived creates a particular kind of isolation. People guard you, watch you for signs of breaking, but they don't really see you."

Her eyes hold mine for a long moment, something shifting in her expression. Understanding, perhaps, or recognition. She returns to the files, but the space between us feels different—charged with shared vulnerability neither of us intended to reveal.

We continue working through documents, the silence now companionable rather than tense. Our hands brush occasionally, neither of us pulling away quite as quickly as before. The storm rages on, isolating us further in this bubble of candlelight and revelation.

"Juan used to hide notes in my lunches," she says suddenly, looking up from a particularly dense file. "Little jokes or riddles. Even when he was away with my father, he'd write them in advance and mother would slip them into my lunchbox." A small smile touches her lips. "I saved every one."

The mention of Juan usually tightens something in my chest—guilt, regret, the weight of blood debt. But tonight, in this storm-battered house with candles guttering in the draft, I find myself wanting to share rather than retreat from his memory.

“He was a natural navigator," I tell her, setting aside the document I've been reading. "In Afghanistan, he could look at mountain ranges and know exactly where we were, which valleys were safe, which paths to avoid." The memory comes easily, unmarred for once by the horror that followed. "He taught me phrases in Pashto to use with local elders—respectful greetings that opened doors American military formality couldn't."

Yelana watches me, her expression hungry for details of the brother she lost too young. "What else?" she asks softly.

"He collected rocks—specific ones with patterns or unusual colors. Kept them in his pockets until they were smooth from handling." I find myself smiling slightly at the memory. "Your father thought it was childish, but Juan had geological theories about mineral compositions in different regions. He was probably right."

"That sounds like him," she says, something like wonder in her voice. "I barely remember him, just... impressions. The sound of his laugh. The way he smelled like cinnamon gum." She looks down at the files between us. "It's strange hearing about him as a person, not just a tragic figure in our family history."

I nod, understanding exactly what she means. We all become simplified after death—reduced to our relationships to the living, our most notable traits, the manner of our passing. The complex humanity gets lost.

Lightning flashes, momentarily overwhelming the candles' glow. In that stark illumination, I see Yelana clearly—not as Emelio's daughter or my protection assignment, but as a woman carrying burdens of her own with remarkable strength.

"There's more here about Juan," she says suddenly, pulling a thick manila envelope from the bottom of the second case. She opens it carefully, sliding out documents protected by plastic sheeting.

Her breath catches audibly. I move closer, leaning in to see what's affected her so strongly. It's a photograph—Juan in military-style gear, standing beside a younger Emelio near a mountain range I recognize instantly. The Hindu Kush, not far from where he died. The boy's smile is wide, excited, proud to be included in his father's world. Emelio's hand rests on his shoulder, his expression a rare display of unguarded affection.

Yelana's finger traces her brother's face through the plastic, following the contours of features that echo her own. I feel my jaw clench involuntarily, memories of that day surging back—the ambush, the crossfire, the moment Juan appeared where he shouldn't have been.

"He looks so young," she whispers. "I always imagined him older, more like you. But he was just a boy."

"A brave boy," I say, my voice rougher than intended. "Braver than many men I've served with."

Her eyes lift from the photograph to meet mine, and something shifts in that moment—the air between us changing like atmospheric pressure before a storm breaks. For the first time, our shared connection to Juan feels like a bond rather than a barrier. The loss that divided us now somehow connects us, a thread of understanding pulling us toward each other.

"He would have liked you," she says, the words emerging before I can analyze their wisdom. "Not just as my protector. As a person."

"Would he?" I say as she holds my gaze, something vulnerable and fierce in her expression. "The man responsible for his death?"

"Yes," she answers honestly. "Because you're not afraid of the truth, even when it hurts. He valued that."

A particularly violent gust of wind slams against the windows, rattling the frames in their moorings. The intrusion breaks our moment of connection, drawing both our attention to the world beyond this candlelit bubble. The storm outside rages on, a mirror to the one brewing between us—powerful, unpredictable, impossible to ignore.

Yelana carefully returns the photograph to its protective sleeve, but something has changed. The tension between us hasn't dissipated—it's transformed, evolved from antagonism to something more complex and dangerous.

"We should finish going through these files," she says, her voice steadier now. "Find everything we can about Ken and what my father suspected."

I nod, returning to the documents spread before us. But as we continue working side by side, the occasional brush of her shoulder against mine carries new significance. The candlelight catches in her hair when she bends over a particularly dense page of notes, creating a halo effect that draws my eye despite my best efforts.

The rain hammers against the roof, the wind howls through the eaves, and we sit surrounded by the ghosts and secrets of Emelio Zentarra's empire. Yet somehow, in this storm-battered safe house, with Juan's memory between us like a bridge rather than a wall, I feel something I haven't experienced in years.

Connection. Dangerous, inappropriate, inevitable connection.

And like the storm outside, I'm powerless to stop it.

TEN
Nightclub Rebellion

Yelana

The walls of the estate have never felt more like a prison than they do tonight. I pace my bedroom like a caged animal, the conversation with Mason at the beach house replaying in my mind on an endless loop. His face in the candlelight, the way his voice softened when he spoke about Juan, the brief touches of our hands over those documents—all of it twists inside me, forming knots I can't untangle. I need out. Need space to breathe. Need somewhere loud enough to drown the whispers in my head that say maybe, just maybe, I'm starting to feel something for the man I'm supposed to hate.

My closet yields the necessary armor—a black dress that hugs every curve like a second skin, heels high enough to make my father roll in his fresh grave. I apply makeup with seductive precision: smoky eyes dark enough to hide in, lipstick the color of warning signs. The woman in the mirror looks nothing like Emelio Zentarra's grieving daughter. She looks dangerous. Untouchable. Free.

I wait until two in the morning, when even Mason's vigilance must have its limits. The security system is top-tier—his doing—but it's still my house. I've spent twenty-one years learning its secrets, finding its blind spots. The service entrance near the east kitchen has a six-second delay when the motion sensors reset—something Mason hasn't discovered yet. I count the seconds in my head, timing my movements with the system's electronic heartbeat, slipping through its arteries like a clot headed for the brain.

The night air hits my bare shoulders like a whispered threat. I don't shiver. Sierra Zentarra's daughter doesn't show weakness, even to the empty garden. My phone buzzes in my clutch—the car service I ordered through a burner app, waiting beyond the property line. Six minutes of strategic movement through the grounds, staying in camera blind spots, hugging shadows like old friends.

The gate cameras pan in predictable sweeps—fifteen seconds east, fifteen west. I count in my head, slipping through the service gate between passes. The freedom on the other side tastes metallic, dangerous. The black sedan waits exactly where I specified, its driver asking no questions when I slide into the back seat.

"Pulse," I tell him, tasting the word like I'm sampling something forbidden. My father's club. My club now. The driver nods, pulls away from the curb. I don't look back at the estate shrinking in the rear window. Tonight isn't about what's behind me.

Los Angeles slides past in neon smears and shadow, the city's pulse accelerating as we approach the heart of its nightlife. We stop at a nondescript building, its exterior deliberately boring—the best camouflage in a city obsessed with appearances. Only a small blue light above a steel door hints at what waits inside. No line, no velvet rope. Pulse doesn't cater to people who wait.

The doorman recognizes me immediately, his eyes widening slightly before his professional mask returns. "Miss Zentarra. It's been some time."

I offer a smile that doesn't reach my eyes. "Not anymore."

Inside, bass hits my chest like a physical blow, so loud my heartbeat adjusts to match its rhythm. Strobe lights fragment the crowd into stuttering freeze-frames—hands raised, bodies pressed, heads thrown back in chemical ecstasy. The air smells like sweat and expensive perfume and spilled alcohol—nothing like the antiseptic cleanliness of the estate or the musty safety of that beach bunker.

I cut through the crowd like a blade, feeling eyes track my movement but not caring whose they are. The bar is my first target. I slide onto a stool, catching the bartender's attention with a subtle gesture my mother taught me years ago. He approaches immediately, recognition sparking in his eyes.

"Miss Zentarra. My condolences about your—"

"Four tequila shots," I interrupt. "Patrón. Lime. Salt." I don't want condolences. Don't want to be reminded that I'm an orphan in a black dress playing at freedom.

The shots appear before me like magic—the perks of ownership. I don't waste time with ceremony. The first burns a path down my throat, the second numbs it, the third makes the club's edges blur pleasantly. The fourth I hold between my fingers, studying the clear liquid like it contains answers instead of more questions.

A man slides onto the stool beside me—designer watch, tailored shirt, eyes that calculate my worth based on obvious metrics. He says something I can't hear over the music. I down the fourth shot instead of responding, letting the liquor's fire spread through my limbs, transforming nervousness into reckless courage.

I leave him mid-sentence, drawn to the dance floor by the pulsing beat and the promise of anonymity among bodies. Here, I'm not Yelana Zentarra, reluctant heir to a dangerous empire. I'm just another girl losing herself under strobe lights, letting the music overwrite thought. I close my eyes and move, letting alcohol and bass carry me away from security protocols and blood debts and the memory of Mason's fingers brushing mine over candlelit documents.

Bodies press against me, strangers seeking connection in the dark. I welcome their touch—it's simple, uncomplicated, nothing like the electric current that jumps between Mason and me whenever we're close. I dance until sweat beads along my spine, until my carefully applied makeup begins to smudge, until the tequila haze makes every sensation more intense and less important.

A man appears before me—tall, dark-haired, with a mouth that curves easily into a smile. Not Mason, with his perpetual vigilance and haunted eyes. This man's hands find my waist without asking permission, pulling me against him with entitled confidence. I let him, draping my arms around his neck, our bodies finding the beat together.

"You're too beautiful to look so sad," he shouts over the music, his breath hot against my ear.

I laugh, the sound lost in the noise. If he only knew how many reasons I have for sadness. Instead of explaining, I press closer, letting his hands roam down my sides, his thigh slipping between mine as we move together. The contact is exactly what I wanted—physical, meaningless, a perfect distraction from the complicated mess of emotions waiting back at the estate. From the dangerous way Mason's eyes soften when he thinks I'm not looking. From the guilt I feel for wanting the man responsible for Juan's death.

The stranger's hands slide lower, cupping my ass, pulling me hard against him. I should feel something—desire, excitement, even disgust—but all I feel is numb relief that for these moments, I don't have to think. Don't have to feel. Don't have to be anything but a body in motion.

And then—like my thoughts have conjured him from shadow—I see Mason.

He stands at the edge of the dance floor, a pillar of stillness in the churning sea of movement. Even through the flashing lights and tequila haze, I recognize his military posture, the set of his shoulders, the intensity of his focus as his eyes lock onto me. The crowd seems to part around him, instinctively giving space to the predator in their midst. His face remains in shadow, but I feel the heat of his anger from across the room.

His fists are clenched at his sides, his jaw tight enough that I can almost hear his teeth grinding even through the deafening music. Beyond the obvious fury at my escape, something else flickers in his expression as he watches the stranger's hands on my body—something possessive and primal that sends a different kind of heat spiraling through me.

Jealousy. Raw and unmistakable, etched into every line of his body as he watches another man touch me.

The realization hits harder than the tequila, making my head swim. Mason Phillips—detached, professional, haunted by my brother's ghost—is jealous. And God help me, some dark part of me is thrilled by it.

A dangerous thrill shoots through me, sharp as broken glass, when our eyes lock across the dance floor. I see the exact moment Mason spots the stranger's hands on my body—the subtle tightening around his eyes, the flash of something possessive and raw behind his professional mask. And in that instant, something wicked and wounded inside me decides to push him further, to see how far I can make him crack. Because if he's going to make me feel these impossible things, he deserves to suffer too.

I hold Mason's gaze deliberately, making sure he's watching as I press my body more firmly against the stranger. My hands slide up the man's chest, around his neck, into his hair. The stranger misinterprets my sudden enthusiasm, his smile widening as his grip on my hips tightens.

"You want to get out of here?" he shouts over the music, his lips brushing my ear.

I don't answer with words. Instead, I pull back just enough to look into his face—not because I care what he looks like, but to ensure my profile is perfect for Mason's viewing angle. Then I press my mouth against the stranger's, parting my lips, making it as filthy and deliberate as possible. The man responds immediately, his hands sliding lower, pulling me against him with new urgency.

Through half-lidded eyes, I watch Mason. The strobe lights catch his face in staccato flashes—jaw clenched, nostrils flared, something primal replacing his usual calculated control. I've hit my mark perfectly. The invisible thread of tension between us pulls taut enough to snap.

And snap it does.

Mason moves like violence personified, cutting through the crowd with lethal precision. Dancers instinctively part for him, responding to some primitive recognition of danger. His eyes never leave mine, even as his body navigates the packed floor with inhuman efficiency. The stranger's tongue is in my mouth when Mason reaches us, but I'm watching Mason's approach, heart hammering against my ribs in a rhythm that has nothing to do with desire for the man I'm kissing.

A hand clamps onto the stranger's shoulder, pulling him back with enough force to break our kiss abruptly. The man stumbles, confusion quickly morphing to anger as he turns to confront the interruption. The words die on his lips when he faces Mason. Even in the chaotic lighting, there's no mistaking the lethal capability radiating from every line of Mason's body.

"Security," Mason says, the word barely audible over the music but carrying enough authority to make the stranger hesitate. "She's leaving."

His hand wraps around my upper arm, firm enough to control but careful not to bruise. The dichotomy is so perfectly Mason—capable of violence but meticulous in its application.

"We were in the middle of something," the stranger protests, though he's already taking a half-step back.

"No, you weren't." Mason's voice remains professionally detached, but his eyes promise consequences if this conversation continues. "She's intoxicated and under my protection. Walk away."

The tequila in my system ignites into fresh rage at being discussed like a package to be handed off. "I'm not going anywhere," I spit, trying to wrench my arm from Mason's grip. His fingers don't budge. "And I'm not under anyone's protection."

The stranger looks between us, survival instinct finally kicking in. "Look, I don't want any trouble—"

"Then don't make any," Mason cuts him off, dismissing him entirely as he turns his attention to me. "We're leaving. Now."

"Fuck you," I shout, loud enough that heads turn even over the pounding music. "Get your fucking hands off me!" I twist violently in his grip, making a spectacle of resistance. Nearby dancers back away, creating a small circle of space around our confrontation. "I'm staying!"

Mason's expression doesn't change, but something dangerous flashes in his eyes—a warning I'm too drunk and angry to heed. When I try to pull away again, his tactics shift. In one fluid motion, his arm slides around my waist, and he lifts me slightly off the ground, neutralizing my leverage. My feet scramble for purchase as he starts moving toward the exit, my body pressed against his side like a rebellious package.

"Put me down!" I shriek, slapping at his shoulder, his chest, anywhere I can reach. "Security! This man is assaulting me!" The irony of calling for security against my own security isn't lost on me, but I'm beyond caring about consistency.

The crowd parts for us, a blur of curious faces and raised phones. Someone steps forward—a bouncer with shoulders like small mountains—but stops when I accidentally call Mason by name in my string of curses. Recognition flickers across the bouncer's face; he knows who Mason is, who I am. He backs away with a nod. No help there. The Zentarra name working against me for once.

Mason's grip doesn't loosen as he navigates through the club. My struggles become more desperate, less coordinated, as we near the exit. The cool night air hits my overheated skin when the door opens, the sudden temperature change momentarily disorienting after the hot press of bodies inside.

"I hate you," I hiss against his ear, close enough to feel him flinch slightly at the venom in my voice. "You don't own me. My father's debt doesn't make me your property."

He says nothing, just continues toward the black SUV idling at the curb. When did he have time to call for a car? The driver opens the back door as we approach, pointedly looking anywhere but at the spectacle of me half-carried, half-dragged by Mason.

"I'm not going back there," I say, a hint of desperation leaking into my anger. "You can't make me."

Mason pauses, finally looking directly at me. His eyes are cold, professional, but something else simmers beneath the surface—concern, anger, and that same possessive heat I saw inside. "Yes, I can."

With that simple declaration, he deposits me into the back seat with surprising gentleness given the circumstances. Before I can scramble across to the opposite door, he's beside me, the door closing with a definitive click. The locks engage with a sound like a prison cell sliding shut.

The driver pulls away from the curb immediately, following some predetermined protocol I wasn't part of establishing. The tinted windows seal us in our private bubble of tension, the bass from the club fading as we put distance between us and my brief escape.

Inside the car, Mason's controlled breathing fills the silence. He sits with military posture, not looking at me, one hand resting on the door handle as if he expects me to try breaking out at any moment. Which, honestly, isn't an unreasonable assumption.

"Take me back," I demand, though the words lack the force they had in the club. The adrenaline is starting to ebb, leaving exhaustion and tequila-fueled nausea in its wake.

"No." One syllable, absolute as gravity.

I turn to stare out the window, watching the neon blur of Los Angeles slide past. My brief taste of freedom evaporating like spilled alcohol on hot pavement. The prison walls of my new reality closing in once more.

But beneath the anger and resentment, a traitorous part of me remembers the look in his eyes when he saw another man's hands on my body. Remembers and savors it, even as I hate myself for caring.

The silence in the car lasts approximately thirty seconds before I can't contain my rage anymore. "Who the hell do you think you are?" I spit, twisting in my seat to face him. My dress rides up my thighs, but I'm too furious to care about modesty. "You embarrassed me in front of dozens of people. You manhandled me like I'm some unruly child. In my own fucking club!"

Mason stares straight ahead, his profile carved from stone in the passing streetlights. His knuckles whiten as he grips the steering wheel—the driver mysteriously disappeared once we were both in the back seat, and now Mason's behind the wheel, putting more distance between me and freedom with every second.

"You compromised your security," he says finally, his voice low and controlled in a way that only fuels my anger. "You deliberately evaded protocols designed to keep you alive. You exposed yourself to potential threats while intoxicated and distracted."

"I'm not some little girl you need to babysit!" The words explode from me, raw and jagged. "I'm twenty-one fucking years old and the head of my father's organization! You don't get to decide where I go or who I—"

"You think your enemies aren't watching?" His voice cuts through mine, still quiet but vibrating with intensity. His eyes remain fixed on the road, but something in his jaw twitches. "You think they wouldn't love to grab you when you're drunk and grinding on some random asshole?"

Heat floods my cheeks, partly from anger, partly from the memory of how he looked watching me with that stranger. "That 'random asshole' wasn't trying to kill me. He was just trying to—"

"To fuck you." Mason's clinical assessment lands like a slap. "And you were using him to what? Forget? Escape? Make me jealous?"

The last question hangs between us, charged and dangerous. I turn away, staring out the window at the empty streets flashing past. "Not everything is about you, Phillips."

"No," he agrees, his voice softening almost imperceptibly. "But that display in the club was. You made sure I was watching."

The accuracy of his assessment burns. I have no response that isn't a lie, so I retreat into silence for the remainder of the drive, letting my anger simmer to a boil.

When we arrive at the estate, I don't wait for him to open my door. I shove it open myself, stumbling slightly on my heels as I storm toward the house. I hear him behind me, his footsteps measured and controlled where mine are fueled by rage and tequila.

The front door slams against the wall as I push through it, the sound echoing through the empty foyer. Kendrick will appear soon, drawn by the noise—he always does—but for now, it's just Mason and me in the vast, hollow space of my inheritance.

"You had no right!" I spin to face him as he closes the door with deliberate gentleness that somehow feels more violent than my slam. "No right to drag me out of there like some misbehaving teenager!"

"I had every right." He advances into the foyer, his voice still maddeningly calm. "Your father—"

"My father is dead!" The words tear from my throat, raw and painful. "And I'm so fucking sick of everyone using him to control me. His wishes. His business. His debts. What about what I want?"

"What you want will get you killed." Mason's face remains impassive, but something flickers in his eyes—frustration, concern, something else I can't name. "You think this is about control? It's about keeping you alive."

"It's about your guilt," I accuse, moving closer, invading his space. "You couldn't save Juan, you couldn't save my father, so now you're obsessed with saving me. But I don't need saving, Phillips. I need freedom!"

We're moving through the house now, our argument echoing off marble floors and high ceilings. Neither of us turning on lights, our shadows stretching and contracting with each pass beneath the security system's dim guidance lamps.

"Freedom to what? Get drunk? Dance with strangers? There are a dozen safer ways to grieve, Yelana."

"Don't you dare tell me how to grieve," I seethe, my voice dropping dangerously low. "You don't know what this feels like. To lose everything and then be handed the keys to an empire built on death."

"I know exactly what it feels like," he counters, something raw finally breaking through his professional veneer. "I lost my entire team in Afghanistan. Every friend I had. Then I lost Kerry. My parents. Don't tell me I don't understand loss."

The revelation should make me soften, should create connection through shared pain. Instead, it fuels my rage. "Then you should understand why I needed one fucking night to forget! One night where I wasn't Emelio Zentarra's orphaned daughter with a target on my back!"

We've reached the main hallway now, the portrait gallery where generations of Zentarras stare down with painted judgment. My heels click against marble, sharp as gunshots in the tense silence between verbal salvos.

"You're nothing but a fucking guard dog," I hiss, getting in his face, close enough to see the muscle jump in his jaw. "A pet my father kept around out of guilt and obligation. That's all this is. A debt being paid in protection services."

Nothing. Not even a flicker of reaction. His control infuriates me further.

"Is that why you look at me the way you do?" I press, poking a finger against his chest. "Guilt? Obligation? Or is it something else, Phillips? Does watching me make you feel something your precious sense of duty can't allow?"

His eyes narrow slightly, the only indication that my words have landed. "You're drunk. You don't know what you're saying."

"I know exactly what I'm saying." I step closer, my finger jabbing harder against his sternum. "I saw your face when that man had his hands on me. That wasn't professional concern. That was jealousy."

"Yelana—" His voice carries a warning I'm too angry to heed.

"What are you going to do about it?" I challenge, my face inches from his. When he remains stone-still, something inside me snaps. My hand cracks across his face before I fully register the decision to slap him.

The sound echoes through the hallway, sharp and final. For one breathless moment, absolute stillness. Then—movement so fast I can't track it. My back hits the wall, both wrists captured in one of his hands, pinned above my head. His body presses against mine, solid and unyielding. Our faces are inches apart, both of us breathing hard, the air between us electric with something that transcends anger.

His free hand braces against the wall beside my head. I can feel the heat radiating from him, smell the faint trace of his cologne mingled with the scent of rain that never quite leaves his skin. His pupils are blown wide, the gray of his irises reduced to thin rings around bottomless black. There's danger in his eyes, but not the kind that threatens physical harm.

"Don't," he says, his voice rough-edged and low. Just that. A single word that contains multitudes.

I lift my chin, defiance warring with the heat pooling in my stomach at his proximity. "I'm not a little girl you need to protect," I growl, my voice barely above a whisper.

His eyes drop to my mouth for the briefest moment before returning to mine. "I am very aware you are not a little girl," he says, each word precise and heavy with meaning. Then he leans in, his lips by my ear, so close I can feel his breath. "So stop acting like a spoiled brat."

For one breathless moment, something shifts between us—the anger transforming into a different kind of tension entirely. His grip on my wrists loosens slightly, his body leaning incrementally closer. I can feel his heart hammering against my chest, matching the frantic rhythm of my own.

Then, like a switch being flipped, he releases me and steps back. The sudden absence of his body heat leaves me cold and unsteady. Without another word, he turns and walks away, his footsteps measured and deliberate down the hallway.

I remain pressed against the wall, trembling from anger and adrenaline and something else entirely—something I'm not ready to name. My skin burns where he touched me, the ghost of his grip lingering on my wrists. I slide down until I'm sitting on the cold marble floor, my dress hiked indecently high, my carefully constructed armor in ruins around me.

In trying to escape my confusing feelings for Mason Phillips, I've only managed to make them infinitely more complicated. And judging by the look in his eyes before he walked away, I'm not the only one struggling with this impossible attraction.

ELEVEN
Midnight Intruders

Mason

I stare at the ceiling of my spartan room, sleep a distant possibility as I replay the scene at Pulse over and over. Her body against that stranger. The rage that surged through me, unprofessional, dangerous, compromising. I tell myself it was about her security, about the mission, but the lie tastes bitter. That wasn't concern for a protectee that burned through me when I saw his hands on her, it was jealousy, raw and primitive. Emotion I can't afford, especially not for Yelana Zentarra. Not for my blood debt. Not for the sister of the boy I couldn't save.

The memory of pinning her against the wall floods back, her wrists captured in my hand, her body pressed against mine. The scent of tequila and expensive perfume. Her eyes, defiant and wanting. The moment hanging between us like a live grenade with the pin pulled.

I sit up, running a hand over my face, sweat cooling on my bare chest in the night air. This is unacceptable. A breach in operational discipline that could—

A scream pierces the silence—high, panicked, unmistakably Yelana.

My body moves before conscious thought, muscle memory from a thousand combat situations. Wearing only sweatpants, I grab my weapon, safety off, and I'm at her door in four seconds flat, mind cataloging possible threats, angles of approach, defensive positions. Her scream wasn't cut off—not an attacker silencing her—but it held genuine terror.

I don't knock. The door gives way under my shoulder, my Sig leading the way as I sweep the room in practiced arcs, identifying and dismissing potential threats in milliseconds. Closet—clear. Bathroom—door open, clear. Windows—intact, no breach.

And then I see her, pressed into the corner of her massive four-poster bed, eyes wide, a towel wrapped hastily around her body, water still beading on her shoulders. She's staring at something on her bedspread with naked terror.

"What is it?" I demand, still scanning for actual threats.

"There!" She points at a small dark shape crawling across her duvet. "Kill it!"

A spider. A fucking spider. The absurdity of the situation—me standing in her bedroom doorway, weapon drawn, heart racing with combat readiness, while Yelana, heir to one of the most dangerous criminal empires in America, cowers from an arachnid smaller that a quarter—hits me like a wave.

I secure my weapon, tucking it back into my shoulder holster, then grab a tissue from her nightstand. "This is what had you screaming like you were being murdered?"

"It's huge," she says defensively, still not moving from her corner position.

I dispatch her eight-legged intruder with a tissue, feeling her eyes on me the entire time. When I turn back to her, something unexpected happens. Her lips twitch, then curve upward, and suddenly she's laughing—a genuine sound I've rarely heard from her. Not the sharp, weaponized laughter she uses in meetings or the bitter version from our arguments, but something almost girlish.

"I'm sorry," she manages between breaths. "But if you could have seen your face—charging in here like Navy SEAL Captain America..."

Despite everything—our fight at the club, the tension between us, the completely unprofessional thoughts I was just having about her—I find myself smiling too. "It's Lieutenant, not Captain."

Her laugh deepens, and something loosens in my chest. This version of Yelana—slightly disheveled, guard down, eyes bright with humor instead of challenge—is a rare sight. One I could get used to.

"Thanks for saving me from the terrifying beast," she says, her smile lingering.

"All part of the service," I reply, moving to leave before this moment of connection becomes something I can't control. "Try not to encounter any more deadly wildlife before morning."

I'm almost at the door when the window explodes inward.

Glass shards spray across the room as two black-clad figures crash through in a synchronized breach. I'm moving before the first piece hits the floor, weapon already in hand, body positioning itself between Yelana and the threat. Time slows, adrenaline sharpening every detail into crystal clarity.

"Down!" I bark at Yelana, identifying the first attacker's knife in the same heartbeat. His stance, grip, the way he balances his weight—trained, professional, not some random thug. The second man has a garrote already looped in his gloved hands.

No time for a clean shot. Too much risk with Yelana behind me. Close quarters combat it is.

I grab the heavy crystal lamp from the nightstand, ripping its cord from the wall and hurling it in one fluid motion. It catches Attacker One in the face, buying me the half-second I need to close distance. His knife slashes air where I was, not where I am. I drive my forearm up into his extended elbow—hard enough to hear the joint crack. The knife clatters to the carpet as he howls.

Attacker Two loops around, trying to flank me to reach Yelana. Not happening.

I hook my foot under the nightstand and kick it into his path, following through with a strike to his throat that has him gasping. But he recovers fast—too fast—and his fist glances off my jaw with enough force to make stars bloom at the edge of my vision.

Professional. Trained. Determined.

I pivot, using his momentum against him, the same move I taught Yelana days ago. When his balance shifts, I drive my knee into his kidney, following with an elbow to the base of his skull. He staggers but doesn't drop.

Behind me, Yelana screams a warning. I duck instinctively as Attacker One—broken arm and all—swings a jagged shard of mirror glass where my neck had been. The movement saves my carotid artery but costs me positioning. I'm off-balance for a crucial second.

Attacker Two seizes the opportunity, tackling me into Yelana's dresser. Wood cracks, perfume bottles shatter, the scent of expensive fragrance mixing with the copper tang of blood as glass cuts into my shoulder. I hook my fingers into his eye sockets—a dirty move, but I'm not fighting for points. He screams, reeling back, giving me space to deliver a palm strike to his nose that sends cartilage crunching into his brain.

One down. Permanently.

The bedroom door crashes open again—Ken Jackson, weapon drawn, face set in hard lines. "Phillips!"

"One more!" I shout, already tracking Attacker One, who's

retreating toward the shattered window, weapon now in his unbroken hand.

Ken's first shot goes wide, splintering the window frame. His second catches the attacker in the shoulder, spinning him but not stopping him. The man dives through the window into the night, leaving a spray of blood in his wake.

"Perimeter breach, east wing!" Ken barks into his radio, already moving to the window to cover the escape route. "Armed suspect, wounded, heading south across the grounds!"

I turn back to Yelana, finding her pressed against the headboard, eyes wide, a thin line of blood on her cheek where flying glass caught her. The room around us looks like a war zone—broken furniture, shattered glass, blood spatter on the cream-colored walls, the body of Attacker Two crumpled near the bathroom door.

"Are you hurt?" I demand, my voice harsher than intended as adrenaline still courses through my system.

She shakes her head mutely, shock evident in her face. This wasn't a random attack. This was coordinated, professional, timed precisely—when she was vulnerable, when security was still adjusting after her nightclub escape. When my focus was compromised by unprofessional feelings.

I survey the chaos of her once-pristine bedroom, tactical assessment warring with the primitive need to get her somewhere safe, to keep her close, to never let her out of my sight again. The jealousy I felt watching her with that stranger at the club suddenly seems trivial, childish. This is the real threat. This is what I need to focus on.

Not the way my heart still hammers at how close I came to losing her.

Combat adrenaline still courses through my system as I kneel before Yelana, my hands steady from years of field medicine despite the tremor of rage still working through my chest. She could have died. The realization hits harder than the attacker's fist did. If I'd been a second slower, if I'd still been brooding in my room instead of rushing to her scream—I shut down that line of thinking. Focus on the now. Assess. Treat. Secure. The tactical checklist resets my breathing, steadies my pulse. My fingers, still tacky with someone else's blood, hover over the cut on her cheek, not touching yet. "I need to check you for injuries," I say, my voice stripped of everything but calm efficiency.

She nods, her usual defiance temporarily erased by shock. "I'm fine," she insists, but the slight quaver in her voice betrays her.

"Let me confirm that," I counter, already examining the cut on her cheek. Superficial. Won't even scar. I find myself absurdly grateful for this small mercy. "Does anything hurt? Did you hit anything when you fell back?"

My hands move with clinical precision, checking her arms for lacerations from the flying glass, her head for contusions, her ribs for potential damage from impact. Each touch is deliberately impersonal, though the warmth of her skin through the thin tank top registers despite my professional detachment. I find a constellation of small cuts on her forearms where she must have raised them instinctively against the shower of glass. None need stitches. A bruise is already forming along her shoulder blade where she hit the wall during the fight.

The intimacy of this examination isn't lost on me. Just hours ago, I had her pinned against a wall, both of us breathing hard with something that wasn't just anger. Now I'm checking her body for wounds with the same hands that just killed a man to keep her safe. The contrast makes my throat tighten.

I clear it roughly. "Nothing serious," I report, forcing my gaze away from the way her tank top has slipped slightly off one shoulder. "But you can't stay here tonight."

Ken stands at the shattered window, directing security personnel on his radio, his back deliberately turned to give us privacy while still covering potential entry points. The room reeks of blood and broken glass and the cloying sweetness of spilled perfume. The dead attacker has been discreetly covered with a sheet, but his presence remains a stark reminder of how close this was.

"The entire east wing is compromised," I continue, helping Yelana to her feet. My hand hovers at her elbow but doesn't quite touch, maintaining necessary distance. "You'll stay in my suite until we can secure new quarters."

I expect argument, rebellion—the Yelana from the nightclub who defied me at every turn. Instead, she nods, wrapping her arms around herself, suddenly looking much younger than her twenty-one years. "Okay."

That simple acquiescence hits me harder than any of her sharp retorts could. Fear has momentarily stripped away her defenses, revealing the vulnerability she works so hard to hide. A surge of protectiveness washes through me—different from professional obligation, more visceral. More dangerous.

Ken approaches, holstering his weapon. "Perimeter team reports no sign of the second attacker. He made it past the south fence. Bleeding badly, though—won't get far." His eyes move to Yelana, softening slightly. "You alright, kid?"

She nods again, a ghost of her usual fire returning at being called "kid." "Nothing that won't heal," she says, unconsciously echoing words I've used about my own combat injuries.

"We need to discuss how they got past our security," I say to Ken, studying his face for any reaction. The timing of this attack is too convenient—right after Yelana's unauthorized club excursion, when protocols were disrupted. When I was distracted by emotions I shouldn't have.

"Already on it," Ken replies, face unreadable. "Initial assessment suggests they used the service road access. Camera was disabled approximately twenty-two minutes before the breach." His eyes narrow slightly. "Convenient timing."

"Very," I agree, the silent question hanging between us. Inside job? Someone with knowledge of our disrupted routine?

Ken's radio crackles with an update from the security team. He listens, then: "I need to coordinate the sweep. We're locking down the entire property. I've doubled guards on all access points." He hesitates, then adds, "Phillips, your room is the most secure location right now. Reinforced door, no exterior windows. Keep her there until I've personally verified the property is clear."

I nod, grateful for his tactical assessment while still maintaining my suspicion. Trust no one completely—a rule that's kept me alive through two wars and countless operations. "Check in every thirty minutes. And Ken—" I lower my voice, ensuring Yelana can't hear, "—I want to know how they knew exactly which room was hers."

A shadow crosses his face, either concern or something darker. "Copy that."

With Ken coordinating the security response, I guide Yelana from the wreckage of her bedroom. My hand finds the small of her back instinctively—a protective gesture that feels too natural. She doesn't pull away, which tells me more about her current state than words could. The Yelana who slapped me hours ago would never allow this touch.

We move through the darkened corridors of the estate, each shadow a potential threat, each corner a possible ambush point. My body remains between her and any angle of approach, my hand now resting on my weapon rather than her back. The walk to my quarters takes exactly seventy-three seconds, each one thick with unspoken tension.

My room—my space—was never meant to accommodate anyone else, especially not Yelana Zentarra. When I push open the reinforced door, I see it suddenly through her eyes: spartan, utilitarian, almost monastic compared to her lavish quarters. No artwork adorns the walls. No decorative pillows crowd the bed. Just a queen-sized mattress with military-precise corners, a desk with my laptop and precisely arranged files, a chair positioned for optimal view of both door and window, and a small dresser containing identical sets of clothing.

The only personal touch is a worn photograph of my SEAL team tucked into the corner of the mirror—all of them gone now, their faces frozen in time before Afghanistan. Before Juan. Before everything changed.

Yelana steps inside, her eyes cataloging details with surprising focus given what she's just experienced. Her gaze lingers on the photo, then drifts to the perfectly aligned row of boots at the foot of the bed, the weapon cleaning kit on the desk, the single book on the nightstand—Sun Tzu, well-worn.

"It's very... you," she says finally, arms still wrapped around herself.

I close and lock the door behind us, engaging three separate security systems with practiced efficiency. "It serves its purpose."

"No, I mean..." She turns, facing me for the first time since the attack. "It's honest. Nothing for show. Nothing unnecessary." Something shifts in her expression—a reassessment. "I didn't mean that as an insult."

"I didn't take it as one," I reply, moving to the closet to find her something to wear. My T-shirt will swallow her whole, but it's clean and doesn't have blood on it like her current clothes. I hand it to her, careful that our fingers don't touch. "Bathroom's through there. First aid kit under the sink for those cuts."

She accepts the shirt, clutching it against her chest. For a moment, she stands there looking strangely lost in the ordered simplicity of my room—this woman who just hours ago was dancing with a stranger to spite me, who faced down her father's lieutenants with regal command, who screamed at a spider but faced armed attackers with surprising composure.

"Thank you," she says softly. "For saving my life."

The simple sincerity in her voice strips away my professional distance for a dangerous second. "Always," I reply, the word carrying more weight than I intended.

Her eyes hold mine for a moment too long before she disappears into the bathroom, leaving me alone with the knowledge that "always" isn't just professional obligation anymore. It's a promise I'm not sure I have the right to make.

When Yelana emerges from the bathroom, the sight of her in my shirt hits me with unexpected force. The black fabric swallows her small frame, falling to mid-thigh, making her look both younger and more vulnerable. Her hair is damp where she's washed away blood and glass, her face scrubbed clean of makeup, the small cut on her cheek now covered with a butterfly bandage from my first aid kit. She's wrapped one of my towels around her shoulders like a shawl, her arms hugging it close to her body as if seeking armor to replace what the attack stripped away. This isn't the fierce, defiant woman who challenged me at every turn. This is someone I haven't seen before—Yelana without her walls, without her father's legacy propping her up, without the anger that's fueled her since I arrived.

I clear my throat, suddenly aware that I'm still wearing clothes stained with blood—both mine and the attacker's. "I should clean up," I say, grabbing a fresh t-shirt and sweatpants from the drawer. "Make yourself comfortable."

In the bathroom, I strip and quickly assess my own injuries—nothing serious, just superficial cuts from the flying glass and what will become an impressive bruise along my ribs where I hit Yelana's dresser. I wash away the blood, watching it spiral down the drain in pale pink swirls. The face in the mirror looks back at me with eyes I barely recognize—something unguarded there that hasn't been present in years.

When I emerge, Yelana has settled on the edge of my bed, my towel replaced by the spare blanket I keep folded at the foot of the mattress. She's wrapped it around her shoulders, legs tucked beneath her, looking impossibly young. My shirt dwarfs her, the collar slipping to reveal her collarbone and the elegant line of her neck. I force my eyes away.

"Ken checked in," she says, gesturing to my phone on the nightstand. "No sign of the second attacker off property. They're still sweeping the grounds."

I nod, maintaining a careful distance as I check the messages myself. "The blood trail ended at the service road. Likely had a vehicle waiting."

A silence stretches between us—not the hostile quiet of our previous encounters nor the charged tension from hours ago against that wall. This is something new, raw with shared trauma and unspoken questions. Yelana stares at her hands, picking at a loose thread in the blanket.

"I thought I could handle this," she finally says, her voice so soft I have to lean closer to hear. "I didn't want to believe it was this bad." She looks up at me, eyes bright with unshed tears she's too proud to release. "When my father died, everyone treated me like I was made of glass. Like I couldn't possibly understand the world he built, let alone run it. I was so determined to prove them wrong."

The confession costs her—I can see it in the way her knuckles whiten against the blanket, in the slight tremor of her lower lip before she stills it. I hesitate, then move to sit beside her on the edge of the bed, close enough that our shoulders almost touch.

"Your father spent decades building defenses against these threats," I say carefully. "Learning the hard way who to trust, who to fear. You can't expect to absorb that knowledge overnight."

She laughs, a brittle sound with no humor. "Is that your polite way of saying I've been an idiot?"

"It's my way of saying you're human." I turn slightly to face her. "Emelio wasn't invulnerable either. He just had decades of hard-won experience you haven't had time to acquire."

Her eyes search mine, looking for the lie, for the condescension she expects. Finding neither, something shifts in her expression. She leans slightly, closing the gap between our shoulders until they touch. The contact is electric—a simple connection that somehow carries more intimacy than any of our previous physical encounters. I don't move away.

"I was trying to escape," she admits, staring at the floor. "At the club. From all of it—the danger, the responsibility. From you."

"From me?" The question escapes before I can stop it.

She lifts her gaze to mine, something vulnerable and fierce in her expression. "From the way you make me feel. Confused. Angry. Safe." Her voice catches on the last word. "I shouldn't feel safe with the man responsible for Juan's death. But I do."

The confession hangs between us, changing everything and nothing. My chest tightens with emotions I can't afford—guilt, hope, desire, all tangled together in a knot I have no right to unravel.

"Yelana—" I begin, not knowing what I'm about to say.

She shakes her head. "Don't. I'm not asking for anything. I'm just tired of pretending." Her eyes drop to my mouth for a fraction of a second. "Aren't you?"

The air between us charges with possibility, with danger more complex than armed attackers or security breaches. I find myself leaning forward slightly, drawn by some force I've spent weeks denying. Her breathing changes, quickens. A flush spreads across her cheeks. Her pupils dilate, dark centers expanding to swallow the brown of her irises.

We're close enough that I feel her breath on my face, close enough that I can see the faint freckles across the bridge of her nose, usually hidden by makeup. Close enough that crossing the remaining distance would be as simple as falling.

Her hand moves from the blanket to my wrist, fingers tracing the tendons there with hesitant exploration. The touch burns through my skin, ignites something in my blood that tactical training can't extinguish. My own hand lifts of its own accord, hovering near her face before gently, so gently, brushing a strand of damp hair behind her ear. Her eyes flutter closed at the contact.

The moment stretches, balances on a knife edge of possibility. I could kiss her. She would let me. Everything in her body language invites it—the slight parting of her lips, the tilt of her chin, the quickened pulse visible at the base of her throat.

And yet—

Juan's baseball cap at the memorial. My promise to Emelio. The memory of Kerry's broken body in Afghanistan. The ghosts and debts that stand between us like physical barriers.

I pull back, my hand dropping away from her face. Her eyes open, something like understanding and disappointment mingling in their depths. She doesn't apologize, doesn't pretend the moment didn't exist. Instead, she nods once and draws the blanket tighter around her shoulders.

"We should sleep," I say, voice rougher than intended. "You take the bed. I'll—"

"Don't be ridiculous," she interrupts, a flash of her usual spirit returning. "We're both adults. The bed is big enough." Before I can argue, she adds, "And I'm not taking your protection detail seriously just to have you sleeping on the floor where you'll be useless if someone else breaks in."

The practical logic is a convenient mask for what we both know—neither of us wants to be alone tonight, but neither is ready to cross the line we just approached.

I nod, conceding. "I'll take the side by the door."

We settle into an awkward dance of preparation—turning down covers, arranging pillows, establishing careful boundaries in the shared space. I position myself on my back, as close to the edge as possible without falling off, hyperaware of her presence mere inches away. The ceiling above us becomes the focus of my attention, its blank surface a canvas for projected doubts and regrets.

"Mason?" Her voice comes softly through the darkness.

"Yes?"

"Thank you. Not just for tonight. For everything since you arrived."

I turn my head slightly, finding her profile in the dim light from the bathroom. "I owe your family a debt."

"Is that the only reason you're here?" she asks, the question weighted with unspoken meaning.

I don't answer immediately, truth warring with protective distance. "It was," I finally admit. "At the beginning."

She nods, accepting this partial confession, then turns away, curling onto her side facing the wall. "Goodnight."

"Goodnight, Yelana."

Sleep comes for her within minutes, her breathing settling into the steady rhythm of exhaustion overcoming fear. I remain awake, senses tuned to every sound in the house, every shift in the security systems I've established. My body is on alert while my mind wages its own battle against memories and desires that have no place in this mission.

In sleep, Yelana's defenses crumble completely. She shifts, turning toward me unconsciously, seeking warmth or safety or both. Her body curls against my side, her head finding my shoulder as if it belongs there. Her hand comes to rest over my heart, small and warm through the thin cotton of my shirt.

I should wake her, should maintain the boundaries between us that professionalism and history demand. Instead, I find my arm wrapping around her, drawing her closer, offering protection even in sleep.

The ghosts watch from the corners of my consciousness—Juan, Kerry, my teammates from Afghanistan. All the people I couldn't save. All the debts I haven't paid. But for the first time since arriving at the Zentarra estate, their accusations seem fainter, drowned out by the steady breathing of the woman in my arms.

I stare at the ceiling, torn between duty and desire, between past and present. Between the blood debt that brought me here and the feelings that make me want to stay for reasons that have nothing to do with obligation.

Sleep won't come tonight. Not with Yelana's warmth against me, not with attackers still at large, not with my own conflicted heart betraying every principle I've lived by since Afghanistan. But as her fingers curl unconsciously against my chest, I find myself wondering for the first time if some debts might be paid in ways neither Emelio nor I ever anticipated.

And whether some ghosts might finally be laid to rest.

TWELVE
The Funeral

Yelana

I stand before my parents' twin caskets, the morning sun cutting across the cemetery's manicured lawns with inappropriate brilliance. The weight of my black Chanel dress feels like armor, not against bullets but against breaking. My face is a careful mask—the one my mother taught me to wear in public, no matter what storms rage behind it. I can feel Mason's presence at my back, a solid shadow moving with practiced precision as he scans the gathered mourners. His hand occasionally brushes my lower back—a touch so light it could be mistaken for accidental if it didn't come precisely when my composure threatens to crack.

The elite of Los Angeles' underworld have turned out in expensive black suits and designer sunglasses, their respect for my father manifesting in solemn nods and calculated silence. Business rivals who would gladly slit each other's throats share the same row of chairs, a temporary truce forged in the shadow of death. I recognize faces from board meetings, charity galas, and my father's more discreet business gatherings—all of them watching me with the same question in their eyes: Will the daughter crumble or rise?

The priest drones on about eternal peace, his words floating over me like debris in a current. I focus instead on the glossy surface of the caskets, each adorned with a spray of white lilies—my mother's favorite. Their sweetness can't mask the metallic smell of freshly turned earth. When I close my eyes, I still see their bodies as I identified them: cold, waxy approximations of the people who raised me.

Last night, sleeping in Mason's arms, I had my first dreamless sleep since their murders. The memory brings heat to my cheeks even here, standing over my parents' remains. The way his arm curled protectively around me, my head finding the hollow of his shoulder as if it had been carved specifically for me. I don't dare look back at him now, afraid my face might betray thoughts too complicated for a funeral.

"And now, Yelana Zentarra will say a few words in remembrance of her parents," the priest announces, stepping aside with rehearsed solemnity.

I move forward, the paper with my prepared eulogy unnecessary. The words are etched into my brain after hours of practice before my bathroom mirror, watching myself break and reassemble over and over until I could speak without crumbling. As I take my position, I catch a flicker of movement from Mason—a subtle adjustment that places him with clearer sightlines to the perimeter of the cemetery.

"Emelio and Sierra Zentarra were known to the world as successful business leaders and philanthropists," I begin, my voice carrying across the silent gathering. "To me, they were simply mother and father."

The faces before me blur slightly as I continue, describing my father's uncompromising principles, my mother's elegant strength. I speak of family dinners and holiday traditions—sanitized versions of a childhood spent in the shadow of an empire built on blood and bullets. These people don't need to know about my father teaching me to shoot on my thirteenth birthday, or my mother explaining which poisons leave no trace while arranging flowers for a dinner party.

"My father believed that true legacy isn't measured in wealth but in respect," I continue, scanning the crowd as I was taught. Know your audience. Watch for threats. Sierra Zentarra's lessons never end, even after her death. "He earned that respect through unwavering loyalty to those who stood with him, and unmistakable consequences for those who stood against him."

The gathered associates shift slightly at this—a collective recognition of the thin veil over my warning. I am my father's daughter. I will honor his debts and settle his scores.

"My mother taught me that real power isn't displayed, but felt." My voice wavers slightly, the first crack in my facade. I see my mother's hands braiding my hair before school, her fingernails painted perfect red, the same color as the blood she once wiped from my father's shirt collar without comment.

I'm nearing the end now, the memorized words running out. Mason's posture changes behind me—a subtle tensing that sends warning prickles across my skin. I keep speaking, but part of my awareness divides, tracking his heightened alertness.

"They leave behind a legacy that I..." The words stick in my throat as I catch Mason's slight head turn toward the eastern perimeter. Something's wrong. "...that I promise to uphold with the same strength and conviction they demonstrated throughout their lives."

My voice cracks on the final words—not from grief, though the mourners will assume so, but from the adrenaline suddenly flooding my system in response to Mason's vigilance. "Goodbye, mother. Goodbye, father. May you find in death the peace that eluded you in life."

The final word barely leaves my lips when the first shot cracks through the air. Mason moves with impossible speed, his body slamming into mine as bullets chip into the marble headstone beside us. I hit the ground hard, the breath knocked from my lungs, Mason's solid weight covering me entirely. His arms cradle my head, protecting it from the impact as gunfire erupts from multiple directions.

"Stay down," he growls into my ear, his body completely shielding mine. I catch glimpses of chaos through the cage of his arms—mourners diving for cover, security personnel drawing weapons, the priest flat on the ground with hands covering his head.

Mason's radio crackles with voices shouting coordinates and positions. Ken's voice cuts through: "East perimeter breached! Three hostiles, automatic weapons—"

The transmission cuts off abruptly. Mason's body tenses further above mine.

"We move on three," Mason says, his mouth so close to my ear that I feel his breath warm against my skin. "Stay low. Crawl exactly where I crawl. Understand?"

I nod, fear and training converging into perfect clarity. On his count, we begin moving—a combat crawl across manicured grass now littered with abandoned flowers and bullet casings. Mason keeps his body between me and the most active gunfire, using tombstones and decorative statuary as cover.

"Vehicle approaching south entrance," Mason barks into his comm. "Confirm friendly."

A static-filled response comes back affirmative. We change direction, moving toward a black SUV racing across the cemetery grounds, tires tearing up pristine grass. The back door flings open before the vehicle fully stops. Mason practically throws me inside, diving in after me as bullets ping against the armored exterior.

"Go!" he shouts to the driver, already positioning himself to continue shielding me as the SUV accelerates away.

It's only when we're speeding through the cemetery gates that I realize something is wrong. I scan the vehicle—driver, front passenger with a bleeding arm, Mason and me in the back.

"Where's Ken?" My voice sounds strange in my own ears, thin and stretched.

Mason's eyes narrow, his gaze meeting mine with an intensity that answers before his words do. "Unknown. Last transmission from the east perimeter, then nothing."

A cold pit forms in my stomach as the implication settles. Ken disappeared right as the attack began. Ken, who has been like an uncle to me since childhood. Ken, who my father suspected. Ken, who would have known exactly where I would be standing, exactly when I would finish speaking.

Mason watches my face as the realization dawns, his expression grim but unsurprised. And suddenly I understand that last night's sanctuary in his arms, the comfort I found in his protection, was merely the calm before a storm that's only beginning to break.

My father's office feels different now—emptier somehow, despite the massive oak desk and leather chairs that still dominate the space. I've changed from my funeral dress into jeans and a black sweater, clothes that feel like admitting defeat. The dress was armor, a costume of control. These clothes are surrender to the reality that today wasn't just about burying my parents—it was about someone trying to ensure I joined them. I perch on the edge of my father's chair—my chair now—and watch Mason pace the room like a caged predator, phone pressed to his ear, muscles tight with controlled fury. When he hangs up, the look he gives me confirms what I already know: this wasn't random violence. This was planned, precise, and personal.

"Three of our security team dead," he reports, sliding his phone into his pocket. His voice carries the clinical detachment of someone who's delivered bad news too many times. "Martinez, Alvarez, and Chen. All veterans, all positioned at strategic points around the perimeter."

I press my fingertips against the smooth wood of my father's desk, tracing the faint impressions left by years of his heavy signet ring striking the same spot when he was angry. "And the attackers?"

"Gone. No shell casings, no dropped weapons, no blood trails." Mason moves to the window, positioning himself to see both the grounds and me simultaneously. The cuts on his face from the earlier bedroom attack have barely healed, and now new bruises bloom along his jawline from today's violence. "Professional hit team. Military precision."

"Costa's organization?" I ask, though I already suspect the answer.

"Possibly." His eyes never stop moving, cataloging threats even here in what should be the safest room in the house. "But the timing was too perfect. They knew exactly when to strike—at the most emotionally vulnerable moment of the service."

The implication hangs in the air between us. Someone gave them that information. Someone who knew the funeral schedule down to the minute. Someone like Ken.

I reach for the bourbon decanter on the side table, then think better of it. I need clarity now, not comfort. Instead, my fingers drum against the leather arm of the chair, a nervous habit my mother would have corrected with a sharp look. "The attack pattern?"

"Three-point formation. East, south, and west approaches." He gestures as he speaks, hands mapping invisible coordinates in the air. "No shots from the north—they wanted to force our retreat in a specific direction."

"Toward what looked like safety but wasn't," I finish for him, the strategy clear even to my less-trained mind.

Mason nods, something like approval flickering briefly in his eyes. "Exactly."

The door opens with that perfect silence that only Kendrick can manage. He enters carrying a silver tray with two tumblers of amber liquid and a carafe of water. His face betrays nothing as he places the tray on the desk between Mason and me, but his eyes take in our positions, the tension in the room, the security diagrams Mason has spread across the desk.

"I thought you might require refreshment after the day's... unfortunate events," he says, his British accent crisp as starched linen. "My condolences on the disruption of the service, Miss Zentarra. Your words for your parents were most moving."

"Thank you, Kendrick," I reply automatically, the social niceties my mother drilled into me surfacing even now.

He arranges the glasses with meticulous precision, lingering longer than necessary. I notice how his gaze catches on Mason's notes—specifically, the circled name "K. Jackson" with question marks surrounding it. His expression doesn't change, but something in the careful way he straightens suggests recognition.

"Will there be anything else?" he asks, hands folded perfectly before him.

"No, thank you," I say, watching as he bows slightly and retreats with that same uncanny silence.

Mason waits until the door closes completely before speaking. "He was reading my notes."

"He always notices everything," I say, reaching for the glass Kendrick left. "It's his job."

"It's dangerous." Mason remains standing, ignoring his drink. "Information flow needs to be contained until we identify the leak."

I take a sip, letting the bourbon burn a path down my throat. "If you're about to suggest that Kendrick is working against us after twenty years of service—"

"I'm not ruling anyone out." His voice hardens. "Especially not after what happened with Ken today."

The bourbon turns bitter on my tongue. "We don't know what happened with Ken. He could be injured. Captured. He could have pursued the attackers."

"Without radio contact? Without backup? Without a single word to his team?" Mason's skepticism cuts through my defenses. "Ken disappeared at the exact moment the attack began, from the exact location where the first shots came from."

"Correlation isn't causation," I snap, my father's favorite phrase when dismissing flimsy evidence. "Ken has been with my family since I was a child. He taught me to ride a bike. He sat with me in the hospital when I broke my arm falling from a tree. He wouldn't—"

"Your father suspected him." Mason's interruption lands like a slap. "The documents we found at the beach house—"

"Suspicions aren't proof!" I slam my palm against the desk, bourbon splashing over the rim of my glass. "My father suspected everyone at some point. It was his nature."

Mason moves closer, leaning across the desk, his face tight with controlled urgency. "Think about it, Yelana. Who knew the funeral arrangements down to the minute? Who positioned the security team? Who had access to every detail of today's service?"

"That doesn't make him guilty." But even to my own ears, my defense sounds hollow. "There are other explanations."

"Give me one that makes sense." His eyes hold mine, demanding honesty I'm not ready to give.

"I don't have to explain anything to you." The words come out harsher than intended. "You work for me, Phillips, not the other way around."

He straightens, something shuttering behind his eyes. The professional mask sliding back into place over whatever personal connection we've been building. "I work for your safety, regardless of where the threat comes from."

"And I'm telling you, Ken isn't a threat." My voice rises despite my efforts to control it. "He's family."

"Family can betray you." His voice drops, taking on an edge I haven't heard before. "Sometimes they're the most dangerous ones of all."

The truth in his words stings more than I want to admit. I think of Ken's empty chair at security briefings, his perfectly timed absences when information leaked, the way he always seemed to know things before anyone told him. I think of my father's notes, the question marks around Ken's name growing more numerous in recent months.

"Get out," I say suddenly, needing space from Mason's certainty, from the doubt he's planting that I can't afford to nurture. "I need to be alone."

He doesn't move immediately, assessing me with eyes that see too much. "Yelana—"

"Please." The word costs me, but I can't bear another minute of his rational suspicion chipping away at the few pillars still holding up my world. "Just... give me some time."

Something softens in his expression—a glimpse of the man who held me through the night, not the tactical officer analyzing threats. "Lock the door behind me. Keep your panic button within reach. I'll be right outside."

I nod, not trusting my voice for more words.

At the door, he pauses, looking back at me with an expression I can't fully interpret. "I hope I'm wrong about Ken," he says finally. "But hope isn't a security strategy."

When the door closes behind him, I sink fully into my father's chair, feeling its leather embrace like a cold substitute for the arms I slept in last night. I trace the wood grain of the desk with numb fingers, trying to find patterns in the chaos like my father would have done. The bourbon sits untouched now, its amber depths reflecting light like trapped fire.

If Ken betrayed us, who can I trust? The question circles my mind like a vulture. Not Kendrick, with his too-observant eyes. Not the remaining security team. Not the business associates who watched me with calculating gazes at the funeral.

Maybe not even Mason, whose presence in my life stems from a blood debt rather than choice. Whose arms I slept in last night despite every reason not to trust him. Whose certainty about Ken's betrayal might be tactical brilliance—or the perfect misdirection from his own agenda.

The panic button sits cold and small in my palm, a direct line to the man standing just outside my door. I set it on the desk, just beyond easy reach, and turn to face the coming darkness alone.

I stand outside Mason's door for a full minute before knocking, my bare feet silent on the cold marble of the hallway. Sleep eludes me despite the bone-deep exhaustion that should have claimed me hours ago. Every time I close my eyes, I see bullets tearing through headstones, hear the screams of mourners, feel the solid weight of Mason's body shielding mine. The argument we had in my father's office echoes in my mind, the tension between us yet another layer of exhaustion I can't shake. When I finally tap my knuckles against his door, the sound seems too loud in the midnight silence of the estate. It opens almost immediately—he wasn't sleeping either.

Mason stands in the doorway, fully dressed despite the late hour, his eyes alert and searching mine. For a heartbeat, we simply look at each other, the argument from earlier suspended between us like a fragile glass bauble. Then something breaks in me—some final wall of resistance collapsing under the weight of the day's horrors.

I step forward without a word, and his arms open to receive me. We collide in an embrace that feels both inevitable and impossible, his arms wrapping around me with a certainty that makes my breath catch. I press my face against his chest, inhaling the scent of gun oil and that indefinable something that is uniquely him. His heart beats steady and strong against my cheek, his chin resting on the top of my head. For several long moments, we simply breathe together, my fingers clutching the back of his shirt like I might dissolve if I let go.

When he finally pulls back, his eyes search my face with an intensity that would have made me flinch days ago. Now, I meet his gaze without armor.

"Come in," he says simply, stepping aside to admit me to his spartan quarters.

His bed is neatly made, untouched, the covers still hospital-corner tight. On the desk, his weapons lie disassembled, parts arranged in perfect rows like surgical instruments awaiting use. A cleaning cloth stained with oil sits beside them. He was preparing, not sleeping.

I perch on the edge of his bed while he returns to the desk chair, the distance between us both physical and metaphorical after the closeness of our embrace.

"I couldn't sleep," I offer lamely, as if midnight visits to his room are something we need to explain.

"Neither could I." He picks up a cloth and resumes cleaning a firing pin with methodical precision. "Days like today make it... difficult."

"Days when people try to kill me at my parents' funeral?" The bitter humor feels strange on my tongue, but the small quirk of his mouth makes it worth the effort.

"Those particularly." His hands never stop their practiced movements, but his eyes lift to mine. "How are you holding up? Actually holding up, not the official Zentarra response."

The question—simple, direct, without agenda—catches me off guard. How long has it been since someone asked how I felt without an ulterior motive? Since before my father died, at least.

"I'm..." I begin, then falter, unable to find words adequate for the storm inside me. "I buried my parents today. Someone tried to ensure I joined them. And the man I've known as an uncle my entire life might have orchestrated it all." I exhale slowly. "I don't know how I am."

Mason nods, understanding without platitudes. "That's honest, at least."

A silence settles between us—not uncomfortable, but weighted with everything still unsaid. I watch his hands as they work, finding strange comfort in their mechanical efficiency.

"I lost my entire SEAL team in Afghanistan," he says suddenly, his voice lower but steady. "Not all at once, lost five the night your father helped me. One by one, over eighteen months."

I stay silent, recognizing the rare gift of his willingness to share this.

"Michael went first—IED on a routine patrol. He collected antique pocketknives, had one for every country he'd served in. Wanted to open a museum someday." Mason's hands continue their work, but his eyes are focused on something I can't see. "Then Dawson—sniper fire during an extraction. He had just gotten engaged, carried her picture everywhere. Would show it to anyone who'd look, tell them she was too beautiful to have said yes to him."

He assembles the firing pin into the weapon with practiced movements, his words continuing in the same steady rhythm. "Chen lasted another four months. Helicopter crash during a sandstorm. Best chess player I've ever known—could beat you in six moves while reciting poetry in Mandarin."

Each name comes with a detail, a humanizing fragment that transforms abstract loss into specific grief. I realize he's giving me something precious—not just stories, but pieces of himself usually kept locked away.

"And then Kerry," I prompt softly when he falls silent.

His hands finally still. "Kerry wasn't in Afghanistan. She was... after. When I thought I might have a life again." He sets the weapon down, fully assembled now. "We were engaged. Had a date set, a house picked out. Then a car accident took her and my parents in one night. Drunk driver."

The clinical way he relates this devastating loss makes it somehow more heartbreaking.

"I'm sorry," I say, the words inadequate but sincere.

He looks up, something vulnerable flickering across his face. "After that, I stopped forming attachments. Seemed safer. Until—"

"Until my father called in his blood debt," I finish for him.

"Until you," he corrects softly.

The distinction hangs between us, significant and dangerous. I find myself moving from the edge of the bed to sit closer to him, our knees almost touching.

"Tell me about Juan," he says, surprising me. It's the first time he's asked about my brother directly. "Not what happened in Afghanistan. Who he was."

The request opens something in my chest—a door long sealed shut. "He loved science fiction movies. The cheesier, the better. He'd make me watch them with him, even when I was too young to understand the plots." I smile at the memory. "He had a rock collection—would bring home specimens from wherever my father took him. Labeled them all with their precise geological classifications."

Mason nods, a small smile touching his lips. "He showed me his collection once, during a briefing break. Knew the mineral composition of every stone."

"He wanted to be a geologist," I say, the words emerging from a place long untouched. "Can you imagine? The son of Emelio Zentarra, arms dealer extraordinaire, wanting to study rocks for a living?"

"What did your father think of that?" Mason asks.

"He bought Juan a professional-grade microscope for his birthday that year. Said any passion pursued with excellence was worthy of the Zentarra name." The memory warms me despite the grief that accompanies it. "My father was complicated."

"Most people worth knowing are," Mason replies, his eyes holding mine.

We talk through the night, trading stories like rare coins—each one valuable, each one bringing us closer together. He tells me about Kerry's terrible cooking and beautiful laugh. I tell him about hiding with Juan in the wine cellar during my parents' more dangerous business meetings. He describes Afghanistan's star-filled skies; I recall my mother teaching me to shoot while reciting Shakespeare.

Grief becomes the bridge between us rather than the wall. With each memory shared, the weight of the day's horror recedes slightly, replaced by something I can't yet name but recognize as vital.

Dawn breaks almost without our noticing, pale light seeping through his curtains to paint the room in soft gold. We've migrated to sit side by side on his bed, shoulders touching, voices grown hoarse from hours of conversation.

"I should go," I say finally, though neither of us moves. "People will start stirring soon."

Mason nods, but his hand finds mine on the bedspread, fingers lightly covering mine. "Thank you," he says simply.

"For what?"

"For trusting me with your memories. With your grief." His eyes meet mine, more open than I've ever seen them. "It's a rare gift."

I don't pull my hand away. "Same to you."

We sit in the growing light, neither willing to break this fragile peace we've constructed from the rubble of our separate tragedies. Outside this room, Ken's betrayal, Costa's threat, and my father's dangerous legacy await. But here, in this moment between night and morning, we've found something unexpected.

Not quite healing. Not quite happiness. But perhaps the beginning of both.

THIRTEEN
Missing Pieces

MASON

The lock gives way with a soft click as I work the tension wrench and pick. Ken's office door creaks in protest when I push it open, revealing a space that reeks of stale cigars and expensive cologne – signature scents of a man who wants others to know he's important. Yelana hesitates at the threshold, her fingers tracing the polished nameplate on the door. I don't rush her; this invasion of her family confidant's private domain can't be easy. But sentiment has no place in security breaches, and Ken's disappearance during the cemetery attack left too many questions that need answers.

"We shouldn't be doing this," she says, but steps inside anyway. Her arms wrap around herself, a defensive posture I've noticed she adopts when her certainties begin to crumble.

"He's been missing for twenty-six hours." I move directly to the desk, opening the top right drawer with gloved hands. "No contact, no trail, nothing. That's not the behavior of an innocent man."

The office is meticulously organized – leather-bound books arranged by height on mahogany shelves, papers stacked in precise alignment on the blotter, pens standing at attention in a sterling silver holder. The space of a man who values control. My fingers work methodically through each drawer, examining folders, testing for false bottoms, checking for anything out of place in this temple to orderliness.

Yelana moves to the computer, jiggling the mouse to wake the screen. "It's password protected," she mutters, fingers hovering over the keyboard. She types a combination – a date I recognize as Juan's birthday – and frowns when access is denied. "He always used family birthdays for his passwords."

"Not this time," I note, filing away this small but significant deviation from pattern.

The bottom drawer yields nothing but expense reports and maintenance logs. I close it and run my fingers along the drawer's frame, feeling for inconsistencies in the wood grain. Years of searching compounds in Afghanistan taught me that secrets hide in plain sight, in the spaces between the obvious.

"Try your birthday," I suggest, still focused on the desk.

The soft tap of keys, then: "Nothing."

My fingers catch on a slight irregularity beneath the right drawer – a depression no larger than a dime. I press it, and a soft click rewards my effort. A false bottom in the middle drawer slides back, revealing three unmarked USB drives nestled in a foam cutout.

"Found something," I say, holding one up for Yelana to see.

Her face pales slightly, but she recovers quickly. "That doesn't mean anything. My father had dozens of those. Standard operating procedure for secure data."

"Hidden in secret compartments?" I plug one into my secure laptop, unsurprised when it requests a decryption key. "This level of security suggests something worth hiding."

Yelana abandons the computer and moves to a filing cabinet, yanking open drawers with increasing force. "Ken ran security for this family for twenty years. Of course he has secure storage protocols."

I let her search, focusing on my own methodical examination. The bookshelf reveals nothing unusual until I notice a volume of Kipling that sits a quarter-inch farther out than its neighbors. I pull it free, feeling its unnatural weight immediately. The pages are hollowed out, creating a cavity that holds a satellite phone – the kind that can't be easily traced through normal telecommunications networks.

"Yelana." My voice is carefully neutral as I hold up the device.

She turns, a folder clutched in her hands, and freezes when she sees what I'm holding. "That's not—"

"A satellite phone hidden in a hollowed-out book? Yeah, it is." I check the call history – empty. Recently wiped. "Any legitimate reason your family's security chief would need untraceable communications kept secret from the rest of the team?"

"Stop it." She slams a drawer shut with enough force to rattle the paintings on the wall. "Ken is family. He's been here since before I could walk. He taught me to ride a bike, for Christ's sake."

"Family doesn't mean shit when money's involved." The words come out harsher than intended, but the evidence is mounting too quickly to ignore. "You think Costa wouldn't pay millions to have someone on the inside? Someone with access to your father's security protocols? To your movements?"

Her eyes flash dangerously. "You don't know him."

"I know patterns." I move to the computer, nudging her aside to try a different approach. "And the pattern here is someone with inside access compromising your security at every turn."

I try variations of common passwords, getting nowhere until I input Ken's birth year followed by the word "revenge" – a shot in the dark that hits its mark. The screen populates with folders, most innocuously labeled until I notice one called "Z_Contingencies" hidden within system files.

"Look at this." I open it, revealing dozens of password-protected documents.

Yelana leans over my shoulder, her hair brushing against my cheek. Her scent – vanilla and something distinctly her – momentarily distracts me before I refocus. The folder contains what appear to be alternate security protocols, estate maps with routes marked in red, and personnel files with notations I can't immediately decipher.

"This could be legitimate contingency planning," she argues, but her voice lacks conviction.

I open the desk drawer again, retrieving a leather-bound logbook tucked beneath stationery. The pages contain columns of numbers and initials – a code I recognize from my military days as a simple cipher for tracking communications.

"Dates, times, and contact codes." I flip through the pages, stopping at an entry from the day before her parents' murder. "This one matches the timeframe when the security system at the main house was 'accidentally' disabled for maintenance."

Yelana snatches the book from my hands, her eyes scanning the entries. "This doesn't prove anything. Ken maintained all our security logs."

"Which gave him perfect cover to document his communications with whoever he's working with." I stand, facing her directly. "Yelana, I know you don't want to believe this—"

"You're right, I don't!" Her voice rises, color flooding her cheeks. "Because Ken Jackson held me when I cried after Juan died. He stayed up all night when I had nightmares. He has been the one constant in a life where people disappear or die or betray us at every turn." Her voice breaks on the last word, and she slams her palm against the desk. "Not Ken. Not him too."

I step closer, keeping my voice even. "Sometimes the people closest to us are the ones with the best opportunity to hurt us."

"Like you?" The accusation hangs between us. "The man responsible for my brother's death, suddenly so concerned with my welfare?"

The words sting, but I don't flinch. "Yes, like me. Which is why you should question everything, including my motives." I pick up the satellite phone again. "But this isn't about me. This is about concrete evidence that the man you trust has been operating outside normal channels, maintaining secret communications, and disappeared the exact moment assassins knew where to find you."

Her eyes fill with tears she refuses to let fall. She reaches for the logbook again, flipping to recent entries with trembling fingers. I watch the last of her certainty crumble as she finds dates matching security breaches, matched with initials that mean nothing to most but clearly trigger recognition in her.

"VC," she whispers. "Vince Costa."

The admission costs her visibly – her shoulders slump, her fingers white-knuckled against the leather binding. I resist the urge to comfort her; that's not what she needs from me right now. What she needs is the truth, however painful.

"I'm sorry," I say, meaning it more than she'll ever know.

She closes the book with a finality that speaks of endings beyond just this investigation. When she looks up, something has hardened in her eyes – a transformation I recognize all too well from my own experiences with betrayal.

"Find him," she says. "Whatever it takes."

The door flies open with enough force to rattle the framed certifications on Ken's wall. Sophia Reyes stands in the doorway, her usual composed demeanor replaced by flushed cheeks and rapid breathing. She clutches a thick stack of papers to her chest like they might try to escape. Her eyes dart between me and Yelana, momentarily surprised to find us in Ken's office before determination resets her features. Without explanation, she strides to the desk and slams the stack of printouts onto the polished surface, sending a pen holder clattering to the floor.

"I've been looking everywhere for you," she says to Yelana, not bothering to acknowledge me. Her voice carries the sharp edge of someone who's discovered something they wish they hadn't. "You need to see this. Now."

I step back, watching both women carefully. Sophia's arrival is either extremely convenient or highly suspicious – my training doesn't allow for coincidences. Her usually immaculate appearance shows signs of distress – blouse partially untucked, hair falling from its severe bun. The logistics director has always struck me as someone who'd rather die than appear disheveled.

Yelana approaches the desk cautiously, as if the papers might bite. "What is all this?"

"Spreadsheets. Financial transfers. Shipping manifests." Sophia taps a manicured finger against the top document – columns of numbers with Ken's electronic signature at the bottom. "These weren't authorized by your father. Not a single one."

I move to Yelana's side, scanning the documents over her shoulder. Years of intelligence analysis kick in automatically, my eyes picking out patterns in the data. Weapons shipments to non-standard locations. Financial transfers to numbered accounts. Inventory adjustments that don't match any legitimate business operation.

"Ken's been moving product off-books for months," Sophia continues, flipping through pages with practiced efficiency. "At first, I thought it was just accounting errors. Small discrepancies. Nothing worth raising alarms over."

"But they weren't small," I observe, noting the cumulative totals highlighted in yellow.

"They were just the beginning." Sophia pulls out a separate folder, this one containing shipping manifests for military-grade weapons. "These went to buyers not on any approved client list. Ghost recipients. Payments routed through shell companies I can't trace."

Yelana's fingers tremble slightly as she takes the manifests, her eyes widening at the listed items. Grenade launchers. Anti-tank missiles. Enough firepower to equip a small army. All bearing Ken's authorization codes.

"This particular shipment," Sophia says, pointing to a line item dated three weeks ago, "was supposedly sent to our warehouse in Arizona. I called the facility manager directly. Nothing arrived."

I watch Yelana's face as she processes this information, the mental calculations visible in her expression as she connects these revelations to what we found earlier. Her defenses are crumbling, reality overwhelming the narrative she's clung to about the man she trusted.

"There's more." Sophia's voice softens slightly, the only acknowledgment that what she's about to present will hurt. She extracts a series of bank statements from the middle of the stack. "Offshore accounts. Five of them, all linked to electronic transfers authorized by Ken."

The accounts show regular deposits – substantial amounts flowing in biweekly increments. Money laundering disguised as legitimate business transactions. Professional work, but not perfect. The pattern is clear to anyone trained to look for it.

"Eight point four million in the last six months alone," Sophia says, tapping the total at the bottom of the page.

Yelana's breathing quickens, her knuckles white against the edge of the desk. "This could be legitimate. Alternative revenue streams my father kept compartmentalized—"

"Yelana." I keep my voice gentle but firm. "You know that's not what this is."

She doesn't respond, but the desperate hope in her eyes dims further. She flips through more documents – inventory discrepancies revealing millions in missing merchandise, authorization codes that bypass normal security protocols, cargo manifests for shipments that vanished into thin air.

"I ran a full inventory check after noticing these discrepancies," Sophia explains, pulling out another spreadsheet. "The highlighted items never reached their destinations, but were marked as delivered in our system. Thirty-seven million in merchandise, just gone."

I examine the missing inventory list with growing concern. "These aren't random selections. This is a targeted acquisition of specific capabilities – anti-personnel, anti-vehicle, surveillance countermeasures." I look up at Yelana. "Someone's building an arsenal designed to take down a specific type of security operation."

"Your father's security operation," Sophia adds unnecessarily.

Yelana reaches the final page, and the color drains from her face completely. It's a transfer confirmation – a substantial sum moved to an account in the Cayman Islands, authorized by Ken Jackson. The transaction date is circled in red: the day before Sierra Zentarra's murder.

"No," she whispers, stumbling backward. Her hip catches Ken's chair, sending it spinning into the wall with a dull thud. "He wouldn't. Not my mother."

The devastation in her voice cuts through the professional detachment I've been maintaining. I want to reach for her, to offer some comfort against this betrayal, but know she needs to process this in her own way. Her world is collapsing around her – again – and platitudes won't help.

"The timing could be coincidental," Sophia offers weakly, not believing it herself.

"When was the last transfer?" I ask, already knowing the answer will be damning.

Sophia hesitates, then flips to another page. "Two days ago. Six hours before the cemetery attack."

Yelana makes a sound – not quite a sob, not quite a gasp – that contains more anguish than a scream could convey. Her hand flies to her mouth, and for a moment I think she might be ill. Then her training reasserts itself, her spine straightening even as her eyes remain haunted.

"He sold us out," she says flatly. "All of us. For what? Money? Power?"

"Both, most likely," I reply, scanning the documents again for any detail we might have missed. "Plus whatever Costa promised him. Probably a significant position in the new hierarchy after your family was eliminated."

The brutally honest assessment earns me a sharp look from Sophia, but Yelana needs truth now, not coddling. The danger is still immediate, and understanding Ken's motives might help predict his next move.

"We need to move these documents to a secure location," I say, gathering the papers into a neat stack. "And we need to alert the remaining security team about Ken's betrayal without tipping off any other potential moles."

Sophia nods in agreement, her professional mask slipping back into place now that the initial shock has passed. Her eyes meet mine over Yelana's bowed head, and we exchange a grim look of understanding. The situation is even worse than we thought, the betrayal more complete, the danger more immediate.

"I'll update the security protocols immediately," Sophia says, her voice steady again. "Change all access codes, revoke Ken's credentials, implement the ghost protocol your father established for leadership compromise."

"Do it," Yelana orders, her voice hollow but determined. Her eyes remain fixed on that final damning document – the financial equivalent of a smoking gun pointing directly at her mother's murder.

I give her thirty seconds of privacy after she storms out of the office. It's a tactical calculation – enough time to respect her need to process, not so much that she could disappear from my protection. When I step into the hallway, I spot her immediately, collapsed against a marble column halfway to the main foyer. Her body shakes with silent sobs, one hand pressed against her mouth to muffle the sound. The controlled, regal woman who faced down her father's lieutenants has momentarily vanished, replaced by someone drowning in betrayal. I approach slowly, making enough noise that I won't startle her.

"Don't," she warns without looking up, her voice raw. "Don't tell me it's going to be okay."

"Wasn't planning to." I slide down the column opposite her, sitting on the cold floor with my back against the marble. The position gives me clear sightlines down both directions of the hallway while maintaining a respectful distance from her grief. "It's not okay. It's fucked up beyond measure."

A sound escapes her – half sob, half surprised laugh at my bluntness. She wipes angrily at her tears, mascara smearing across her cheek like war paint. "I trusted him with everything. Every secret. Every vulnerability." Her voice cracks. "He held my hand at my brother's funeral."

I nod, letting the silence stretch between us. The weight of betrayal is familiar territory – a landscape I've traversed too many times to count. In Afghanistan. In intelligence briefings gone wrong. In waking up alive when teammates died because someone talked to the wrong person.

"I've been there," I say quietly, rolling a tension knot from my shoulder. Old habits from old wounds. "My team in Kandahar – our intel officer sold us out for a promotion."

Her head lifts at this, eyes locking onto mine with sudden interest. "What happened?"

"Operation went sideways. Ambush waiting exactly where we were told the area was clear." The memory resurfaces with crystalline clarity – dust kicked up by helicopter rotors, the smell of gun oil and fear, radio chatter suddenly silenced. "Found out later he'd been feeding information to a rival agency, positioning himself for a lateral move up the chain. Four good men died because he wanted a bigger office and a better parking space."

"What did you do to him?" There's something dangerous in her question – a hunger for retribution I recognize all too well.

"Nothing." I meet her gaze steadily. "System protected him. He got his promotion. Last I heard, he was running operations in Eastern Europe."

"That's it? You just... accepted it?" Disbelief colors her voice.

"Didn't say that." I flex my right hand, remembering the satisfaction of knuckles connecting with smug certainty. "Said I did nothing officially. Unofficially, he needed facial reconstruction surgery before taking his new post."

The ghost of a smile touches her lips before fading. She pulls her knees to her chest, making herself smaller against the column. We sit in silence, the distant sounds of the estate – staff movements, security patrols, the perpetual hum of surveillance equipment – creating a backdrop to our shared understanding of betrayal.

"Tell me about Juan," she says suddenly, her voice different somehow. Softer. More vulnerable. "What really happened that day?"

The request catches me off guard. We've circled this topic since my arrival, approaching it obliquely, never directly. The blood debt between us acknowledged but unexamined. I consider deflecting, offering the sanitized version Emelio approved for his daughter. But something about this moment – her raw grief, the parallel betrayals connecting us – demands honesty.

"You sure you want this?" I ask, giving her one last chance to maintain the protective narrative she's lived with.

She nods, eyes never leaving mine.

I exhale slowly, organizing memories I've spent years trying to compartmentalize. "After your father pulled me from the wreckage of our ambushed convoy, he hid me in a back room of your family's compound." I lean my head back against the marble, focusing on a distant point. "I was barely conscious. Multiple shrapnel wounds, two bullet grazes, severe concussion."

"How long were you there?" she prompts when I pause.

"Three days. Your father treated my wounds himself." The tactical assessment comes automatically, professional distance from the horror that followed. "Then Taliban scouts tracked us down. Someone had given them intel about an American soldier being sheltered nearby."

Her breathing has stilled completely, her entire focus on my words.

"Emelio decided we needed to move immediately. Said they'd burn the whole compound, kill everyone inside to get to me." I meet her gaze. "Juan insisted on coming with us. Your father wanted him to stay behind with you and your mother."

I describe those frantic moments in careful detail – Emelio wrapping me in local clothing, Juan checking the street, the whispered argument between father and son that ended with Juan saying something that made Emelio reluctantly nod.

"We made it three blocks before they spotted us. Fighters appeared at both ends of the narrow street. We ducked into an abandoned shop, but there was no rear exit." The words come mechanically now, muscle memory from after-action reports. "Your father barricaded the door while Juan and I searched for another way out. The only option was a half-collapsed stairwell leading to the roof."

"But you couldn't climb," she whispers.

"Juan..." I have to pause, the image so vivid it could be happening before me now. "Juan insisted on staying behind with your father, said I should go first. Seven years old with more courage than men four times his age."

Her hand covers her mouth, eyes wide with both dread and desperate need to know.

"He reached me just as a Taliban fighter with a clear shot took aim. I was reloading, didn't see the threat until it was too late." I trace the jagged scar along my jaw unconsciously. "Juan saw it. He pushed me down and took three bullets meant for me. Center mass, no chance."

The clinical description fails to capture the reality – the surprised look in Juan's eyes, the way his body jerked with each impact, the terrible stillness that followed.

"I caught him as he fell." My voice roughens despite my efforts to maintain composure. "Tried to stop the bleeding, but there was... too much. He said something – I couldn't understand the words. His eyes stayed on mine until they didn't see anything anymore."

The silence that follows feels sacred somehow, heavy with shared grief across years and circumstances. When I finally look at Yelana again, tears stream unchecked down her face, but something has shifted in her expression – a weight lifted or perhaps transformed.

"Thank you," she says simply. "For telling me the truth."

She uncurls from her position, moving across the space between us with fluid grace to sit beside me against the column. Our shoulders touch, a point of warmth in the cold marble hallway. Her hand finds my jaw, fingers tracing the scar left by the bullet that grazed me after passing through Juan.

"He saved you," she says, her touch feather-light along the ridged tissue.

"Yes." I resist the urge to lean into her touch, though every nerve ending fires at the contact. "I didn't deserve it."

"That's not how saving works." Her fingers linger on my face, eyes tracking their movement before meeting mine again. "We don't save people because they deserve it. We save them because we see something worth preserving."

The insight strikes deeper than she could know, penetrating defenses built over years of survivor's guilt. Her face is close now, close enough that I can see the gold flecks in her brown eyes, count individual lashes still spiky with tears.

"What did he see in me?" I ask, the question emerging from some wounded place I rarely acknowledge.

"Maybe the same thing I'm starting to see." Her voice drops to a whisper, her gaze dropping briefly to my mouth before returning to my eyes.

The air between us charges with something electric and inevitable. I find myself leaning forward, drawn by some gravity beyond tactical assessment or professional distance. She meets me halfway, her breathing shallow, eyes fluttering closed as the space between us narrows to mere millimeters. I can feel her breath against my lips, catch the faint trace of coffee and salt tears. Time suspends in that narrow gap between almost and happening.

A throat clears at the end of the hallway, the sound precise and deliberately timed. We jerk apart, the moment shattered as Kendrick materializes like a ghost from the shadows. His face betrays nothing – professional discretion perfected over decades – but something knowing lingers in his eyes.

"Dinner is prepared, Miss Zentarra," he announces, his British accent crisp in the silent hallway. "I've taken the liberty of setting places in the small dining room, as I assumed you might prefer privacy this evening."

Yelana straightens, composure returning with visible effort. "Thank you, Kendrick. We'll be there shortly."

He bows slightly and retreats, footsteps fading with that uncanny silence that seems to follow him everywhere. The interruption has broken whatever spell held us moments ago, reality rushing back into the space between us.

I stand first, offering her a hand up that she accepts after only a moment's hesitation. Her fingers linger against mine longer than necessary before she withdraws, smoothing her clothing with practiced motions.

"We should go," she says, though her eyes tell a different story. "Much to discuss about... security arrangements."

I nod, falling into step beside her as we head toward the dining room, both of us knowing that whatever almost happened in that hallway has only been delayed, not prevented. The ghost of Juan between us has transformed from barrier to bridge, and neither Kendrick's interruption nor Ken's betrayal can undo that fundamental shift.

FOURTEEN
Business and Pleasure

Mason

Miguel Costa's restaurant gleams like a trap baited with crystal and gold. I scan the room systematically as we enter, cataloging exit points, security personnel positions, and potential cover options—habits ingrained from years of combat zones that serve me well in places like this where danger wears designer suits instead of tactical gear. Yelana walks beside me, her sleek business attire a modern armor that accentuates both her authority and the dangerous curves beneath. The confidence in her stride belies the weight she's carrying—the recent discovery of Ken's betrayal, the constant threat against her life, and now this high-stakes meeting with the brother of her father's most dangerous rival.

"I count six security personnel," I murmur, my lips barely moving. "Two at the bar, one by each exit, two circulating among the tables. Armed, concealed carry."

"I see them," she replies just as quietly, a smile fixed on her face as she nods to the maître d'. "Miguel wouldn't risk his legitimate business with sloppy security. This place is his crown jewel."

The restaurant interior unfolds around us in calculated opulence—crystal chandeliers casting honeyed light over marble tables, plush velvet booths secluded by ornate privacy screens, waitstaff moving with practiced discretion between them. But beneath the veneer of exclusivity, I note the bulletproof glass subtly integrated into the architectural features, the angles of the security cameras disguised as decorative elements, the slight bulges beneath the tailored jackets of select staff members. This place is as much a fortress as it is a five-star establishment.

We're led to a corner booth where Miguel Costa awaits, a man whose smooth exterior could make you forget the blood on his hands if you didn't know better. He rises as we approach, his smile practiced and perfect. Beside him stands a younger man—same eyes, same jawline, but lacking the weathered edges that come from decades in a business where mistakes mean death.

"Yelana Zentarra." Miguel takes her hand, kissing it with old-world formality. "Even more beautiful than your mother, may she rest in peace."

I watch the subtle tightening around Yelana's eyes—the only sign that the mention of Sierra affects her. "Mr. Costa. Thank you for agreeing to meet on such short notice."

"How could I refuse Emelio's daughter? Please, sit." He gestures to the booth. "This is my son, Antonio. He's been overseeing our import operations for three years now."

Antonio's eyes linger on Yelana with undisguised interest as we slide into the booth. I position myself at the edge, maintaining sightlines to both exits while staying close enough to intervene if necessary. The younger Costa's gaze tracks Yelana's movements with the hungry appreciation of a predator assessing prey, though there's something else there too—a genuine spark of admiration that sets my teeth on edge.

"My condolences for your loss," Antonio offers, his voice carrying the silky timbre of practiced charm. "Your father was a formidable businessman. The entire industry feels his absence."

"Some more acutely than others," Yelana replies, her tone carrying just enough edge to establish boundaries without breaking diplomacy. "Which brings us to why I requested this meeting."

Miguel signals a waiter who materializes with a bottle of wine so expensive I could probably buy a car with what it costs. I decline with a subtle gesture—on duty means stone sober, always. Yelana accepts half a glass, touching it to her lips without actually drinking. Smart. She's learning.

"Vince sends his regrets that he couldn't join us," Miguel says as the waiter retreats. "Business in Colombia required his personal attention."

"Convenient timing," I comment, unable to help myself.

Miguel's eyes flick to me, assessing and dismissive in the same glance. "And you are?"

"My head of security," Yelana answers before I can, her hand briefly touching my arm in a subtle warning to stand down. "Mason Phillips. He goes where I go."

"A wise precaution in these uncertain times." Miguel's smile doesn't reach his eyes. "Though I assure you, you're perfectly safe in my establishment."

"Forgive me if recent events have made me cautious," Yelana replies, smoothly redirecting the conversation. "Now, regarding the territorial arrangements my father had established with your organization—"

I watch her transform before my eyes, the young woman I've been protecting shifting into a business leader with the same dangerous competence her father wielded. She speaks with authority beyond her years, navigating complex negotiations about distribution channels and non-compete territories with the precision of someone who's been doing this for decades rather than weeks.

"The San Diego corridor remains under Zentarra control," she states, not a question but a declaration. "The pricing structures my father established with your southern suppliers will continue, with the agreed-upon quarterly adjustments."

Miguel leans back, fingers steepled beneath his chin. "Those arrangements were made with Emelio personally. With his passing, perhaps it's time to... renegotiate terms."

"Perhaps." Yelana's smile reminds me of a knife's edge catching light. "But first, we should discuss the three shipments diverted from our Arizona warehouse to your facilities in Tijuana."

Miguel's expression doesn't change, but I notice the slight tightening of his jaw. Antonio shifts in his seat, eyes darting to his father then back to Yelana.

"I'm not sure what you're implying," Miguel replies, his voice cooled by several degrees.

"I'm not implying anything. I'm stating facts." Yelana removes a thin folder from her briefcase, sliding it across the table. "Manifests. Serial numbers. Destination confirmations. All products diverted from Zentarra inventory through a very specific security vulnerability that only recently came to my attention."

I watch Miguel's hands as he opens the folder, noting how his right drifts slightly closer to his jacket where a weapon almost certainly rests. My own hand edges toward my holster, hidden but accessible beneath my sport coat.

"These could be fabricated," Miguel says carefully, though his eyes betray recognition.

"They could be," Yelana agrees, taking a deliberate sip of her wine. "But we both know they aren't. Just as we both know Ken Jackson didn't suddenly develop a taste for expensive real estate in Bogotá on his Zentarra salary."

Antonio watches Yelana with newfound intensity, reassessing her as a threat rather than a potential conquest. Good. Let him see her for what she truly is—not just a pretty face inheriting daddy's business, but a force in her own right.

"What exactly are you proposing, Miss Zentarra?" Miguel asks, his tone shifting to something more respectful.

"A return to established boundaries. Compensation for the diverted merchandise. And information about who authorized payment to Ken Jackson from Costa accounts."

The restaurant continues its elegant performance around us—waiters gliding between tables, champagne corks popping at a celebration across the room, pianist playing something classical and subdued. But at our table, the air has changed, charged with the dangerous electricity of power shifting hands.

I watch Yelana with growing admiration as she leverages every advantage, counters every evasion, and gradually pulls Miguel Costa into a position where cooperation becomes the only viable option. She's magnificent in her calculated precision, channeling Emelio's strategic mind while adding something uniquely her own—a perceptiveness about human nature that allows her to read Miguel's reactions with uncanny accuracy.

Antonio leans forward, inserting himself into the conversation with practiced ease. "Perhaps we could discuss these matters further over dinner?" His eyes never leave Yelana's face. "I find business always flows more smoothly with good food and better company."

The invitation carries layers of meaning, his interest in Yelana barely disguised beneath business courtesy. I resist the urge to step in, to assert some claim that I have no right to make. Instead, I focus on the security personnel positioned around the room, on the exits and entrances, on anything but the way Antonio looks at her or the way something in my chest tightens at his obvious interest.

"I believe that could be arranged," Yelana replies, her tone giving nothing away. "Assuming we reach preliminary agreements on the core issues first."

As the conversation shifts to specific pricing structures and territory lines, hushed tones disguising the lethal nature of the merchandise being discussed, I maintain my vigilance while acknowledging an uncomfortable truth: I'm no longer just watching Yelana to protect her. I'm watching her because I can't look away, because something fundamental has shifted between us since that night in the hallway when truth about Juan created a bridge instead of a wall.

And that realization makes me more dangerous to her than any Costa ever could.

The business portion of our meeting concludes with tentative agreements that benefit neither side completely—the hallmark of successful negotiation according to Emelio's playbook. Miguel signals his approval with a slight nod, and Antonio immediately summons a waiter carrying a tray of champagne flutes. The amber liquid catches the light as he offers a glass to Yelana with a practiced smile that's shown too many women the same rehearsed charm. She accepts with appropriate business courtesy, but I notice the subtle shift in her posture—a slight opening toward him that makes something in my chest constrict.

"To new partnerships," Antonio proposes, raising his glass with eyes fixed solely on Yelana. "And to honoring old traditions while creating better ones."

The double meaning isn't lost on anyone at the table. Miguel watches his son with the calculating assessment of a chess master seeing a promising move unfold. Yelana touches her glass to Antonio's with practiced grace, taking the smallest sip possible while maintaining appearances.

"Your father would be proud," Miguel tells her, his tone carrying unexpected sincerity. "Few could step into Emelio Zentarra's shoes with such... natural authority."

Before Yelana can respond, the pianist transitions to something slower, more intimate. Antonio sets his barely-touched champagne on the table and extends his hand toward her.

"Would you honor me with a dance?" he asks. "I find business creates tension that music helps dissolve."

I watch Yelana hesitate, her eyes briefly flickering toward me before returning to Antonio. The question in her glance is clear: security risk assessment. But before I can subtly signal my professional opinion, Miguel interjects.

"An excellent idea. Nothing builds trust like stepping away from the table." He gives Yelana an encouraging nod that borders on expectation. A test, perhaps, of her willingness to solidify this fragile truce with social niceties.

"One dance," she agrees, placing her hand in Antonio's.

I remain seated, fighting to keep my expression neutral as Antonio guides her to the small dance floor where three other couples already sway to the music. His hand settles on her lower back, fingers splayed possessively against the fabric of her suit jacket. The touch is professionally appropriate but personally presumptuous. I catch myself grinding my teeth and force my jaw to relax.

"She's quite remarkable," Miguel observes, watching me watch them. "Beauty and brilliance in equal measure, just like her mother."

"She is." I keep my response minimal, unwilling to engage beyond necessity with the man whose brother likely ordered the attack at the funeral. My focus remains on Yelana and the room's security parameters, refusing to acknowledge the third, entirely unprofessional concern burning in my chest.

Antonio pulls Yelana slightly closer than business etiquette dictates, his mouth moving near her ear as he speaks words I can't hear. Whatever he says makes her laugh—not the performative social laugh she uses in business settings, but something more genuine that transforms her face with brief, unguarded lightness. My fingers tighten around my water glass, knuckles whitening with pressure I don't intend to exert.

This reaction is unprofessional. Dangerous. A compromise to the singular focus required for her protection. I force myself to conduct another systematic scan of the restaurant, deliberately pulling my attention from the dance floor to assess the broader security situation.

The bar area remains consistent—two security personnel maintaining positions with clear sightlines to both entrances. The main dining room holds steady at forty-seven guests, three waitstaff, and one security detail accompanying what appears to be a Latin American diplomat near the western wall. Nothing unusual, nothing—

Movement near the kitchen entrance catches my attention. A waiter emerges, carrying a covered silver tray with unusual stillness. Most servers balance trays with a slight compensatory sway, adjusting continuously to maintain equilibrium. This one moves with rigid precision, body too tense for someone simply delivering dinner.

I track him peripherally while pretending to listen to Miguel's commentary about wine vintages. The waiter's eyes dart around the room, not making the normal visual check for his assigned tables but instead sweeping systematically toward the dance floor. His right hand grips the tray handle from below rather than supporting from above—a position that would allow for quick removal of the cover while maintaining control of whatever lies beneath.

"Excuse me," I murmur to Miguel, rising smoothly while maintaining visual contact with the waiter. "Need to check on something."

The waiter's path becomes clear as he angles directly toward the dance floor, specifically toward Yelana and Antonio. His left hand now shifts to the edge of the silver cover, thumb positioned for quick removal. I've seen this approach before—in Baghdad, in Kabul, in a dozen security briefings about covert assassination techniques.

I move casually at first, not wanting to trigger premature action, positioning myself to intercept while tracking his increasingly nervous eye movements. A slight sheen of sweat appears on his upper lip despite the restaurant's perfectly regulated temperature. His right hand shifts, revealing a momentary glimpse of what appears to be a modified trigger guard beneath the tray.

Twenty feet separates us as his pace quickens. Fifteen feet. Ten.

He reaches the edge of the dance floor, his target now clear as he approaches Yelana's back while she remains focused on Antonio. His thumb hooks under the silver cover, beginning to lift.

Training takes over. I launch across the remaining distance, driving my shoulder into his midsection with controlled force. The silver cover clatters to the floor, revealing a compact semi-automatic pistol with suppressor attached, now spinning across polished marble as I take the would-be assassin down.

My momentum carries us both to the ground, dishes and silverware crashing around us as the tray's contents scatter. I pin him with practiced efficiency—right knee driving into his solar plexus, left hand securing his dominant wrist, right forearm pressed against his throat with just enough pressure to immobilize without crushing his trachea.

"Don't move," I growl, applying additional pressure when he attempts to buck beneath me. His eyes widen with the sudden realization that his oxygen supply depends entirely on my restraint.

The restaurant erupts in chaos—women screaming, men shouting, chairs scraping against marble as guests scramble away from the confrontation. I maintain focus on the attacker, aware of Yelana's position in my peripheral vision as security personnel converge from all directions with weapons drawn.

"Gun!" I shout to the approaching security team. "Check for backup weapons and secure the weapon on the floor!"

Costa's security responds with professional efficiency, two men taking control of the attacker while another retrieves the fallen pistol. I roll smoothly to my feet, immediately moving to Yelana who stands frozen several feet away, Antonio's arm around her shoulders in what could be either protection or possession.

"Are you hurt?" I demand, eyes quickly scanning her for any sign of injury.

She shakes her head, shock giving way to the anger I've come to expect from her in crisis situations. "What the hell just happened?"

Before I can answer, Miguel's voice cuts through the chaos, sharp with fury as he barks orders to his security team. The restaurant is rapidly emptying, guests hurried out by staff while the remaining security creates a perimeter around our group.

"In my establishment," Miguel seethes, watching as his men secure the would-be assassin. "They dare to attempt this in my house?"

Antonio's arm remains around Yelana, his face a mask of concern that reads as genuine even to my suspicious assessment. "Are you alright?" he asks her, his attention focused entirely on her face.

"I'm fine," she assures him, though her voice carries the slight tremor of adrenaline. She steps away from his protective embrace, moving closer to me instead. The small victory this represents is entirely inappropriate given the circumstances, yet I can't help but register it.

"We need to leave," I tell her quietly but firmly. "Now. This location is compromised."

For once, she doesn't argue. The slight nod she gives me carries more weight than any verbal agreement could—a recognition that tonight's events have escalated the danger beyond even her willingness to challenge my security protocols.

As Costa's men lead the attacker away for what will undoubtedly be a painful interrogation, I guide Yelana toward the exit, my hand instinctively finding the small of her back where Antonio's had been minutes earlier. The gesture is professionally justified but personally satisfying in ways I refuse to examine as we step into the night, leaving behind broken glass, scattered silverware, and whatever illusion of safety the Costa restaurant might have offered.

Chaos erupts around us like a tactical flashbang—disorienting, immediate, complete. Miguel Costa bellows orders in rapid-fire Spanish, his security team forming a protective circle around him and his son while simultaneously securing the would-be assassin. "Find out who sent him!" Miguel demands, face contorted with the particular fury of a man whose sovereignty has been violated. "Nobody attacks guests in my establishment!" I keep Yelana close, one hand on her elbow, body angled to shield her from any secondary attack while guiding her toward the exit. The restaurant's other patrons press against the walls, their evening of fine dining transformed into a front-row seat to the violent reality that underwrites the luxury they enjoy.

Antonio steps forward, his earlier charm replaced by cold efficiency. "Let me arrange an escort for you—"

"We have our own security protocols," I cut him off, already assessing the street through the glass doors. Our SUV waits at the curb, driver alert and engine running per standard procedure. "Keep your men back. Any approach will be considered hostile."

Miguel nods sharply, professional respect momentarily overriding his anger. "I give you my word, this was not authorized by the Costa family. We will find who is responsible."

"I'm sure you will," Yelana replies, her voice steady despite the slight tremor I can feel through my hand on her arm. "We'll be in touch about our findings as well."

We exit into the cool night air, my body maintaining protective position as we approach the vehicle. I scan rooflines, shadows, nearby cars—the thousand potential hiding spots that make urban security a nightmare. The driver opens the rear door at our approach, and I usher Yelana inside before following, maintaining visual coverage of all angles until the armored door seals us in comparative safety.

"Go," I order the driver, who pulls smoothly into traffic without question. The restaurant recedes behind us, its elegant façade now tainted by violence—like everything else in Yelana's world.

Silence fills the vehicle interior, heavy with unspoken accusations. Yelana stares out the window, her profile sharp in the passing streetlights, jaw clenched tight enough that I can see the muscle working beneath her skin. The calm after action has always been the most dangerous time—when adrenaline recedes and emotions rush in to fill the void. I brace myself for what's coming.

"What the hell was that?" she finally asks, voice deceptively quiet as she turns to face me.

"An assassination attempt," I answer simply. "The waiter was carrying a modified Glock 26 with suppressor under that serving tray. Standard close-quarters elimination technique."

"I'm not talking about the assassination attempt." Her eyes flash dangerously. "I'm talking about how you handled it. Tackling someone in the middle of a high-level business negotiation? Creating a scene that destroyed any credibility I might have established with the Costas?"

The unfairness of the accusation stings more than it should. "Would you prefer I'd let him shoot you?"

"I'd prefer you exercise some goddamn judgment!" Her voice rises slightly, control slipping. "You could have discreetly intercepted him before he reached the dance floor. You could have alerted Costa's security. You could have done anything other than diving across the restaurant like some action movie hero!"

"There wasn't time for subtle," I counter, struggling to keep my own tone even. "He was seconds from drawing. I made a tactical decision based on immediate threat assessment."

"Bullshit." The curse sounds sharper in her cultured voice. "You've been watching Antonio like a hawk all night. This was about him touching me, not about legitimate security concerns."

The accusation hits too close to home, igniting my own anger. "I've been doing this a lot longer than you've been running your father's business, Yelana. Don't confuse your personal discomfort with professional assessment."

"Professional?" She laughs without humor. "Was it professional when you couldn't take your eyes off us dancing? When your knuckles turned white around your glass? When you practically knocked Antonio away from me after tackling that waiter?"

"I was doing my job," I insist, heat rising in my voice despite my best efforts at control. "The job your father gave me. The job you remind me of every time I make a decision you don't like."

"My father hired you to protect me, not embarrass me in front of potential business partners!"

"Your father hired me to keep you alive, regardless of your feelings about my methods." I lean forward, the space between us charged with something more volatile than mere disagreement. "Those 'potential business partners' are connected to the same organization that's tried to kill you twice now."

"You don't know that," she fires back. "Miguel seemed genuinely shocked by the attack."

"Of course he did. He's been perfecting that performance for decades." My frustration builds with each exchange. "Their shock doesn't mean they weren't testing you, seeing how you'd react under pressure, assessing your security vulnerabilities."

"So now I'm not allowed to conduct business at all? Should I just hide in the estate while you decide who I can speak to, where I can go, who I can dance with?"

The mention of dancing reignites something dangerous in my chest. "Antonio Costa isn't interested in business with you. He's interested in getting you into bed, using you to gain leverage over the Zentarra organization, or both."

"And that's your professional assessment, is it?" Her eyes narrow, seeing too much. "Not jealousy? Not possessiveness? Just pure tactical analysis?"

"What I feel doesn't matter," I growl, the words scraping my throat. "My job is to keep you alive."

"Then answer the question," she demands, moving closer across the seat, her perfume filling the space between us. "Was that tackle about protecting me, or about Antonio's hands on me?"

"Both," I admit, voice rougher than intended. "I was jealous, okay? Seeing you with him—" I cut myself off, horrified at the admission I nearly completed.

Her eyes widen, anger momentarily replaced by shock as we stare at each other in the dim interior. The SUV slows, turning into the estate driveway, the security gates opening to admit us. Neither of us moves as the vehicle comes to a stop in front of the main entrance.

The driver clears his throat awkwardly. "We've arrived, Miss Zentarra."

Yelana exits without another word, storming toward the house with the furious grace that's become so familiar. I follow, signaling the driver to stand down as I pursue her through the front door and into the main hallway.

"Yelana, wait." My voice echoes off marble floors and high ceilings.

She spins to face me, color high in her cheeks, eyes bright with anger and something else I can't—or won't—identify. "What? What could you possibly have to say that justifies treating me like a child who can't make her own decisions?"

"I'm trying to keep you alive!" I close the distance between us, frustration overriding caution. "Why can't you understand that everything I do is to protect you?"

"I never asked for your protection!" She steps toward me, close enough that I can feel the heat radiating from her body. "I never asked for any of this!"

"Well, neither did I!" The words burst from some place deeper than professional restraint can reach. "You're half my age! I didn't ask to care about what happens to you beyond a security assignment. I didn't ask to lie awake wondering if you're safe. I didn't ask to feel sick watching another man touch you!"

Her breath catches, the argument suspended in the charged air between us. We stand toe to toe in the hallway, both breathing hard, neither willing to retreat. Something shifts in her expression—anger softening into a different kind of intensity, one that pulls at something primitive in my chest.

"Mason," she says, my name half whisper, half challenge.

Whatever restraint I've maintained shatters completely. My hands find her waist, pulling her against me as my mouth claims hers in a kiss that begins as an extension of our argument—fierce, demanding, angry. Her response is immediate, hands clutching my shoulders, body arching into mine as if the contact is as essential to her as it suddenly is to me.

The kiss transforms, anger giving way to something more vulnerable as her lips soften beneath mine. My hand slides up her back to cradle her head, fingers threading through her hair as the last of my professional distance crumbles. She makes a small sound against my mouth—part surrender, part demand—that reverberates through my entire body.

Reality crashes back when we break apart, both breathing heavily, staring at each other with identical expressions of shock. Her lips are slightly swollen, her pupils dilated, her professional composure completely undone. I've never seen anything more beautiful or more terrifying.

Without a word, she steps back, the space between us expanding into a chasm of professional boundaries I've just dynamited beyond repair. She turns and walks away, footsteps quick and uneven on the marble floor, until she reaches her bedroom door. It closes behind her with a decisive click that sounds like the final period on a sentence I'll regret for the rest of my life.

I remain in the hallway, alone with the ghost of her taste on my lips and the certainty that I've just compromised everything—her security, my integrity, the oath I made to her father. I lean against the wall, closing my eyes as self-recrimination floods in to replace desire.

"Fuck," I whisper to the empty hallway, the single word containing everything I can't allow myself to feel and everything I suddenly can't deny.

FIFTEEN
Traitor Revealed

YELANA

I pace my father's office like a caged animal, fingers tracing my lips where Mason's mouth burned against mine minutes ago. The taste of him still lingers—gunmetal and desperation and something dangerously addictive. My body vibrates with conflicting impulses: to run back to him, to slap him, to finish what that kiss started. Instead, I'm hiding in my father's sanctum, seeking answers in the ghost of his presence while my world crumbles in new and unexpected ways.

The massive oak desk looms before me, its surface still arranged exactly as my father left it—pen aligned precisely with the leather blotter, crystal paperweight catching the dim light. I've avoided changing anything, as if preserving this room might somehow keep him with me. Foolish. As foolish as letting Mason Phillips breach every defense I've built.

The door crashes open with enough force to shake the hinges. I spin around, heart slamming against my ribs as Ken Jackson staggers in, one hand braced against the doorframe. Blood spatters his once-immaculate shirt, his face a mess of purpling bruises and half-dried blood. His right eye has swollen nearly shut, his lip split and crusted.

"Jesus Christ," I gasp, frozen in place.

Mason appears behind him like a shadow, hand already moving toward the weapon concealed beneath his jacket. His eyes meet mine for a split second—the first time since that kiss—and something electric passes between us before his focus snaps back to Ken.

"Help me," Ken croaks, stumbling forward. He collapses into one of the leather chairs across from my father's desk, his breath coming in ragged bursts. "They had me. Costa's men. After the funeral..."

I rush to him, professional training overriding personal shock. "Get the first aid kit," I order Mason, who hesitates, his eyes narrowing slightly as he assesses Ken. There's something in his stance—a coiled readiness that suggests he doesn't entirely believe what he's seeing.

"I'm fine," Ken waves away my concern, though nothing about him looks fine. "Had to get back... warn you." His fingers fumble inside his torn jacket, extracting a small flash drive that he clutches like salvation. "Evidence. They let their guard down... thought I was unconscious." He presses the drive into my palm. "The traitor. I found him."

Mason hasn't moved to get the first aid kit. Instead, he's circling slowly to position himself where he can see both Ken and the door, his shoulders set in a way I've come to recognize as combat-ready.

"Who?" I demand, clutching the drive. "Ken, who betrayed us?"

Ken's eyes dart toward the door, then back to me. "Kendrick," he rasps. "Your butler. Been feeding information to Costa for months. I found the communications."

The accusation hits like a physical blow. Kendrick, who has served my family with quiet dignity for over twenty years. Kendrick, who taught me to tie my shoes and waited up with hot chocolate when nightmares kept me awake after Juan died.

"That's impossible," I say, even as doubt creeps in. Ken wouldn't make this accusation lightly. Would he?

"Check the drive," Ken insists, gesturing weakly toward my father's computer. "Emails. Bank transfers. Meeting logs. All there."

I move to the computer, flash drive clutched in my suddenly cold fingers. Mason steps closer, and I feel the heat of him at my back, not quite touching but present enough that my skin prickles with awareness.

"Convenient timing," he murmurs, low enough that only I can hear. "Right when we were starting to build a case against him."

Before I can respond, the office door opens again—this time with the silent precision that only one person in this household has mastered. Kendrick enters bearing a silver tray with a carafe of coffee and three cups, his timing impeccable as always. His eyes widen slightly at the sight of Ken, the only break in his perfect composure.

"Mr. Jackson," he says, voice steady despite the shock evident in his eyes. "You've returned to us. Shall I fetch the medical supplies?"

"You treacherous bastard," Ken snarls, struggling to push himself upright in the chair. "Don't pretend. I found your communications with Costa. The payment records. Everything."

The accusation hangs in the air like smoke after gunfire. I watch Kendrick's face, searching for guilt, for the confirmation that would make Ken's accusation true. For a moment, his expression remains perfectly blank, the consummate professional.

Then something shifts. His hands—always steady, always controlled—begin to tremble. The silver tray rattles, coffee sloshing against fine china. His eyes dart to me, then to Mason, then to the door.

"Miss Yelana," Kendrick says, his voice barely audible. "I don't understand."

"Like hell you don't," Ken spits. "Your encrypted communications. The meetings in Santa Monica. The offshore account where they've been paying you to sell out this family."

Kendrick's normally immaculate posture seems to collapse inward, shoulders hunching as if under an invisible weight. The tray trembles more violently in his hands.

"Perhaps you should set that down," Mason suggests quietly, his tone neutral but his body language anything but. He's positioned himself between Kendrick and me, his stance casual to anyone who doesn't know how quickly he can move.

Kendrick places the tray on a side table, the china rattling against silver. When he straightens, his face has aged a decade. "Miss Yelana," he says again, her eyes pleading. "I've served your family faithfully for twenty-three years."

"Then explain what's on this," I say, holding up the flash drive. I want to believe him. God help me, I want any explanation that doesn't add another betrayal to the mountain I'm already carrying.

"I cannot explain what I haven't seen," Kendrick replies, a hint of his usual dignity returning. "But I can assure you, my loyalty has never wavered."

From my peripheral vision, I see Mason studying both men with clinical detachment. His eyes track Ken's injuries, lingering on the bruising patterns, the blood spatters that don't quite match the story of captivity and escape. His gaze shifts to Kendrick, noting the butler's shaking hands, the barely perceptible beading of sweat at his temples.

"Check the drive," Ken urges again, more forcefully. "Everything you need is there."

I hesitate, caught between Ken's certainty and something in Mason's expression that whispers caution. Ken has been family to me since childhood. I watched him bleed for my father countless times. But the way Mason's eyes narrow as he catalogs inconsistencies in Ken's appearance, the subtle head shake he gives me when our eyes meet—it plants a seed of doubt I can't ignore.

"We will," I say finally, pocketing the drive instead of immediately plugging it in. "But first, you need medical attention, Ken. And Kendrick isn't going anywhere."

Ken's face tightens with frustration, but he nods, slumping back in the chair. Kendrick stands perfectly still, his usually impeccable poise fractured by the gravity of the accusation against him.

Between them, Mason remains watchful, his body oriented toward me like a compass finding north. I feel the phantom pressure of his lips against mine and wonder if I've already made too many mistakes to salvage what matters most—my father's legacy, my own survival, and perhaps something else I'm still afraid to name.

I stand in the corner of my father's office watching Ken loom over Kendrick, who sits rigidly in my father's chair—a visual violation that makes my stomach turn. We've moved from accusation to impromptu interrogation without even checking the flash drive, Ken's urgency sweeping us along like a rip current. Mason remains by the door, his body a coiled spring, eyes constantly moving between Ken, Kendrick, and the windows. He hasn't mentioned our kiss, but something has shifted between us—a new awareness that crackles like static electricity whenever our eyes meet.

"Start talking," Ken demands, his voice a razor despite his apparent injuries. "How long have you been feeding information to Costa?"

Kendrick's posture remains impeccable even under duress, his spine straight against the leather chair that has cradled three generations of Zentarra patriarchs. Only his hands betray him, fingers twisting together on his lap like pale, frightened animals.

"I've served this family faithfully for—"

Ken slams his palm against the desk, sending my father's crystal paperweight jumping. "Spare us the loyalty speech. We have the evidence."

I pace the perimeter of the office, grief transmuting into a white-hot anger that threatens to consume my rationality. If Kendrick betrayed us—Kendrick, who cut the crusts off my sandwiches and taught me how to polish silver—then there's no one left to trust. The thought is a cold void opening beneath my feet.

"Miss Yelana," Kendrick says, turning to me with eyes that have witnessed every significant moment of my life. "Whatever Mr. Jackson believes he's found, I assure you—"

"We found your offshore accounts," Ken interrupts. "The meeting logs. The access codes you provided to Costa's team. It's over, Kendrick. The only question now is how much more damage you'll cause before we end this."

I stop pacing, studying Kendrick's face. Something isn't right. We haven't even examined the flash drive yet, and Ken is speaking as if the evidence is irrefutable. My eyes find Mason's across the room, and I see my own doubt mirrored there.

"Ken," I say, "maybe we should verify what's on the drive before—"

"There's no time," Ken snaps, eyes never leaving Kendrick. "We have a confession to secure before Costa's people realize their inside man has been compromised."

Kendrick's gaze drops to his hands, and something in his expression fractures. "They threatened my sister's children," he says so quietly I almost miss it. "My nieces in London."

The confession hangs in the air like smoke. Ken straightens, vindication hardening his features.

"They showed me photographs," Kendrick continues, his voice hollow. "Outside their school. In their bedroom. Said they would start with the youngest and work their way up if I didn't cooperate." He looks up at me, eyes glistening. "I never gave them anything vital. Just enough to satisfy them. Schedule changes. Staff rotations. Never security codes or safe room locations."

"You son of a bitch," Ken snarls. "How many people died because of what you shared? The attack at the funeral—"

"I knew nothing about that," Kendrick insists, a flash of the dignified man I've known all my life returning. "I would never endanger Miss Yelana. Never."

He turns to me fully now, ignoring Ken's looming presence. "Your father would have understood, Miss Yelana. Family was everything to him. Everything." His voice breaks on the last word, and the sound pierces something in my chest.

I step forward, uncertain what I'm about to say or do, when the lights abruptly cut out. The office plunges into perfect darkness, the sudden absence of the security system's ambient hum creating a vacuum of silence that raises the hair on my arms.

"Don't move," Mason's voice comes from closer than expected, and then his hand is on my arm, pulling me away from the windows. The warmth of his palm burns through my sleeve, an anchor in the disorienting blackness.

"Backup generator should kick in," Ken says, but the seconds stretch with no sign of emergency lighting.

"It won't," Mason replies, his breath warm against my ear. "They've disabled it. We're compromised."

My eyes adjust gradually to the darkness, moonlight filtering through the office windows providing just enough illumination to make out shapes. Mason has positioned himself between me and the glass, his weapon already drawn. The solid weight of his presence beside me is both comfort and confusion after everything that's passed between us.

"There," Ken says, pointing toward the grounds. "Movement by the eastern perimeter."

I squint through the gloom and see them—dark figures moving with military precision across the manicured lawn, the occasional glint of moonlight on metal betraying their weapons.

"How many?" I ask, my voice steadier than I feel.

"At least six that I can see," Mason answers. "Probably more coming from other angles."

"We need to get to the panic room," Ken says immediately, reaching for my arm. "Now, before they breach the house."

Mason shifts slightly, his body blocking Ken's approach. "The secret passage to the garage is faster," he counters. "Less exposed. We can be in a vehicle and away before they secure the perimeter."

The two security strategies hang in the air between them like invisible swords. I look from Ken's blood-streaked face to Mason's watchful profile, both men tasked with keeping me alive, both suggesting opposite courses of action.

"The panic room is designed for exactly this scenario," Ken insists, his voice rising with urgency. "Your father built it to withstand anything short of a direct missile strike."

"And it has one entrance, one exit," Mason replies, his tone deliberately measured in contrast to Ken's intensity. "Perfect place to trap someone you want to eliminate."

Ken's face contorts with sudden anger. "What are you implying, Phillips?"

"I'm not implying anything. I'm stating facts." Mason's hand remains on my arm, solid and warm. "The garage route gives us options. The panic room is a dead end if they know we're in there."

"They won't know if we move now," Ken argues, stepping closer. His hand drifts toward the holster at his side, a movement so subtle I almost miss it in the darkness. But Mason doesn't miss it. His posture shifts microscopically, weight transferring to the balls of his feet.

I look between them, my heart hammering against my ribs. Ken—who taught me to drive, who carried me to bed when I fell asleep in the car, who's been my father's right hand for two decades. Mason—who's barely been in my life two months, who I barely trust with my feelings, let alone my life.

Yet something in Ken's insistence sets off warning bells I can't ignore. The eager way he pushes for the panic room. The flash drive we still haven't verified. The injuries that suddenly seem too precisely placed, too theatrical.

"Yelana," Mason says quietly, using my first name without the usual formality. "We need to move. Now."

Kendrick hasn't moved from my father's chair, his eyes tracking the silent battle of wills unfolding before him. When he catches my gaze, something passes between us—a lifetime of small kindnesses and shared grief, culminating in this moment of terrible clarity.

"Trust your instincts, Miss Yelana," he says softly. "As your father always did."

Ken's hand moves closer to his weapon, his patience visibly thinning. "We don't have time for this. The panic room. Now."

I take a deep breath, decision crystallizing as the first sounds of breaking glass echo from somewhere deeper in the house. Armed men are inside. Time has run out.

Ken's hand flies to his holster, and the world slows to a terrible, crystalline clarity. "You've been a pain in my ass since you got here, Phillips," he snarls, drawing his weapon with the practiced ease of someone who's imagined this moment for a long time. The gun swings toward Mason—black and deadly and certain—and my breath freezes in my lungs. Everything collapses into this single, horrifying moment: Ken, my surrogate uncle, pointing a gun at Mason, the man I just kissed, while armed intruders close in on us from all sides.

Mason doesn't flinch, doesn't blink, his own weapon already raised. Two trained killers in perfect deadly symmetry across my father's office. The standoff stretches for one heartbeat, two, three—

"Run, Miss Yelana!"

Kendrick erupts from my father's chair with shocking speed for a man his age, launching himself at Ken with reckless abandon. His dignified reserve vanishes as he throws himself into Ken's gun arm, disrupting his aim. The weapon discharges with a thunderous crack that reverberates through my bones.

Then again.

Kendrick jerks twice, his body absorbing the bullets meant for Mason—for me. Blood sprays across the room, splattering the family portraits that line my father's wall. My grandfather's stern face, my father's proud smile, Juan's childhood innocence—all baptized in Kendrick's sacrifice. He crumples to the floor without a sound, his loyal service ended with the same quiet dignity with which he lived.

"No!" The scream tears from my throat, raw and primal.

Mason moves like violence personified, tackling Ken before he can recover his aim. They crash into my father's antique desk, sending papers and crystal flying. The heavy oak groans under their combined weight, decades of Zentarra business decisions weathering this final, brutal negotiation.

"The bookcase!" Mason shouts as he grapples with Ken, one hand locked around Ken's wrist, trying to control the weapon. "Go! Third shelf, green book!"

I scramble toward the bookcase, my body moving on instinct while my mind remains frozen on Kendrick's fallen form. Blood spreads beneath him in a dark pool, soaking into the Persian carpet my mother imported from Istanbul. The room fills with the copper-penny smell of death, overwhelming the leather and paper scent that's always defined this space.

Behind me, Ken drives his knee into Mason's side, eliciting a grunt of pain. They roll across the desk, sending my father's prized Montblanc pen clattering to the floor. Mason's elbow connects with Ken's jaw, snapping his head back.

My fingers find the leather spine of the green book—Kipling's collected works, my father's favorite—and pull. Something clicks within the shelving, a mechanism releasing with a soft snick that would be inaudible if not for my heightened senses. The entire bookcase shifts slightly, revealing a seam in the paneling.

"Hurry!" Mason growls, his voice tight with effort as Ken slams his head against the edge of the desk. The sickening crack makes my stomach lurch, but Mason responds by driving his knee upward into Ken's ribs.

I shove against the bookcase, feeling it give way on hidden hinges. Cool air rushes from the dark passage beyond—my father's insurance policy, a secret route to the garage built when I was still in diapers. The passage yawns before me, dark and uncertain, but not as dangerous as what's behind.

Ken breaks free of Mason's grip momentarily, reaching inside his jacket. The knife appears in his hand like a magician's trick—thin and lethal. Before Mason can react, Ken slashes downward, opening a vicious line across Mason's side.

"Mason!" I cry out, frozen halfway into the passage.

Blood immediately soaks through Mason's shirt, spreading like spilled wine across the fabric. But he doesn't yield. Instead, he drives his forearm into Ken's throat, pinning him against the desk with renewed fury.

"Go!" he commands, not looking at me, all his focus on keeping Ken's knife from finding its mark again. "I'll find you!"

I hesitate, torn between the desperate need to escape and the sickening certainty that I'm abandoning Mason to a losing fight. Ken knows this house, knows its secrets. He's been planning this betrayal for months, maybe years. And now Mason is bleeding, outnumbered, fighting for both our lives.

Ken must see my indecision. "He's already dead," he spits, struggling against Mason's grip. "Just like your father, just like your mother. The Zentarra legacy ends tonight."

Something in his words—the cold satisfaction, the calculated cruelty—finalizes my decision. I slip fully into the passage, fingers finding the small flashlight my father installed on the inner wall. The dim beam illuminates rough concrete walls, a utilitarian escape route disguised behind my father's refined office.

Behind me, the fight intensifies. Glass shatters. Bodies slam against furniture. A grunt of pain—Mason's or Ken's, I can't tell.

Then comes the unmistakable sound of gunfire from elsewhere in the house. The intruders have breached our inner defenses. Time has run out.

"They're in!" Ken shouts, not to me but to someone else—to the invaders he's invited into my home. He breaks away from Mason with a final violent shove, diving toward the office door instead of pursuing me.

Through the narrowing gap in the bookcase, I see Mason struggle to his feet, one hand pressed against his bleeding side. He staggers slightly, leaving crimson handprints on my father's desk as he uses it for support. His shirt is soaked with blood, his face pale but determined as he lurches toward the passage.

Heavy footsteps pound down the hallway toward the office. Multiple men, moving fast. Ken has disappeared, leaving Mason to face whatever forces are approaching. I should run—every survival instinct screams to flee deeper into the passage, to save myself.

Instead, I wait those critical seconds, holding the bookcase open as Mason half-falls into the passage beside me. His breath comes in ragged gasps, his weight nearly taking us both down as he stumbles against me. I catch him, feeling the warm wetness of his blood seeping into my own clothes.

"Close it," he manages, reaching back with bloody fingers to grab the interior latch.

Together, we pull the bookcase shut just as shadows appear in the office doorway. The mechanism clicks with terrible finality, sealing us in darkness broken only by my small flashlight. Blood trails across the expensive carpet mark Mason's path to our hiding place—a neon sign for anyone looking closely enough.

Mason sags against the passage wall, his breathing labored. "Need to keep moving," he says, though his legs seem barely able to support him. "Garage is... hundred yards... end of passage."

I slip my shoulder under his arm, taking some of his weight. "Together," I insist, feeling his blood soaking into my sleeve, my side, my resolve.

Behind us, muffled voices filter through the bookcase. They're in the office now, discovering Kendrick's body, seeing the blood trail. We have minutes, maybe seconds before they find the passage mechanism.

"He betrayed us," I whisper, the reality of Ken's treachery still impossible to fully comprehend. "All this time..."

"Tell me something I don't know," Mason mutters, attempting gallows humor despite the pain evident in his voice. He pushes away from the wall, determined to keep moving despite his injury. "Like why the hell I waited so long to kiss you."

The inappropriate timing of his comment startles a half-sob, half-laugh from me as we stumble forward into the darkness, leaving behind Kendrick's cooling body, my father's violated sanctuary, and whatever remains of the life I once knew. Ahead lies only uncertainty, danger, and a slim chance of survival—but at least I'm not facing it alone.

SIXTEEN
Wounded Hearts

Mason

My vision blurs at the edges as I stumble through the door of the beach safe house, one hand pressed against the slick warmth spreading beneath my shirt. The knife wound pulses with each heartbeat, a constant reminder of Ken's betrayal. Salt air hits my face, grounding me momentarily as Yelana's arm tightens around my waist, bearing weight I can't manage alone. "Almost there," she says, voice steadier than her trembling hands. The irony doesn't escape me—I'm supposed to be protecting her, not bleeding all over her expensive clothes while she drags my sorry ass to safety.

The safe house materializes around me in fragments, weathered floorboards groaning under our combined weight, sparse furniture positioned for optimal defensive coverage, windows with clear sightlines to all approach vectors. Even half-conscious, I catalog escape routes and potential cover spots. Old habits.

"Sit down before you fall down," Yelana orders, guiding me to a faded couch that's seen better decades. I comply without argument, a testament to how badly I'm hurt. The cushions exhale dust as I collapse, sending pain knifing through my side.

Yelana moves with unexpected efficiency, securing the door with three separate locks before disappearing into what must be a bathroom. I hear cabinets opening, water running. The constant crash of waves against the shore outside provides a rhythmic counterpoint to the pounding in my head. This place is remote—one of Emelio's off-book properties. No paper trail, no digital footprint. If we're lucky, Ken doesn't know about it.

If we're lucky. Luck hasn't exactly been on our side lately.

She returns with an armful of supplies—gauze, antiseptic, suture kit. Her face is set in determined lines, fear pushed beneath a veneer of control that reminds me of her father. "This needs to come off," she says, producing scissors and attacking my shirt without waiting for permission.

The fabric peels away from the wound with a wet, sucking sound that makes her inhale sharply. I look down to assess the damage. The gash runs six inches along my ribs, deep enough to need stitches but not deep enough to hit anything vital. I've had worse. Not much worse, but still.

"Looks like he missed the important parts," I mutter, trying for humor that falls flat in the sterile reality of blood and betrayal.

Yelana's hands hover over the wound, suddenly uncertain. "I've never actually done this before."

"First time for everything," I reply, taking the antiseptic bottle from her. "Pour this. Don't be gentle—it needs to be clean."

She bites her lower lip, nods once, and uncaps the bottle. The liquid fire hits my open flesh and steals my breath. My vision whites out for a second, muscles seizing as I fight to remain conscious.

"I'm sorry," she whispers, and I'm not sure if she's apologizing for the pain or for something larger, something neither of us can fully articulate yet.

"You should've let me handle Ken," I say through gritted teeth as she prepares the suture kit, my voice strained against the pain. "I knew something was off."

Her head snaps up, eyes flashing with sudden anger. "And you should've trusted me when I said he was loyal." The words lash out, sharp as the needle she's threading. "I've known him my entire life. He taught me to ride a bike. He sat with me in hospitals. He was family."

The raw hurt in her voice cuts deeper than Ken's knife. I watch her hands as they work—steady now, anger providing focus her fear couldn't. She cleans the wound with precise, economical movements, her face inches from my torso. I focus on her eyebrows, the small furrow of concentration between them, anything to distract from the coming pain.

"The first stitch is the worst," I warn as she positions the needle. "Don't hesitate once you start."

She nods, takes a deep breath, and pierces my skin. Fire races along my nerve endings, but I hold still, jaw clenched so tight I might crack teeth. Her fingers work with surprising dexterity, pulling the edges of my flesh together with neat, even stitches. My abdomen tenses with each pierce and tug, muscles jumping involuntarily beneath her hands.

"I should have seen it," I admit, needing to fill the silence with something besides my controlled breathing. "All the signs were there—his convenient absences during security breaches, the missing inventory that passed through his office, his push for the panic room instead of escape."

"Stop," she says without looking up from her work, halfway through the line of stitches. "This isn't your fault."

"It's literally my job to spot threats. I failed." The confession tastes bitter on my tongue. "I let my focus get... compromised."

Now she does look up, her face close enough that I can see the gold flecks in her brown eyes, smell the faint trace of her perfume beneath the metallic tang of my blood. "Ken fooled everyone," she says firmly. "Even my father."

The words hit me like a physical blow. Emelio Zentarra, the most paranoid, calculating bastard I've ever known, suspected everyone. His trust was a resource more precious than the millions he made selling death around the globe. If Ken fooled him...

"Your father suspected him," I remind her, wincing as she starts another stitch. "Those documents at the beach house—"

"Suspicion isn't certainty," she counters. "Dad suspected everyone periodically. He investigated me once when inventory numbers didn't match. It was just... how he operated."

The admission surprises me. I hadn't known that part of their relationship—the careful distance of suspicion even between father and daughter. It explains something about her, the defensive walls she builds and the calculated risks she takes to prove herself.

"Hold still," she murmurs, focused on the final stitches. Her breath whispers across my skin, raising goosebumps that have nothing to do with pain. The intimacy of the moment strikes me suddenly—her hands on my bare skin, her face inches from mine, the vulnerability of allowing someone else to literally stitch you back together.

"Almost done," she says, and I'm not sure if she's talking about the stitches or trying to reassure herself that this nightmare might eventually end. She ties off the final suture and sits back to examine her handiwork—a neat line of black thread holding me together.

Our eyes meet, and something electric passes between us. Recognition, maybe. Understanding. We're both victims of the same betrayal, both orphaned by violence, both struggling to rebuild something from the wreckage. The moment stretches, dangerous with possibility, before she breaks it by reaching for the gauze.

"This needs to be covered," she says, voice carefully neutral as she presses the bandage over my wound. Her fingers brush against my skin, lingering a fraction longer than necessary. I feel each point of contact like a brand.

I look away first, uncomfortable with the vulnerability between us. "You did good work, Zentarra. Didn't know arts and crafts was part of your fancy education."

She almost smiles, the ghost of it touching her lips before fading. "There's a lot you don't know about me, Phillips."

The challenge in her voice is unmistakable, an invitation I'm not sure I should accept. But sitting here, bleeding and broken in her father's forgotten safe house, I wonder if I've been fighting the wrong battle all along.

Yelan's hands still against my skin, the medical supplies scattered on the couch beside us. Something shifts in her expression, determination replacing the clinical focus from moments ago. "I know there's something between us," she says abruptly, the directness catching me off guard. "And I know you're fighting it because of my age, because of my father." No preamble, no retreat. It's the same fearless approach she brings to everything, charging headfirst into danger rather than circling it cautiously. My pulse quickens, not from blood loss but from the precipice we're suddenly standing on.

"Yelana—" I start, my voice rougher than intended.

"Don't deny it," she interrupts. "Not here. Not after everything." Her eyes hold mine, refusing to let me look away. "We might be dead tomorrow. Ken's men could find us any minute. I don't want to die without saying this."

Twenty-two years separate us. Twenty-two years of life, of mistakes, of blood and violence she's only beginning to understand. My hand rises almost of its own accord, fingers brushing her cheek in a touch too intimate to be professional, too gentle to be casual. "I'm too old for you," I say, the words hollow even to my own ears.

"That's not a real objection," she fires back. "It's an excuse."

"I promised your father I'd protect you." Another fragment of resistance, crumbling even as I offer it.

"And you are. But that's not all you want to do." The challenge in her voice strips away pretense, leaves nowhere to hide.

"I've failed everyone I've ever cared about." This admission cuts closer to truth. "My team in Afghanistan. Kerry. Your brother." The names form a litany of ghosts between us. "I can't fail you too."

"So you'd rather not try at all?" Her voice softens, but her eyes remain fierce. "That's cowardice, Mason. Not protection."

The accusation lands with the accuracy of a bullet, finding the vulnerable point beneath my armor. "You don't understand what you're asking for," I warn, even as my hand slides to the back of her neck, fingers threading through her hair.

"Then show me." Three words, offered like a dare.

Something snaps inside me, restraint, resistance, resolve, all breaking under the weight of desire I've fought since first seeing her. My hands find her hips, pulling her onto my lap in a single fluid motion despite the protest from my wounded side. She straddles me, thighs pressed against mine, the position immediately intimate.

"This is a mistake," I murmur against her mouth, even as I pull her closer.

"Then make it," she whispers, and closes the final distance between us.

Her lips meet mine with surprising gentleness that quickly ignites into something hungrier. Months of tension, of fighting this pull between us, collapse into this single point of contact. My hands roam her back, her waist, learning the curves I've forced myself not to acknowledge. Her fingers tangle in my hair, her body arching against mine as the kiss deepens into something primitive and necessary.

Pain from my wound fades beneath a more urgent heat. I taste her desperation, her relief at finally breaking through the walls between us. Her hips rock against mine, creating friction that pulls a groan from deep in my chest. Everything accelerates, hands everywhere at once, breath coming in short gasps between kisses that grow more demanding with each passing second.

I grip the hem of her blouse, breaking the kiss just long enough to search her eyes for any hesitation. Finding none, I tear the fabric upward, revealing smooth skin and black lace. She helps, arms raising, the garment discarded somewhere behind the couch. Her fingers attack my belt buckle with single-minded determination that would make me smile if I weren't so consumed by need.

Standing becomes imperative, despite the protest from my injured side. I lift her with me, our mouths still connected, turning to press her against the nearest wall. Her legs wrap around my waist, ankles crossing at the small of my back. The position brings us into perfect alignment, only frustrating layers of clothing preventing the connection we both want.

Those barriers don't last. My hands make quick work of her remaining clothes, tactical efficiency serving a much more pleasant purpose than usual. She's equally determined, pushing my pants down my hips until I kick them free. The first touch of skin against skin pulls sounds from both of us, half relief, half desperate hunger for more.

I stand her up and I drop to my knees before her, ignoring the sharp pain from my wound. Her eyes widen, understanding my intent a moment before my mouth finds hers. One leg drapes over my shoulder as my hands grip her hips, steadying her against the wall. She tastes like salt and sweetness, like everything I've denied myself. Her fingers tangle in my hair, nails scraping my scalp as I work her toward the edge with single-minded focus.

"Mason," she gasps, the sound of my name in that breathy voice nearly undoes me. Her body tenses, trembling on the precipice, and I know she's close.

I rise in one fluid motion, lifting her against me. Her back presses against the wall as I position myself, eyes locked with hers in one final moment of certainty. She nods, a small movement that changes everything, and I thrust forward, joining us in a single smooth motion that steals the breath from both our lungs.

For a moment, we're perfectly still, adjusting to this new reality where there's no space between us, no pretense, no barriers. Then her hips shift, a small, impatient movement that breaks the spell. I begin to move, finding a rhythm that makes her eyes flutter closed, and her head fall back against the wall.

"Look at me," I command, needing to see her, to know this is real and not some blood-loss hallucination.

Her eyes open, dark with desire but absolutely present. The connection transcends physical; something raw and honest passes between us with each movement. This isn't just sex; it's acknowledgment of everything we've been circling for months.

We don't make it long against the wall. The bed beckons—a proper surface to explore each other without the limitations of vertical positioning. I carry her there without breaking our connection, laying her back against the cool sheets. The new angle draws sounds from her that I immediately commit to memory, determined to hear them again.

Time loses meaning. There's only sensation, only her body moving with mine, only the building pressure that promises release. When it comes, it crashes through us both with an intensity that borders on violent, every muscle tensing, every nerve ending firing at once. Her name tears from my throat, a confession and a prayer.

Afterwards, we lie tangled together, her head on my chest, my fingers tracing idle patterns on her back. The constant rhythm of waves outside matches our gradually slowing heartbeats. I should feel guilt. Should be planning our next move. Should be securing the perimeter. Instead, I find myself present in a way I haven't been for years, anchored by her weight against me.

"You're thinking too loud," she murmurs against my skin.

"Old habits," I reply, pressing a kiss to her forehead. The tenderness of the gesture surprises me more than the passion that preceded it.

She shifts, looking up at me with eyes that see too much. "Regrets already?"

"No," I answer honestly. "Just wondering how long we have before reality crashes back in."

The question hangs in the air between us, neither of us having an answer. For now, it's enough to hold her, to breathe in the scent of her hair, to pretend the world outside this room doesn't exist. Reality and its consequences will find us soon enough.

Yelan's breathing has settled into the even rhythm of exhausted sleep, her body warm against mine, when something changes. A subtle shift in the ambient noise outside, the pattern of waves interrupted by something else. Footsteps. Careful, measured, trying not to be heard. My body tenses, combat instincts overriding the peaceful moment. I place my hand gently over Yelana's mouth as her eyes snap open, already reaching for the gun on the nightstand with my other hand. "Someone's outside," I whisper, holding her gaze to convey the seriousness without causing panic. "Get dressed. Quickly."

To her credit, she doesn't question or hesitate. In seconds, she's sliding from the bed, gathering clothes silently while I do the same, ignoring the burning protest from my stitched side. The wound will have to wait. Survival first, pain later. I pull on pants, not bothering with a shirt, and motion Yelana toward the kitchen area, the most defensible position with access to both potential weapons and the back exit if needed.

She understands without explanation, moving low and fast to position herself behind the counter. I toss her a knife from the block on the counter, better than nothing, and signal for absolute silence. The footsteps have reached the wooden deck that wraps around the safe house, boards creaking, amateur mistake. Professionals know to step at the edge of planks near support beams to minimize noise.

Which means either this isn't a professional, or they want us to hear them coming. Neither option feels reassuring.

I position myself beside the window, back to the wall, weapon ready. The angle gives me visual coverage of the approach without exposing my position. Three figures would be ideal, one at each entrance with a third providing overwatch, but I'm working solo with a wounded side and a civilan to protect. Not ideal odds, but I've survived worse.

The footsteps pause at the back door. I hear the soft scrape of metal on metal, someone testing the lock or inserting a pick. I raise three fingers where Yelana can see them, counting down. Two. One.

The door creaks open, hinges protesting from years of salt air exposure. I launch forward, leading with my weapon, prepared to neutralize the threat with extreme prejudice. My finger tightens on the trigger—

“Jesus Christ!” A familiar voice yelps as I pull up short, barrel of my gun stopping inches from Sophia Reyes’ forehead. She stands frozen in the doorway, hands half-raised, eyes wide with shock and fear. “It’s me! Don’t shoot!”

I lower my weapon slightly, but don't holster it. "Identify yourself," I demand, still blocking her entrance. In my peripheral vision, I see Yelana rise slightly from behind the counter, knife still gripped in white knuckles.

"Sophia Reyes, logistics director for Zentarra Enterprises," she says, voice steadier now but still pitched high with adrenaline. "Employee ID 774-385. My first car was a red Mazda that I wrecked the day I got my license. You told me that yesterday when we were reviewing security protocols."

The personal detail—one I specifically asked her as a verification question—confirms her identity. I step back, lowering the weapon completely but keeping it in hand. Old habits die hard, and today's friends have a tendency to become tomorrow's enemies in this business.

"Thank god you're both alive," she says, closing and locking the door behind her. Her usually impeccable appearance is in disarray —hair windblown, clothes wrinkled, dark circles beneath her eyes suggesting she hasn't slept. "I've been driving all night trying to find you."

"How did you know we'd be here?" Yelana asks, emerging from behind the counter but keeping the knife visible. Smart girl.

Learning fast.

"Process of elimination," Sophia answers, dumping her backpack on the small dining table with a heavy thud. "Ken's men have the main house, the downtown condo, and the mountain property under surveillance. This was the only safe house from your father's confidential file that they hadn't located yet."

She begins pulling items from the backpack—a laptop, several file folders, a satellite phone. Her movements are precise despite her obvious exhaustion, arranging the items in neat rows on the table's scarred surface.

"What happened after we escaped?" I ask, moving to check the windows and ensure we weren't followed.

Sophia's face hardens. "Ken seized control. He's telling everyone you two murdered Emelio and Sierra, then tried to kill Kendrick when he discovered the truth." She pulls a flash drive from her pocket, holding it up like evidence. "He's running the entire organization now, with Costa's backing. Anyone loyal to Yelana has been eliminated or is in hiding."

"Costa's?" Yelana repeats, sinking into a chair as the implications hit her. "Miguel was just negotiating with us yesterday."

"Not Miguel," Sophia corrects, opening the laptop and inserting the drive. "Vince. The older brother. Miguel was just the public face for the negotiations." The screen illuminates her tired features as she navigates through files. "Ken has been working with the Vasquez cartel for years, using them to move product off the books while using Vince Costa's network for distribution."

I join them at the table, scanning the documents as she pulls them up. Financial records showing payments to offshore accounts that match the ones we found in Ken's office. Shipping manifests for weapons that never reached their official destinations. Surveillance photos of Ken meeting with a man I recognize as Alejandro Vasquez, head of the cartel that controls much of the Mexican border.

"How did you get this?" I ask, impressed despite myself.

"I've been keeping my own records for months," she admits. "Something felt wrong with the inventory numbers, and your father taught me to always have backup documentation." She nods to Yelana. "I was going to bring it to you once I had concrete proof, but then... everything happened at once."

Yelana reaches across the table, gripping Sophia's hand. "You risked your life coming here."

"They would have killed me eventually anyway," Sophia says with surprising calm. "Ken's been systematically eliminating everyone loyal to your father. I was on the list—just further down than some others."

The implications settle around us like ash from a battlefield. Ken hasn't just seized control; he's orchestrating a complete purge of the old guard, consolidating power with ruthless efficiency.

"They're saying you stole fifty million in bearer bonds before murdering Kendrick," Sophia continues, pulling up news reports that show our faces plastered across financial crime bulletins. "There's an international warrant out for both of you. Every port, airport, and border crossing has your photos."

"Clever," I mutter, reluctantly impressed by the thoroughness of Ken's frame job. "He's cut off any legitimate escape routes."

Outside, the first light of dawn breaks over the ocean, pale gold filtering through the windows. We huddle around the table, three survivors of a catastrophe still unfolding, facing a decision that will define everything that follows.

"We have two options," I say, laying it out with tactical precision. "Run and disappear—new identities, new lives, leave the Zentarra empire to Ken and his cartel friends." I look directly at Yelana, seeing the fire in her eyes that tells me what she'll choose before I offer the alternative. "Or we fight back. Clear our names. Take back what's yours."

"That's not even a choice," she says, chin lifting with the same determination I've come to expect from her. "That organization is my family's legacy. My legacy."

Sophia nods, her exhaustion momentarily masked by resolve. "I have contacts who remained loyal. People who don't believe the lies about you two."

I study the evidence spread before us, weighing our resources against the massive operation Ken now controls. The odds are terrible. We're outnumbered, outgunned, and officially fugitives. Success would require perfect execution, unshakable loyalty from what few allies remain, and the element of surprise.

"If we do this," I warn, "there's no half measures. We go all in. And some of us might not make it out alive."

Yelana's hand finds mine under the table, fingers interlacing in a grip that's both a question and an answer. The touch carries the weight of everything that's passed between us—the grief, the betrayal, the unexpected connection we've found in the wreckage of her family's empire.

"Then we better not die," she says simply, as if it's a decision as easy to implement as to make.

The rising sun paints the room in shades of gold and promise. I don't tell them that dawn has always been the preferred time for executions. Some truths don't need sharing.

Instead, I squeeze Yelana's hand and begin planning a war.

SEVENTEEN
The Alliance

YELANA

Miguel Costa's yacht cuts through the water like a knife—all sleek lines and gleaming surfaces that scream money louder than any voice could. I straighten my shoulders as we approach, ignoring the tremor in my hands that hasn't fully subsided since Ken's betrayal three days ago. The vessel represents everything I need right now: power, resources, and the kind of muscle that can help me take back what's mine. It also represents everything that should terrify me—another Costa, another potential betrayal, another man who sees me as either a conquest or a threat. Maybe both.

"You sure about this?" Mason mutters beside me, his body close enough that I feel his warmth but not so close that the guards scanning us from the deck will notice. His eyes never stop moving, cataloging threats, exits, angles of fire. Even injured, he radiates the kind of lethal competence that makes my skin prickle.

"No," I admit, matching his quiet tone. "But we're out of options unless you've got a private army hidden somewhere."

Sophia adjusts the backpack containing our bargaining chips—digital records of Ken's betrayal, detailed maps of my father's compound, and security protocols that only a longtime insider could provide. Her usually immaculate appearance has been replaced by practical clothes and haunted eyes. "Miguel isn't Vince," she reminds us. "Different Costa, different agenda."

"Same bloodline," Mason counters, his hand brushing the concealed weapon at his back—the one that took thirty minutes of arguing before I convinced him to bring aboard. "Same business model."

I step onto the floating dock, feeling it shift beneath my weight. The evening air carries salt and diesel and expensive cologne—the signature scent of power in my world. "We need him more than he needs us," I remind them both. "So let me do the talking."

Two guards in tailored suits that don't quite hide their shoulder holsters escort us up the gangway. Their eyes linger on me a beat too long—assessing the daughter of Emelio Zentarra, now a fugitive, now desperate enough to seek help from a family that's been both business partner and rival for decades. I meet their gaze without flinching. Let them look. Let them wonder. Let them underestimate me.

The yacht's teak deck gleams in the fading twilight, each board polished to a soft glow that speaks of daily maintenance by people who are paid very well to remain invisible. Security cameras track our movement from discreet mounts designed to blend with the vessel's sleek architecture. I count four armed men positioned at strategic points—professionals who stand with the relaxed readiness of predators who don't need to posture.

We're led to the main cabin, a space of breathtaking luxury that manages to avoid the tackiness that often plagues the nouveau riche. Floor-to-ceiling windows offer panoramic views of the darkening sea, the last rays of sunset painting the water in shades of amber and blood. Miguel Costa rises from behind a glass table covered with maps and documents, his smile practiced but his eyes calculating.

"Miss Zentarra," he says, extending his hand. "I've been expecting you."

I take his hand, matching his firm grip. "Mr. Costa. Thank you for agreeing to meet."

"The daughter of Emelio Zentarra doesn't request meetings every day." He gestures to the leather chairs surrounding the table. "Especially not when she's wanted for murder in three countries."

"Four, actually," I correct him, taking a seat directly across from him. "Tunisia just issued their warrant this morning."

A flicker of appreciation crosses his features before he masks it. Behind me, I feel rather than see Mason position himself where he can watch both Miguel and the door. Sophia takes the seat to my right, already reaching for her backpack.

"You understand my brother is... displeased about the situation at the restaurant," Miguel says, diving straight into business. "The assassination attempt was neither authorized nor appreciated by me."

Miguel's fingers tap a rhythm against the glass tabletop. "Vince has always had his own approach to business matters. As, I believe, did your Mr. Jackson."

"Ken is not my anything," I reply, ice coating each word. "Which is why I'm here."

I lean forward, sweeping aside a satellite map of what appears to be my family's compound to create space between us. "I'm offering you exclusive distribution rights in Oregon, Washington, and British Columbia once I regain control of the Zentarra Organization." The words flow with more confidence than I feel, my father's lessons in negotiation surfacing when I need them most. "First right of refusal on any new product lines for the next five years. And a twenty percent discount on all transactions for the first twelve months."

Miguel's eyebrows lift slightly—the only indication that my offer has surprised him. "Generous," he acknowledges. "But ultimately worthless if you can't deliver."

"I can deliver."

"Can you?" He leans back, studying me with the practiced ease of a man who has sized up countless opponents across similar tables. "Ken Jackson controls your organization. Your assets are frozen. Your loyal personnel are either dead or in hiding. You're offering territories you don't control with resources you don't have."

I don't blink. Don't shift. Don't show the fear that churns beneath my practiced calm. "I'm offering the future. Ken is offering the past."

Miguel tilts his head, considering. "I require Northern California as well. And thirty percent discount for eighteen months."

"Northern California is non-negotiable," I counter immediately, knowing it's one of our most profitable territories. "The discount stops at fifteen percent for twelve months. But I'll throw in preferential supplier status with our Southeast Asian connections."

A slight smile plays at the corner of his mouth. "Twenty percent for fifteen months. And I want your father's contact in Jakarta."

"Eighteen percent," I counter, feeling Mason shift behind me. "And you get the Jakarta contact after Ken is removed. Not before."

Sophia opens her laptop, the screen's glow illuminating her face in the dimming cabin. "I've brought the security protocols for Ken's current operation," she says, her voice steady despite the tension radiating from her posture. "Complete building schematics, guard rotations, access codes to the lower levels." She slides an encrypted drive across the glass table. "Everything you need to coordinate a successful infiltration."

Miguel takes the drive, examining it between manicured fingers before passing it to one of his security personnel. "And in return, you want...?"

"Manpower," I state flatly. "Vehicles. Weapons. Logistical support for an operation tomorrow night."

"Tomorrow?" His surprise seems genuine. "That's ambitious."

"Ken thinks we're still regrouping," I explain. "Still licking our wounds. The longer we wait, the more time he has to consolidate power and eliminate anyone still loyal to me."

Miguel studies me for a long moment, his expression unreadable. I feel the weight of his assessment—not just of my offer, but of me. My capability. My resolve. My worthiness as an ally or an adversary.

"You are very much your father's daughter," he says finally. "But with your mother's spine." The observation carries a strange mix of admiration and calculation. "I'll provide what you need. On one additional condition."

Here it comes—the twist, the demand, the poison pill. I steel myself. "Which is?"

"When this is over, we renegotiate our families' territorial agreements. All of them. A fresh start."

The request hides a thousand potential traps, but also opportunities. I nod slowly. "Agreed. But I select the negotiation location."

Something that might be genuine respect flickers in his eyes. "Done." He extends his hand across the table.

I take it, feeling his grip tighten around mine, holding a beat too long. His thumb brushes across my knuckles in a gesture that manages to be both business-appropriate and uncomfortably intimate.

"To successful ventures, Miss Zentarra," he says, his gaze holding mine.

I retrieve my hand with deliberate calm. "To success," I echo, feeling Mason's presence behind me like a physical touch—solid, protective, and radiating a tension that has nothing to do with the armed men surrounding us.

Sleep refuses to find me tonight, though my body aches with exhaustion. I stare at the yacht's ceiling, listening to water lap against the hull and wondering if I'll be alive this time tomorrow. The plans are set. Miguel's men have their orders. Weapons have been distributed and routes memorized. There's nothing left to do but wait—and waiting has always been my personal hell. I swing my legs over the edge of the too-soft bed, my bare feet meeting cold floor. The silk pajamas Sophia scrounged for me whisper against my skin as I stand, decision made before I can second-guess myself. If I might die tomorrow, I'm not spending my last night alone with my fear.

The yacht's corridor is dimly lit, the luxury that seemed ostentatious by day now shrouded in shadows that make the space feel almost intimate. I count doors as I pass—Sophia's cabin, then the empty one Miguel offered "in case plans need to be adjusted overnight," his eyes lingering on me as he said it, and finally Mason's. I hesitate, suddenly aware of my racing heartbeat, my tangled hair, the thin silk covering my body. This isn't a tactical decision. This is something else entirely.

I knock before I can lose my nerve.

Silence stretches long enough that I consider retreating when the door opens, revealing Mason in cargo pants and nothing else. His chest bears a constellation of scars—some old and silvered, others fresh and angry, including the knife wound from Ken that I stitched myself. His hair is damp, like he's recently showered, and the scent of him—soap and gun oil and something essentially him—hits me with physical force.

"Can't sleep?" he asks, voice rough at the edges.

I shake my head. "Too much thinking."

He steps back, inviting me in without words. The cabin is smaller than mine, with just enough room for a narrow bed, a desk, and the weapons laid out in precise rows on a cloth. A cleaning rod still sits in his hand, and I realize I've interrupted his methodical preparation.

"Sorry," I gesture to the disassembled gun. "I can go."

"Stay." The word hangs between us, simple and complex all at once. He returns to the desk but doesn't immediately resume his work. "You should be resting. Tomorrow won't be easy."

I sit on the edge of his bed, the only other surface available. The mattress dips beneath my weight, and moonlight streams through the small porthole, painting silver streaks across the floor. "That's why I can't sleep. Keep thinking about everything that could go wrong."

"That's my job," he says, the ghost of a smile touching his lips. "Professional worrier."

"And what are your professional worries telling you about tomorrow?"

His hands move automatically, reassembling the weapon with practiced efficiency. "That it's high-risk. That Miguel's men are wildcards. That Ken has home-field advantage." The pieces click together under his fingers, becoming deadly with each connection. "That you should be somewhere far away while we handle this."

"Not happening," I counter immediately. "It's my organization, my fight."

"Your funeral if things go bad." His bluntness doesn't surprise me anymore. It's one of the things I've come to value about him—no sugar-coating, no gentle lies.

"Maybe." I draw my knees up, wrapping my arms around them. "What happens after? If we succeed, I mean."

He sets the now-assembled gun down, his movements deliberate. "You take back control. Rebuild what Ken destroyed. Move forward."

"And you?" The question emerges smaller than I intended, betraying more than I meant to reveal. "Is that when you walk away? Debt paid in full?"

His eyes find mine in the dim light, his expression unreadable. "Is that what you think this is? A debt?"

"Isn't it?" I challenge, heart hammering against my ribs. "My father saved your life. You promised to protect me in return. Sounds like a debt to me."

He stands, crossing the small space to sit beside me on the bed. The mattress shifts with his weight, sliding me closer to him until our thighs press together. "It started that way," he admits, voice low. "But that's not what it is now."

"What is it then?" I press, needing to hear him say it.

His hand lifts, hesitates, then brushes a strand of hair from my face with surprising gentleness. "Complicated."

"That's a cop-out answer." I turn to face him fully, gathering my courage. "I'm in love with you, Mason. That's not complicated. It just is."

The confession hangs in the air between us, impossible to take back. His eyes widen slightly, the only indication that I've surprised him. For one terrible moment, he says nothing, and I feel myself teetering on the edge of humiliation.

Then his hand cups my face, calloused palm warm against my cheek. "You deserve better than me," he says roughly. "Someone who isn't broken. Someone closer to your age. Someone with less blood on their hands."

"I don't want better," I whisper. "I want you."

Something breaks in his expression then, restraint crumbling like a dam giving way. He pulls me onto his lap in one fluid motion, his mouth finding mine with desperate hunger. I wrap my arms around his neck, pressing myself against the heat of his chest, feeling his heart hammer against mine.

"I love you," he murmurs against my lips, the words dragged from somewhere deep and hidden. "Not because of any debt. Because of you. Only you."

His hands slide beneath my silk top, finding skin that burns for his touch. I gasp as his fingers trace my spine, my ribs, the curve of my breast. We move together with a sync that speaks of bodies recognizing their match, of souls finding harbor after too long adrift.

"Are you sure?" he asks as I tug at his belt, his voice strained with the effort of restraint.

"I've never been more sure of anything," I answer, and the last barrier between us dissolves.

Clothes fall away under urgent hands. His fingers find scars I've never shown anyone—the bullet graze along my hip from a kidnapping attempt at sixteen, the thin white line beneath my ribs from a broken bottle in a club fight. I explore his body with equal reverence, tracing the map of violence written across his skin—shrapnel pockmarks across his shoulder, the puckered circle of an old bullet wound near his collarbone, the fresh pink line where I stitched him together myself.

When I straddle him, taking him inside me with a gasp that he captures with his mouth, the world narrows to this cabin, this man, this moment stolen from the jaws of death that wait for us tomorrow. I move above him, finding a rhythm that makes his hands tighten on my hips, his breath catching in his throat. His eyes never leave mine—this connection more intimate than the joining of our bodies.

"Yelana," he breathes, my name a prayer and a plea as I rock against him.

I lean down to kiss him, our bodies sliding together in the silver moonlight that paints us in monochrome—light and shadow, life and death, love and war all compressed into this single point of connection. His hands guide my movements, sometimes gentle, sometimes urgent, always reverent.

When release claims us both, it's like breaking the surface after too long underwater—gasping, desperate, alive with a clarity that only proximity to death can bring. I collapse against his chest, his arms wrapping around me with fierce protectiveness, both of us trembling with the aftershocks of pleasure and the weight of what we've admitted to each other.

"Stay," he whispers against my hair, echoing his earlier invitation with new meaning.

I nod against his skin, knowing he means more than just tonight. Knowing that whatever happens tomorrow, whatever blood is spilled or victories claimed, we've already won something precious and unlikely—something worth fighting for beyond revenge or reclamation.

His fingers trace idle patterns on my skin as our breathing slows, the gentle rock of the yacht on night waters lulling us toward a peace neither of us expected to find on the eve of war.

Mason

Yelana's breathing settles into a rhythm against my chest, her body curled into mine like she's always belonged there. The yacht rocks gently beneath us, moonlight painting silver streaks across her bare shoulder where it peeks above the thin sheet. I trace my fingers along her skin, memorizing the texture, the warmth, the reality of her. Twenty-four hours ago, I wouldn't have allowed myself this—this moment, this woman, this fragile hope for something beyond survival. But death has a way of clarifying priorities, and tomorrow carries enough risk to justify tonight's surrender.

The cabin feels impossibly small with her in it, every molecule of air charged with her presence. Outside, water slaps against the hull in a steady rhythm that reminds me we're suspended between worlds—not quite on land, not fully at sea. A fitting metaphor for where we find ourselves: between her father's legacy and her future, between my duty and my desire, between yesterday's ghosts and tomorrow's uncertainty.

Her fingers draw idle patterns on my chest, circling old scars like she's connecting constellations. The touch sends electricity racing beneath my skin, a reminder that I'm still alive despite numerous attempts by various parties to change that status. Each scar tells a story she hasn't asked for yet—the jagged line from a knife fight in Baghdad, the puckered circle where a bullet passed clean through my shoulder in Kandahar, the fresh pink seam where she stitched me together herself after Ken's betrayal.

She shifts suddenly, propping herself up on one elbow. Her hair falls in a dark curtain around her face, and the moonlight catches in her eyes, turning them to liquid silver.

"Promise me something," she says, voice low but intense.

"Depends on what you're asking," I answer honestly. Some promises I can't make, won't make, even for her.

Her hand flattens against my chest, right over my heart. "Don't sacrifice yourself tomorrow. Don't play the hero." The pressure of her palm increases, fingers digging slightly into my flesh. "I've lost everyone else. I won't lose you too."

The request hits me like a physical blow. It's the one promise I'm not sure I can keep, the one that conflicts directly with my core mission—keeping her alive, whatever the cost.

"Yelana—"

"Promise me," she insists, eyes never leaving mine. "I need you to come back. Not just for the mission. For after."

I cover her hand with mine, feeling her pulse through our joined fingers. "I promise I'll do everything possible to come back to you," I say carefully, threading the needle between comfort and commitment.

She studies my face, looking for the lie. She's getting better at reading me—a fact that's both endearing and dangerous. I hold her gaze steadily, letting her see enough truth to satisfy her. Yes, I want to come back. Yes, I want an after with her. What I don't let her see is the absolute certainty that if it comes down to her life or mine, I've already made my choice.

"Okay," she says finally, settling back against me.

I pull her closer, burying my face in her hair to hide the shadows I know must be visible in my eyes. The scent of her—something floral mixed with the saltwater air and our shared exertion—fills my senses, anchoring me to this moment when my mind tries to slip forward to tomorrow's potential outcomes or backward to past failures.

Kerry's face flashes unbidden behind my closed eyelids—her body in the hospital bed, broken beyond repair by the drunk driver who took her and my parents in one senseless moment. The steady beep of monitors counting down to a flatline I couldn't prevent. The cold weight of her engagement ring in my palm after they finally convinced me to leave her side. The suffocating certainty that everyone I love eventually pays the price for that love.

I tighten my arms around Yelana, suddenly desperate to feel her warmth, her life, her presence. She responds immediately, pressing closer, as if sensing the ghost that's slipped into the cabin with us.

"Tell me about her sometime," she whispers against my chest, startling me with her perception. "Kerry. When you're ready."

I swallow hard, nodding against her hair without speaking. Another time. Another night. If we get that luxury.

"Let's go through the plan once more," I say instead, needing the solid ground of tactics and strategy beneath my feet again. "Miguel's men will create a diversion at the east entrance of the warehouse compound. Automated security systems will redirect guards to that location."

Yelana shifts, not pulling away but adjusting to see my face. "While we enter through the delivery bay on the west side using Sophia's access codes," she continues, accepting the change in topic. "The security cameras loop for eight minutes—that's our window to reach the server room."

Her finger traces the outline of the warehouse on my chest, mapping our infiltration route across my skin. The gesture is oddly intimate—planning death and reclamation while skin touches skin.

"Once we secure the server room," I add, "Sophia downloads the files that prove Ken's embezzlement and ties to both Costa organizations. Those go to your father's allies in three different agencies."

"And Miguel's team moves to secure the main floor while we head for my father's vault," she finishes, her finger now circling the spot over my heart. "Where we find the contingency protocols and the list of loyal contacts Dad kept for emergencies."

I catch her hand, bringing her fingers to my lips. "You stay with me at all times. No exceptions. If we get separated, you retreat immediately to extraction point Charlie."

She starts to protest, but I shake my head. "Non-negotiable. Miguel's men are there for the warehouse and its contents. I'm there for you."

"I'm not helpless, Mason." A flash of that Zentarra fire in her eyes. "I can handle myself."

"Never said you were helpless," I counter, brushing hair back from her face. "But Ken wants you dead more than he wants anything else. You're the only legitimate threat to his control of the organization. He'll have given specific orders concerning you."

She considers this, then nods reluctantly. "Fine. But the same goes for you. No unnecessary risks."

I don't respond directly, instead pulling her down for a kiss that starts gentle but quickly deepens with the urgency of everything we're not saying. Her body melts against mine, the heat between us building again despite the exhaustion weighing our limbs.

Later, as she finally drifts toward sleep, her breathing evens out against my neck. I remain awake, one hand stroking her hair, the other resting near the gun I've placed within easy reach. The yacht rocks gently in the harbor, and distant lights from the shore cast intermittent patterns across the cabin ceiling.

I watch her sleep and wonder about impossibilities—a future where age differences and violent pasts don't matter, where the daughter of an arms dealer and a broken ex-NAVY SEAL might build something lasting from the wreckage of their separate tragedies. It seems as unlikely as surviving tomorrow's mission unscathed, yet I find myself planning for it anyway. Mapping escape routes to a life I've never allowed myself to imagine.

The night deepens around us, the hours before dawn ticking away toward whatever fate waits at the warehouse. I hold her against me, this woman who's somehow become the center of a world I thought had lost its axis, and make silent promises I hope I can keep.

EIGHTEEN
Infiltration

Mason

The maintenance uniform itches against my skin as I adjust the collar for the tenth time in five minutes. Too tight around the throat, too loose in the shoulders. Not built for someone with my frame, but that's the point—we're not supposed to stand out. I check my concealed Glock, making sure it sits snug against my lower back, then glance at Yelana and Sophia beside me. Miguel's security badges dangle from our belts, tickets to a party where we're definitely not welcome guests. Yelana catches my eye and gives me a small nod, her face set with determination that reminds me why I'm here, why I'll always be here as long as she needs me.

"Three guards at the south entrance," I murmur, scanning the warehouse exterior. "Two more patrolling the fence line. Standard formation, minimal overlap in sight lines. Sophia, you ready?"

Sophia nods, her fingers dancing across the tablet she's cradled against her chest like a newborn. "Security feed loop engaged. We've got eight minutes before the system refreshes."

The warehouse door beeps green when Sophia swipes Miguel's borrowed access card. We slip inside, immediately engulfed by the cavernous space with its dimly lit pathways between towering stacks of shipping containers. The air hangs heavy with the smell of gun oil, metal, and cardboard—the distinct scent of weapons in storage that I'd recognize blindfolded. My eyes adjust quickly, picking out the red pinpricks of security cameras and the shadowy outlines of crates labeled in languages from across the globe.

"Spread out," I instruct, keeping my voice low. "Fifteen feet maximum separation. Priority locations are marked on your tablets. Place bugs, confirm signal, move on."

I take the center aisle, Yelana the left, Sophia the right. Each step is measured, careful. Years of combat operations have taught me how to move silently even in standard-issue boots that squeak on polished concrete. I reach the first target—a metal support column near what appears to be an inventory control station—and press the first surveillance device against the underside of a desk. The adhesive makes a soft suctioning sound as it attaches.

"Bug one active," Sophia confirms in my earpiece. "Signal strength optimal."

I move deeper into the warehouse, placing devices behind electrical panels, beneath tables, inside hollow sections of support beams. Reaching for a high spot above a shipping container, pain lances through my side where Ken's knife found me days ago. The stitched wound pulls and burns, forcing me to grit my teeth against a hiss of discomfort. I adjust my stance, using my shoulder instead of stretching fully, and manage to place the bug without reopening anything.

"You okay?" Yelana's voice comes through my earpiece, somehow knowing I'm hurting without even seeing me.

"Fine," I reply automatically, though the persistent throb tells a different story. "Four minutes left on the loop. Keep moving."

From my position, I can see Yelana across the warehouse floor, moving with a grace that surprises me despite having seen her in action before. Gone is the socialite who once complained about broken nails; in her place moves a predator—sleek, focused, aware of her surroundings in a way that speaks of instinct rather than training. She places her bugs with efficient precision, never hesitating, never second-guessing. Pride swells in my chest, followed immediately by fear—she's too good at this, too comfortable in this dangerous world.

"North section clear," Sophia reports. "Moving to secondary targets."

"Copy that," I respond, working my way toward the central office space where Ken likely conducts his business. "Yelana, stay in visual range."

She acknowledges with a slight hand gesture without breaking stride, already anticipating my concern. We've developed a shorthand that transcends verbal communication, our bodies intuitively understanding each other's movements. It should scare me how quickly this happened, how deeply she's embedded herself in my tactical awareness.

The warehouse reveals its secrets as we progress—crates of Russian RPGs stacked next to Israeli ammunition, Chinese-manufactured electronics beside American body armor. Ken's been building an arsenal that crosses every international boundary, enough firepower to supply a small war or topple several governments. I place bugs near inventory lists, shipping manifestos, anything that might capture conversations about destinations or buyers.

"Two minutes," Sophia warns as I approach the final target—Ken's private office, a glass-walled space overlooking the warehouse floor.

The door yields to Sophia's electronic skeleton key, and I slip inside, immediately assessing the room. Desk positioned to see anyone approaching. Computer screen angled away from the windows. Two exits, including what appears to be a private back door. I place bugs beneath the desk, inside a lamp base, and behind a framed photo of Ken shaking hands with a South American official I recognize from intelligence briefings.

"Final placement confirmed," Sophia says. "Signal strong. Thirty seconds to system reset. Move to extraction point."

We converge at our predetermined exit point, moving with practiced efficiency that speaks to hours spent reviewing floorplans and security protocols. So far, so good. Almost too good.

That's when I hear it—the sharp intake of breath from a man to our left.

"Hey! You're Zentarra's kid!"

The burly security guard's hand is already reaching for his radio when I step between him and Yelana, but it's too late. His shout echoes across the warehouse floor, and suddenly the space erupts with activity. Alarm klaxons wail, bathing everything in pulsing red light. The rhythmic thunder of boots announces guards converging from every direction.

"Move!" I grab Yelana's arm, pulling her toward our secondary exit route as Sophia bolts ahead, already tapping commands into her tablet that might buy us precious seconds.

We sprint through the labyrinth of shipping containers, my body operating on muscle memory and adrenaline that temporarily silences the protest from my injured side. Yelana matches my pace stride for stride, her hand finding mine as we round a corner and come face-to-face with two guards. Without breaking momentum, I drop to one knee, forming a platform with my interlaced fingers. She steps into my hands with perfect timing, and I launch her upward. She catches the top of the shipping container, swinging her legs over in one fluid motion before reaching back to grasp my outstretched arm, pulling me up beside her.

Below, guards shout in confusion, momentarily losing sight of us.

"This way," I whisper, leading her across the tops of containers, mapping an aerial route through the warehouse.

At the edge of one container, I drop first, breaking her fall as she follows. We slide beneath a stationary forklift just as flashlight beams sweep the area. Her body presses against mine in the narrow space, her breath warm against my neck. For a second, the world narrows to just this—her heartbeat against my chest, her eyes meeting mine in silent communication. Then we're moving again, her pulling me through a gap between crates that my broader shoulders barely fit through.

"Six o'clock," I warn as a guard appears behind us.

Yelana doesn't hesitate, grabbing a loose pipe from nearby and hurling it across the warehouse. The clattering distraction buys us precious seconds to duck behind a stack of wooden pallets. We move in perfect synchronicity, each anticipating the other's movements. When I pause to check our flank, she watches our rear. When she stumbles slightly on an uneven floor grate, my hand is already there to steady her.

"Exit route compromised," Sophia's voice crackles through our earpieces. "Redirecting to loading bay. Twenty meters east of your position."

Red emergency lights strobe overhead, throwing disorienting shadows as we run. A bullet sings past my ear, embedding itself in a crate inches from Yelana's head. I pull her behind a forklift, shielding her body with mine as I draw my weapon.

"Stay low," I instruct, firing twice to force our pursuers into cover.

The loading bay doors loom ahead, Sophia's silhouette barely visible as she waves us forward. Yelana sprints beside me, neither of us breaking stride as we hurtle toward escape, the sounds of pursuit closing in behind us with every passing second.

I drag Yelana behind a stack of wooden crates as bullets pepper the metal containers above us. My lungs burn with exertion, the knife wound in my side screaming in protest at our frantic escape. The warehouse has transformed from quiet infiltration to chaotic battleground in less than two minutes—guards shouting coordinates, alarms wailing, the metallic echo of bullets ricocheting off steel. I check my weapon, nine rounds left. Not enough for a prolonged firefight, especially not with Yelana to protect. I need a better exit strategy, and fast.

"Sophia," I whisper into my comm unit. "Position?"

Static crackles in my ear before her voice breaks through. "Northeast corner. Guards have cut me off from your location. Working on alternate route."

A flash of movement in the adjacent aisle catches my eye—not guards, something else. I press Yelana further into cover, my body shielding hers as I peer through a narrow gap between crates. Five men gather in what appears to be an impromptu meeting space, their backs to us. The central figure's posture is unmistakable even at this distance—Ken Jackson, his silver hair gleaming under the emergency lights.

"That's him," Yelana breathes against my ear, her body tensing like a coiled spring. "And those men with him—"

I see it the moment she does. The mercenaries flanking Ken are the same ones from the funeral attack—I recognize the tall one with the distinctive scar running down his neck, the compact figure who moved with unmistakable ex-military precision. These aren't random hired guns; they're the same team that tried to kill Yelana at her parents' grave.

Her hand clutches my arm with bruising force, body trembling with rage rather than fear. I feel her shift, preparing to move, and clamp my arm across her midsection, holding her firmly against me.

"Don't," I whisper, my lips nearly touching her ear. "We need evidence, not revenge. Not yet."

She's rigid against me for three heartbeats before the tension partially drains from her muscles. Not surrender, but strategic patience. I feel a surge of pride even as concern tightens my chest—she's learning to channel her impulses, but each lesson makes her more dangerous, more like her father.

Ken's voice carries across the space between us, clear enough that I can make out every damning word. "The timetable has accelerated. She's made her move with Costa's people faster than anticipated."

"We have men inside Miguel's organization," the scarred mercenary responds, his accent vaguely Eastern European. "But we haven't pinpointed her location yet."

"Find her," Ken snaps, handing over a thick manila folder. "This contains everything—security codes to her remaining safe houses, known associates, the kill order with payment confirmation."

The smaller mercenary flips through the folder, nodding with professional assessment. "And the timeline?"

"Immediate elimination," Ken replies without hesitation. "Once this is done, the organization is mine. Emelio and Sierra had to go, and now their precious daughter needs to disappear too."

Beside me, Yelana's breath catches, the only outward sign of the emotional impact of hearing Ken casually discuss her parents' murders. Her hand slips into her pocket, extracting her phone with slow, deliberate movements. She activates the recording function, angling the device toward the conversation while remaining hidden behind our cover.

"Vince Costa is getting impatient," the scarred mercenary warns. "He expected control of the Los Angeles corridor as payment for his assistance."

Ken's laugh is cold, dismissive. "Vince will get exactly what we agreed upon—twenty percent of distribution rights, nothing more. Once the girl is eliminated, I'll have the board's full confidence. They'll fall in line or join her parents."

The explicit confession sends a chill down my spine despite the stuffy warehouse air. Yelana's face hardens into a mask of control that would make her father proud, her hand steady as she continues recording. This is the evidence we need—Ken's own words confirming the conspiracy, the connection to Vince Costa, the premeditated murder of Emelio and Sierra. Enough to turn Miguel's organization fully against Ken, enough to convince the remaining Zentarra loyalists to rally behind Yelana.

The crunch of a boot on concrete splinters the moment. A guard rounds the corner behind us, his surprised intake of breath preceding his shout by milliseconds.

"Here! They're over here!"

Everything accelerates to combat speed. I tackle the guard before he can raise his weapon, driving my elbow into his throat to silence him, but it's too late—Ken and the mercenaries have heard. Shouts erupt from multiple directions as our position is compromised.

"Run!" I pull Yelana to her feet, pushing her ahead of me as gunfire erupts behind us. We sprint down the narrow corridor between shipping containers, bullets splintering wood and sparking off metal around us.

"This way!" Yelana veers suddenly, pulling me toward an emergency exit sign glowing red in the distance. Smart—she's remembering the building schematics we memorized, identifying the shortest route out.

We dodge between forklifts and pallets, guards converging from multiple directions. Ken's voice rises above the chaos, cold with fury: "Shoot to kill! Don't let them escape!"

The exit door is thirty feet ahead when I spot the guard taking position at the intersection of two aisles—kneeling, weapon raised, sighting directly at Yelana's back. Time compresses into crystalline focus. I lunge forward, shoving Yelana hard toward the door while pivoting to face the threat.

The impact feels like a sledgehammer to my shoulder, spinning me halfway around. Hot wetness immediately spreads across my chest, the familiar copper scent of blood filling my nostrils. Not my first bullet, probably not my last, but the shock of it still steals my breath for crucial seconds.

"Mason!" Yelana's scream seems distant through the sudden ringing in my ears.

I stumble, catching myself against a shipping container, leaving a smeared handprint of blood on the metal. Tactical assessment is automatic: left shoulder, through and through, no arterial spray. Painful but not immediately fatal. I can still move, still fight, still get her out.

"Go," I manage to growl, pushing off the container and forcing my legs to cooperate. "Get to the door."

Instead of obeying, she's suddenly beside me, her arm around my waist, taking my weight. "Not without you." The steel in her voice brooks no argument.

Pain radiates from the wound with each step, blood soaking through my uniform, making the fabric stick to my skin in a nauseating way I've experienced too many times before. I want to argue, to force her ahead, to fulfill my promise to her father to keep her safe at any cost. But my body betrays me, growing heavier as blood loss begins to take its toll.

"Almost there," she encourages, practically dragging me the final ten feet to the exit.

The door crashes open under Yelana's shoulder, spilling us into the cool night air. A van screeches to a halt mere feet away, its side door sliding open to reveal Sophia behind the wheel.

"Get in!" she shouts, eyes widening at the sight of my blood-soaked uniform.

Yelana heaves me into the van, climbing in after me as bullets ping against the vehicle's reinforced exterior. The door slides shut, and Sophia floors the accelerator, tires screeching against asphalt as we lurch away from the warehouse.

"They're following!" Sophia warns, swerving sharply onto a side street as headlights appear in our rearview mirror.

I pull myself up enough to check through the rear window. Two black SUVs in pursuit, gaining quickly. My vision blurs at the edges, but training keeps me functional despite the pain.

"Take the alley three blocks ahead," I instruct, pressing my hand against the wound to slow the bleeding. "Too narrow for their vehicles."

Yelana tears strips from her uniform, creating a makeshift pressure bandage that she presses firmly against my shoulder. Her hands are steady, her face set with determination, but her eyes betray her fear when they meet mine.

"You promised," she whispers, accusation and concern mingling in her voice as Sophia's driving throws us against each other with each turn. "No heroics."

"Technically," I manage through gritted teeth, "I promised to come back to you." The van rattles over potholes, sending fresh waves of pain through my injured shoulder. "Still keeping that one."

Her face softens slightly, even as she maintains pressure on my wound. The van lurches into the narrow alley, scraping against brick walls as Sophia navigates the tight space at dangerous speed.

Behind us, our pursuers' headlights disappear as they're forced to find alternate routes.

"Stay with me," Yelana commands, her free hand cupping my face, forcing me to focus on her eyes. "We got what we came for. Now stay with me."

I nod, the movement requiring more effort than it should. The recording on her phone combined with our planted bugs gives us everything we need to destroy Ken. But first, I need to stay conscious long enough to make it to safety. For her. Always for her.

Miguel's safehouse swims into focus as the van's side door slides open, revealing a modern apartment building with the kind of security features that speak my language—reinforced windows, multiple cameras with overlapping fields of vision, controlled entry points. My tactical assessment is automatic despite the bullet hole in my shoulder, turning each movement into an exercise in pain management. Blood has soaked through Yelana's makeshift bandage, creating a sticky mess that pulls at my skin when Sophia helps me from the vehicle. I bite down on a groan that threatens to escape as my feet hit concrete, refusing to show weakness even as my vision temporarily grays around the edges.

"Lean on me," Yelana instructs, sliding her shoulder under my good arm. Her voice carries that specific blend of command and concern that reminds me of field medics I've known—people who understand that their care isn't optional.

We move through a service entrance, bypassing the main lobby where civilian eyes might notice a blood-soaked man being half-carried by two women. The service elevator hums as it carries us to the top floor, the building's systems humming with the quiet efficiency of expensive security. My training notes exit routes, camera positions, potential defensive choke points—information cataloged for later even as blood continues seeping through my fingers.

The apartment itself is a testament to Miguel Costa's understanding of what constitutes proper security. Floor-to-ceiling windows that most would consider a vulnerability are made from ballistic glass thick enough to stop small arms fire. The entryway features a reinforced door with three separate locking mechanisms. Inside, the sleek modern furniture is arranged to provide clear sightlines throughout the open-concept living area. Nothing that screams "safe house" to civilian eyes, but everything a professional would want.

"Bathroom," Sophia directs, already pulling a medical kit from beneath the kitchen sink. "Better light, contained space for blood cleanup."

They guide me to a bathroom larger than some apartments I've lived in, all gleaming white tile and chrome fixtures that will soon be stained with my blood. Yelana helps me onto the edge of the massive soaking tub, her hands gentle but insistent as Sophia lays out medical supplies on the marble counter with practiced efficiency.

"This needs to come off," Sophia says, producing trauma shears from the kit and attacking my uniform without waiting for permission. The blood-soaked fabric yields easily to the sharp blades, peeling away to reveal the mess beneath.

Yelana's sharp intake of breath is the only reaction to the sight of my torso—a roadmap of old scars now featuring a fresh, angry hole just below my left collarbone. Blood continues to seep from both entry and exit wounds, creating crimson rivulets down my chest and back.

"Through and through," Sophia assesses professionally, already pulling on nitrile gloves. "Clean entry, slightly jagged exit. Missed major vessels but there might be bone fragments."

"Just patch it enough so I can function," I instruct, my voice rougher than intended. "We don't have time for proper medical care."

Sophia ignores me, preparing an antiseptic solution. "Hold him steady," she tells Yelana, who positions herself behind me, hands firm on my good shoulder and waist.

The antiseptic hits like liquid fire, sending fresh waves of agony radiating from the wound. My muscles seize involuntarily, a grunt escaping through clenched teeth despite my best efforts to remain stoic. Yelana's grip tightens, her fingers digging into my skin to keep me from jerking away from Sophia's ministrations.

"Do you want something for the pain?" Sophia asks, already probing the wound with forceps, searching for bullet fragments.

"No." The answer is automatic, born from years of experience. "Need to stay sharp."

The forceps find something embedded in muscle, and my vision momentarily whites out as Sophia extracts a small metal fragment. The clink as she drops it into a metal dish seems unnaturally loud in the tense silence of the bathroom.

"I've done this before," Yelana says softly as Sophia continues working. "With you. After Ken stabbed you."

The memory surfaces through the pain haze—her hands steady as she stitched the knife wound, her face set with determination, the intimate moment that followed. Different circumstances, same determination in her eyes now.

"You're getting too much practice," I manage, attempting humor that falls flat when Sophia extracts another fragment, sending fresh blood oozing down my chest.

The wound cleaning and stitching continues in tense silence, interrupted only by my controlled breathing and occasional instructions from Sophia. The bullet took a clean path through muscle, missing bone and major blood vessels—lucky by combat injury standards, though it doesn't feel particularly fortunate as Sophia drives the needle through my flesh again and again, pulling the edges of the wound together with neat, even sutures.

"You need blood," she says as she applies the final bandage, "but this should hold if you don't do anything stupid in the next twenty-four hours."

"No promises," I reply, already testing my range of motion, cataloging exactly how much function I've retained. Enough to fight. Not enough to win easily. But winning has never been about physical perfection—it's about will, about the ability to push through pain when necessary. And tomorrow, it will be necessary.

"Go check the footage," I tell Yelana, who hovers uncertainly as Sophia cleans up the medical supplies. "See what our bugs captured."

She nods, disappearing into the main living area where her laptop waits. I pull myself to my feet, refusing Sophia's offered hand, and follow more slowly, each step a careful negotiation between movement and pain management.

In the living room, Yelana has already connected her phone to the laptop, downloading the recording of Ken's damning confession. The audio plays with crystal clarity through the apartment's sound system, Ken's voice filling the space with evidence of his betrayal.

"Once this is done, the organization is mine. Emelio and Sierra had to go, and now their precious daughter needs to disappear too."

Tears well in Yelana's eyes as she hears her parents' murders discussed so callously, but she blinks them away quickly, focusing instead on the technical aspects of enhancing the audio and creating backup copies. Her hands move with purpose across the keyboard, grief transmuted into action. I recognize the coping mechanism—channeling emotion into tactical response, something I've done countless times in the aftermath of losing teammates.

"We have him," she says, voice steady despite the moisture still clinging to her lashes. "This plus the surveillance footage from the bugs gives us everything we need to destroy him."

Sophia returns from the bathroom, her hands clean but her expression grim. "I need to check the perimeter and verify our exit routes for tomorrow. The building has blind spots in the security coverage that need manual verification."

She disappears through the front door, leaving Yelana and me alone in the suddenly quiet apartment. The adrenaline that's been carrying me begins to ebb, leaving behind pain that pulses with each heartbeat and fatigue that makes even standing an act of will.

"Come with me," Yelana says, noticing my deteriorating condition. She takes my hand, leading me toward a glass door that opens onto a rooftop terrace.

The night air hits my skin with surprising coolness after the apartment's warmth. The terrace offers a panoramic view of Los

Angeles spread below us, lights twinkling like fallen stars against the darkness. Tactically, it's exposed—but the surrounding buildings are lower, making it defensible. She guides me to a cushioned bench where I can lean back, taking weight off my injured side.

"You took a bullet for me," she says quietly, her fingers brushing the edge of the bandage visible above the clean t-shirt Sophia found for me. "Again."

"Occupational hazard," I reply, attempting to lighten her mood.

"Don't." Her eyes harden slightly. "Don't dismiss it like it doesn't matter. Like you don't matter."

Her hand finds mine, our fingers intertwining with the easy familiarity that still surprises me. How quickly she's become essential, how completely she's dismantled the professional distance I maintained for decades.

"We've got him now," I say, squeezing her fingers gently. "The recording, the bugs, Miguel's backing—it's enough to end this."

She nods, her gaze drifting over the city lights before returning to my face. Her free hand reaches up to trace the line of my jaw, the touch feather-light yet grounding. "I thought I'd lost you when I saw you get hit. For a second, I couldn't breathe, couldn't think."

"I'm harder to kill than that," I assure her, leaning into her touch despite myself. "It'll take more than Ken's hired guns to keep me from coming back to you."

Her eyes search mine, finding whatever confirmation she needs before she leans forward, pressing her lips gently against mine. The kiss is different from our previous ones—not driven by desperate passion or the fear of impending death, but by something deeper, more certain. A promise.

When she pulls back, her expression has shifted from vulnerability to determination. "Tomorrow we end this," she says, hand still cradling my face. "We take back what's mine, and we make Ken pay for everything—my parents, your shoulder, all of it."

I nod, knowing that tomorrow carries risks that neither of us can fully calculate. Ken will be desperate, cornered, at his most dangerous. But looking at Yelana now, backlit by the city she was born to command, I find myself believing in something I haven't trusted in years: a future beyond the next mission, the next fight, the next day.

"Together," I say, the word carrying more weight than any tactical plan or strategic assessment could convey.

Her smile carries equal parts tenderness and steel as she leans her head against my good shoulder, both of us looking out over the city that will become our battlefield all too soon.

NINETEEN
Confrontation

YELANA

I move like a ghost through the halls of my own home, the marble floors cold and familiar beneath my feet. Each step brings a flood of memories—running down these corridors as a child, walking them in grief after Juan died, and now stalking them with vengeance in my heart. The bulletproof vest beneath my tailored suit feels like armor, heavy and reassuring against my skin. My father's voice echoes in my head: "In business, Yelana, timing is everything." Never has his wisdom felt more relevant than now, as we prepare to reclaim what Ken stole from us—from me.

Miguel's men file behind us like shadows, their movements precise and silent. These halls weren't built for stealth—they were designed to impress, to intimidate, to announce the power of the Zentarra name with every gleaming surface and priceless artwork. Now those same features work against us, forcing us to hug the walls where the marble won't betray our footsteps.

"Security cameras disabled for the northeast corridor," Sophia whispers, her fingers dancing across her tablet. The blue glow illuminates her face from below, casting strange shadows that make her look both younger and older than her years. "Four minutes until the system resets."

I nod, not trusting my voice in this moment. It's surreal being back here—a place where I once felt untouchable, now infiltrating it like a thief. The paintings watch our progress with judgmental eyes—my grandfather's stern portrait, my mother's elegant commission, even little Juan's school photograph that my father insisted on displaying alongside priceless art. My family bears witness to what I've become: a fugitive in my own legacy.

Mason moves ahead of me, his injured shoulder creating a slight hitch in his usually fluid stride. The bandage beneath his tactical shirt hasn't started bleeding through yet—a good sign, but the night is young. His eyes never stop moving, cataloging threats, exits, contingencies. I watch him check his weapon for the third time in as many minutes—not nervousness but thoroughness. That attention to detail is why he's still alive, why I'm still alive.

"Stop here," he instructs, voice barely audible as we reach the junction that will lead us to the conference room. He points to an ornate alcove—my mother's idea, a decorative niche that once held a Ming dynasty vase worth more than most people's homes. "This gives me direct line of sight to the doors and enough cover if things go sideways."

I slip into the space beside him, close enough that our arms brush. Even in this moment of extreme danger, my body betrays me with a flash of awareness at his proximity. Ridiculous. Inconvenient. Undeniable.

"The recording?" he asks, eyes still scanning our surroundings.

I pat my jacket pocket. "Here. And backed up on Sophia's systems, just in case."

"And the contingency plans?"

"If he doesn't take the bait, if he doesn't incriminate himself further, we still have enough evidence from the warehouse recording to convince the lieutenants," I recite. "If the lieutenants side with him despite the evidence, Miguel's men create an exit corridor while you and I retreat to extraction point Alpha."

He nods, finally looking directly at me. His eyes soften for just a moment—a private expression I've only recently learned to recognize. "You ready for this?"

Am I ready? To face the man who murdered my parents? Who tried to kill me? Who betrayed everything my father built? Who forced me to become a fugitive in my own life?

"I've been ready since the moment he put a knife in your side," I answer.

Sophia approaches, tablet still in hand. "The lieutenants are all present. Ken's giving his weekly status update." She shows me the screen, a grainy feed from one of our reactivated bugs showing the conference room. Ken stands at the head of the table—my father's place—gesturing as he speaks to seven men whose loyalty will determine the future of the Zentarra organization. "Now's the ideal window. He's just starting his presentation on quarterly numbers. Maximum impact if you interrupt now."

Miguel's men spread out with silent efficiency, taking positions that give them coverage of all approach vectors to the conference room. Their leader—a stone-faced man with eyes that have seen too much violence to be impressed by more—gives me a slight nod. Ready.

Mason's hand finds mine, a brief squeeze that contains everything we can't say aloud. I think of last night in Miguel's safe house, his body curved protectively around mine despite his injured shoulder, his lips against my hair whispering promises neither of us knows if we can keep.

"Don't get shot again," I tell him, aiming for lightness but landing somewhere closer to plea.

"Don't give him a reason to shoot you," he counters, his thumb brushing across my knuckles before he releases my hand. He moves into position, his weapon held low but ready, his eyes already focused on what's coming rather than what might have been.

I adjust my suit jacket one final time, ensuring the recording device is accessible but the bulletproof vest remains hidden. The weight of my father's watch presses against my wrist—the one possession I refused to leave behind when we fled the estate that night. Its steady tick marks the seconds toward whatever future awaits on the other side of those mahogany doors.

Sophia takes her position at a terminal tucked into an administrative alcove, ready to broadcast the evidence to every screen in the building if necessary. Her fingers hover over the keyboard like a pianist before a concerto. "Ready when you are."

I straighten my shoulders, feeling the soft cashmere of my suit jacket stretch across the hard ceramic plates beneath. The fabric cost more than some cars—another lesson from my father. "Always dress better than everyone in the room, Yelana. Power recognizes power." My hair is pulled back in a severe style that adds years to my appearance, making me look less like the "girl" Ken dismisses and more like the woman who will end him.

With one last deep breath, I step away from the safety of shadows and walk directly toward the conference room doors. Each step feels simultaneously like surrender and advance, like I'm marching toward both my birthright and my potential execution. The carved mahogany panels loom larger with each step, the gold Zentarra emblem at their center catching the light like a winking eye.

Behind me, I feel rather than see Mason shift to maintain visual coverage. Ahead, through those doors, sits the man who destroyed my family. Between us lies only wood, opportunity, and the thinnest margin for error.

I place my hands against the cool surface of the doors, feeling the grain of wood my father touched countless times. Then, with one fluid motion, I push them open and step into my inheritance.

The conference room falls silent as I step through the doorway, eight heads turning in perfect synchronicity like some macabre ballet. Ken freezes mid-gesture at the head of the table—my father's chair, my father's place—his mouth still open on whatever lie he was spinning. For one perfect moment, shock renders his face completely unguarded, and I see what I came for: fear. It flashes across his features like lightning before his mask of control slides back into place. Around the table, the lieutenants' expressions range from disbelief to calculation to something that might be relief. I let the silence stretch, savoring the power of interruption before I finally speak.

"Don't stop on my account, Ken." My voice carries in the silent room. "I'm curious about how the organization my father built is performing under your... stewardship."

Ken recovers with the smooth adaptability that's kept him alive in this business for decades. His surprise transforms into a practiced smile, the kind reserved for business associates you plan to betray later.

"Well, look who's decided to join us," he says, voice dripping with false warmth. "Our wayward heiress returns—or should I say, our traitor?" He gestures to the empty chair beside him, not the one at the head of the table. "Come, sit. We were just discussing the unfortunate financial discrepancies that appeared during your brief tenure before your... hasty departure."

I ignore the offered chair and move deliberately toward the head of the table. Antonio Krane, our distribution chief, shifts slightly to make room, his eyes never leaving my face. Beside him, Marcus Webb—my father's oldest lieutenant—watches with the calculating patience of a man who's survived three decades in this business by choosing the winning side.

"I believe this is my seat," I say, placing my hands on the back of my father's chair but not sitting yet. "Unless someone would like to dispute that?"

The challenge hangs in the air. Ken's smile tightens but doesn't fade.

"No one's disputing your birthright, Yelana," he says, pivoting smoothly. "But perhaps now isn't the time for a reunion. We're discussing sensitive matters—specifically, your collaboration with the Costa family to undermine our Southern distribution networks."

I finally sit, the leather chair still molded to my father's form rather than mine. Too big, like everything I've inherited. But I don't let it show. Instead, I cross my legs and rest my elbows on the armrests, mirroring my father's posture from a hundred meetings I observed from the shadows.

"Please," I gesture magnanimously. "Continue with your explanation of my alleged treachery."

Ken seizes the opportunity, spinning a narrative for the lieutenants about how I've been working with Miguel Costa to funnel Zentarra weapons through competitive channels, undermining our pricing structures and profit margins. His performance is masterful—concern rather than accusation, regret rather than anger. If I didn't have the evidence in my pocket, I might almost believe him myself.

I scan the faces around the table while Ken speaks. Rodriguez shifts uncomfortably, eyes darting between Ken and me. He's new, promoted after my father's death—Ken's man. Diaz maintains a perfect poker face, though his fingers drum softly against the polished mahogany—his tell when he's hearing bullshit, something my father taught me to watch for. Chen sits perfectly still, the only indication of his attention the slight narrowing of his eyes as Ken mentions specific shipment numbers that don't align with the books Chen oversees.

"—which is why we've had to reroute the Singapore shipments through alternative channels," Ken concludes, spreading his hands in a gesture of reluctant disclosure. "The evidence is irrefutable, unfortunately. I take no pleasure in revealing these things."

I let the silence stretch again after he finishes, long enough for discomfort to seep into the room. Then I slowly reach into my jacket pocket, removing the small recording device.

"Before you continue with your lies, Ken, I think everyone should hear what you have to say when you think no one's listening." I place the device on the table, the action deliberately unhurried. "This was recorded three days ago at the Costa warehouse. Your warehouse now isn't it?"

Ken's expression doesn't change, but his right hand twitches slightly—reaching for a weapon that isn't there. Security protocols for these meetings: no firearms except for external guards.

I press play.

Ken's voice fills the room, crystal clear and unmistakable: "The timetable has accelerated. She's made her move with Costa's people faster than anticipated."

Another voice—the scarred mercenary: "We have men inside Miguel's organization. But we haven't pinpointed her location yet."

Ken again: "Find her. This contains everything—security codes to her remaining safe houses, known associates, the kill order with payment confirmation."

The lieutenants shift in their seats, some glancing at each other, others staring directly at Ken whose complexion has grown increasingly pale.

Then the most damning evidence plays: "Once this is done, the organization is mine. Emelio and Sierra had to go, and now their precious daughter needs to disappear too."

Marcus Webb's hand flattens against the table, his wedding ring clicking against wood—the only sound in the room besides the recording. Antonio Krane's posture changes subtly, angling away from Ken, distancing himself physically from the exposed traitor.

The mercenary's voice continues: "Vince Costa is getting impatient. He expected control of the Los Angeles corridor as payment for his assistance."

Ken's cold laugh: "Vince will get exactly what we agreed upon—twenty percent of distribution rights, nothing more. Once the girl is eliminated, I'll have the board's full confidence. They'll fall in line or join her parents."

I stop the recording, letting the final words hang in the air. The conference room has transformed into a pressure cooker, tension building with nowhere to escape.

"I have more," I say into the silence. "Financial records. Communication logs. Weapons shipments diverted to the Vasquez cartel. Everything." My voice remains steady, though my heart hammers against my ribs. "But I don't think we need to waste any more time, do we, Ken?"

Ken's face contorts, the mask of civility crumbling to reveal the rage beneath. His eyes dart around the table, searching for allies and finding none. Even Rodriguez won't meet his gaze now.

"You think they'll follow you?" Ken spits, abandoning pretense. "A child playing dress-up in Daddy's clothes? You have no idea what it takes to run this organization."

"No," I agree calmly. "I don't have your experience betraying people who trust you. Murdering your friends. Selling out to rivals." I lean forward, placing my palms flat on the table. "But I am my father's daughter. And unlike you, I don't need to kill to command loyalty."

Ken's eyes narrow to slits, calculating even in his exposure. I watch him process options, trajectories, possibilities. I see the moment when he realizes there's only one play left—the desperation option.

"This recording proves nothing," he says, his voice dropping to a dangerous register. "Anyone can be made to say anything with the right editing. What these men need is leadership, not accusations."

"What we need," Marcus Webb says slowly, "is an explanation, Ken." His weathered hand moves toward the inside of his jacket—reaching for the weapon I know he always carries despite the protocols.

The room balances on a knife's edge, everyone sensing the imminent explosion of violence. Ken's eyes dart to the door, measuring distance, calculating odds.

I've seen that look before—in prey animals when they realize they're cornered. In my peripheral vision, I see Mason shift slightly in the alcove, anticipating what's coming next.

Ken's smile returns suddenly, too wide, too bright. "Of course. You deserve an explanation."

His hand moves like lightning.

Ken moves with a predator's speed that belies his age, lunging across the table and seizing Marcus Webb by his silk tie. Before anyone can react, he's dragged the older man backward, producing a small pistol from somewhere inside his jacket. The muzzle presses against Marcus's temple, the older man's eyes wide with surprise rather than fear. The room freezes in tableau—lieutenants half-risen from their chairs, hands moving toward concealed weapons, all motion suspended by the immediate threat. Ken's smile has transformed into something feral, a cornered animal showing its teeth.

"Nobody moves!" Ken shouts, backing toward the wall with his human shield. "Anyone twitches, and the loyal Mr. Webb gets to see if there's an afterlife."

My mind races, cataloging variables with the cold calculation my father drilled into me. Ken's position. The distance to cover. The other lieutenants' locations. The secret signal button beneath the table that would have already summoned Ken's personal security team. From my peripheral vision, I see Mason in position, his weapon raised but unable to take the shot with Marcus in the way.

"This isn't going to end well for you, Ken," I say, remaining deliberately still while keeping his attention on me rather than the others in the room. "The recording is already backed up on servers across three countries. Killing Marcus—killing me—changes nothing."

Ken adjusts his grip, wrapping his arm tighter around Marcus's throat. The older man's face reddens slightly, but his eyes meet mine with surprising clarity. There's a message there—something beyond fear. Trust, perhaps. Or calculation.

"You've always underestimated me," Ken snarls. "Just like your father did. He thought I was content to be his errand boy forever, handling his dirty work while he played the respectable businessman." His voice rises with each word, decades of resentment bubbling to the surface. "Twenty-five years I gave him! Twenty-five years of loyalty, and what did I get? Passed over for his spoiled brat, who doesn't know the first thing about this business."

I take a half-step forward, drawing his attention completely to me. "Is that what this is about? Your wounded pride?" I infuse my voice with every ounce of my mother's aristocratic disdain. "You always were second-best, Ken. My father knew it. I know it. That's why you'll never run this organization."

The barb strikes precisely where intended. Ken's focus narrows to me, his eyes burning with hatred that momentarily overshadows his calculation. His grip on Marcus loosens fractionally as rage overtakes strategy—exactly as I hoped.

"You little bi—"

The crack of a single gunshot cuts through his words. Ken screams, his shoulder jerking backward as blood blooms across his expensive suit jacket. Marcus seizes the opportunity, driving his elbow into Ken's solar plexus and dropping to the floor as Ken staggers back.

Chaos erupts like a detonation.

The conference room doors burst open, Ken's personal security team flooding in with weapons drawn. Gunfire erupts from multiple directions at once—Miguel's men engaging from their hidden positions, lieutenants diving for cover, bullets splintering the mahogany table and shattering the glass display cabinets that held my father's prized antique weapons.

I drop instantly, rolling beneath the heavy table as slugs tear through the space where I stood seconds before. From somewhere across the room, I hear Antonio Krane shouting orders to his own men. Glass rains down as a chandelier takes a stray round, sending crystal daggers scattering across the polished floor.

"Yelana!" Sophia appears beside me, crawling beneath the table's protection, her tablet still clutched against her chest. Blood trickles from a cut on her forehead where flying glass caught her. "Are you hit?"

"I'm fine." My voice sounds distant to my own ears, drowned beneath the percussion of gunfire and the strange ringing that follows extreme violence. "The lieutenants?"

"Most made it to cover." She angles the tablet so I can see, its screen displaying a tactical map of the room with heat signatures showing positions. "Miguel's men have engaged Ken's security. The odds are even."

A bullet punches through the table inches from my hand, sending splinters into my palm. I barely feel it, my focus entirely on Ken. Through the chaos, I spot him staggering toward the eastern wall, one hand pressed against his bleeding shoulder, the other still gripping his pistol. Marcus has taken cover behind an overturned chair, blood staining his collar but moving with purpose—alive.

"There!" I point, watching as Ken reaches a bookcase that I've seen a thousand times but never questioned. His bloody hand presses against a specific volume, and suddenly the entire case slides sideways, revealing a narrow passage beyond. "He has an escape route!"

Mason materializes from the smoke and confusion, vaulting over a fallen lieutenant to land in a combat crouch beside our position. His tactical shirt shows a spreading stain of fresh blood—his wound reopened in the exertion. His eyes meet mine for a fraction of a second, conveying everything words can't in the middle of a firefight.

"Stay down," he orders, already moving toward Ken's escape route. "Sophia, keep her alive."

Before I can protest, he's gone, weaving through the battlefield with the efficient grace of someone who's navigated countless warzones. I watch him drop a guard with a precise strike to the throat, take another's weapon in a disarming move too fast to follow, and launch himself toward the secret passage where Ken is disappearing.

"Mason, wait!" My voice is lost in the cacophony of battle.

He doesn't hesitate, diving through the narrow opening seconds after Ken vanishes into its depths. The bookcase begins sliding closed behind him—some automated security measure triggered by Ken's escape.

"No, no, no," I mutter, preparing to follow, but Sophia's hand clamps around my wrist with surprising strength.

"You can't," she says, her eyes on the tactical display. "More hostiles approaching from the west corridor. If we don't secure this room now, there won't be an organization left to reclaim."

I hesitate, torn between following Mason and securing my position here. The rational choice is clear, but rationality feels distant when the man I love is pursuing a cornered killer through unknown passages with a reopened wound leaving a trail of blood behind him.

A massive explosion rocks the room—one of Miguel's men deploying a flashbang to disorient Ken's remaining guards. In the momentary confusion, I make my decision.

"Help me rally the lieutenants," I tell Sophia, pulling myself into a crouch behind the bullet-riddled table. "We need to end this now."

As if to punctuate my words, a final shot echoes from the secret passage before the bookcase seals completely, cutting off any possibility of following Mason. All I can do now is secure this room, consolidate power, and pray that Mason's uncanny ability to survive extends to one more impossible situation.

The lieutenants who've taken cover nearby look to me with varying degrees of shock and calculation. This is the moment—either I take control or the organization fragments into chaos. Despite the bullets still flying, despite the blood seeping through Mason's reopened wound somewhere behind that sealed passage, despite everything, I force myself to focus on the immediate battle.

My father's daughter. My mother's spine. My own destiny.

"Antonio!" I call out to Krane, who has positioned himself behind a fallen cabinet. "Take the east flank. Rodriguez, cover the doors. Anyone loyal to the Zentarra name, rally to me now!"

Blood and broken glass crunch beneath my knees as I crawl toward the overturned credenza where Antonio Krane has taken position. Bullets continue to fly overhead, peppering the walls with holes that destroy priceless artwork my mother spent decades collecting. The irony doesn't escape me—my parents' killers desecrating their treasures even in defeat. Sophia stays close behind me, her tablet clutched protectively against her chest like a shield, though the only protection it offers is informational. When I reach Antonio, his eyes widen at my approach, weapon half-raised before recognition dawns.

"Jesus Christ, Yelana," he hisses, pulling me deeper into cover as a spray of bullets stitches the floor where I just crawled. "What the hell is happening?"

"Exactly what it looks like," I reply, keeping my voice steady despite the adrenaline coursing through my veins. "Ken killed my parents, tried to kill me, and now he's trying to kill all of us to keep control."

Sophia positions herself between us, angling her tablet so Antonio can see the screen. "We have proof beyond the recording," she explains, swiping through financial documents with bloodstained fingers. "Ken's been embezzling from the organization for years. Look here—" she points to highlighted transfers, "—funds moving to offshore accounts tied directly to the mercenaries who attacked at the funeral."

Antonio studies the screen, his expression hardening with each swipe. A lifetime in this business has taught him to process information quickly, to make decisions that mean life or death in seconds. I watch the calculation in his eyes, the weighing of loyalty against survival.

"And these?" he asks, pointing to another document.

"Weapon shipments diverted to the Vasquez cartel," Sophia explains. "Twenty percent of our Asian pipeline, rerouted through shell companies Ken controls personally."

A bullet embeds itself in the wood inches from Antonio's head. He doesn't flinch.

"Antonio," I press, knowing this moment will define everything that follows. "My father trusted you for fifteen years. I'm not asking for blind loyalty. I'm showing you proof."

His eyes meet mine, searching for something—weakness, perhaps, or uncertainty. I don't look away.

"What do you need us to do?" he asks finally.

Relief floods through me, but I don't let it show on my face. Instead, I shift immediately to command mode, the role I was born for but never thought I'd assume so soon or under such circumstances.

"Secure the east exit," I instruct. "We have men in the courtyard—we need them inside now."

Antonio nods, already speaking rapid instructions into his comm unit. Around us, the gunfire begins to shift, becoming more sporadic as Miguel's men systematically neutralize Ken's security personnel. Through the broken windows, I hear sirens approaching—local police responding to gunfire at the Zentarra estate, no doubt already bought off by Ken to look the other way if necessary.

Marcus Webb crawls toward our position, blood seeping from a graze across his temple where Ken's gun pressed moments ago. His expression carries none of the doubt I expected—just grim determination and something that might be respect.

"The lower levels need to be secured," he says without preamble. "Ken keeps his most loyal men in the sublevels. They'll be coming up through the service elevators."

"Already handling it," Sophia responds, showing him the tablet where red dots representing Miguel's men are moving into position around the elevator access points. "We've overridden the security protocols. Those elevators won't move without our authorization now."

More lieutenants converge on our position as the gunfire gradually subsides. Rodriguez arrives last, his expression guarded but his weapon pointed safely away—a tentative alignment rather than full commitment. Blood spatters his expensive suit, though whether it's his own or someone else's is impossible to tell.

"Show them," I instruct Sophia, who immediately begins displaying the evidence in a methodical presentation that leaves no room for doubt. Financial records, communication logs, security footage from the warehouse—a damning tapestry of Ken's betrayal woven together with the precision of someone who's been gathering evidence for months.

The lieutenants' expressions harden with each new revelation. These men aren't moved by moral outrage—they've all done things that would shock civilians—but betrayal of the organization, theft from their common enterprise, collusion with rivals? Those are unforgivable sins in our world.

"The Costa connection?" Chen asks, his normally impassive face showing rare emotion.

"Vince Costa provided backing and mercenaries," Sophia explains. "In exchange for territorial concessions Ken never intended to honor."

"Miguel Costa is a separate entity," I clarify quickly. "He provided support for our operation today, with agreements for renegotiation of boundaries once stability is restored."

A practical concern, immediately understood by men who navigate these waters daily. Business continues, alliances shift, only the disloyal are punished.

Miguel's security chief approaches, his tactical gear showing signs of the recent firefight but his posture still alert. "Building secure, Miss Zentarra. Ken's men are either neutralized or have surrendered." His eyes flick to the sealed bookcase. "No sign of Jackson or your man who pursued him."

My heart clenches at the reminder of Mason disappearing into that passage, blood already soaking through his shirt from his reopened wound. I force myself to maintain my composed expression despite the fear clawing at my insides.

"We need to find where that passage leads," I say, gesturing toward the bookcase that swallowed both Mason and Ken minutes ago. "Building schematics, original blueprints, anything."

"The house plans are in your father's private safe," Marcus offers. "But there may be hidden passages not documented officially."

"My father would have had contingencies," I say, thinking aloud. "Escape routes, safe rooms..." I turn to Sophia. "Check the security system for blind spots—areas without camera coverage or motion sensors."

She's already working, fingers flying across the tablet. "There's a dead zone beneath the eastern gardens. No cameras, no sensors, nothing on any security grid. That's not accidental."

The sirens grow louder outside. We have minutes at most before local authorities create complications we don't need.

"Antonio, take four men and secure the eastern gardens. If that passage exits there, I want to know." I turn to Rodriguez. "Call your contact at the police department. Tell them there was a security drill that got out of hand. Offer the usual compensation for their discretion."

He hesitates briefly before nodding, already pulling out his phone. The immediate compliance speaks volumes about the shifting power dynamics in the room.

"Chen, I need a comprehensive inventory check, immediately. Whatever Ken's been skimming, I want to know the full extent."

"Marcus, contact our international clients. Assure them that the Zentarra Organization is stable and operations continue without interruption."

I issue orders in rapid succession, each one acknowledged with increasing deference. With each command obeyed, my position solidifies. The transition of power happens in real-time, blood still wet on the marble floors.

Through it all, my thoughts keep returning to Mason, pursuing Ken through dark passages with a bullet wound already reopened. The man who stood between me and death multiple times, who taught me to shoot properly, who held me through nightmare-filled nights, whose lips I can still feel against mine from our last desperate embrace before this mission began.

A lieutenant I don't immediately recognize approaches with a tablet displaying security camera footage. "Miss Zentarra, we've found something. There's movement in the eastern garden tunnels."

I peer at the grainy night-vision image, my breath catching at the sight of two figures emerging from what appears to be a concealed entrance beneath an ornamental fountain. One walks with the confident stride of someone who knows he's won. The other follows at a distance, stalking rather than pursuing.

Ken and Mason.

"Send everything we have to that location," I order, already moving toward the door. "Now!"

As I stride through the bullet-riddled conference room, lieutenants fall in behind me without question—the rightful heir reclaiming her kingdom, leading her forces into battle. Blood drips from a cut on my cheek I don't remember receiving. Glass crunches beneath my heels. Outside, the sirens wail closer.

Whatever happens next, Ken's reign ends tonight. And Mason—my Mason—better keep his promise to come back to me, or I'll drag him back from whatever afterlife claims him.

I am Yelana Zentarra. My father's daughter. My own woman. And this is just the beginning.

TWENTY
The Final Showdown

Mason

The passage narrows as I follow the blood trail—Ken's blood from my shot in the conference room, dark droplets marking his escape like breadcrumbs. My own wound throbs in rhythm with my heartbeat, warm wetness seeping through the hastily applied pressure bandage. The tunnel air hangs heavy with dust and disuse, but I push forward, tracking my prey through the darkness with single-minded focus. The path slopes gradually upward, old stone giving way to newer concrete, until moonlight filters through a gap ahead. I emerge silently into the Zentarra family mausoleum, a cathedral of marble monuments to power and wealth where Emelio and Sierra were laid to rest barely weeks ago.

My boots make no sound on the polished floor—a lifetime of training rendering me nearly ghostlike as I move between shadows. Moonlight spills through stained glass windows, painting the white marble in fractured colors that shift with passing clouds. The space feels both vast and claustrophobic, tombs of Zentarra ancestors stretching back generations creating a maze of blind corners and potential ambush points. I catalog them automatically, my mind mapping escape routes even as my eyes adjust to the dimness. The air carries the scent of fresh-cut flowers and cold stone, underlaid with something metallic—Ken's blood or my own, I can't be sure.

Then I see him, a dark silhouette against the pale marble of the newest tomb. Ken stands before Emelio's final resting place, his fingers tracing the freshly engraved letters of his former boss's name. There's something almost reverent in his posture, a parody of mourning that makes my jaw clench. His suit is torn at the shoulder where my bullet found him, dark stain spreading across the expensive fabric.

I move closer, keeping stone angels and ornate columns between us until I'm ready to reveal myself. My weapon is drawn but held low at my side, steady despite the pain radiating from my reopened wound. One clear shot would end this—justice delivered in the house of the dead. But something stays my finger. I need to hear him say it. Need to know why.

"Took you long enough, Lieutenant," Ken says without turning, his voice echoing against marble surfaces. Not surprised, then. He knew I was here.

I step into a shaft of colored moonlight, no longer concealing my presence. "It's over, Ken. The lieutenants have seen the evidence. Yelana has control of the organization now."

He turns slowly, a cruel smile playing on his lips. Blood has soaked through his shirt, but he stands tall, showing no signs of weakness. "Nothing's over until I say it's over."

We begin circling each other, two predators in a killing ground of tombs. Our footsteps whisper across the marble floor, a ritual dance of death performed beside the bodies of those already claimed by violence.

"Twenty-five years," Ken spits, his face contorted with bitterness. "Twenty-five years I gave to Emelio, doing the work he was too squeamish to handle himself. The interrogations. The eliminations. Building his empire while he played benevolent father figure." His eyes never leave mine as we continue our slow orbit. "And then you show up—the noble soldier he saved. His precious 'debt of blood.'"

"This isn't about me," I say, keeping my voice level despite the rage building in my chest. "You murdered him. You murdered Sierra."

Ken laughs, the sound bouncing off stone angels and marble slabs. "I did what was necessary. What Emelio himself would have done in my position." His hand moves inside his jacket, but I already have my weapon trained on him. He stops, smiling. "Still quick, even with that shoulder. But are you quick enough to save her this time? Unlike in Afghanistan?"

The words hit like a sledgehammer, finding the tender spots in my psyche with surgical precision. Ken sees my flinch, slight as it is, and presses his advantage.

"Your team died because you failed them," he continues, voice dripping with false sympathy. "All those men, following you into an ambush. How many were there? Five? Six? All dead because Lieutenant Phillips couldn't read the signs."

Memories flash unbidden—George's laugh during a sandstorm in Kandahar, Riley's collection of foreign coins, Michael's wife pregnant with their first child. Faces of men I couldn't save. I push the images down, but Ken is already moving to the next wound.

"And poor Kerry. Waiting for you to pick her up that night, wasn't she? If you'd been on time, maybe the drunk driver would have never crossed your path. Maybe she'd still be alive." His smile widens as he sees the impact of his words. "And little Juan, of course. Emelio's pride and joy, running into gunfire because you were too slow to secure the perimeter."

My finger tightens on the trigger, but I resist the urge to silence him permanently. He's trying to provoke me, to make me sloppy with anger. I've seen this tactic before—psychological warfare designed to unbalance an opponent.

"You think killing me will end this?" Ken asks, taking a step closer. "You're a temporary solution to a permanent problem. As long as Yelana lives, there will always be someone coming for her. The Costa family. The Vasquez cartel. Former clients with grudges. You can't watch her forever."

"I don't need forever," I reply, steadying my aim. "Just long enough to eliminate threats like you."

Ken's eyes narrow, calculating as ever. "You know what your problem is, Phillips? You believe in things. Honor. Duty. Love." He spits the last word like it's poison. "Emelio believed too. Look where it got him." He gestures to the tomb beside us, Emelio's name carved in cold stone.

"And what do you believe in, Ken?"

"Survival," he answers immediately. "Power. The only things that matter in this world." He takes another step toward me, close enough now that I can see the sweat beading on his forehead despite the chill in the mausoleum. "You couldn't save them then. You can't save her now."

The words slide between my ribs like a knife, finding the fear I've carried since the moment I realized my feelings for Yelana went beyond duty. The fear that history will repeat itself, that everyone I care for is doomed by that very connection. I feel my wounded side protesting as tension builds in my muscles, ready for the violence that hangs between us like an unspoken promise.

"You're wrong," I tell him, and I see genuine surprise flicker across his face at the conviction in my voice. "I couldn't save them. That will haunt me until I die. But Yelana?" I allow myself a small smile. "She doesn't need me to save her. She's her father's daughter. And that's what you never understood about Emelio—he didn't just build an empire. He built a legacy."

Rage distorts Ken's features, the calculated manipulation giving way to raw hatred. His hand moves again, faster this time, drawing a weapon from his bloodstained jacket.

We lunge toward each other simultaneously, my bullet wound screaming in protest as we crash into the first devastating blows of what's about to become a fight to the death.

My fist connects with Ken's jaw, the impact reverberating up my arm as his head snaps back. But he recovers faster than I expect, ducking under my follow-up strike and driving his shoulder into my midsection. Pain explodes from my bullet wound as we crash backward into a stone angel, its cold wings digging into my spine. I taste copper as the impact forces blood into my mouth, but training overrides pain. I bring my knee up sharply, catching Ken in the ribs and pushing him off balance just enough to create separation.

"Getting slow, Phillips," Ken taunts, circling again, his breath visible in the cold air of the mausoleum. "Guess that shoulder's bothering you."

I don't waste energy responding. Every word is oxygen I can't afford to lose. Instead, I feint left before pivoting right, landing a solid hook to his kidney. Ken grunts but counters immediately, his elbow catching my temple with a precision that speaks to years of dirty fighting. Stars explode across my vision, but muscle memory keeps me moving, blocking his follow-up strike and shoving him backward into a marble headstone.

We crash between the monuments to Zentarra wealth, trading vicious blows that echo through the cavernous space. Each impact tells a story of hatred, betrayal, and the inevitable violence that underlies the world we both inhabit. Blood—mine and his

—spatters across white marble like some deranged artist's brush-strokes, desecrating the pristine surfaces meant to honor the dead.

Ken's next strike finds my left side, precisely targeting the half-healed bullet wound from the warehouse fight. White-hot agony shorts out my nervous system for a crucial second, my guard dropping just enough for him to slam his palm into my chin, snapping my head back. I stumble, struggling to maintain my footing on the polished floor now slick with our blood.

"Did I tell you how she cried for Emelio?" Ken asks, pressing his advantage as he stalks forward. "Sierra, I mean. When I told her why she had to die, she begged for Emelio. Called his name right before I put a bullet in her head."

Rage floods my system, providing a temporary barrier against pain. I launch myself at him, tackling him into a waist-high crypt. The impact knocks the wind from both of us, but I recover first, driving my fist into his face once, twice, a third time. Blood erupts from his nose, coating my knuckles in warm crimson.

Ken bucks beneath me, somehow getting a knee between us and creating enough space to slam his forehead into mine. The head-butt sends me reeling backward, vision blurring as he capitalizes on my disorientation. His boot connects with my ribs, the distinct crack of bone yielding under pressure followed by a flash of pain so intense I nearly black out.

"You should see yourself," Ken laughs, circling as I struggle to rise. "The great protector, bleeding out in a tomb. Poetic, isn't it?"

Each breath sends daggers through my chest where his kick broke at least one rib. My movements grow sluggish, the combined blood loss from the reopened bullet wound and this new fight draining my strength with each passing second. I catalog my injuries with clinical detachment: broken rib, possible concussion, reopened bullet wound, contusions to the face and torso. Survivable individually. Potentially fatal in combination, especially with an opponent who shows no signs of slowing down.

Ken sees my assessment, reading the realization in my eyes. "Finally understanding your situation? Good." He feints right, and when I move to counter, drives his knee directly into my wounded side.

The pain steals my breath completely this time. My legs buckle as my body instinctively curls around the injury. I drop to one knee, fighting to remain conscious as dark spots dance at the edges of my vision. My gun—still clutched in my right hand despite the battering—suddenly feels like it weighs a hundred pounds.

Ken doesn't hesitate. His foot lashes out, connecting with my wrist with surgical precision. My fingers go numb instantly, the weapon clattering across the marble floor, spinning away into the shadows between tombs. Defenseless now, I try to push myself upright, but my body refuses to comply, muscles trembling with exhaustion and blood loss.

"Look at you," Ken says, standing over me with contempt twisting his features. "Emelio's chosen one. His trusted protector." He delivers another kick, this one catching me in the shoulder and sending me sprawling onto my back. "Twenty-five years I served that man."

He retrieves my gun from where it landed, checking it with the practiced ease of someone who's handled weapons all his life. "But when he needed someone to watch his precious daughter, who did he call?" The barrel swings toward me, centered on my forehead. "Not his right-hand man. Not the person who built his empire alongside him. He sent for you. 'El Protector.'"

He spits the nickname like it's poison, his face contorted with decades of resentment finally finding its voice. Blood continues to seep from his shoulder where my bullet found him earlier, but adrenaline and hatred seem to render him immune to its effects.

"You want to know the real reason I killed him?" Ken asks, crouching beside me, pressing the gun barrel against my temple. "It wasn't just business. It was personal. He never trusted me like he trusted you. A man he knew for what—fifteen years? While I stood by him for twenty-five."

I taste blood pooling in my mouth, feel it trickling warm down my neck from a cut above my eye. "Trust... isn't about time," I manage, each word a struggle against the pressure in my chest. "It's about character."

Ken's laugh echoes off the marble crypts. "Character? In this business?" He presses the gun harder against my skin. "There's no room for character in what we do. Only survival and power. Emelio forgot that. You never learned it. And his daughter? She'll die just like her parents, thinking honor means something in a world built on blood money."

His finger tightens on the trigger, and I find myself strangely calm in what should be my final moments. My thoughts turn to Yelana—not to our failure, but to what we found together. If this is my end, at least I experienced that connection, however briefly.

"I wanted you to understand before you die," Ken continues, almost conversational now. "Why it had to be this way. Why—"

The soft sound of footsteps interrupts him, the distinct click of heels on marble echoing through the mausoleum. Ken's head snaps up, his attention momentarily divided between finishing me and addressing the new arrival.

Yelana stands framed in the entrance, moonlight silhouetting her slender form. Even from this distance, I can see the steel in her posture, the determined set of her shoulders. Her face reveals nothing, but her eyes—her father's eyes—burn with cold fury as they take in the scene before her. No fear, just calculation and resolve.

"Yelana, run," I try to shout, but it emerges as little more than a hoarse whisper.

Ken rises slowly, my gun still trained on me but his attention now split. "Perfect timing," he calls to her, voice echoing through the marble chamber. "I was just explaining to your guard dog why your entire family needs to be erased."

I struggle to rise, to place myself between them, but my body betrays me, responding with agonizing slowness to my desperate commands. All I can do is watch as Ken begins to turn the gun toward the woman I love, his lips curling into a triumphant smile.

Ken's attention shifts to Yelana, the gun in his hand beginning to pivot away from my head toward her slender figure. Time slows to a crawl, pain and exhaustion falling away beneath a surge of desperate clarity. I've failed too many people I cared about—my SEAL team in Afghanistan, Kerry, Juan. Not her. Not Yelana. With one final, desperate surge of strength born from something beyond physical reserves, I launch myself upward, slamming into Ken's legs as his finger tightens on the trigger.

The gun discharges, the bullet sailing wide as we both crash to the marble floor. Ken's skull connects with stone, momentarily stunning him, but he recovers with the resilience of a man who's survived decades in a business where hesitation means death. His knee drives into my broken rib, sending white-hot agony through my torso. I barely suppress a scream, channeling the pain into fuel as I grapple for control of the weapon.

"You just don't know when to die, do you?" Ken snarls, smashing his elbow against my wounded shoulder.

We roll across the floor, locked in a desperate struggle that carries us directly into Sierra's tomb. The impact rattles ancient marble, sending fresh flowers cascading across our tangled bodies. The gun fires again, the report deafening in the enclosed space, the muzzle flash momentarily blinding us both. Somewhere, stone chips spray as the bullet ricochets off a marble angel, embedding itself in the ceiling.

Through the blur of combat, I glimpse Yelana circling us like a predator, her eyes never leaving the weapon we fight for. Smart girl. Positioning herself. Waiting for her moment rather than rushing in.

Ken manages to get his knee on my chest, pinning me against Sierra's tomb with his full weight. The pressure against my broken rib sends nausea rolling through me in waves, blurring the edge of my vision into a Rorschach inkblot. His free hand clamps around my throat, fingers digging into flesh with murderous intent.

"Watch her die first," he gasps, swinging the gun toward Yelana again. "Then you can join her."

I drive my palm up into his wounded shoulder, fingers digging into the bullet hole I put there hours ago. Ken's agonized howl fills the mausoleum as fresh blood spurts between my fingers. The gun discharges again, another wild shot that shatters a stained glass window, sending colored fragments raining across the marble floor like frozen rain.

Yelana ducks behind a stone sarcophagus, then moves with surprising speed toward where my original weapon skidded earlier. Her hands close around the grip, and she rises in a smooth motion that speaks of the training I've given her over these past weeks—feet planted shoulder-width apart, arms extended, weapon gripped firmly in both hands.

Neither Ken nor I see her move into position. We're too consumed by our mutual determination to kill each other, locked in a primitive struggle that has transcended tactics into pure survival instinct. Ken smashes his forehead into mine, temporarily stunning me. The momentary advantage is all he needs to wrench free of my grip on his wounded shoulder.

He straddles me fully now, one hand still crushing my windpipe while the other brings the gun barrel directly to my temple. Blood from his reopened shoulder wound drips onto my face, mingling with my own injuries in a grotesque baptism.

"You failed them all," Ken hisses, his face inches from mine, spittle and blood spraying with each word. His weight shifts as he prepares for the kill shot, finger tightening on the trigger. "And now you'll fail her too."

Three shots crack in rapid succession, the sound amplified by marble surfaces into something physical enough to feel against my skin. Ken's body jerks with each impact, his eyes widening in shock rather than pain. He turns his head slowly, almost curiously, toward Yelana who stands twenty feet away, my gun still extended in a perfect firing stance. Smoke curls from the barrel, rising like incense in the moonlit mausoleum.

Ken's weight shifts as he topples sideways, blood blooming across his chest in three distinct roses. His back connects with Emelio's tomb, the symmetry not lost on any of us as he slumps against his former boss's final resting place. The gun falls from his nerveless fingers, clattering against marble with shocking finality.

"You're your father's daughter," he gasps, blood bubbling at the corners of his mouth. His eyes remain clear despite the mortal wounds, fixing on Yelana with something like perverse pride. "I always knew you had it in you."

I drag myself to a sitting position, every movement sending fresh waves of agony through my battered body. Blood streams from a gash on my forehead, running into my left eye and forcing me to blink it away.

Yelana approaches cautiously, weapon still trained on Ken though it's clear he has only moments left. Her face reveals no regret, no horror at taking a life—only the cold resolve of someone doing what's necessary. In this moment, she is entirely Emelio's heir.

"You'll never escape this life," Ken continues, each word forcing more blood past his lips. "It'll corrupt you like it did him. Like it corrupts everyone who touches it." His gaze shifts between us, a grotesque smile forming. "You think it ends with me? Others will come for you. The Vasquez cartel. Vince Costa. Former clients with grudges against your father."

"Let them come," Yelana replies, her voice steady as a surgeon's hand. "They'll find what you found."

Ken laughs, the sound wet and horrible. "You think... you're different..." His eyes begin to lose focus, death's approach evident in his slackening features. "You're not... You're just... beginning..."

His body goes still, eyes fixed on some distant point beyond the mausoleum's stained glass windows. In death, the lines of bitterness smooth from his face, leaving only the man who once stood loyally at Emelio's side for twenty-five years before ambition corrupted whatever honor he might have possessed.

The sudden silence feels oppressive, broken only by our ragged breathing and the distant call of night birds outside. I pull myself to my feet, using Sierra's tomb for support, leaving bloody handprints on the white marble that her caretakers will discover with horror tomorrow. Each movement sends fresh pain radiating through my body, but I force myself upright.

Yelana and I lock eyes across the blood-spattered space, something profound and wordless passing between us. I see the weight of what she's done settling on her shoulders—not regret, but acknowledgment of the line she's crossed. There's no going back from this moment. No pretending the world is anything other than what it is.

I limp toward her, each step a negotiation with pain, leaving bloody footprints across the floor that once held only the solemn dignity of death, not its violent reality. When I reach her, she lowers the weapon, letting it hang at her side as her free hand reaches for mine.

"Are you okay?" she asks, the simple question containing layers of meaning beyond the physical.

"I will be," I answer, the truth in its simplicity. I take the gun gently from her hand, securing it at my waist. "We should go. The shots will bring attention, even out here."

She nods, slipping her arm around my waist to support me as I drape my arm across her shoulders. We move toward the exit, two broken bodies finding strength in their connection. The pain in my side flares with each step, but I focus on the warmth of her against me, on the simple fact of our survival.

At the mausoleum entrance, Yelana pauses, looking back at the carnage we're leaving behind—Ken's body slumped against her father's tomb, blood staining the pristine marble, broken glass from shattered windows glittering in moonlight like scattered diamonds.

"He was right about one thing," she says quietly. "Others will come."

I tighten my arm around her shoulders, a gesture of protection and promise. "Let them."

We step out into the night air, leaving death behind us but carrying its lessons forward. The weight of her against my side feels like an anchor in a world where everything else has proven temporary or false. Tomorrow will bring new threats, new battles, new wounds. But tonight, we walk away together, physically and emotionally exhausted but alive—and in this business, sometimes that's the only victory that matters.

TWENTY-ONE
The Aftermath

Yelana

I sit in my father's leather chair, the dawn light filtering through bullet-resistant windows, casting long shadows across the mahogany desk that still smells faintly of his cologne. The surface is buried under dossiers, security reports, and personnel files—the paper empire beneath the real one. My fingers trace the edges of a folder marked "CONFIDENTIAL," nails clicking against the cardstock in a rhythm that matches my racing thoughts. Three days since Ken's blood stained the marble of my family's mausoleum. Three days of reclaiming what's mine piece by methodical piece.

"The security team assignments for the ceremony," Sophia says, placing another folder beside my right hand. Dark circles shadow her eyes, matching my own. Neither of us has slept much since Ken's betrayal tore our world apart.

I flip it open, scanning names and positions. "Rodriguez stays in logistics. I don't want him anywhere near the main floor during the transition announcement."

"He's been cooperative since the confrontation," Sophia points out.

"Cooperative isn't loyal." I strike his name from the security detail with a single line of my pen. "Move Chen to oversee the east entrance. Double the guards at all access points. Anyone who worked closely with Ken gets reassigned or removed."

Miguel Costa leans against the wall, arms crossed over his expensive suit, watching me with the calculating eyes of someone assessing an investment. "Purging too quickly creates vulnerabilities," he observes. "Empty spaces that others rush to fill."

"I'm not purging," I correct him without looking up. "I'm restructuring. There's a difference."

Sophia's fingers dance across her tablet, implementing my changes in real-time. "The guest list is finalized. All major clients and partners have confirmed attendance. The Vasquez delegation requested additional security clearances."

"Denied," I snap. "Standard protocol for everyone. No exceptions." I shuffle through another stack of papers, pulling out shipping manifests that require immediate attention. "What's the status on the Singapore shipment?"

"Rerouted through the Macau channel," Sophia answers. "Arriving on schedule with Marcus Webb personally overseeing the transfer." She hesitates, then adds, "There are still inconsistencies in the financial records from Ken's—"

"That chapter's closed," I cut her off, my voice sharper than intended. I soften slightly, adding, "Focus on the current operations. The past will keep until we've stabilized the present."

Miguel pushes himself off the wall, approaching the desk with the fluid grace of a predator. "The Zentarra Organization under new leadership presents... opportunities for some of your rivals." His fingertips rest lightly on the edge of my desk—familiar, presumptuous. "Several factions will test your resolve in the coming weeks."

I meet his gaze directly. "Let them. Testing me would be a costly mistake." I return to the papers, dismissing his concern with a flick of my wrist. "The Costa partnership remains as we discussed. No adjustments necessary unless you're having second thoughts?"

A ghost of a smile touches his lips. "Not at all. My brother may have been short-sighted, but I recognize the value in our arrangement."

The door opens without a knock—only one person would dare. Mason enters, and I straighten reflexively, a reaction I can't seem to control despite my best efforts. He moves with the careful precision of someone still recovering from serious injuries, but his eyes sweep the room with the same tactical assessment I've come to rely on.

"Perimeter check complete," he reports, standing at parade rest near the doorway rather than approaching the desk. "All security measures in place for the ceremony. I've assigned additional teams to monitor roof access points and underground entrances."

I nod, pretending to focus on the papers before me rather than the way his presence immediately changes the atmosphere in the room. "And the digital security protocols?"

"Implemented as directed," he answers, his voice professionally neutral. "New firewalls are active. Communications have been rerouted through secure channels only. All devices have been screened for surveillance equipment."

"Good." The single word hangs between us, loaded with everything we're not saying.

Miguel watches this exchange with unconcealed interest. "And what about you, Phillips? Now that the blood debt is paid, what are your plans? Return to private security? Or perhaps back to military contracting?"

The question lands like a grenade in the center of the room. Sophia suddenly finds her tablet absolutely fascinating. I shuffle papers with deliberate focus, though the words blur before my eyes.

Mason's expression doesn't change, but I notice the slight shift in his stance—weight moving to the balls of his feet, ready for quick movement. Fight or flight. "My immediate concern is ensuring Miss Zentarra's security during the transition of power," he says, neatly sidestepping the actual question.

"Of course," Miguel replies, his tone suggesting he's noted the evasion and finds it interesting. "Loyalty is such a rare commodity these days."

I tap the edge of a folder against the desk, bringing attention back to the business at hand. "The ceremony begins at 7 PM sharp. I want final security checks completed by 5. Sophia, prepare the statement for distribution to our international partners immediately following the announcement."

"Already drafted," she confirms.

"And the modifications to the lieutenant structure?" I ask.

"All outlined in the blue folder," she replies. "Waiting for your final approval."

I nod, conscious of Mason's presence by the door, neither fully in the room nor out of it—a perfect metaphor for our current situation. "Miguel, I'll need your security detail to coordinate with ours. No overlapping jurisdictions, no confusion about chain of command."

"Naturally," he agrees smoothly. "Though I doubt anyone would challenge your authority after recent... demonstrations of your resolve."

My fingers unconsciously touch the bandage on my left arm, a souvenir from the final confrontation with Ken. "Authority isn't demonstrated once and assumed forever. It's reinforced daily." The words come from my father's lips through mine, wisdom passed down like the organization itself.

Sophia checks her watch. "We should review the ceremony seating arrangements. Several factions have made specific requests about proximity to you."

I stand, gathering key documents into a neat stack. "Politics disguised as protocol. Put everyone exactly where they don't want to be. It keeps them off-balance." I turn to Mason. "I need a moment to review the security detail privately."

Miguel takes the cue, pushing himself away from the desk. "Until this evening, then."

As they leave, Sophia gives me a look that says she knows this isn't just about security details. The door closes behind them, leaving Mason and me alone in my father's office with the weight of everything unsaid pressing down like a physical force.

The morning light has strengthened, illuminating dust particles floating between us like the fragments of whatever we had—or might have had—before reality reasserted itself. I straighten papers that don't need straightening, and he stands motionless, waiting for whatever comes next in this careful dance we've been performing since the mausoleum.

I pause at the threshold of the main hall, adjusting the cuffs of my tailored black suit—my father's style reimagined through my eyes. The jacket cuts sharply at the waist, the red silk lining a flash of color visible only when I move, like blood beneath skin. My mother's diamond earrings catch the light, a subtle reminder of what was taken and what remains. Beyond the double doors, two hundred people wait—lieutenants, business partners, rivals, allies—all gathered to witness the official transfer of power. All wondering if Emelio Zentarra's daughter has what it takes to hold what she has claimed.

"Ready, Miss Zentarra?" Maria asks.

I give her a single nod, drawing my shoulders back. "Open them."

The heavy doors swing wide, and every conversation stops mid-sentence. Two hundred faces turn toward me, two hundred assessments begin simultaneously. I feel their eyes measuring the cut of my suit, the straightness of my spine, the focus in my gaze. I take the first step forward, then another, my heels striking the marble with deliberate, unhurried precision. The sound echoes through the sudden silence.

The main hall of the Zentarra estate has hosted countless gatherings—business deals disguised as social events, celebrations masking power plays, alliances formed and broken over expensive champagne. Tonight, the crystal chandeliers burn a little brighter, the security presence a little heavier. Faces arranged in careful expressions of respect mask calculations running behind every pair of eyes.

Antonio Krane stands with his team near the eastern windows, his posture indicating cautious alliance. Marcus Webb holds court with several international clients, his bruised face from the confrontation with Ken now a badge of loyalty he wears proudly. The Costa family occupies a prime position near the center of the room—Miguel flanked by advisors, his expression revealing nothing but polite interest.

My eyes find Mason before I consciously look for him. He's positioned against the back wall, one shoulder leaning against a column, his stance casual to anyone who doesn't know what to look for. I see the contour of his concealed weapon, the way his eyes never stop moving, cataloging every person, every movement, every potential threat. His suit can't quite hide the bandages I know wrap around his torso, evidence of wounds gained protecting what's mine—protecting me.

The podium awaits at the front of the hall, my father's emblem emblazoned across its front. I take my place behind it, allowing the silence to stretch for three deliberate heartbeats before speaking.

"My parents weren't saints." My voice carries clearly through the perfect acoustics of the hall. No hesitation, no apology. "They built this organization with blood and steel. I won't insult their memory or your intelligence by pretending otherwise."

A ripple passes through the crowd—surprise at this deviation from the expected platitudes. Several lieutenants shift uncomfortably, glancing at each other.

"Emelio and Sierra Zentarra understood what many forget: In our world, respect isn't requested—it's earned. Trust isn't given—it's verified. Loyalty isn't declared—it's demonstrated." I let my gaze sweep across the gathering, meeting the eyes of key figures. "My father earned your respect through consistent action. My mother verified your trustworthiness with meticulous attention to detail. And I—" I pause, allowing the weight of what's coming to build, "—have demonstrated what happens to those who mistake my youth for weakness."

No one mentions Ken's name, but his absence hangs heavy in the room. I don't flinch from it.

"You all know what happened. A trusted lieutenant betrayed his position, murdered my parents, and attempted to seize control of what wasn't his." My voice remains level, each word precise. "He miscalculated. That error cost him everything."

Miguel Costa's expression remains carefully neutral, but something like appreciation flickers in his eyes. The lieutenants who wavered during the crisis stand straighter, as if proximity to my certainty might erase their hesitation.

"The Zentarra Organization stands at a crossroads," I continue. "We can cling to old methods, old grudges, old limitations—or we can evolve. Under my leadership, we will expand beyond traditional markets while strengthening our core operations. We will forge new alliances while honoring proven partnerships. We will adapt to changing global realities while maintaining the principles that built our success."

I place my hands flat on the podium, leaning forward slightly. "Some of you are wondering if I have what it takes. Good. Keep wondering. Keep watching. I'll be doing the same." The threat beneath the statement isn't hidden, just elegantly wrapped. "Prove your value, and you'll find no more loyal ally than me. Prove otherwise..." I let the implication hang in the air.

Marcus Webb nods almost imperceptibly from his position near the front. Antonio Krane's posture subtly shifts, aligning himself more visibly with my statement. From the back wall, I feel Mason's eyes on me, his expression unreadable at this distance.

"The world believes organizations like ours exist in shadows," I say, straightening to my full height. "They're wrong. We don't hide in darkness—we control it. We harness it. We direct it toward our purposes." A line from my father, repurposed for this moment. "Today marks not just a transition of leadership but an evolution of vision. Those who align with that vision will prosper. Those who resist it will not."

Sophia steps forward from her position behind me, carrying a small velvet box. She opens it to reveal my father's signet ring—the physical symbol of Zentarra authority, worn by him for decades until Ken's betrayal took it from his finger. I remove it from the cushion, feeling its substantial weight before sliding it onto my hand.

"With this, I formally accept leadership of the Zentarra Organization in all its operations, territories, and interests," I state, holding up my hand so the ring catches the light. "Let no one question its legitimacy or mine."

Applause breaks out, starting near the front where the most loyal lieutenants stand and spreading through the hall. I step away from the podium as Sophia announces the commencement of the reception portion of the evening. Immediately, people begin moving toward me, faces arranged in congratulatory smiles, hands extended in performative solidarity.

I navigate the currents of power with practiced ease—a firm handshake here, a subtle rebuff there, careful attention paid to who approaches and who hangs back. Miguel Costa makes his way through the crowd with deliberate patience, watching my interactions with calculating eyes. I'm performing and I know it—every gesture, every word measured and weighed for its political value.

In a brief moment between conversations, my eyes drift back to Mason's position by the wall. The space stands empty now, his absence like a sudden drop in air pressure. I scan the room while maintaining my smile for the shipping director currently speaking about expanded Asian routes. There—a side door closing, a glimpse of broad shoulders slipping away unnoticed by anyone except me.

Something cold settles in my chest despite the warmth of the crowded room. Victory tastes like ashes when there's no one to share it with who sees past the crown to the person beneath it.

I find him exactly where I knew he'd be. The eastern balcony has always been his thinking spot—far enough from the main security routes to offer privacy, high enough to give tactical advantage, yet still within response range if something goes wrong. Mason leans against the railing, whiskey glass dangling from fingers that bear fresh bruises from the fight with Ken. His shoulders create a rigid line beneath his black shirt, attempting casual relaxation but achieving military readiness instead. He doesn't turn when I step through the glass doors, though I know he heard me coming. He's always hearing, always watching, always ready.

I approach with two fresh glasses and the bottle I took from my father's private collection. The crystal catches the distant city lights as I set everything on the small table beside him. The night air carries the scent of the gardens below, jasmine and gunpowder from the security team's evening drills.

"You disappeared," I say, pouring amber liquid into both glasses.

"You had it handled." His voice holds the careful neutrality I've come to hate. "Impressive speech."

I push a glass toward him, taking mine with deliberate casualness that matches his pretense. "So are you out?"

The question lands between us like a grenade with the pin half-pulled. Mason's fingers tighten around his glass, his profile sharp against the backdrop of city lights. He takes too long to answer.

"The debt's paid," he finally says without meeting my eyes, repeating the words Miguel used earlier. As if our relationship could be reduced to a ledger entry: life saved, debt owed, balance cleared.

"Bullshit." I take a sharp sip that burns all the way down. "That's not what I asked."

He turns then, his face half in shadow, half illuminated by the lights from the estate behind us. The bruising along his jaw has faded to yellowish-green, a physical reminder of what we survived together. "What do you want me to say, Yelana?"

"The truth would be refreshing." I lean against the railing beside him, close but not touching. "Or is that too much to ask from the man who's seen me at my absolute worst and still came back for more?"

"It's complicated."

"It's really not." My voice hardens with frustration. "You're using our different worlds as an excuse because you're afraid."

His jaw tightens. "You don't understand what you're asking for."

"I understand exactly what I'm asking for." I set my glass down harder than necessary. "I'm asking for you to stop pretending that what happened between us was just adrenaline or convenience or whatever bullshit you've been telling yourself."

"I never said—"

"You didn't have to. You've been looking for the exit since we killed Ken." My knuckles whiten around my glass. "Mission accomplished, debt paid, time to disappear before things get messy, right? Before you have to actually deal with feelings instead of bullets."

Mason slams his drink down, liquid sloshing over the edge onto the concrete. "You think I want to leave? Your world swallows people whole, Yelana. I've watched it happen. Your father, your mother, Ken—everyone gets corrupted eventually. The power, the money, the constant looking over your shoulder—it changes people."

"My world?" I step closer, voice dropping dangerously. "You've been in it since Afghanistan. You were in it the moment you took my father's help, the moment you promised to protect me. You don't get to act like this is some foreign country you just stumbled into."

His eyes flash with something raw and wounded. "It's different now."

"Why? Because we slept together? Because you actually care? Because for once in your life, you can't pretend this is just another job?" Each question pushes closer to the truth we're both circling.

"Because I can't lose anyone else!" The words explode from him, shocking us both with their force. His chest rises and falls rapidly, control momentarily shattered. "I couldn't save Kerry. I barely saved you. Every time I close my eyes, I see you bleeding out in that mausoleum, or getting gunned down by the next Ken, or disappearing into your father's world until you become someone I don't recognize."

The confession hangs between us, his fear finally exposed to the night air. I want to reach for him, to bridge the physical gap that mirrors the emotional one, but something holds me back—pride or self-preservation, I'm not sure which.

"You think I'm not scared?" My voice softens despite my intention to remain hard. "Everyone in that room tonight looks at me and sees my father. They measure everything I do against his legacy. They're all waiting for me to fail or succeed spectacularly, but none of them see me. You're the only one who does."

His expression shifts, vulnerability replacing anger. "Yelana—"

"No, let me finish." I set my glass down, needing both hands free for what comes next. "I've spent my whole life being Emelio Zentarra's daughter. The princess in the tower, protected and prepped to inherit a kingdom built on blood money and back-room deals. And then you showed up—this angry, damaged man who looked at me and saw past all that. Who pushed me to be stronger, who trusted me to handle the truth, who didn't treat me like I would break."

I step closer, close enough to feel the heat from his body but still not touching. "And now you want to walk away because it's messy and complicated? Because we might fail? Because you're scared of losing me?" I shake my head, disappointment burning behind my eyes. "I thought you were braver than that."

His hand moves as if to reach for me, then stops, suspended in the space between us. "I've buried everyone I've ever loved," he says quietly. "I can't bury you too."

"So your solution is to bury us instead? While we're both still breathing?" I laugh, a sharp sound with no humor. "That's cowardice, I thought you were braver than that."

The words hit him like a physical blow. His eyes darken, jaw clenching as he absorbs the accusation. For a moment, I think he might reach for me, might bridge the gap we've both created. Instead, he turns back to the railing, hands gripping the metal with white-knuckle force.

"You deserve better than me," he says to the night sky rather than to me.

"That's for me to decide." I straighten, gathering my dignity around me like armor. "When you figure out what you actually want—not what you're afraid of, but what you want—you know where to find me."

I turn and walk away, my footsteps echoing on the concrete. Each step feels heavier than the last, but I don't look back. Can't look back. The sound of the glass door sliding open and closed marks the boundary between us as clearly as our fears.

Through the glass, I catch a glimpse of his reflection—fractured by the beveled edges of the door panels, a man broken into pieces by forces he can't control. Part of me wants to return, to gather those pieces and hold them together with my bare hands if necessary. But I've spent too long chasing people who won't be caught, and my new role demands more from me than that.

I am Yelana Zentarra. I've reclaimed my father's empire, avenged my parents' deaths, and established my authority over those who would challenge me. I can't make one stubborn, damaged man see what's right in front of him.

At least, not tonight.

TWENTY-TWO
Crossroads

MASON

I fold each item with military precision, creasing edges sharp enough to cut. Shirts, pants, underwear—all condensed into the smallest possible footprint in my duffel. Old habits from too many deployments where space meant survival. The Glock comes next, field-stripped, cleaned, and reassembled in ninety seconds flat before I secure it in its holster. Another muscle memory I can't shake. I check the spare magazines, counting bullets like rosary beads. Fifteen rounds, plus one in the chamber. More than enough for whatever's waiting outside these gates. If only bullets could protect against what I'm really running from.

My knuckles whiten around the grip of the Glock before I slide it home. The movement pulls at the half-healed wounds across my ribs, a sharp reminder of Ken's knife, his bullets, his final moments in the mausoleum. Pain I can handle. It's familiar, quantifiable. What I can't handle is the look in Yelana's eyes on that balcony last night. Disappointment. Hurt. Understanding.

Coward.

The word hangs in the air of this too-elegant room I never belonged in. She hurled it at me like a throwing knife, and like all her aims lately, it struck true. Am I running because I'm scared? Because it's easier than staying? Because the thought of watching her transform into her father terrifies me almost as much as the thought of losing her?

My phone buzzes with a text notification. I pull it from my pocket, already knowing who it's from. Sophia, confirming security rotations for the next week. Professional to the end. I swipe past it and find myself staring at the photo I can't bring myself to delete—Yelana at the safe house, hair loose around her shoulders, eyes challenging the camera, a half-smile playing on lips I can still feel against mine. My thumb hovers over the screen, tracing the outline of her face without touching it.

"Fuck," I mutter, shoving the phone back in my pocket. This is exactly why I need to leave. I'm compromised. Emotional. Making decisions based on feelings instead of tactical assessment. Everything I've trained against for twenty years.

I zip the duffel with more force than necessary, the harsh sound cutting through the quiet room. This space never felt like mine anyway—too much mahogany and silk for a guy who spent most of his adult life sleeping on canvas cots and desert sand. The bathroom still holds her scent from the night she helped stitch my wounds. The chair by the window bears the imprint of her body from late strategy sessions. Every inch of this room is haunted by her presence.

I make a final sweep, checking drawers and closets with practiced efficiency. Nothing left behind except memories I can't pack away. My gaze catches on the view through the window—the carefully manicured gardens stretching toward the security perimeter, the spot where I first trained Yelana to shoot, the eastern section where Juan's memorial stands beneath an ancient oak tree.

Juan. The boy I couldn't save. The death that bound me to this family through blood and obligation.

I shoulder the duffel, decision made. I need to see the memorial one more time before I go. A private goodbye to the ghost that started all this.

The hallways of the Zentarra estate are quiet in the early evening. Most staff have retreated to their quarters after the ceremony yesterday. Those who remain give me respectful nods as I pass—the man who helped their young mistress reclaim her birthright. If only they knew I'm deserting her less than twenty-four hours after her triumph.

I note the security cameras tracking my movement, the subtle pressure plates beneath the marble flooring, the infrared sensors at each junction—all measures I helped implement. The estate is a fortress now, designed to prevent another Ken from ever getting close to her again. She'll be safe here, safer than with me and all the chaos I inevitably bring.

The garden air hits my face as I step through the terrace doors, heavy with jasmine and approaching rain. Long shadows stretch across the manicured lawns like grasping fingers. The grass muffles my footsteps as I follow the stone path that winds toward the eastern section, past fountains and sculptured hedges that cost more than my entire Chicago apartment.

Juan's memorial appears as I round a flowering hedge, nestled beneath the spreading branches of an oak tree old enough to have witnessed generations of Zentarra power. Not a grave—Juan's actual remains rest in the family mausoleum where Ken met his end—but a peaceful remembrance space Emelio created after the Afghanistan ambush that claimed his son.

The weathered bronze plaque catches the dying light, Juan's name and dates glowing warm against the green patina. Fourteen years since that day. Fourteen years since a father sacrificed his son to save a stranger. The weight of that debt settles across my shoulders like a physical thing, heavier than any tactical gear I've ever carried.

Around the plaque, arranged with careful reverence, sit the totems of a life cut short: a collection of small metal cars Juan collected as a child; a baseball signed by players whose names have long since faded; a framed photo of Juan with his father, both smiling at the camera with identical expressions. And newer additions—fresh flowers in crystal vases, their scent mingling with the garden's natural perfume. Yelana's work. She comes here often, I know. Talking to the brother she lost too young, seeking guidance from a ghost.

I crouch before the memorial, knees protesting after too many injuries and not enough rest. My fingers brush against the cool metal of the plaque, tracing the engraved letters of Juan's name.

"I tried," I tell him quietly. "I kept her alive. Got her through the worst of it." The words feel inadequate in the face of his permanent silence. "Your father saved my life, and I repaid the debt. But somewhere along the way, it stopped being about duty."

Wind rustles through the oak leaves above, nature's only answer.

"She's stronger than all of us," I continue. "Smarter too. She'll rebuild what Ken tried to destroy. Make it better, probably." I pause, throat tight with emotions I rarely allow myself to acknowledge. "I can't stay and watch her become someone she'll hate. Or worse, watch her die because I wasn't fast enough, smart enough, good enough."

A child's marble rests among Juan's belongings, blue glass swirled with white like a miniature earth. I pick it up, rolling it between my fingers, feeling its perfect smoothness. The kind of innocent treasure a boy would value, now preserved as a sacred object.

"I couldn't save you," I whisper. "And I almost lost her too many times already."

The decision to leave still feels wrong, like tearing off a limb. But staying feels equally impossible. I place the marble back exactly where I found it, arranging it with careful precision.

I stand, muscles protesting, wounds aching. The duffel weighs against my shoulder like a sentence as I turn to leave. One last look at the memorial, at this piece of Zentarra history that changed my life's trajectory forever.

"I'll still protect her," I promise the silent plaque. "Just from a distance where I can't destroy her too."

As I walk away, the garden shadows lengthen behind me, stretching like hands trying to pull me back to what I'm leaving.

I'm halfway back to the main path when I see her. Yelana sits perfectly still on the stone bench facing Juan's memorial, her spine straight as a blade, shoulders set in that rigid posture she adopts when forcing herself not to break. She doesn't turn at my approach, though I know she hears me—the slight tilt of her head, the almost imperceptible tension in her neck betraying her awareness. For a moment, I consider retreating, slipping away without disturbing her grief. But running got me labeled a coward once already. I won't earn that title twice in twenty-four hours.

I approach slowly, giving her time to dismiss me if that's what she wants. When she doesn't, I set my duffel down and lower myself onto the bench beside her, leaving careful inches between us. Neither of us speaks. The silence stretches, weighted with everything we've been through together—bullets and blood, betrayal and vengeance, grief and desire—compressed into this small space between our bodies.

She's changed from her business attire into dark jeans and a simple black sweater, hair pulled back in a loose ponytail. Without makeup, the shadows beneath her eyes are more pronounced, the small scar at her temple from the warehouse fight more visible. Her hands rest in her lap, fingers interlaced so tightly the knuckles show white. She looks both younger and older than her years, vulnerability and strength coexisting in impossible balance.

"I've been thinking about what Ken said," she finally says, voice soft but steady. "In the mausoleum, before I shot him." Her eyes never leave Juan's memorial, as if addressing her brother rather than me. "About being trapped in my father's world. About becoming corrupted by it."

I remain silent, recognizing that whatever she's working through requires space, not interruption.

"I don't want to just be Emelio's daughter anymore," she continues, fingers unclasping to trace Juan's name on the plaque. "I don't want to be defined by his legacy or his mistakes. Or by what I had to become to survive Ken's betrayal."

"That's understandable," I offer carefully, uncertain where this is heading.

She turns to face me fully, her eyes clear and determined in a way that makes my chest tighten. "I'm selling the organization's illegal operations. All of them. The weapons distribution networks, the black market channels, the offshore accounts—everything that isn't legitimate."

The words hit me so unexpectedly that for a moment I wondered if I'd misheard. "You're... what?"

"Miguel Costa is buying most of it," she continues, watching my reaction closely. "The Asian pipeline goes to Chen, who's wanted independence for years. Marcus Webb takes over European distribution until retirement next year."

I struggle to process what she's saying. After everything—the bloody fight for control, Ken's death, yesterday's ceremony where she claimed her father's throne—she's walking away from the empire that cost her parents' lives?

"You fought so hard to take it back," I say, searching her face for signs of coercion or undue influence. "You risked everything."

"I fought to take it back so I could decide what to do with it," she clarifies, a hint of the old fire flashing in her eyes. "Not to let Ken steal it, not to watch it destroy more lives. To control its fate." Her voice softens. "There's a difference between reclaiming your power and becoming what took that power from you in the first place."

"Your father—"

"Built what he thought would protect his family," she interrupts. "But it didn't. It got him killed. It got my mother killed. It almost got me killed." She looks back at the memorial. "I won't let it define me, either."

Understanding dawns slowly. This isn't surrender—it's liberation. Not weakness, but a different kind of strength than I expected from her.

"What will you do instead?" I ask, genuinely curious about her vision.

"Expand the legitimate businesses. Technology, pharmaceuticals, shipping, real estate." Her eyes light with an enthusiasm I haven't seen before. "My father used those as cover, but they're profitable on their own. Without the risk, without the constant looking over our shoulder for the next Ken or the next cartel hit squad."

I find myself nodding slowly, impressed despite my surprise. "It's a bold move."

"It's the only move that lets me sleep at night," she says simply. "The only one that honors what my parents died protecting—not their business, but their family."

Something shifts between us, the air charged with possibilities neither of us anticipated. I look down at my duffel, the physical manifestation of my intention to run, and feel a flush of shame.

"My security business in Chicago feels like a fucking empty shell compared to being here with you," I admit, the words scraping raw against my throat. "Has for a while now."

Her eyes soften at the admission, but she doesn't reach for me as I half-expect. Instead, she studies me with careful consideration. "I think we both need time," she says after a moment. "Me to transform the organization, you to figure out if what you feel for me is real or just an extension of your duty to my father."

The suggestion stings, but I can't honestly deny the validity of her concern. How much of my feeling for her is tied to the debt I owed Emelio? To the adrenaline of fighting alongside her? To the intensity of protecting someone through life-or-death situations?

"How much time?" I ask, voice rougher than intended.

"Six months," she says, her voice steady despite the emotion visible in her eyes. "I need to dismantle the illegal operations, establish the new direction, prove to everyone that I'm serious about this change. You need to go back to Chicago, rebuild your life there, see if it still fits." She pauses, vulnerability breaking through her composed exterior. "See if you still want this—want me—when there's no blood debt or family obligation involved."

I want to argue that I already know, that my feelings transcended duty weeks ago, but she's right. We both need clarity that can only come with distance and time. The realization doesn't make it any easier to accept.

"Six months," I repeat, the words tasting bitter and sweet simultaneously.

"If you still feel the way you do now," she continues, looking down at the bench where our hands rest inches apart, "meet me at the beach house. The one in Malibu where my parents used to take me as a child."

My fingers inch closer to hers on the stone surface, not quite touching but close enough to feel the heat of her skin. "And if you change your mind? If this new direction takes you somewhere I can't follow?"

"Then we'll both know it wasn't meant to be," she says simply. "But at least we'll know for certain."

The logic is impeccable, the emotional cost almost unbearable. I look at her profile in the fading light—the proud lift of her chin, the strength in her shoulders, the vulnerability she allows only me to see—and realize I've never met anyone like her. Never will again.

Our fingers drift closer on the bench, pinky fingers almost but not quite touching. The small space between us charges with electricity, with possibility, with the weight of decisions that will shape both our futures.

"When would we start?" I ask, already dreading the answer.

"Tonight," she says, eyes meeting mine directly. "Clean break. Fresh start."

I nod slowly, accepting the inevitability of it. Six months apart to discover if what we've found is real or merely the product of extraordinary circumstances. Six months to live in our separate worlds and see if they can ever truly align.

Our hands remain close but separate on the stone bench between us, a physical representation of everything unsaid.

Dusk falls around us like a velvet curtain, the garden transforming in the fading light. Long shadows stretch across the lawn, merging into the growing darkness while the western sky burns with final streaks of amber and gold. Neither of us moves from the bench, as if by mutual unspoken agreement, we're extending these last moments together until night forces us apart. Someone—Maria probably, with her impeccable timing and discretion—has lit the memorial candles around Juan's plaque. The small flames flicker in glass containers, creating pools of warm, unsteady light that catch in Yelana's eyes and turn them to liquid gold.

The air grows cooler as darkness deepens, bringing with it the night scents of jasmine and distant rain. A few stars appear overhead, faint pinpricks against the darkening blue. We sit in companionable silence, watching the candle flames dance in the slight breeze, both aware that each passing minute brings us closer to separation. Six months suddenly feels like an eternity, each hour stretching impossibly long when measured against the absence of her presence.

My hand moves of its own accord, finally crossing the small distance between us on the bench. My calloused fingers cover hers, skin against skin after the restraint we've both maintained. Her hand turns beneath mine, our fingers intertwining with familiar ease, fitting together like puzzle pieces designed for each other. The simple contact sends electricity up my arm, a reminder of everything I'm choosing to walk away from.

"I'll be there," I promise, my voice rough with emotion. "Six months from today, at the beach house."

She meets my gaze directly, vulnerability mingling with challenge in her expression. "But what if you're not? What if Chicago pulls you back in? What if you decide this was all just adrenaline and obligation?"

The questions hang between us, legitimate fears that neither of us can simply dismiss. I tighten my grip on her hand, anchoring us both to this moment, to what feels real despite all rational doubts.

"I've been running my whole life," I tell her, each word drawn from some deep well of honesty I rarely access. "From my parents' expectations, into the military, away from Kerry's death, from one war zone to the next." I pause, gathering the courage to continue. "I'm tired of running. When I'm with you, I don't feel that urge to escape. For the first time in my life, I want to stay somewhere. With someone."

Her eyes soften at the admission, though she doesn't immediately respond. Instead, she shifts closer on the bench, the barrier of space between us dissolving by increments. The candles cast dancing shadows across her face, highlighting the strength in her jawline, the delicate curve of her lips, the intensity that has always drawn me to her despite my best defenses.

"Six months to be sure," she says softly. "For both of us."

I pull her closer, unable to maintain distance any longer. One hand cups her face, my thumb brushing across her cheekbone with a gentleness that surprises even me. I study her features in the flickering light as if committing them to memory—the small scar near her temple from the warehouse fight, the precise arch of her eyebrows, the way her lashes cast shadows on her cheeks when she looks down.

"I've survived deployments longer than that," I say, trying for lightness and missing by miles, my voice too raw with emotion to carry the pretense. "But none that mattered this much."

Her hand rises to cover mine against her cheek, her palm warm against my knuckles. "This isn't a deployment, Mason. This is a choice. For both of us."

"I've already chosen," I tell her, the certainty in my voice surprising me with its conviction.

The distance between us collapses entirely as I lean forward, capturing her lips with mine. The kiss begins gently, almost hesitant, before transforming into something deeper, more desperate. Her arms wind around my neck as mine circle her waist, pulling her against me until I feel her heartbeat against my chest. We pour everything we can't say into this contact—all the fear and hope, doubt and certainty, regret and promise that words can't adequately express.

Her fingers thread through my hair, holding me to her with surprising strength as the kiss deepens. I taste salt—her tears or mine, I'm not sure which—and the faint sweetness that's uniquely her. Time suspends around us, the garden fading to background noise as we cling to each other with the knowledge of our impending separation burning between us like a physical presence.

When we finally break apart, both breathing heavily, her eyes are bright with unshed tears that catch the candlelight like diamonds. One escapes, trailing down her cheek, and I brush it away with my thumb, my own vision suspiciously blurred. We remain close, foreheads touching, sharing breath in the narrow space between us.

"Six months," she repeats, the words both promise and plea.

"I'll be waiting," I assure her, voice barely above a whisper. "However long it takes."

She pulls back slowly, her hands sliding down to rest against my chest for a moment before dropping away entirely. The physical separation feels like tearing a bandage from a wound not yet healed—necessary but painful beyond words.

"I need to go inside," she says, composure returning to her voice though her eyes remain unguarded. "Rodriguez and the lieutenants are waiting for details about the transition."

I nod, understanding that she's already shifting back into her role as leader, as Zentarra. It's what she needs to do, what she's been trained her entire life to do. I release her, my hands feeling empty without her to hold.

She stands, smoothing nonexistent wrinkles from her jeans in a gesture that betrays her need for something to do with her hands. "Goodbye, Mason," she says, the formality not quite masking the emotion beneath.

"Until the beach house," I correct gently, refusing to make this a final farewell.

A hint of a smile touches her lips. "Until then."

I watch her walk away, her slender figure silhouetted against the estate lights as she moves toward the main house. Her steps are measured, her spine straight, shoulders back—every inch the leader she was born to be, reclaiming her power on her own terms. Pride swells in my chest, tempered with a sharp ache of separation already setting in.

Only when she disappears through the terrace doors do I turn back to Juan's memorial. The candles still flicker around his plaque, casting warm light across the weathered bronze.

"I'll take care of her," I whisper to the silent marker, the same promise I made fourteen years ago to his father. "Just in a different way than either of us expected."

I shoulder my duffel bag, its weight insignificant compared to the invisible burden of leaving. My feet carry me along the garden path toward the gates, each step requiring deliberate effort not to turn back, not to run after her, not to abandon this plan that feels simultaneously like the most sensible and most painful decision I've ever made.

At the edge of the property, I pause for one last look at the Zentarra estate—the garden where Juan's memorial stands, the balcony where Yelana called me a coward, the rooms where we fought and bled and found each other against impossible odds. Six months to discover if what we've built can survive normal life, separate paths, distance and time.

I turn toward the waiting car, not looking back though every instinct screams at me to stay. Some battles can only be won by retreating first—regroup, reassess, return stronger. Six months. One hundred and eighty-three days. I've counted longer countdowns with less worthy rewards waiting at the end.

TWENTY-THREE
Full Circle

MASON

The weathered deck creaks beneath my boots as I set my duffel down, salt air filling my lungs with each breath. Six months to the day. I scan the horizon where the Pacific swallows the sun in slow, deliberate bites, turning the sky into bleeding watercolors. Nothing's changed here – same peeling paint on the railings, same hidden panel beneath the welcome mat where Emelio kept a Glock 19 for emergencies. Same hollow feeling in my chest as I check my watch for the fifth time in twenty minutes.

One hundred and eighty-three days. That was the countdown I've been running in my head since walking away from the Zentarra estate, each number crossed off. Chicago welcomed me back with indifferent arms – my apartment collecting dust, my security business running on autopilot thanks to Rodriguez, my old second-in-command, who never asked why I suddenly needed to expand operations with such intensity.

I run my finger over the new scar on my forearm, a jagged line where Ken's knife caught me during our final confrontation. The wound healed cleaner than expected, leaving just enough of a mark to serve as a permanent reminder. Some scars are meant to be kept.

The floorboards squeak as I pace the length of the deck, my reflection ghosting across the sliding glass doors. I look different than I did six months ago. Not just the new lines around my eyes or the silver threading through my temples, but something deeper. I move differently, like some of the weight I've carried for decades has finally been set down.

Three months ago, I visited the graves of my SEAL team for the first time since their funerals. Laid white roses on each headstone, spoke their names aloud like a roll call. George. Riley. Michael. Craig. Fynn. The guilt still came, but it didn't drown me like it used to. Progress, not perfection – something my new therapist keeps reminding me when I slip into old patterns of self-blame.

Kerry's grave was the hardest. I stood there for hours, telling her everything – about Yelana, about Ken, about finally understanding that loving someone new doesn't erase what we had. The groundskeeper eventually asked if I was okay, finding me sitting cross-legged on the grass, empty whiskey flask beside me, laughing through tears as I told stories to a marble slab about the woman who taught me it was okay to be human in a world that demanded I be a weapon.

"You'd like her," I told Kerry's headstone. "She calls me on my bullshit just like you did."

Back in Chicago, I threw myself into rebuilding. Hired four veterans with combat experience and PTSD diagnoses no private security firm would touch. Expanded our client list to include three tech startups and a women's shelter that couldn't afford our rates but got them anyway. Bought the building next door to our headquarters and renovated it into additional training space.

All the things that should have filled the emptiness. All the things that didn't.

I check my watch again. 5:47 PM. The sun hangs lower now, balanced on the edge of the horizon like it's deciding whether to stay or go. I know the feeling.

The beach house itself stands exactly as I remember – Emelio's idea of "modest" still meaning three bedrooms, panoramic ocean views, and enough security features to withstand a small invasion. I'd already swept the place upon arrival, old habits refusing to die. Found the weapons cache still tucked beneath the living room rug. Checked that the panic room behind the kitchen pantry remained operational. Verified the security cameras positioned at strategic points along the property line.

The place doesn't just look the same – it smells the same. Salt and cedar and that particular mustiness of a house closed up for too long. Beneath it all, I catch the faintest trace of perfume, embedded in the fabric of the couch where we sat during our last visit here years ago, when I was still just her father's hired gun, and Yelana was still just Emelio's little girl being groomed for an empire she didn't want.

The sound of tires on gravel snaps me to attention. My heart rate spikes, combat instincts kicking in before I can suppress them. I move to the side of the deck, positioning myself with clear sightlines to the approaching vehicle while minimizing my exposure – another habit that refuses to die.

A sleek black car winds up the private drive, sunlight glinting off tinted windows. Not the usual armored SUV the Zentarra security detail favors. Something more elegant, less conspicuous. More in line with the legitimate businesswoman she's becoming than the arms dealer's daughter she was.

The car stops. For several heartbeats, nothing happens. Then the driver's door opens.

She steps out, and six months of carefully constructed composure threatens to crumble inside me. Yelana moves differently too – her shoulders squared but not rigid, her chin lifted with confidence rather than defiance. Her hair falls loose around her shoulders, longer than before, catching the wind off the ocean. She wears simple dark jeans and a white blouse that billows slightly in the breeze – no tactical gear, no concealed weapons, no armor against the world.

She spots me on the deck and pauses, one hand resting on the car door. Something passes across her face – relief, uncertainty, determination – before her lips curve into that half-smile that's haunted my dreams for six months.

I don't remember deciding to move, but suddenly I'm at the stairs, descending toward her with measured steps that belie the earthquake happening in my chest. She closes the car door and walks toward me, each step deliberate, her eyes never leaving mine.

We meet at the bottom of the stairs, stopping with three feet of charged air between us. Close enough to touch, far enough to retreat if necessary. Both of us strategic to the end.

"You came," she says, her voice steady but soft, carrying that hint of husky depth that never fails to unravel something in me.

"I said I would." My voice sounds rougher than intended.

The wind lifts a strand of her hair, and I resist the urge to reach out and tuck it behind her ear. Six months of distance has done nothing to diminish the pull she exerts, like gravity personified in this woman who stands before me, both familiar and new.

"You're on time," she observes, glancing at her watch with something like teasing in her eyes. "That's new."

The tension breaks slightly, a smile tugging at my lips despite my best efforts. "I've been here for three hours."

Her laugh – that genuine, unguarded sound I've heard too rarely – fills the space between us. "Of course you have."

The setting sun paints her in gold, highlighting the changes six months has wrought. There's a serenity to her I've never seen before, a centeredness that speaks of hard-won battles with herself rather than others. Her eyes hold mine, searching for whatever changes she can read in my face.

"It's good to see you, Mason," she says finally, my name on her lips sending electricity down my spine.

"You too." Two simple words carrying the weight of everything I can't yet say.

The ocean crashes against the shore below us, constant and rhythmic like a heartbeat. Neither of us moves to close the distance, both understanding that whatever happens next will be deliberate, chosen, not rushed by the emotions crashing against our carefully constructed walls.

We stand facing each other as the last slice of sun disappears beneath the horizon, the first test of our reunion passed simply by both of us showing up as promised.

The whiskey burns a familiar path down my throat as we sit on opposite ends of the weathered deck sofa, distance maintained like a mutual agreement. Yelana swirls her glass, amber liquid catching the last light as darkness settles over the ocean. Six months of stories hang between us, neither quite knowing where to begin.

The waves provide background noise, filling silences that aren't exactly uncomfortable but aren't comfortable either – the awkwardness of two people relearning each other's presence.

"So," I finally offer, "Z-Corp. Saw your logo on a building downtown last week."

Her lips curve slightly. "Legitimate businesses only now. Security consulting, tech development, specialized logistics." She gestures toward the coastline where lights blink in the distance. "That's our new research facility. Clean energy solutions, if you can believe it."

"Emelio would be surprised."

"Maybe." She takes a sip, considering. "Or maybe not. He always adapted when necessary. Survival required it."

I watch her face in the fading light, noting the confidence behind her words. This isn't theoretical for her anymore – she's lived it, built it, proven it works.

"I kept the parts worth saving," she continues, leaning forward slightly, animation entering her voice. "The connections, the infrastructure, the loyalty. Turned the rest to ash." She meets my eyes directly. "Miguel Costa handles the old business now. We have a non-interference agreement. Clean break."

The implications sink in. She really did it – transformed a criminal empire into a legitimate corporate one. Cut ties with the world that killed her parents without destroying what they built.

"And the lieutenants?"

"Most adapted. Some retired with generous packages. A few..." Her shrug communicates their fate clearly enough. "Chen runs Asia Pacific operations now. Completely above board. Marcus Webb finally took that retirement he'd been threatening for years." She pauses. "Your turn. Chicago?"

I set my glass down, organizing thoughts that suddenly feel inadequate compared to her transformation. "Expanded the business. Hired four new operatives – all veterans, all skilled, all carrying their own ghosts. Doubled our client list. Bought the building next door." Facts, not feelings – my default setting.

Her eyes don't leave mine, waiting for what I'm not saying. She always could see through my tactical reports to the human beneath.

"Visited the team's graves," I continue, voice rougher. "Kerry's too. Talked to a therapist about Afghanistan. About Kerry. About Ken." The admission costs me, but I make myself say it. "About you."

Her eyebrow raises slightly, but she doesn't interrupt.

"Stopped having the nightmares. Mostly." I rub the back of my neck, discomfort with emotional disclosure never quite conquered. "Still wake up reaching for a weapon sometimes, but I don't always grab it anymore. Progress, according to Dr. Levine."

"You're seeing a therapist?" Genuine surprise colors her voice. "Voluntarily?"

"Don't sound so shocked. I'm evolving too." The corner of my mouth twitches. "Slowly. Painfully. With considerable resistance."

Her laugh breaks the remaining tension, genuine and unguarded. We both reach for our glasses at the same time, hands briefly crossing paths, the slight contact sending electricity up my arm.

"Remember Rodriguez? My second-in-command?" I continue, retreating to safer topics. "He's basically running day-to-day operations now. Freed me up to focus on strategic planning. Turns out I'm not terrible at it when I'm not constantly watching for threats."

"I could have told you that." Her smile turns wistful. "I learned strategy from watching you, you know. When you thought I was just being stubborn, I was studying how you assessed situations, predicted outcomes."

"Could've fooled me," I reply, warmth spreading through my chest that has nothing to do with the whiskey. "Thought you were just arguing with everything I said on principle."

"Oh, that too." She lifts her glass in mock salute. "Multi-tasking."

As the sky darkens fully, the automatic deck lights activate, casting us in a soft glow that feels both intimate and exposing. Yelana kicks off her shoes, tucking her feet beneath her on the sofa, the casual gesture somehow more revealing of her comfort than any words.

"I've been thinking," I say, reaching into my pocket for the folded napkin I've carried for weeks. "About the future. About a partnership."

Her eyes sharpen with interest as I unfold the napkin and slide it across the low table between us. The sketch is rough – my company logo merged with Z-Corp's, creating something new while preserving elements of both.

"Professional and personal," I explain, watching her study the drawing. "Your technology, my tactical experience. Your global connections, my specialized security knowledge. Your vision, my execution." I pause, gathering courage. "Your heart, my protection. If you still want it."

She looks up, eyes meeting mine with an intensity that steals my breath. "Took you long enough to figure it out."

The distance between us vanishes as she moves across the sofa, closing the gap that separated us. Her hand finds my face, thumb tracing the new scar along my jaw from Ken's final attack. The touch carries both tenderness and possession, gentle exploration and certain claim.

"I knew before I left," I admit, voice dropping lower as she moves closer. "Knew when I walked away that I was walking away from the best thing I'd ever found. But I needed to be sure I could be what you deserve. Not just what you needed in a crisis."

"And what did you decide?" Her question falls against my lips, our faces now inches apart.

"That I belong wherever you are. In whatever capacity you'll have me."

Her kiss is nothing like our previous ones – not desperate, not adrenaline-fueled, not colored by the possibility of imminent death. It's deliberate, unhurried, certain. Her lips move against mine with the confidence of someone who knows exactly what she wants and intends to claim it. My hands find her waist, drawing her closer until she's straddling my lap, her weight settling against me in perfect alignment.

"I missed you," she breathes against my mouth, fingers threading through my hair. "Missed this. Missed us."

Words fail me, so I answer with actions instead. My hands slide beneath her blouse, finding the warm skin of her back, tracing the familiar topography of her body – the curve of her spine, the slight ridge of scars from battles fought together, the perfect dip of her waist. She arches into my touch like a current completing its circuit.

Our mouths never separate as she begins unbuttoning my shirt, fingers nimble and certain. No fumbling, no hesitation – just the deliberate unveiling of what belongs to her. When her hands find my chest, tracing the scars from wounds she witnessed and some she didn't, something breaks open inside me. The control I've maintained for six months – hell, for most of my life – crumbles beneath her touch.

I stand in one fluid motion, lifting her with me. Her legs wrap around my waist, her soft laugh against my neck sending shivers down my spine as I carry her through the sliding glass doors into the beach house. The bedroom is fifteen steps away – I've already mapped it, already calculated the most efficient path, old habits refusing to die even in this moment.

We fall onto the bed together, a tangle of limbs and half-removed clothing. Moonlight spills through uncovered windows, painting her skin silver as I push her blouse from her shoulders. She's beautiful in ways that transcend the physical – fierce and vulnerable, powerful and yielding, completely herself in every moment.

Her hands work at my belt, impatient now despite our unhurried beginning. "Too many clothes," she mutters against my collarbone, teeth grazing sensitive skin.

I help her remove the barriers between us, each piece of clothing discarded revealing more of what we've both been missing. When we're finally skin to skin, I pause to look at her – really look at her

– memorizing every detail like a man who once thought he'd never have this again.

"Stop analyzing and start touching," she commands, pulling me down to her with surprising strength.

I obey, losing myself in her. Our bodies remember each other, finding rhythm with the ease of long-time lovers despite our months apart. Her fingernails dig into my back as I trace paths down her body with my mouth, relearning every sensitive spot, every way to make her breath catch and release. She's equally relentless, finding the places that make me forget my own name, much less the strategic calculations that usually run through my mind.

When we finally join, the sensation is overwhelming – physically and emotionally. Her eyes hold mine, refusing to let me retreat into the safety of physical pleasure without emotional connection. This isn't just sex – it's a reclaiming, a promise, a future written in the language of bodies that understand each other completely.

"Stay with me," she whispers, and I know she's not just talking about this moment.

"Always," I promise, meaning it with every fiber of my being.

We move together, building toward something that feels both like coming home and setting out on a new journey. When release finally claims us both, it's with a completeness I've never experienced before – as if the final walls between us have crumbled, leaving nothing but truth in their wake.

Afterward, she lies across my chest, her heartbeat gradually slowing against mine. My fingers trace lazy patterns on her back as the ocean crashes rhythmically outside our window.

"So," she murmurs against my skin, "about that partnership..."

I laugh softly, pulling her closer. "I think we just signed the agreement."

Morning light filters through half-drawn blinds, painting stripes across the tangled sheets. Yelana sleeps beside me, her breathing deep and even, one hand still resting on my chest like she's afraid I might disappear. I trace the curve of her shoulder with my fingertips, barely touching, not wanting to wake her yet. Today we face our ghosts together. The visiting order was her idea – "a pilgrimage," she called it last night as we lay wrapped in each other's arms. A journey through our shared past before we can fully claim our future.

She stirs beneath my touch, eyes opening with immediate awareness – no gradual transition from sleep to wakefulness. Another trait we share, born from lives where letting your guard down completely could be fatal.

"You're thinking too loudly," she murmurs, voice husky with sleep. Her hand slides up to my face, thumb brushing across the perpetual stubble on my jaw. "Having second thoughts about today?"

"No." I turn to kiss her palm. "Just thinking about how far we've come to get here."

She sits up, sheet falling away as she stretches. Sunlight catches the network of scars across her skin – some from before I knew her, some I witnessed her receive, all part of the map that makes her who she is. My hand finds the jagged line along her ribs from the warehouse fight, a tactile reminder of how close I came to losing her before I truly had her.

"We should go," she says, catching my hand and pressing a kiss to my knuckles. "Before we find reasons to stay in bed all day."

The drive to the Zentarra family mausoleum is quiet, both of us sinking into our own thoughts as the coast road winds beneath a cloudless blue sky. Yelana wears a simple black dress, elegant without being formal. I opted for dark slacks and a button-down – as close to funeral attire as my wardrobe gets. The flowers rest on the back seat – white roses for Emelio and Sierra, red for my team, a single yellow one for Kerry who always claimed they were "obnoxiously cheerful in a world that needed more obnoxious cheer."

The mausoleum stands as I remember it – white marble gleaming in the morning sun, imposing yet somehow welcoming. The scene of our final confrontation with Ken, now washed clean of blood and restored to its solemn purpose. Yelana's hand finds mine as we climb the steps, her grip tightening slightly when we push open the heavy doors.

Inside, shafts of colored light filter through stained glass windows, casting rainbow patterns across generations of Zentarra wealth and power laid to rest. Emelio and Sierra's tombs occupy the newest section, their marble markers still noticeably whiter than the weathered monuments of ancestors. Yelana approaches them with measured steps, her back straight, shoulders squared – the posture of someone determined to show strength even in private grief.

She places white roses on each marker, fingers lingering on the engraved names. "They would have approved," she says quietly, her voice echoing slightly in the cavernous space. "Eventually."

I stay back, giving her this moment of privacy while remaining close enough to support. My relationship with her parents was complicated at best – Emelio saved my life at the cost of his son's, then later called in that debt. Sierra nursed me back to health while simultaneously assessing whether I was a threat to her family. They were criminals and killers, but also fiercely loyal parents who loved their daughter enough to build an empire to protect her.

"Your father once told me he wished his daughter would meet someone like me when she was older," I say, stepping forward to stand beside her. "It was years ago, when you were still in school and had your first boyfriend."

Yelana turns to me, surprise evident in her raised eyebrow. "You never told me that."

"Nothing to tell. He just wanted someone who could protect you." I place my hand beside hers on Emelio's tomb, a gesture somewhere between respect and challenge. "I was broken, angry, looking for redemption in all the wrong places when we were last together."

"And now?" she asks, a hint of amusement in her voice.

"Now I'm still broken, but the pieces fit together better." I look directly at Emelio's name carved in marble. "And I protect what matters, just like you taught me."

We stand in silence for another moment before Yelana presses a kiss to her fingertips, then touches each marker one last time. "Goodbye," she whispers, though whether to her parents or to the weight of their legacy, I'm not certain.

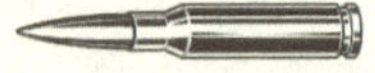

The military cemetery presents a stark contrast to the Zentarra mausoleum – uniform white headstones in perfect alignment, American flags fluttering at attention in the gentle breeze. No grand monuments to wealth and power here, just the solemn recognition of lives given in service. My team rests in the section reserved for special operations personnel, their graves arranged in the same formation they took in combat – a detail I requested and the military honored.

I move between their headstones with practiced efficiency, laying a single red rose on each. George Harris, whose stupid jokes kept us sane during the worst missions. Riley Peters, who could disarm any explosive device with the same concentration he used to solve crossword puzzles. Michael Anderson, whose wife was pregnant when he died, whose child now turns fourteen without ever knowing his father. Craig Ackers, who dreamed of opening a bar when he got out. Fynn Chalmers, youngest of us all, who followed me into hell because I asked him to.

Yelana follows silently, bearing witness to my ritual. She doesn't offer platitudes or unnecessary comfort, understanding that this moment isn't about grief but respect.

Kerry's grave sits apart from my team but within the same section – Lieutenant Kerry Gaston, Naval Intelligence, my fiancée who died in a drunk driving accident while waiting for me to pick her up. I was running late. Always running late when it mattered most.

I kneel before her headstone, positioning the yellow rose carefully against the white marble. "Hey, Kerry," I say, my voice rougher than intended. "I brought someone to meet you."

Yelana steps forward, her hand finding my shoulder in silent support.

"This is Yelana," I continue, the surreal nature of introducing one woman I love to the memory of another not lost on me. "She saved me when I couldn't save myself. Just like you used to."

Yelana kneels beside me, her dress pooling around her on the grass. "Hello, Lieutenant," she says with simple dignity. "Thank you for loving him first. For showing him how."

Something tight in my chest loosens at her words, a knot of guilt and grief I've carried for years unraveling slightly. Kerry would have liked her – would have appreciated her directness, her refusal to sugarcoat reality, her fierce protection of what she considers hers.

"I think she would have approved too," I say as we stand to leave. "Eventually."

Yelana's smile holds a hint of mischief. "I'm growing on the ghosts in your life, one by one."

Our final stop requires the longest drive – back to the Zentarra estate where Juan's memorial stands beneath the ancient oak tree. The guards recognize Yelana immediately, snapping to attention as we pass through security checkpoints she once ruled over. The estate itself looks different – security still evident but less militaristic, more corporate headquarters than armed compound.

The garden remains as I remember it, though the flowers have changed with the season. Juan's memorial appears through the trees, sunlight dappling the bronze plaque where we stood six months ago to make our agreement.

Together, we approach the memorial, our hands joined. The single red rose we brought rests between our intertwined fingers, neither fully holding it, both supporting its weight. We place it among Juan's treasures – the toy cars, the signed baseball, the blue marble I carefully positioned six months earlier.

"He's the reason we met," Yelana says softly. "The most innocent catalyst for the most complicated journey."

"I've spent fourteen years trying to make up for not saving him," I admit, the truth easier to speak here than anywhere else. "Trying to pay a debt that could never be balanced."

"And now?" She turns to face me, her eyes searching mine.

"Now I understand some debts aren't meant to be paid. They're meant to be transformed." I take both her hands in mine, turning her to face me fully. "Into something new. Something better."

Her eyes widen slightly, sensing the shift in my voice, the subtle change in my posture. "Mason?"

The small box feels heavy in my pocket, though I've carried heavier burdens with less purpose. I hadn't planned this moment – not here, not now – but standing before the memorial that connects our past while discussing our future, the rightness of it settles over me with absolute clarity.

I drop to one knee, ignoring the twinge from old injuries, focusing instead on her face as realization dawns in her eyes.

"I've spent most of my life looking backward," I tell her, voice steadier than I feel. "Trying to atone for failures, trying to protect myself from more loss, trying to outrun ghosts that never stopped chasing me." I pull the small black box from my pocket, opening it to reveal the ring I bought in Chicago three months ago – a simple platinum band set with a single diamond flanked by two smaller sapphires. Nothing ostentatious, nothing that would interfere with handling a weapon or running an empire.

"With you, for the first time, I'm looking forward," I continue, watching as her composure falters slightly, her eyes brightening with unshed tears. "I can't promise we won't face more battles. Can't promise I won't still wake up reaching for a weapon sometimes. Can't promise I'll ever be completely whole." I take a breath, centering myself in this moment that matters more than any mission. "But I can promise you'll never face another battle alone. I can promise to be broken beside you rather than perfect without you. I can promise to choose you, every day, for whatever days we have left."

I hold the ring up, sunlight catching in the diamond's depths. "Yelana Zentarra, will you marry me?"

For one terrifying heartbeat, she's completely still, her expression unreadable. Then a smile breaks across her face, radiant and fierce and absolutely certain.

"Yes," she says, dropping to her knees to meet me at eye level, cupping my face between her hands. "Yes, I will marry you, Mason Phillips."

I slide the ring onto her finger with hands that don't shake, despite the earthquake happening in my chest. It fits perfectly – of course it does. I've memorized every detail of her hands, just as I've memorized every detail of her.

She pulls me into a kiss that tastes of salt and promise, of endings and beginnings woven together into something new. When we finally break apart, we're both smiling with a lightness that feels foreign yet perfectly right.

We stand together, turning away from Juan's memorial toward the path that leads back to the waiting car, back to our future. My arm slides around her waist, her head resting against my shoulder as naturally as if we've walked this way for years rather than days.

Behind us, the graves and memorials stand as silent witnesses to what brought us together. Ahead, the path stretches toward possibilities neither of us could have imagined six months ago. For once, I don't look back.

Also by Laci Mae Wyld

Beneath These Ruined Walls: Whispers in the Highlands

In a quest for solace, Fi MacPherson's journey to the Scottish Highlands leads her to the haunting ruins of Sutherland Castle. A chance encounter with a Highland warrior, who fades into thin air before her eyes, initially seems like a mere illusion.

Yet, as his presence lingers in her dreams and his touch ignites a fire within her, Fi is thrust into a realm where time blurs and souls entwine across centuries.

As Fi unravels the entangled memories of Isla—a woman torn between two brothers in a bygone era—she realizes that she is destined to relive their tragic tale over and over. Lachlan, the loyal and fierce warrior, and Hamish, his jealous and vengeful brother, are forever linked with her fate.

I Do...Hate You

In the heart of a city ruled by crime, survival means embracing the darkness within.

Meli Vasquez, a fierce and clever young woman, has long been confined to a life of servitude within the walls of a notorious crime family's stronghold. When the ruthless and feared Corbin Argyros, known as "The Executor " for his lethal efficiency, unexpectedly claims her as his bride to fulfill an ancient family decree, Meli is thrust into a world of opulence, danger, and power beyond her wildest dreams.

To Corbin, Meli's defiance is an intriguing challenge, her sharp wit a valuable asset. But to Meli, he is nothing more than a monstrous captor with haunted eyes and hands that stoke a dangerous fire within her. Their fiery clashes soon give way to forbidden passion, blurring the lines between loathing and longing.

In Corbin's brutal world, where compassion is weakness and love is a liability, Meli and Corbin realize that their unlikely partnership may be their most potent weapon yet. As betrayals mount, they must stand together against all who seek to tear them apart.

Content Warning: Contains explicit language and sexual scenes, including light choking, oral sex, manual stimulation, sexual violence, murder, kidnapping, torture, physical and sexual abuse, and themes of parental death.

Mark Me

35-year-old Mica Greer harbors a talent for intricate designs and a shield against emotional entanglements. But when Nyah Summers, with her haunting past and hidden pain, walks into his life, the flames of change flicker to life.

In a bold stand against Nyah's abusive past, Mica's defiance sets off a spark that neither of them can ignore. Drawn together by shared scars and unspoken desires, their connection deepens as they navigate the shadows of their histories.

Offering Nyah refuge within his sanctuary and a role in his creative world, Mica finds himself unraveling the layers of his own defenses. As their bond intensifies from friendship to something more, they must confront the looming threat of Nyah's vindictive ex-lover.

Experience a tale where redemption emerges from chaos, and the brightest flames are forged from the depths of darkness.

Good Girl To Goddess: Dancing with Desire

Cast aside on her birthday for not fitting in a mold, Elara James sheds her timid skin and overnight becomes a bold enchantress. Guided by her loyal confidante, she swaps modest clothing for daring outfits and quiet behavior for a fearless, take-no-prisoners attitude.

For six months, Elara indulges in fleeting affairs and casual flings, vowing to avoid emotional entanglements to protect her heart. One golden rule guides her nights: never stay until dawn.

Then enters Ryker Davis—confident, commanding, and undeniably captivating. In the heat of passion, he awakens her submission to his every whim. But beyond the bedroom, he reveals a tenderness that challenges the barriers guarding her heart.

As her former lover seeks reconciliation and her closest friend leaves town, Elara faces her deepest fears alone. Will she embrace the vulnerability that comes with true desire, or retreat into the safety of emotional distance?

www.ingramcontent.com/pod-product-compliance
Lightning Source LLC
LaVergne TN
LVHW050917080826
845145LV00001B/117

* 9 7 8 1 7 6 4 5 1 6 8 6 0 *